DANIEL PRICE

SLICK

A NOVEL

Villard Books V New York

Copyright © 2004 by Daniel Price

All rights reserved under International and Pan-American Copyright Conventions. Published in the United States by Villard Books, an imprint of The Random House Publishing Group, a division of Random House, Inc., New York, and simultaneously in Canada by Random House of Canada Limited, Toronto.

VILLARD and "V" CIRCLED Design are registered trademarks of Random House, Inc.

LIBRARY OF CONGRESS CATALOGING-IN-PUBLICATION DATA
Price, Daniel
  Slick : a novel / Daniel Price.
    p.   cm.
  ISBN 1-4000-6234-9
    1. Public relations consultants—Fiction. 2. Rap musicians—Fiction.
    3. Celebrities—Fiction. I. Title.
  PS3616.R526S65 2004
  813'.6—dc22   2004041889

Villard Books website address: www.villard.com

Printed in the United States of America

987654321

FIRST EDITION

Book design by Casey Hampton

For Ricki.
For Yona.

SLICK

When people ask me what I do for a living, I have a few ways to answer without lying. The quick and easy response is that I'm a publicist, of sorts. I'll only add "of sorts," of course, if I feel like teasing the more elaborate answer. "Of sorts" is just a silly passive-aggressive trick I use to encourage extended interest in me, a verbal hyperlink to click on for more information. Almost everyone clicks. Ironically, the few who don't are the ones I'm more interested in talking to. It takes a certain amount of social defiance to see a conversational green light and simply park the car. I've learned to cherish those people, especially in Los Angeles. Mostly I'm left talking to duds.

"Of sorts?"

All right. Here we go . . .

I work in the field of perception management, although the less colorful term is "media manipulation." We're the CIA of PR, the sublime little gremlins who live just outside your senses, selling you products and concepts without you even knowing. Example: if I told you how great Palmolive was, and you knew I worked for Palmolive, you'd obviously take my praise with a healthy amount of skepticism. But if I paid a friend to hand you an article citing a third-party consumer report that deemed Palmolive-brand dishwashing liquid to have the least amount of harmful ammonium sulfate, that would sneak past your filters. Never mind that the study was funded by me, or that the lazy journalist was just parroting my press release, or that ammonium sulfate is only harmful to those who squirt it repeatedly into their mouth and eyes (see: Darwinism); you'd remember my little factoid the next time you pushed your cart past the cleaning products. You might even be subconsciously swayed toward Palmolive just because I mentioned it four times in the course of one paragraph. That's called product placement. You're soaking in it.

There are thousands of people who do what I do, but over the course of my career I've earned a reputation for being something of a devious bastard; "devious" for my choice of methods and "bastard" for my choice of clients. Admittedly, I was never one to discriminate. I've conspired with the gun people, schemed with the liquor people, toiled for tobacco, and moiled for Monsanto. I've pushed polluters and promoted porn. I've shilled for Shell and lied for Tide. I've helped a major pharmaceutical company sell a drug that does nothing by promoting a disease that doesn't exist. And that's just the old stuff on my résumé. That was before I went freelance, and got really creative.

It's usually at this point in the conversation that the duds I'm talking to slowly let the air out of their smiles and desperately cling to their sense of courtesy. Most of them force an interested grunt, adding my picture to their mental file of What's Wrong With America Today. Others gaze back in subdued horror, as if they just figured out what happened to Rosemary's Baby. I've even gotten the dark stare of judgment from entertainment lawyers. Imagine.

In February 2001, a bright and peculiar woman asked me what my origin was. Most people would have found that question a little vague (geographic? ethnic? cosmic?), but I knew exactly what she meant. Like me, she had a longtime love for comic books. In the superhero world, the origin is the tale of the fateful circumstances that gave the hero (or villain) their extraordinary powers and set them on their never-ending path of good (or evil). It was a clever choice of words on her part, a simple way of asking how I got to be me. Amused, I simply told her I was bitten by a radioactive asshole.

She didn't think I was an asshole at all. Then again, she didn't know what I was working on at the time. In February 2001, I was hired to save the public character of a certain man by destroying the character of a certain woman. Despite my nefarious accomplishments, I'd never used my talents to ruin another human being before, and I didn't want to start. So instead of getting nasty, I got clever. I came up with an ambitious alternative, a grand and epic hoax that would have saved all and destroyed none. It would have been my greatest achievement to date, had it worked.

Unfortunately, it didn't. Somewhere along the way, it took a bad turn and just kept going. Once that happened, a lot of people thought I was an asshole. At the lowest point of the operation, a dark and famous woman told me that she didn't care what had happened in my life to make me this way. There was no excuse. There was no excuse for a man like me.

The thing is, I never offered any excuses. I never justified myself through heartbreaking tales of trauma and adversity. I never even claimed to have an origin. I simply was the man I was. What I didn't tell the woman—what I should have told her on that awful day—was that despite the buzz, despite my foiled plans, and despite all my nefarious accomplishments, I was actually a man who meant well.

That's all right. Even if I had told her, she probably wouldn't have believed me. She was certainly entitled to her mistrust. After all, this is a cynical age we live in. This is a media-driven world. And in the media business, they teach you that every good story has two things: a victim and a villain. My story has more than one victim. I guess that makes me the villain. Of sorts.

FLACK

1
SAVE THE MONK SEAL

For millions of years, the Keoki Atoll sisters had struggled with a shared inferiority complex. It's not that they weren't pretty. They were gorgeous. God just put them in a bad place. In the Hawaiian chain, they were two of the farthest-outlying landmasses, separated from the main islands by over twelve hundred miles of ocean. They weren't even touched by human feet until 1827, when Captain Stanikowitch of the Russian freighter *Moller* took a leg-stretch pit stop on Kaikaina, the little sister. For reasons beyond me, he named both islands George. From 1876 to 1932, both George and George (aka Kaikua'ana, the big sister) were courted by the Australian Guano Company, which was just using them for their mineral-rich animal shit.

World War II was a particularly busy time for the sisters. The U.S. Navy commandeered the islands, renamed them Keoki Atoll (Keoki is Hawaiian for "George"), and set up quite an elaborate outpost. After the war ended, the Keoki base was maintained by a skeleton crew for forty-three more years, until the navy shut the place down.

In May 1988, Keoki Atoll was reborn as a national wildlife refuge, housing such endemic but dwindling species as the blue hornbill turtle, the green hornbill turtle, and the Hawaiian monk seal. The sisters were now well protected from human meddlers, who needed a special permit just to come near them. But for all the government's best intentions, the hornbill turtle—both blue and green—left the islands without explanation.

In November 1997 the U.S. gave up on Keoki and leased the islands to Nomura, a Japanese holding company. Animal activists raised a loud stink in Washington, but that lasted about as long as Divx. Luckily for Nomura, the good people at Fairmont Hotels & Resorts were hot to add a Hawaiian dig to the franchise. The sisters were in for a serious makeover.

They had one last year of peace and quiet before an army of developers swarmed all over them in a swirling frenzy of hammering and sawing. By October 2000 the Fairmont Keoki had risen: a 29-acre resort with 450 one-bedroom suites, 55 private beachfront villas, 40,000 square feet of function space, two full-service spas and fitness centers, six restaurants, twelve boutiques, a year-round children's program, full wedding coordination services, and a 140-foot waterslide. It was like a giant luxury cruise ship that wouldn't sink or go anywhere. The one remnant from the sisters' past lives was the navy airport on Kaikua'ana, fully expanded and upgraded to accommodate daily shuttles to and from Honolulu.

The grand opening was set for Friday, February 2, 2001. To ensure that the resort got off to a running start, Fairmont had offered major incentive packages to their Platinum Club members and favored travel agents. Unfortunately, due to internal mismanagement, their promotion coincided with a massive PR blitz for the illustrious Fairmont Plaza in New York. As if stealing their own thunder wasn't bad enough, media operatives for the Landmark Hotels Group—still bitter that Fairmont didn't acquire their own Kea Lani Hotel in Maui—launched a covert, preemptive strike against the sisters. On January 12, *The New York Times* Sunday magazine ran a spoon-fed article on the "troubled" history of Keoki Atoll, focusing on the recent invasion of rats and deadly ants.

As usual, this was painted air. The inexplicable rat epidemic occurred in 1987, while Keoki was still a wildlife refuge, and was permanently solved by a commercial pest-control gestapo. As for the ants, they came with the lumber, but the article failed to mention that they're only deadly to people who happen to be beetle-sized or smaller.

For Fairmont, this was all bad mojo. Based on advance reservations, the Keoki would open at a paltry 30 percent guest occupancy. That's the kind of lame start that can haunt a hotel's reputation, a self-fulfilling omen of doom. Panicked, Fairmont ran to Mertens & Fay, a Los Angeles PR firm that specialized in crisis management. Never too busy to take on a six-figure job, the nice folks at M&F decided to outsource the whole Fairmont mess. To me. My mission, should I choose to accept it, was to bury the bad buzz under a wave of counterhype. They didn't care how I did it as long as I turned Keoki Atoll into a shiny new star on the map. I had two weeks. Mahalo.

That was January 19th. On February 1st, shortly after dawn, custodial workers left the employee dorm on Kaikaina and took the twelve-minute ferry ride to the main hotel on Kaikua'ana. The 250-person staff had settled in shortly after the new year and had the run of both islands. But that would end tomorrow, when over 400 guests and 300 corporate executives would be arriving to christen the resort. For the crew, morale was low. They had uprooted themselves from their mainland jobs just to be here, and now it seemed the Fairmont Keoki was already destined to go the way of EuroDisney.

So you can imagine their surprise when they arrived at the lagoon dock only to find a crowd of 128 naked young women gathered in front of the hotel. From inside a vast rope cordon, they yelled with excited energy as more than six dozen college boys cheered them on.

This was new. On first glance, one might think it was nothing more than a shameless promotional stunt. However, if one were inclined to look up from all the naughty bits, one would notice the many placards the women brandished with righteous pride. They spelled out their cause in large, marker-drawn letters: SAVE THE MONK SEAL!

Masking corporate propaganda as social activism is one of the trade's earliest tricks. In February 1929 the American Tobacco Company hired legendary PR pioneer Edward Bernays to help break the taboo against female smoking. Back then it was considered unladylike, a habit of whores. Two months later, spectators at Macy's New York Easter Day Parade gaped in succession as a battalion of beautiful debutantes proudly puffed their way down Fifth Avenue. They were heralded worldwide as the Torches of Liberty brigade. Another stigma bit the dust. After that, even the most demure femmes were free to wave their Lucky Strikes around. Ah, Edward Bernays. He was Sigmund Freud's nephew and never let anyone forget it. To this day, the tobacco companies still target women by drawing a two-way arrow between smoking and independence. We've come a long way, baby.

For my purpose, I knew the *Monachus schauinslandi*—the monk seal—would be the Trojan horse. But it was currently a cause without a rebel. A quick scan through the Nexis news database pointed me to the University of Maine at Orono, where a formidable all-girl squad of student upstarts made headlines by picketing a local mink farm in raw-meat bikinis. That may sound like no big deal, but this was mid-Maine in mid-November. Wow. Now *that's* activism. It's also a good way to get freezer burn. I figured these young ladies could use a change of climate.

Two days later, I was sitting in an Orono campus dining hall with Deb Isham, the buxom Robespierre of the pro-critter protest. On behalf of a philanthropic party who wished to remain anonymous, I offered her and 130 of her sisters two thousand dollars each, plus airfare, to stage an eye-catching demonstration on the other side of the country. I told her my employer was most displeased with the Fairmont's eviction of the endangered monk seal. The least we could do was send a loud and clear message on behalf of those persecuted pinnipeds.

Deb was easy to gauge. From her faded sweatshirt, which hid her Massachusetts money and California body, I could tell she wasn't just a self-satisfied poser. She was a true and modest do-gooder, emphasis on "modest." She was all for the cause but, despite her stint in a tenderloin two-piece, had some grave concerns about the nudity. Do we really have to go, you know, the full monty?

Sadly, yes. This wasn't just for my gratification. If you want to know what it's like to be a journalist reading the newswires, try standing in a room with a thousand people yelling "Over here! Over here!" It's maddening, especially since so much of it is blatant promotional crap from amateur agents. All the press has time to do is race through headlines. In this day and age, *Bikini-Clad* isn't even a speed bump. Changing it to *Topless* would certainly get some hits, but not enough to justify the expense. NAKED YOUNG WOMEN PROTEST BEACH RESORT: Now that would stop the presses.

Fortunately, Deb's cohorts were a much easier sell. They were poor. Maine was cold. And their second semester didn't start until February 7. That gave them almost a week to bum around Hawaii, with cash, all for one day's rage against the corporate machine. Screw modesty. In one afternoon, Deb managed to fill every slot on the roster. Half the girls opted to bring along their highly supportive boyfriends, who I later enlisted to serve as crowd control. In record time, I had my army.

Right after Deb dropped me off at the Portland airport, she rolled down the window of her beat-up Tercel and eyed me uncomfortably.

"Scott, do you know why I organized that rally against the mink farm?"

"Because they're killing minks."

"It's not the killing itself that bothers me. I'm not a vegetarian. If minks tasted good, I might even try one. But we don't kill minks for nourishment. We kill them for luxury. In the end, they're being exploited for their skins by people who just want more luxuries. Do you understand what I'm saying?"

It wasn't exactly a rebus. "What would you like to know?"

"Just promise me this is the real thing," she said. "That this isn't all just some big smear campaign by Marriott or something."

See, there's a difference between being smart and being wise. Deb was smart. I swore to her from the bottom of my heart that I wasn't working for any of Fairmont's competitors. After she drove off, I sighed steamy air and quietly hoped she wouldn't get wise.

February 1 was a perfect day for mass nudity. Thursday was a big TV night in itself, but this was also the first day of sweeps. The reruns were gone. *Survivor: Australia* was premiering in its regular time slot, followed by surprise hit *CSI* in its new choice location. You had *Who Wants to Be a Millionaire?* on ABC, *WWF Smackdown!* on UPN, and, of course, the eternal Must See lineup on the Peacock. The ten and eleven o'clock newscasts would have over ninety million viewers to tease.

It was also my thirty-fifth birthday. That only mattered to me, of course, especially since I didn't tell anyone. But what a way to celebrate. My work wasn't always this much fun. And my fun wasn't always this much work. I had to play shepherd for a flock of two hundred coeds. They had all arrived in Honolulu in scattered shifts on January 30. The next day I loaded them all onto a chartered booze cruise, which certainly lived up to its name. By the third hour, every stretch of railing was occupied by a heaving undergrad. The rest of the trip, thankfully, was dead quiet. It was an eighteen-hour ride from Oahu to Keoki. We wouldn't get there until dawn.

One of the few other noncollegiates on the boat was David Green, a staff writer at *Maxim*. I owed him a favor so I gave him a heads-up exclusive on the before-and-after of this noble endeavor.

For a man who wrote pieces like "How to Ogle Her Breasts and Get Away with It," David was the furthest thing from a regressed frat boy. He was a soft-spoken, agreeable fellow with a cardiologist wife, two teenage daughters, and one serious midlife crisis. Every time I saw him, he had done something different to his head. First it was the long hair/mustache retro thing, which should have died with Sonny Bono. Then it was the shaved head/goatee combo, which has yet to work on a white man. Now it was a buzz cut and stubble beard, which made him look like an A-list screenwriter. This was progress.

No stranger to PR machinations, David was able to see straight through my seat-of-the-pants operation, all the way to my ulterior. That was fine. I knew he had no intention of tipping the hand that fed him. Honestly, it wouldn't have bothered me if he hinted at the truth in his article. Just not here. Not in front of the girls. It wasn't the boat ride that was making me queasy. If even half of these women backed out, this would be the *Heaven's Gate* of promotional stunts. It would maim my career.

After the students had passed out, David and I enjoyed the quiet night breeze from the bow. Even when standing on the first rung of the railing, he was still shorter than me. Men often did strange, unconscious things to try to match my height.

"So how much has this whole thing cost so far?"

"About the same as two thirty-second spots on *Law and Order,*" I bragged. "Or four on *Special Victims Unit.*"

He whistled. "That's quite a bargain."

"We'll see."

My cautious attitude was echoed—loudly—by my clients at Mertens & Fay. In high-turnover industries like advertising and PR, most account executives (read: accountable executives) tend to be risk-averse. I certainly don't blame them. But you have to keep evolving the craft or the audience will catch on to your methods. Even Sprite's anti-marketing marketing campaign (*Image Is Nothing, Thirst Is Everything.*) soon became transparent to the savvy teen market. A sledgehammer approach like mine would be a great trick, but you could only get away with it once.

At 6:00 A.M. the boat reached the Kaikua'ana port. By then everyone was happy to be back on terra firma. One of the many ironies of the day was that the girls, who had traveled five thousand miles to protest the evils of upscale development, were all mesmerized by the sheer beauty of this place. So was I. It was heavenly. Fairmont had spared no expense to get the world's most talented landscape and structural designers. I had expected a Vegas-like artificiality, or at best San Jose, but it was more like airbrushed nature. Every brick, every fountain, was strategically placed to enhance the native environment. We stood under a pink dawn sky in a majestic stone courtyard that would make Zeus jealous. And we had the whole damn place to ourselves. It occurred to me that the sisters might actually be happy with their new look. Who were we to say?

I joined Deb as she watched the men set up the rope cordon. Unlike her friends, she seemed nervous and bothered. I could already smell the issue, but I played it simple.

"You okay?"

She tied her hair back tight. "Yeah. I just . . . I'm just wondering if we're doing the right thing. I mean, what if this just brings more people here?"

"It probably will."

"It will?"

"Probably," I said. "Look, I'm a realist. I never expected to shut this place down. What we're doing is slapping a scarlet 'A' on the whole franchise. Corporations are really vain. They hate controversy, even if it doesn't hurt their bottom line. My guess is that in three weeks Fairmont will make some big announcement about a new seal-friendly initiative."

"Like what?"

I didn't know. I hadn't thought that far ahead. But it was a good excuse to send out another video news release in three weeks.

"We'll see," I told her. "The important thing is that the next company to develop a luxury resort is going to go out of its way to do something decent for the animals, just to avoid the kind of noise you guys are about to make here today."

Admittedly, that was crap. This story had the shelf life of raw scrod. But Deb took it on faith. My words didn't inspire her, but they at least gagged that quiet, nagging voice that was bothering both of us.

By then the cordon was all done. Symbolically, it was David, the *Maxim* guy, who spoke for all the men. "So, you gals getting naked or what?"

After returning from Maine, I had asked my friend Ira to estimate how many of the nascent nudists would chicken out at the last minute. Ira was my secret weapon. My Nostradamus. Calling him an expert market analyst was like calling *Network* a cute little flick. He was a mad genius, years ahead of his craft, and utterly impossible to be around for more than an hour at a time. But he wasn't infallible. He said he'd be surprised if less than twelve of them deserted the cause. He'd be shocked, then, to learn that only three women fatally succumbed to their poor body image.

Not that it was a figurative day at the beach for the others. It didn't help that David and a few of the less considerate boyfriends had their cameras in prime position. I'd gone out of my way to convince the women that all private parts would be obscured. David even had them all sign release forms that specifically promised the black-bar treatment. *Maxim* may be a T&A mag extraordinaire but any clear-cut nudity would subject them to porn-level marketing restrictions. As for the TV news, it was a no-brainer. The digital nipple blur would be the star of the evening.

After ten minutes of hemming and hawing, I got antsy. I made all the men put down their cameras and turn around while the women got undressed. David didn't like that one bit. He felt he was entitled to a shot of the stripdown. I quietly suggested that he could just capture them putting their clothes back on. It was a photo. Nobody would know. He caved. We all turned away.

By 7:00 A.M., it was a done deal. The girls were naked and inside the cordon. With synchronized trepidation, they folded their strategically held clothes into neat little bundles and placed them by their feet. The boyfriends cheered, David snapped his pictures, and I had a momentary attack of humanity. I hate those. I swore a very long time ago not to judge myself by other people's moral standards, because they're virtually always the product of some faulty, outdated, inconsistent, shrink-wrapped bullshit value system. I'm not talking about religious dogma. That's the devil we know. I'm referring to Hollywood ethics. No, Senator, it's not an oxymoron. Everyone who was raised by their TV and cineplex has been stuffed like foie gras with an unending supply of predigested moral pap, a dizzying tableau of Tinseltown tenets. Corporations are evil. Cripples are nice. Ambitious executives always learn to loosen up and "seize the day." And liars always come clean in the end, usually in front of a big crowd. Screw that. You want one to grow on? Repeat these words: free will. Free will. Free will.

And I'll tell you something else for free: the whole nude experience was more rewarding for the women than it was for the men. Trust me. I was there. It wasn't that sexy. And I'm saying this as a securely heterosexual man who, until that night, hadn't been laid in three years. There was just too much skin. It desensitized me pretty fast.

I wasn't alone. It took five minutes for the boyfriends' raucous cheering to die down to obligatory applause. Once the hotel staff arrived, the guys were completely faking it. By then the whole thing was about as sexy as macramé.

"It'll be better once we start obscuring the nipples and stuff," David told me while snapping pictures. "Strange, isn't it? *Maxim*'s selling like hotcakes while *Penthouse* keeps losing half its subscribers. Gee, you think maybe men are starting to use their imaginations again?"

"That's crazy talk."

"I'm serious. Look around. This is it. You hit the nadir. It doesn't get any more naked than this. Where the hell else can we possibly go from here but back?"

Where indeed? If there's one thing I learned from *Jurassic Park*, it's that life finds a way. But David did convince me of one thing: he wouldn't be around at *Maxim* much longer. Midlife crises aside, burnout was extremely common in the magazine trade. I mean how many times can you write the same "Please Your Man in Bed" piece for *Cosmo* before developing a facial tic?

Meanwhile, the Orono women were off on their own journey. At first they struggled to hide. The most exposed girls fought their way deeper into the crowd, causing the new outer layer to fight their way in. From above it must have looked like a kaleidoscope. Or Busby Berkeley's dry dream. I'm not sure what psychological force took over, but it spread like current. In eerie synchronization, they simply stopped hiding and started cheering.

Makes sense, I suppose. The weather was gorgeous. They were out in large numbers. And they were defiantly breaking convention, like the Torches of Liberty brigade. By the time the men stopped hooting and hollering, the women euphorically took over. Some of the guys even asked me if they could join in on the nude thing and, you know, help the cause. Uh-uh. I was all for equal rights, really, but if we made this thing coed it would seem more like an MTV Spring-Break Special than a social protest. People would smell the marketing.

By 7:30 the next wave of staff arrived on the scene. Then the next. And the next. Within the hour, the courtyard was overflowing with spectators. As I'd hoped, the employees showed no ill will toward the protesters. It was kind of hard to take this seriously when being confronted with signs like FAIRMONT UNFAIR TO MONK SEALS!, HEY FAIRMONT! 'ALOHA' ALSO MEANS GOODBYE!, and my personal favorite: DON'T YOU KNOW YOU'RE GONNA SHOCK THE MONK SEAL?

At 9:15, a DC-10 touched down on the airstrip. The press had finally arrived. The demonstrators were quite surprised to learn that the fourth estate, in this case, was simply a petite reporter and a three-man production crew. The reporter, Miranda Cameron-Donnell, worked for the Associated Press. The production crew worked for me.

"That's it?" yelled one of the boyfriends. "You said the media was gonna be all over this!"

And now they were. Yesterday, while most of the students were booting into the Pacific, I called the producers at each of Hawaii's four major TV news markets. Since the Fairmont Keoki was a four-hour flight from Honolulu, I figured I'd give them ample lead time, just as a courtesy.

Naturally, they all went nuts for my premise. "Wow! Really? Cool!" "Way cool," I replied. "Swing on by."

As I expected, they sighed and stalled: "Yeah, well, I don't know. Keoki Atoll's kind of far, dude. Tell you what, just send the VNR and the B-roll, and we'll definitely use it. Just make sure to send it early enough so we can tease it."

Ninety-nine percent of the world couldn't translate that request for the life of them. That makes the other one percent of us very, very happy.

As you know, the news has changed dramatically over the last ten years. The media outlets have merged and merged and merged into what are (as of now) six multinational überconglomerates that control virtually everything you see and hear. This has led to an unprecedented streamlining of the news industry. It's still going on. Just one month before, the newly consummated AOL Time Warner cut four hundred jobs at CNN. Why? The quick and easy answer would be profitability, but it's also because of people like me. Publicists and journalists used to be flip sides of the same coin. Now we're sharing space on a one-sided nickel. This isn't a bad thing at all. It's made both our jobs a hell of a lot easier. With the exception of AP and *Maxim,* I'm all the media I need for this event.

The video news release (VNR) is the dirty little secret that all flacks and hacks share. It's do-it-yourself coverage. Using my own crew, my own script, even my own voice, I serve as the on-the-scene (but never seen) reporter. When all is said and done, I've got a professional-looking two-minute news piece, the kind you see every night at eleven. From there we use a portable uplink to shoot the whole thing into space. The final step is faxing notice to all the newsrooms. *Hi. We've got a sweet piece on a mob of angry naked chicks. Interested? Here are the satellite coordinates. Go nuts.*

For the budget-conscious news director, this is manna from heaven. It takes just minutes for Graphics to add their custom network overlays and Sound to dub a local reporter's voice over mine. Presto. The station runs the piece as their own. There's no legal requirement to cite the source, and that's just the way we like it. The producers often mix it up a little to cover their tracks. That's what the B-roll is for. It's a no-frills collection of relevant interviews and visual clips, a media LEGO set they can put together any way they want. It's a great system. On a slow news day, a thirty-minute show can squeeze in a good seven to eight minutes of VNRs, as compared to five or six minutes of real news. It's pretty easy to tell the two apart. That fire in Century City? News. That new laser technique to remove wrinkles? VNR. If it promotes a product or company, it's a VNR. If the reporter never appears in any of the on-scene footage, that's because it ain't his story. It came from outer space.

I was glad the cavalry finally arrived. Keoki Atoll was six hours behind the East Coast. I wanted to get this out by 11:00 A.M. so the eastern affiliates could tease the story all through prime time.

The video crew was from an L.A. production house called Metropia. Its three principals—Denny, Gray, and Vivek—were your standard ponytailed AV geeks. But they were masters of their craft. I flew them out here at great expense because I didn't want to take a chance with an untested local outfit. If the final piece looked like crap, the stations wouldn't run it.

I wished I had filmed their faces as soon as they broke through the outer shell of the brouhaha and got a look at the chewy, creamy center. Hearing about my plans was one thing. Seeing them in action was quite another. Even Vivek, the gay one of the bunch, was stunned by the unprecedented display of natural breasts.

The last one into the fray was the AP's own Miranda Cameron-Donnell. Established in 1848, the Associated Press was a nonprofit collective owned by more than fifteen hundred newspapers. In effect, they did what I did: ship their stories off to others. Unlike me, they got credit for their work. Also unlike me, their reach extended to over one billion people. That was why I called Miranda. Once she put her piece on the wire, it would get picked up by newspaper, radio, and Web outlets all over the world. There was quite a lot of power packed into that small frame.

Miranda was an old friend of mine. Actually, she was an old friend of an old flame, but we remained chummy. Since I was the one who'd been cheated on and dumped, Miranda didn't have to play the allegiance card and freeze me out. To her, I was only an asshole by profession.

Inviting her to Keoki Atoll had been a cruel pleasure on my part. It was always fun to crack her carefully maintained appearance. Miranda was a power dresser. Even in tropical weather, she looked ready for the catwalk in her sleeveless white Donna Karan blouse and three-hundred-dollar Gucci slacks.

Predictably, her jaw dropped. "Oh my fucking God. I can't believe you really did this."

"Miranda. Hey!" I went to hug her.

"Don't. Don't even touch me. You are the scum of the earth. I've stepped in better things than you."

That was just how New Yorkers said hello. "How are you, hon?"

"Jet-lagged. And thoroughly repulsed. What the hell did you do, hire strippers?"

"Nope. These are genuine New England student activists."

"Pathetic, Scott. Am I the only real journalist here?"

"You and David Green from *Maxim*."

"I'll take that as a yes. Here."

She handed me a DVD-ROM. The AP GraphicsBank was one of the world's most extensive video image libraries. You try finding stock footage of a monk seal.

"Oh, perfect," I said. "I really needed this. Thank you."

"I don't even know why I'm helping you. Jesus."

"Hey, where's your photo guy?"

"That would be me." Proving her point, she extracted a five-thousand-dollar digital camera from her leather bag, holding it as if it were somebody else's baby. "There weren't any photographers available from the Honolulu pool. And my goddamn bosses wouldn't pay to fly Armand out here."

Typical. "All right. Hope you know how to use that thing."

"I hope I don't."

It was finally time to get started. I gave Denny and Vivek a list of required shots, and they immediately sicced their cameras on the pool of nudes. No doubt there would be an unedited C-roll added to their personal collection. I made a note to get a copy for Ira.

Meanwhile, Gray set up his editing station: a titanium G4 Power-Book, complete with satellite uplink terminal. As I handed him the monk-seal disc, Miranda yanked my script out of my pocket. She paced the pavement, reading aloud.

" 'You know the old expression: it's not what you say but how you say it. This morning on the beautiful Hawaiian islands of Keoki Atoll, over two hundred young female activists staged a "cheeky" demonstration against the brand-new Fairmont Keoki, a ninety-million-dollar, twenty-nine-acre luxury'—God, Scott!"

"Keep reading."

" '—luxury beach resort scheduled to open tomorrow. Their gripe? Fairmont's treatment of Keoki's oldest occupant, the endangered monk seal. Now in order to save the critters' hides, these lovely young women . . . are baring theirs.' "

She handed the script back. "You're going to burn in hell."

"Only if they use my tit-for-tat pun."

"So how much did you spend on this whole sham?"

"Who says I spent anything?"

"Right. I'm sure these kids just cashed in their beer bottles. Do they know you're using them?"

"Who says I'm using them? God, Miranda. Relax. You're in Hawaii."

Over the years, I've taught myself to observe people's subtle nuances, to read between their lines. Now I can't turn those powers off. I suffer from Terminator vision, a red-screen overlay with constant streaming data on the side. At the moment that data was telling me Miranda had issues. Not with me or the gratuitous T&A. She was having problems at home. Of course that wasn't a blind guess. I'd met her husband many times. Quite the prick.

Speaking of pricks, the cameras brought out the worst in some of the spectators. One of the hotel workers shouted NC-17 compliments from outside the cordon until a pair of Orono guys got on his case. Fortunately security broke it up before it became a brawl.

Miranda shook her head at the spectacle. "Scott, give me one good reason why I shouldn't blow this farce wide open."

"Because you like me."

"Not after this."

The real reason was because, like David, she knew that 200 WOMEN STRIP NAKED was a hell of a lot more interesting than PR GUY MANIPULATES NEWS. You have to understand something about Miranda. Prior to AP, she spent five years at *USA Today,* until she had a four-color meltdown. Now she liked to tell herself that she was doing real journalism. For all I know, she could be. Just not today. Today she was working for me. Deep down she knew my story would be fluff—imitation fluff—from the moment I tipped her off. Deep down she wanted a paid trip to Hawaii as much as anyone else. And really deep down she was just giving me a hard time so she could feel better about her own role in this so-called farce. I try not to get in the way of other people's rationalizations.

"So who's the ringleader of this thing?" she asked. "Besides you."

"I'll take you to her."

I hadn't seen Deb since the stripdown, and I was having a hell of a time locating her now. Fortunately, she found me.

I waved for Denny as Deb worked her way to the rope border. She was definitely getting airtime. The movement needed a voice, a face, and *that* body. Good Lord. In my preemptive defense, I'll say that the sexiest woman I'd ever known was an A cup. With that out of the way, I feel better in expressing my fervent belief that Deb's stunningly large breasts could stop air traffic. In L.A., women spent thousands to get what she got. I found myself getting resensitized.

"Deb, this is Miranda Cameron-Donnell, from the Associated Press. Miranda, Deb Isham, I-S-H-A-M. She's a senior at U. Maine, Orono. This is her show."

"Hi, Miranda."

"Hi, Deb. Thanks for the complex. I need my tape recorder."

While Miranda rooted through her bag, I threw Deb a cautious look. *Remember what we talked about, hon. Keep your answers short. Play up your conviction. Never speculate. And never, ever say anything off the record. There's no such thing as "off the record."*

Miranda found her recorder. "All right. Here we go. Don't worry, Deb. This'll be painless, especially if you have nothing to hide. Obviously, you don't. You ready?"

"Sure."

"All right. Let's start basic. Why are you doing this?"

"Because the Hawaiian monk-seal population is down to twelve hundred and shrinking fast. They need space and privacy in order to breed. Keoki Atoll has been their home for millions of years. Now, because of yet another resort this state doesn't need, these animals have nowhere to mate."

"Uh-huh. And what does this have to do with you girls getting naked?"

"Well, Miranda, let me ask you. If we were fully clothed, would you even be here?"

"Actually, yes. But that's a good line." Miranda grinned and gave me a thumbs-up. "A-plus on the prep work, handsome."

"Thank you."

Yet another advantage of the VNR: my crap was read-only. They would only see what I wanted them to see. Although Miranda was barred from the conspiracy angle, she still had the power to tarnish my paint job. It was a calculated risk to bring her here. I was hoping our friendship, plus a break from the miserable New York weather, would make her go easy on the story. No such luck. She was going to take her marital rage out on us.

Denny arrived and gladly turned his camera on Deb. Miranda kept going: "By the way, how many of you are there?"

Crossing her arms, Deb nervously looked to the camera. I had to wave her gaze back. "Uh, two hundred and three."

"Are you sure? It looks like less."

I cut in. "If you want to count them, go ahead. They're all here."

Fact: there were 128. But if Miranda wanted to call my bluff, she would have a most difficult time. Counting a crowd of homogenous nude women was like counting a floor full of ball bearings, except fun. I had correctly banked on the assumption that Miranda would not see it as fun.

"All right. I'll let you guys have that one. Here's a question, Deb. Why now?"

"What do you mean?"

"I mean if you're really concerned about the monk seal, wouldn't it have been smarter to stage the protest three years ago, before the construction crew even got started?"

"Come on," I griped.

"No, it's okay," Deb replied, trying hard not to get flummoxed. "Three years ago, I was just a freshman. I didn't know about it. Now that I do, I'm hoping this demonstration will at least slap a scarlet 'A' on the whole franchise. I want these corporations to, you know, think twice before they infringe on the rights of indigenous species."

"I see. So you're punishing Fairmont by showing them your trim, naked bodies."

"We're just . . . we had to resort to this to get your attention. We just want the world to know what Fairmont did to those seals."

"Aren't you afraid you're just giving them free publicity? I mean Fairmont, not the seals."

"Well . . . no. I mean it's bad publicity. Corporations are really vain. They—"

"Who paid for all your travel costs?"

"Uh, Scott. Through an anonymous donor."

Denny looked to me. I waved him on. Keep filming. It's not like this was live.

"And you have no guesses as to who the donor is."

"I have no idea. And I wouldn't want to speculate."

"But you know Scott's a publicist, right?"

"Miranda . . ."

"Yes," said Deb. "Why? What are you getting at?"

"Nothing. I just think it's odd that an anonymous donor would need a publicist. You don't have any idea who's behind this?"

"Objection. Asked and answered."

That was me. With a devilish smirk, Miranda continued. "Okay, Deb. Hypothetically—"

"All right. Stop." Me again. That was enough. It was obvious Miranda wouldn't let the issue drop.

"Scott, would you butt out? I'm conducting an interview."

"No, you're digging for information you know you won't be able to use. What's the point? Just stick to the facts."

She let out a flustered laugh. "Facts?! What facts? I don't see any facts! Oh, wait. I forgot. The number of naked women here. Two hundred and three. That's apparently a fact. Hey, what about the fact that you're working for Fairmont? No. Shit. That fact's only speculation. Sorry."

Daunted, Deb turned to me. "What is she talking about?"

"Forget it. She's just trying to get a rise out of you."

And succeeding. "Is it true?"

"It's not, Deb, I swear to you. I'm not working for Fairmont. They're not paying me a dime."

"Not directly, anyway," Miranda added. "Scott usually works through the big PR agencies. He's a freelance flack. A media mercenary. Ronin."

"Hey, Miranda. How's Jim?"

"Cheating on me."

Thought so. In my book, the definition of "prick" is someone who's both dumb enough and mean enough to screw around on an investigative reporter. Jim certainly fit the description. What do you expect? He's a producer for *Dateline NBC*.

Of course, in Deb's book, the definition of "prick" was now me. Shame, really. She had worked so hard to dodge the hints. Now she was painted into a corner. With wet eyes, she threw me an expletive and disappeared into the sea of flesh.

Denny filmed her telegenic backside, then shut off the camera. "Well, that was dramatic. What now?"

"Now we look for Amber LaPierre. She'll give us some good quotes." I turned to Miranda. "Care to meet the number two girl?"

She shook her head at me in wonder. "You're not even mad at me."

I shrugged. "You know my motto: don't get even, get over it."

"That always drove Gracie nuts, you know. That she could never get you mad."

"Yeah, well, she found a way. Sorry about Jim, incidentally."

"I don't want to talk about it."

That was okay. I wasn't offering. Now, where the hell was Amber?

The rest of the job took longer than expected. I spent fifteen minutes looking for Amber only to discover that she wasn't in the crowd anymore. The public nudity had gotten her so aroused that she made her boyfriend smuggle her back to the boat for a quickie. By the time she returned, all rosy-cheeked, I had already gotten several good quotes from Lorna Noonan, a comely sophomore who would have just as gladly flown out here to protest world peace.

After the incident with Deb, Miranda decided to behave herself. The only person she harassed was fellow journalist David Green. She thanked him and his magazine for keeping millions of useless men in their homes, masturbating, instead of bothering real women. David simply apologized on behalf of *Maxim* for raising the standard of female attractiveness well above Miranda's head.

By 11:00, the whole nude thing had gotten stale. Most of the staff had already gone inside to work. The protesters complained about hunger and sunburn. The boyfriends were just bored. At 11:15 I called it a wrap but told Amber, Lorna, and a dozen others to stick around in case we needed pickup shots.

While Miranda wrote up and sent her wire release, and David shot four rolls of the reverse stripdown, I worked with Metropia to cut the final VNR. I annoyed all three of them with my artistic perfectionism. I'll admit it, I've done one too many of these things. I was getting creative just to alleviate my own boredom. Eventually, Gray snapped. "Jesus, man! Who are you, Kubrick? Step back!" I casually relented, then pointed out that Kubrick would have certainly enjoyed a scene like this.

At high noon, the piece was done. I was happy with it. We launched it into the heavens. I announced it through MediaFAX. It was out of my hands. Boy did that feel good. It felt even better to read Miranda's three-hundred-word submitted draft, which ended up supporting my facts and figures. I knew she'd come around.

I saluted the crowd. "Ladies and gentlemen, that is a wrap."

Students and staff alike rejoiced at a job well done. Giddy at the thought of all the press calls he'd soon be fielding, James Dmitriov—executive director of the Fairmont Keoki—offered the demonstrators free lunch, plus full use of the pool and waterslide. Within seconds of announcing his offer, poor James was almost trampled by the stampede into the hotel.

Miranda shook her head. "That was the most pathetic social protest in human history."

"You outdid yourself, man," said David, clapping my back.

"Thanks, but I'm not going to celebrate until I see how many stations pick us up."

I wouldn't get a sense of that until much later that night. The true count wouldn't start until Friday, when the first Nielsen SIGMA results came in. It's an impressive process. Metropia lojacks the VNR with a digitally encoded tag, then Nielsen tracks it all over the broadcast spectrum. They even calculate the comparative ad value of all that free airtime. Anything over two million dollars would officially be a job well done. Over three million would be a gold star on my forehead. If my story got picked up in all top one hundred markets, on multiple affiliates, the ad value could hit six million. That would make me Jesus.

But I tried not to get too starry-eyed. It was all up to the news directors now. I had to tell myself to loosen up. Out of the many things that could have gone wrong with the production, only one or two did. Silly, insignificant things.

Mostly.

Rare is the day that I have more than one moral relapse. For no reason other than self-justification, I felt the need to achieve some kind of closure with Deb. I knew she wouldn't be dining with her friends, so I looked for her on the boat.

She leaned against the railing of the bow, staring somberly out at the cool blue waters of the lagoon. She was now dressed in a simple white tank top and khaki shorts, an ensemble that made her look very . . . Damn, and here I thought her best color was clear. Maybe David was right. Maybe the visualization was better than the visual. Or maybe three years of circumstantial celibacy were finally taking their toll on me.

No, that was too easy an answer. I was pretty sure these feelings, though not altogether deep, were quite specific to Deb. I suppose I should also mention in my own defense that the sexiest woman I'd ever known (you know, the A cup) was fourteen years older than me, not younger. Is this what happens to us as we inch toward middle age? Was I headed toward an obligatory crisis, where I'd suddenly get the urge to change my hair, grow a beard, buy a fancier car, or have meaningless carnal relations with a well-endowed collegian? This may not have been the best day to turn thirty-five.

Deb didn't acknowledge me, even as I stood next to her, following her gaze across the water. From her vantage, stretching out to sea, it was all nature. No signs or logos. No wheelchair ramps or drinking fountains. I couldn't help but wonder if this was intentional on her part or unconsciously symbolic.

I took a deep breath. "Deb—"

"Fuck you."

Okay. New approach. I let a few seconds pass.

"Look, I wanted everyone to come away from this happy. You guys got an all-expense paid trip to Hawaii. Fairmont got cheap advertising. The press got good filler. And millions of men and women will get a nice little story to distract them from their mundane lives. And if you want more honesty, yes, this will be a nice shot in the arm for my career. The bottom line is that everybody benefits from this."

"Except the monk seal."

I sighed. "Deb, the world isn't that simple. Trust me. There are—"

"Don't give me that paternalistic bullshit! You—"

"There are twelve sides to every story. And a million layers to every side. So tell me, how much truth do you want? How much are you prepared to deal with? Some of it, or all of it?"

"All of it! But I doubt you're capable of—"

"You don't know what I'm capable of. And you'd be surprised at some of the things I know. In my job you've got to learn the facts in order to distort them. I'll start with the easy one. You know what happened to the monk seals when the big construction barges showed up three years ago? They left. That's it. They swam off to Kure Atoll, a bunch of uninhabited, navy-owned islands a hundred miles to the northwest. They have just as much privacy and protection as they ever did. The U.S. government made sure of that before they leased Keoki. But that's old news. That's the happy layer. Do you want to go deeper?"

She kept her hot glare forward.

"The deeper truth is that the Hawaiian monk seal is going to be extinct within fifteen years, and there's not a damn thing we can do about it. Okay, no. If we got rid of the tuna nets that sometimes snag them, they'd probably die off in eighteen years. We might be able to buy another five if we killed off all the tiger sharks in the area, but that creates its own issues. And it's still futile. You know why? Because the monk seal's number one enemy is the monk seal. Surprise! They may look cute, but they are one of the most sexually malevolent species on the face of the planet."

That earned me a quick, distrustful glower.

"During sex," I explained, "the males bite. I'm not talking about love nibbles, I mean they chomp their honeys hard. Often fatally. This has led to a serious skew in the guy/girl ratio, worse than any technical college. But instead of being wooed, the few females left can look forward to a short life of perpetual gang bangs. Oh yes. These monks do that. It's called mobbing. And when there aren't enough women around for the old screw-and-chew, the men move on to the girls. Then the boys. Then each other. This isn't Sammy the Seal you're crying over. These are rapists with flippers. Their entire society is like a bad prison drama. And by 2016 their show is going to be canceled. Because of Fairmont? No. Because there are no more women. They've been on this crash course for fifteen million years. They haven't learned. Now Darwin says it's their time to go. But that's not even the worst part. Do you want go deeper?"

"Shut up."

"The truth is that all of the information I just gave you is out there. It took me ten minutes to get it off the Web. It would have taken you the same—"

"Shut up!"

"—time to find it. But you didn't look. And I know it's not because you're dumb or lazy. Quite the opposite. You're an extraordinary woman. You just didn't want to know. You were offered a free trip to Hawaii to do something you believed in. Something you could feel good about. How often does a chance like that come along? I'm only sorry it got ruined for you, that's all. That's what too much truth can do. That's why people like me exist."

Deb pressed her fist against her lips. I wasn't sure if she was going to cry or deck me. Either way, I figured the greatest gift I could give her now was my lifelong absence.

"You're going to go far, Deb. You're going to do wonderful things. But my well-meaning advice is to get over it, join your friends, and have one hell of a vacation. You deserve it, okay? Take it easy."

She resumed her westward gaze. I took a short breath, nodded, and started on my merry way.

"Scott . . ."

I stopped and turned around. She approached me, chewing on her words.

"I appreciate what you no doubt saw as an attempt to cheer me up. And I also appreciate the wisdom you shared. You're right. There are twelve sides to every story. Here's mine. You're a bastard. You're a bastard who took advantage of my good nature in order to get my clothes off, in order to make more money for your corporate overlords, in order to make more money for yourself. The fact that you think a free vacation could possibly make up for how disgusting I feel shows how little you understand women. Or anyone, for that matter. You may excuse yourself for being such a moral cripple because that's the way you think the world works, but there's another layer to that. Do you want to go deeper?"

"Deb—"

"The deeper truth is that you are going to live a long, destructive life. You're going to keep doing terrible things. And when you're in your deathbed at a hundred and three, you're going to realize that it didn't mean a damn thing. None of it. You know why? Because it'll finally occur to you that nobody's going to miss you. You could die today and nobody would miss you. I certainly wouldn't. In fact, I'll be happy if I forget you even existed. Why don't we get that process started, okay? Get the hell out of my sight. Get the hell out of my life. And Scott? For the sake of the world, please don't live to be a hundred and three."

Fifteen minutes later, I joined Miranda and the Metropia crew at the airstrip. David was staying behind with the students. I wasn't. My work here was done. I'd had quite enough of the sisters.

"Where were you?" asked Miranda.

"Talking to Deb."

"Oh, boy. Did she rip you a new one?"

"She wasn't happy."

"You think she'll sue?"

"Nah."

I figured Deb would be hard-pressed to ever mention it again, for whatever reasons. Shame. Embarrassment. Melodramatic self-pity. Take your pick. She wouldn't even tell her fellow coeds what she had learned. She'd think she was being noble in hiding the truth from them, in not killing their fun. She wouldn't see the utter hypocrisy. She'd just hate me for trying to do the same thing.

Whatever. I've learned not to take these things personally. It would be vain, ludicrous, and an all-around waste of time to treat her harsh opinion as some accurate reflection of who I was. Her final words to me—which she was no doubt proud of—had been shaped by a thousand of her own biases, neuroses, insecurities, generalities. She didn't know me. Instead of facts, she just filled in the blanks with whatever she found lying around. All the salespeople who vexed her. All the men who tried to talk her out of her clothes. All the corporate bad guys she saw on TV. Snakes and snails and puppy-dog tails. There's a mile of difference between truth and judgment, hon. Maybe she'd figure that out for herself someday. She was young. She had time to learn.

2
BITCH FIEND

"So aren't you going to ask about her?"

That was Miranda, sitting next to me in the Tiki Bar at the Honolulu International Airport. We were both waiting for flights to Los Angeles. Once there, she would hop her connecting plane to New York, and I would go home and go to bed. I looked forward to that.

Currently I was staring up at the mounted TV, waiting for the five o'clock news. I loved being out in public when my stories hit the air. I would listen to the reactions of everyone around me. I didn't give a crap what they thought about the nudity or the monk seal. I just wanted to hear them say the word "Fairmont." That would mean I got them. I scored a hit. It was a wonderful thing to see my own mojo at work. Sometime within the next thirty-five minutes I would be hawking my product to everyone in this bar, without saying a word.

"Scott?"

"I'm sorry. What?"

"Aren't you going to ask me how Gracie's doing?"

"Oh," I replied innocently. "No."

"Why not?"

"Because if she's good, I might feel bad. And if she's bad, I might feel bad about feeling good. That's the thing about being raised by German Jews. I feel guilt at my own schadenfreude."

Miranda laughed. "Fine. But she asked me to get the 411 on you. To see how you're doing."

"So what are you going to tell her?"

"I don't know yet. If you had more than one mood or facial expression, I might be able to get a better reading."

"Well, you're a reporter. Ask me some questions."

"Sorry, no. I said I wanted the 411. You only give the 412."

"What's that?"

"The number for Disinformation."

I chuckled. "I like that."

Miranda fought her own smile. "Yeah. You would."

It was 4:50. The Channel 9 news team had yet to plug my story once between the slices of *Judge Judy*. That wasn't encouraging.

"For the record," Miranda added, "she's good."

I knew that. And I was glad for Gracie. There was really no reason for me to stay angry. It was a waste of energy. We had what we had. From the beginning we'd agreed to be the Anti-Couple. We weren't going to meld into one freakish entity or follow any preconceived notions of how to properly coexist. No FranklinCovey tenets. No magazine quizzes. No chicken soup for our souls. And most important, no theatrics. We knew that melodrama was the leading cause of death in all relationships. Our one nonwedding wedding vow was to avoid all cinematic highs and lows. We were two individuals whose lives would not imitate art.

That was the real pity. That she broke her oath. The tale of how she met and fell in love with her legitimate husband could have come straight from a beginner screenwriting class: a smarmy, syrupy pastiche of every Meg Ryan vehicle. Fortunately I was off-screen for most of it. The plot was eventually relayed to me by Miranda, who played the heroine's blunt but supportive friend. She didn't tell me what climactic stunt he had used to win Gracie's heart. Rode a balloon to her office building. Dressed up in a bunny suit. Who knows? He got her. I got over it. To me, she was just backstory now.

"So is there someone else in your life?"

I checked my watch, then the TV. Come on already. "Nope."

"Why not?"

"Because nobody likes me."

"That's bullshit. You're tall. You're smart. You're funny. And you've got that sexy 'evil' thing going on. The problem is that you're just not looking. You've got to be more aggressive."

"I'll make a note."

The young bartender refreshed my Diet Pepsi. I dropped a lemon wedge in the glass, then stirred it all up with a straw.

"Whatever," said Miranda. "Maybe I'll fix you up with someone. I don't know many eligible women. But apparently my husband does."

"Jim's a prick."

"No kidding."

She took a long sip of her mai tai. "What's wrong with me, Scott?"

"Your taste in men."

"It's that simple, huh?"

"He's beneath you and he knows it. I mean, he's not that smart. Or interesting. And he chuckles at his own jokes. Nervously."

She laughed. "I know, I know. He just got me at a good young age. When I was still wet cement. Now I feel like I'm stuck with him, even if we split up. I feel like I'll always be carrying him around."

The credits were running on *Judge Judy*. Still no teaser.

"It's just bullshit," she continued. "I'm getting tired of all the bullshit. And I don't just mean his kind. Or even your kind. My job is just . . . fuck. I don't know, Scott. I'm just sick of the whole business."

Short of faking a seizure, there was nothing I could say or do to prevent her from elaborating.

"There was this woman who died last week. Pika Kumari. She was eighty-four and blind as a bat, but she died just hours after finishing her three thousand eight hundred and twenty-eighth clay sculpture. They were all of Ganesha, the Indian god of fortune. She'd been working on them day in and day out for seventeen years. Her granddaughter told me that Pika had been blinded in that 1984 Union Carbide accident in Bhopal. You know, the poison leak. You know how many people died in that thing?"

"Three thousand eight hundred and twenty-eight," I guessed.

"Very good. She stayed alive just long enough to finish her tribute to those victims. I cried when I found that out. I wrote this thousand-word piece on her. It wasn't just an obituary, it was my tribute to her. Do you know how many newspapers ended up running it?"

"Zero."

"Four. But they all whittled it down to a little nub before sticking it in the back, right below the pet obituaries." She pushed away her drink. "Assholes. Too bad there weren't any naked women involved."

I checked the TV yet again. Why weren't they plugging my story, goddamn it? I gave them plenty of lead time.

Miranda went on. "Human interest. What a bullshit term. Have people really gotten so dumb that we need mass slaughter or full-frontal nudity just to get their attention?"

"There's this book by Bruno Bettelheim. *The Uses of Enchantment.* Ever read it?"

"No."

"It's basically a hyper-Freudian analysis of all the classic fairy tales. Screwed-up stuff. He has a whole chapter on 'Jack and the Beanstalk,' how it's basically an unconscious allegory about maturing into a sexual being."

"You're kidding."

"No. For example, Jack's mother makes him sell the cow because she doesn't provide milk anymore. Are we talking about the cow or the mother? Aha. Then he buys some magic testicular beans, plants them in the fertile ground, and then overnight . . ." I rose a hand from my groin to the sky.

She laughed. "That is such crap."

"That was my first reaction, too. But Bettelheim goes on to make a good point. There have been thousands of fairy tales written over the course of history, but only a handful have survived to become classics. How did that happen? It wasn't good marketing. There was never a GrimmCo pushing these things. They were simply the stories that stuck in the minds of kids who grew up and passed them on to their own kids, again and again and again. Why do you think that is?"

Miranda rolled her eyes. "Because on a deeper human level, sex and violence sell."

"We didn't create the need. We're just filling it."

"Whatever happened to a need for the truth?"

"Yeah, right. Out of the millions of people who love Big Macs, how many would want a list of all the industrial-strength chemicals that go into one? How many of them would jump at the chance to see their favorite burger get put together by some hygienically challenged teenager who probably just fondled himself in the restroom without—"

"All right. All right!" She held up her hands, repulsed. "Bastard."

"See, that's the problem. You're like a media fry cook. You can't enjoy your own product because you see all the shit that goes into it."

"Well, you're the one who puts it there!"

"And you're the one who serves it."

"Tell me, Scott. Was any of this conversation designed to cheer me up?"

"I don't think so. No."

She laughed again, snagging her drink back. She took a long sip, then studied me. "You know, you think you're such a bad-ass."

"I don't think I'm a bad-ass at all. I actually think I'm quite a good-ass."

"Well, you're an ass. Let's just leave it at that."

Good enough. At the moment I was just ass-tired. The whole Keoki operation had taken a lot out of me, and not because of Deb's little tongue-lashing. I was impervious to the scorn of others, but when it came to the media, I was a smitten little boy. If you asked anyone in the world to personify American culture, they'd probably describe the stereotypical supermodel: moody, shallow, vacuous, easy to make fun of, but shamefully hot. Face it, everybody wanted her attention. She didn't have to respect us, she just had to let us touch her. Personally, I didn't even care if she knew my name. I was a grand-scale Cyrano. I wooed her through others. But today I had sent her one hell of a note. I was dying to know what she thought of it.

At the stroke of five, I got my answer.

The most frustrating part of my job was that I had absolute control over every part of the story except the outcome. I thought my timing would be brilliant. I figured February 1 was a perfect day for mass nudity. And it would have been, if it weren't for a fifteen-year-old girl named Annabelle Shane. She trumped me. The goddamn kid had an even better trick than mine.

———

This morning, as I led my army of coeds toward the beaches of Kaikua'ana, young Annabelle decided that today would be the last day of her life. She'd been thinking about death for a couple of weeks, we assume, but was waiting for February sweeps to begin. Like me, she knew her TV business. Like me, she had a carefully planned agenda. Now was the time. The news crews were extra hungry. Technically, she had all month to stage her event, but I suppose, like me, she was anxious to get her story out.

At 7:00 A.M. Los Angeles time, she told her mother she wasn't feeling well and was staying home. Annabelle had been missing a lot of school lately. The maternal instinct would have been to haul her ass out of bed, but Mom—a data-entry operator who was studying at night to get her master's in social work—took a clinical approach. All right, Anna. I'll make you a deal. I'll let you stay home again but tonight you have to tell me what's going on with you. We need to talk about this. Okay?

No problem, said Annabelle. A few hours after her mother and eleven-year-old sister left the house, Annabelle decided to go to school after all. She was a slip of a girl. Stick-thin, short, and surprisingly pale for a Tiger Woods–like crossbreed of African and Asian (Dad was black, Mom was Thai).

But Annabelle knew she was pretty. She had sharp features, great skin, and her mother's exotic eyes. She wasn't happy with her chest, but whatever nature had cheated her of, science would provide. Annabelle had often told her friends that she was getting augmented as soon as she turned eighteen. After that, men would be her lapdogs. They'd conquer France if she asked them to.

Today, she had chosen to make herself sexy. Her mother's mascara. That hot little spaghetti-strap number she'd worn to the 'N Sync concert. She took an extra hour to superstyle her short, raven hair. That was it. She was primed and ready.

For the first time ever, she walked to school. She trekked a mile and a half through Hollywood in high heels. No doubt she was feeling it by the time she got to Melrose Avenue High School, a sprawling three-story complex just east of Fairfax. By then it was already 12:15. Miranda's plane was just touching down on the Keoki airstrip when little Miss Shane primped herself up one last time and entered the crowded cafeteria. With an "odd intensity" (quoth witnesses), she joined her friends at their usual table. "Hey, where have you been? Are you okay? Why you all dressed up?"

Annabelle smiled awkwardly and then retrieved a Sony camcorder. It was her father's toy. Ever since those digital video numbers hit the market, the old-school VHS-C cameras had plummeted in both price and size. This one was $299 at Circuit City and small enough to fit in a teenager's crowded book bag. Annabelle gently placed the camera in Gina's hands. Do you care about me, Gina? Of course, sweetie. Why?

"Just film me."

Those were Annabelle Shane's last words. She kissed Gina on the forehead, took her book bag, and crossed to where the basketball crowd sat. Melrose High was 50 percent African American, 20 percent Hispanic, 20 percent Caucasian, and 10 percent other. The Melrose Raiders (3-1 so far this season) were similarly represented, but the coach and team cocaptains were white as snow.

The Raiders were oft-discussed figures at school, and not just for their winning record. When the prying ears of adults were far out of range, the players—plus qualified friends—went by a different name. This had been the student body's best-kept secret until today.

And this is where my affinity with Annabelle ends. I can't even begin to imagine the thoughts in her head when she pulled out a Glock 17 9mm pistol, a product I had personally helped position into one action film and three video games. The gun was her father's other toy. His only weapon. She didn't hesitate in firing it at the Melrose Raiders, otherwise known as the Bitch Fiends.

A Glock 17 is a powerful handgun, the weapon of choice for a number of law-enforcement agencies because of its ease of use and accuracy. In the hands of a 101-pound neophyte shooter, however, it's not the most precise instrument. Her first shot went through the cafeteria window, puncturing a dumpster. The second bullet missed Bryan Edison, the strapping cocaptain of the b-ball team, by a matter of inches before embedding itself into brick. The third round, also intended for Bryan, hit his teammate Gary Halperin in the right collarbone, shattering it. All three shots happened within three seconds. The Glock 17 is also known for its super-light trigger.

From that moment on, accounts vary widely. Some students say Annabelle was icy calm in the chaos she had caused. Others say she was crying and screaming along with everyone else. The only fact was that she kept shooting. At Bryan Edison. In retrospect, there's no doubt that Bryan knew exactly what her mission was. While half the students ducked under tables, Bryan fled with the rest. And Annabelle followed.

Expanded in 1992, the Melrose High cafeteria accommodated more than six hundred students. It was twenty times the size of the school's basketball court. In the thirty seconds it took Bryan to make it to the doors, Annabelle fired twelve more rounds. Four of them hit walls. Seven hit bystanders. The final shot hit Brian in the back of the head just as he reached the exit. He died before he even hit the ground.

The Glock 17 is so named because its standard clip holds seventeen bullets. Annabelle—who had brought no backup ammo—was obviously saving the last shot for herself. Nobody will ever know whether she chose to stop after Bryan's death or had simply lost count of the number of bullets remaining. Either way, the second-to-last shell was the one that pierced her troubled mind, into her left temple (she was a southpaw) and out through the right.

Before she ended her own life, Annabelle had turned to Gina and was no doubt relieved to see that the whole incident had been caught on tape.

In the coming days, a lot of outspoken public figures would harp on Gina's ability to play camerawoman to her best friend's carnage. She couldn't have frozen in shock, they'd say, because she followed the action like a seasoned war journalist. She panned and scanned the whole thing without uttering so much as a scream. Do you see? Do you see how disconnected our children are?

Bullshit. More thoughtless drumbeating. Only one expert will eventually go on-air to explain the obvious: there's more than one kind of shock. In reality, Gina kept shooting long after Annabelle did. Like a living motion sensor, she blankly pointed the camera at whatever caught her eye, even after the tape ended. Mentally, she was lost in space, failing to respond to teachers and students alike when they called her name. It wasn't until a policeman pried the camera out of her hands that she crashed back to earth.

In the end, there were five dead students, including Bryan Edison and Annabelle. Five others were rushed to Cedars-Sinai with moderate to critical wounds. Out of all nine victims, three were eventually confirmed as Bitch Fiends. The remaining six had never even spoken to Annabelle. They only had the misfortune of standing near Bryan Edison.

At 1:11 P.M. Pacific, the first hints of trouble hit the AP wires. No names. No figures. Just shots fired and casualties reported. Local newsteams had flooded the scene by 1:30. This wasn't a VNR affair, this was the hardest of hard news. By 2:00 P.M., the number of deaths had been confirmed, as was Annabelle's identity as the assailant. The story cracked wide open at 3:00, when reporters around the nation first spoke the words "Bitch Fiend." In New York, viewers heard it from their favorite six o'clock newscast. In L.A., the kids coming home from more fortunate schools got their first glimpse of the tragedy. And at Keoki Atoll, right at that moment, I was cluelessly faxing every news center in the country with my super-hot announcement: NAKED YOUNG WOMEN PROTEST BEACH RESORT.

"Damn."

That was Miranda, at the Tiki Bar, watching the news. By then the story was hours old. It had already mushroomed into the heavens. I wasn't sure if she was cursing at the tragedy of the situation or the fact that she may have very well been the last reporter in the United States to get wind of it.

"Shit."

That was me, next to Miranda. I was cursing at the tragedy of the situation. I had worked damn hard on my VNR. I'd spent over half a million dollars of my client's money. And thanks to one disturbed but media-savvy little girl, my Trojan horse became a big white elephant.

So what is a Bitch Fiend?

To most of the reporters on the scene, it was simply the phrase that Annabelle had inscribed on the label of the controversial mini-tape. Although the LAPD would seize her video forever, its two-word title had made its way to the press by three o'clock, along with the rumor that the movie included more than just a killing spree. Some heard she'd filmed a tell-all suicide note. Others reported that there was *allegedly* a video-taped sex act involving Annabelle and one of the victims. Or two of the victims. Or one of the teachers. Who knew? The cops weren't talking. It would have to stay a mystery for now.

But the title was quickly cracked by the minority of reporters who knew their hip-hop. "Bitch Fiend" was the name of a breakout song by Hunta, a young L.A. rapper whose platinum-selling debut album, *Hunt-away,* had been released the year before through Mean World Records and distributed by Interscope. I'd never heard of the man myself, but then I wasn't really a rap aficionado. I only knew the marquee names, mostly through their controversies: Sean "Puffy" Combs (gun/assault/bribery charges), Eminem (gun/assault/homophobia), Snoop Dogg (gun/murder, acquitted), Ice Cube and Ice T (anti-cop sentiments, movies), and Dr. Dre (various punching/slapping offenses).

Welcome to the big list, Hunta. Hope you survive.

The many news stations under the CBS/Viacom aegis were given quick access to Hunta's music video for "Bitch Fiend," courtesy of sister network MTV. Only a few stations played clips from the raunchy thing. Others broke the plot down to its bare essence: Hunta gets jiggy with bitch. Hunta secretly records bitch. Hunta shows videotape of bitch to all his homeys. Lather, rinse, repeat.

The uncut version of "Bitch Fiend" was first released on the Playboy Channel last September. A strategically edited/blurred version—complete with radio-safe lyrics—soon made the rounds on MTV and BET. There was still enough sex and nastiness to keep the video in heavy rotation, enough to make Hunta more than just a fleeting new face on the scene.

By the time Miranda and I finally caught up with the nation, several Melrose students had spoken to the media. Once again wildly conflicting stories filled the airwaves, all under the *alleged* banner. The whole basketball team was secretly known and feared as the Bitch Fiends. No, it was only a few of them. No, it was all of them, plus at least ten other guys. And they had a sex club. I heard it was an S&M club. Well, I heard they videotaped all their sexual encounters and showed them to each other, just like in the music video. Yeah, it was like a membership requirement. No, I think it was more like a competition to see who could get the most airtime with the most bitches. They told me it was a rape club, man.

Shit, Annabelle. You really knew your media. Not only did you deliver a long-awaited sequel to Columbine, but you gave it a sordid sex twist and a hip-hop soundtrack. Too bad you cast yourself as the lead. The first rule of the media operative is never become part of the story. You should have consulted me.

All in all, it was an ugly situation that would only get worse. The police had just begun their investigation. The press was on full-tilt boogie. And you could just hear the politicians sharpening their knives. They were all fixing to close in on one target: Hunta.

Poor guy. All he wanted to do was get it on with American culture, that hot and surly supermodel. Well, he got her. But this time he was the one who was in for a rough fucking. She was about to show him what a Bitch could really do.

3

MRVL GRL

Although she had rained on my parade, Annabelle Shane also managed to end a personal dry spell.

Miranda caught up with me at the LAX baggage claim. By then it was two in the morning. I'd been thirty-five thousand feet above Catalina when it stopped being my birthday.

"Take me to a hotel," she said.

"You're staying now."

"I called my editor. He's putting me on the Melrose High shooting. I told him I deserved some real news after putting up with your crap."

"Aren't you stepping on toes?"

"It's a big story. There's plenty of room. You parked in long-term, right?"

And just like that, I inherited Miranda. And her baggage.

While airborne, I had received a voice-mail message from Craig Mertens, my contact at Mertens & Fay. Turns out the Keoki campaign wasn't a complete disaster. Although my VNR had bombed in the States, it was all over the morning news in Europe and got considerable airplay in Canada, Mexico, Israel, and Japan. In fact, Japan's only angle on the Melrose massacre was how obsessed we were over it. They harped on the fact that there had been 28 other shooting deaths and 113 gun-related injuries on American soil today. Not that we would ever know that. In Israel, a newscaster had even wider statistics: out of the 150,000 Americans murdered by gunfire in the past ten years, only 150 or so were shot in or around a school. The anchorman snickered at our schoolviolence "epidemic." Why don't you try hanging out at the West Bank sometime? You stupid overreacting Americans. Still, your women are hot. Here's a neat story from Hawaii.

Craig was overjoyed by the international exposure. Affluent foreigners were always a welcome market for Fairmont. He also graciously reminded me that newspapers had much more room for filler than your standard thirty-minute broadcast. Where my VNR failed, Miranda's wire piece would take over. The bottom line was that Fairmont would be happy with what they got: a B+ effort. Still, it could have been an A if it weren't for Annabelle.

Oh well. Life moved on. For most of us, anyway. While in transit, I had also received a message from Keith Ullman, the head of worldwide marketing and distribution for MGM Studios. After two weeks he was finally getting back to me. "Sorry, Scott. It's been crazy here. Let's get together as soon as possible, and we'll talk about this thing of yours."

That "thing" wasn't really mine. It was Ira's. Believe me, if it were mine, I wouldn't have named it Move My Cheese. That was my next priority.

In the meantime, a funny thing happened on the way to adultery.

"I can't believe you drive a Saturn."

I couldn't believe Miranda was still awake. She'd been in the air for eighteen of the past twenty-four hours, crossing back and forth through six different time zones. Her inner clock must have been blinking at 12:00. Now, at 2:30 A.M., she somehow found the energy to dis my ride.

"What would you rather I drive?"

"You're in Los Angeles. You should have an SUV."

"Short people drive SUVs. I don't need to feel bigger."

I figured that Miranda, at 5' 1", would respond with a flip comeback, or at least a flipped finger. Instead, she merely stretched and curled in a way that was seductively catlike. I kept my eyes on the road, but I knew she was looking at me.

"What?"

"You liked Deb Isham," she teased. "I could tell."

"Go to sleep."

"No shame in it, man. Her tits were huge."

"If that's all it took, I'd have a crush on every woman in L.A."

"I mean naturally huge. I think you could have had her, too. If I didn't ruin it."

"I doubt it."

"So what was it you liked about her? Besides her knockers. Is it that she's young and naïve? That she could gaze upon you with a sense of awe and wonder?"

I would not entertain this conversation. Not at 2:30 A.M.

"Scott?"

"Oh, me? I'm sorry. I thought you were talking to Jim."

She laughed hysterically, not without bitterness. "That was *so* rude!"

"I know. I'm sorry. Would you prefer pity?"

"No. That's why I like you."

"Wow," I said. "You actually admit it. How many drinks did you have on that flight?"

"None. I'm just really tired. Why? Are you trying to take advantage of me?"

"Always."

"Good. I don't feel like checking in to a hotel."

I thought of several quips, all ranging from cute to provocative. Instead, I merely shut up. It had been a long day. I was too drained to handle the dilemma that was turning from humor to reality.

From the 405, I took the Wilshire East exit. I lived in Brentwood, only a few minutes away. Miranda had reserved a room at the Hotel Claremont, even closer. The sooner I got her out of my car, the better.

"So this is the famous Wilshire Boulevard," she said, to my relief. That was her way of applying the hand brake.

"Yeah. Do you know who it was named after?"

"Mr. Wilshire."

"Mr. H. Gaylord Wilshire. He was an active socialist but that didn't stop him from being a great capitalist. He invented the I-ON-A-CO magnetic belt, an expensive little doodad that was supposed to heal almost any physical problem. Made millions off of it. He bought so many buildings on this one street that they finally just named it after him. They even called his district the Miracle Mile, because they thought he was such a wizard. You want to know what the funniest part is?"

She didn't answer. I turned to her. She kept her cold stare forward, fighting back tears. Losing.

"Ah, shit. I'm sorry, Miranda."

"No. No pity. Come on. You were doing so well."

I sped through a yellow light. A dark SUV tailgated me. Its brights were on. I had to reposition my mirror to keep from going blind.

"Is there something I can say or do to make you feel better?"

"Depends," she said.

"On what?"

"On whether or not you want to have sex with me."

BAM! Both of our heads jerked back. I almost swerved onto the sidewalk.

Miranda turned around. "Jesus! What happened?"

I wasn't sure until I looked in the rearview mirror again. The SUV quickly pulled back, signaling to the right.

"I think we just got rear-ended," I said.

"Holy shit."

I pulled over, right in front of the Avco cineplex. In this part of town, Wilshire was an eight-lane street. At this time of night, it was deserted. It had taken an extraordinary amount of incompetence to hit me.

I turned on the hazards and looked to Miranda. "You okay?"

"Yeah. Did you hit the brake or something?"

"No. He just knocked into us."

"Well, be careful," she said as I opened the door. "It could be a gang thing."

Silly New Yorker. Crips don't drive sport utility wagons. I was more concerned about an irrational drunk. The last thing I needed was to deal with somebody's beer-fueled rage.

I got out. A small woman emerged from the driver's side. With the headlights on me, I could only see her shape.

"Are you okay, ma'am?"

She didn't move or respond. Once I shielded my eyes, she reached into her car and shut off the brights. She'd done a fair amount of damage to my trunk, and virtually none to her front bumper and grille. Another reason to hate SUVs.

I was idly intrigued by her license plate: MRVL GRL. I never quite understood the allure of vanity plates. First of all, they're vain. Second, they're dated. And finally, they're esoteric. Although in this case, it was a code I was qualified to crack. It was easy enough to add the proper vowels and get MARVEL GIRL, but you had to be a longtime comic-book reader in order to put the name to a face. Marvel Girl was the very first alias of Jean Grey, the only female member of Stan Lee and Jack Kirby's original X-Men. She dropped the moniker in *Uncanny X-Men* #101, when she merged with an interstellar entity to become the all-powerful Phoenix. Since then, she's gone on to become Dark Phoenix, dead Phoenix, resurrected Phoenix, and Famke Janssen.

The driver looked like none of them. Whereas Jean Grey was a statuesque beauty with a large mane of flame-red hair, MRVL GRL was a pixie of a woman, a cropped-cut brunette. If it weren't for her mid-length denim skirt and hoop earrings, I might have assumed she was a teenage boy. Then I would have studied her face, also outdated. Her small features, combined with contrastingly large eyes, gave her a naïve, golden-age charm. She would have been considered beautiful back in the silent-movie era. Today she was merely cute and pleasant in a Katie Couric sort of way.

She gave me a frustrated but apologetic shrug and then examined the damage.

"Well, it's ugly," I told her, "but it could have been worse. You do have insurance, right?"

She didn't answer me. She kept looking at my dented trunk.

"Excuse me? Do you have insurance?"

Shrugging at me again, she took a handheld PDA out of her blouse pocket, then had second thoughts. That's right, honey. It's too dark to be taking notes. Who the hell are you?

I held my arms out. "Uh, hello?"

She abruptly motioned to the dark figure in the passenger seat. *Get your ass out here, will you?*

The door opened, and an icy young blonde stepped out into the night. Very young. Her exaggerated crossed-arm stance pegged her at around fifteen. She was rail-thin and, unlike MRVL GRL, a little more hip with the times.

She studied me, then my car, and muttered an obscenity. MRVL GRL knocked on the hood to get her attention.

"What do you want me to do about it?"

Frustrated, MRVL GRL moved her hands in blunt but methodical patterns that clearly said volumes to the girl. They told me a few things as well.

"Wait a second. You're deaf?" I looked to the girl. "She's deaf?"

"Yes, she's deaf. My mother wants me to tell you that she's sorry for hitting you. It was totally her fault. As if that wasn't obvious."

"I didn't . . ." I looked to the mother, then back at the daughter. "I didn't even know deaf people could drive."

"Yeah. It's blind people who have the problems."

"No. I know, but . . ." This was too strange. "Can you tell her I need her insurance information?"

Annoyed, the girl signed to her mother while talking. "He wants your insurance information."

MRVL GRL nodded impatiently. *Yeah, yeah. Obviously. But consider this.*

Unlike all the interpreters I'd seen (on TV), the girl waited until her mother was done before translating.

"She says she has insurance, but she thinks it's a total rip-off. They're only going to raise her premiums until she pays back twice whatever they end up shelling out for this."

That seemed like an awful lot of information for such a quick bit of sign language. But she was right on about the insurance companies.

"I agree. But if she's proposing some kind of split—"

"You're actually supposed to talk to her."

"What?"

"My mother. She's the one you're dealing with."

I looked to the woman. She threw me an edgy smirk and a wave. *Hi.*

"Uh, are you proposing some kind of . . . split . . . ? Because that's . . ." As I spoke, the mother watched the daughter, who interpreted my words. It was very disconcerting. The mother signed back.

"No no," said the daughter, "she says she'll pay for all the damage. She'd rather pay under the table, that's all. Just get an estimate and she'll send you a check. She's good for it."

Nothing invites cynicism more than the assertion that someone is "good for it." Reading my face, MRVL GRL held up a finger and went back to her car. Awkwardly, I turned to the daughter.

"I've never really talked to a deaf person before."

"You hide it well."

"What are you doing out so late on a school night?"

"Long story."

"Oh. Don't tell me you go to Melrose High School."

"I don't. I'm in eighth grade."

"Really? You look older."

"Thanks. You know, you're awfully polite for someone who just got rammed."

I grinned. "I'm on Prozac."

"Good. Maybe you can lend some to my mother."

MRVL GRL reemerged from the car with her insurance slip and a business card. After handing both to me, she signed to her daughter.

"She says if you want insurance, there it is. But please trust her. If you give her an estimate, she'll give you a check. Or better yet, she can pay in services. She's a professional Web designer. Or so she likes to think."

I looked at the card. JEAN SPELLING, ORIGINAL X WEB DESIGN. Cute. She was definitely a comics fan.

She signed some more. "Again, she says she's really sorry. I told her not to talk and drive. She was in the middle of chewing me out, as usual."

Sensing that her daughter was going off-script, Jean tapped the hood again. The girl rolled her eyes.

"Anyway, please don't report this until she has a chance to pay you. Deal?"

I glanced at Jean. "Look, I don't care how I get paid. If you can go out of pocket, that's fine."

On reading the translation, Jean pressed her hands, shining her relief at me. *Thank you. Thank you.*

"Just drive carefully," I said.

She smiled and quickly signed to her daughter.

"What's your name?"

"Scott. Scott Singer. Yours?"

"Madison. I was the one asking. My mom wants your business card in case she needs to reach you."

I took a card from my wallet and gave it to Jean. She looked younger up close. Early thirties at the most. I noticed her plain silver wedding band. I wondered if Madison's father was deaf, too. Could deaf parents even have a hearing child?

Jean touched my wrist and, with a hint of strain in her face, mouthed "Sorry."

I shrugged. "Take it easy."

They waved and got back in the car. Back to their own drama, already in progress. Meanwhile, I still had mine. With a sigh, I returned to my damaged Saturn and shut the door.

Miranda cocked her head at me. "So what happened?"

"Did you ever see *The Piano*?"

"No."

"It sucked."

"So what happened? Was this woman drunk?"

"No. Just deaf."

"She rear-ended you because she couldn't hear you."

"Apparently she was talking while driving."

"That's messed up."

"You know what's really messed up? That I know the history of Wilshire Boulevard. I know the mating habits of the Hawaiian monk seal. And yet I didn't know deaf people could drive."

"That's fascinating. So are we sleeping together, or am I just ugly?"

I took a deep breath and then a good look at Miranda. She wasn't ugly.

I moved to Los Angeles in 1991. Before that, I had never even been to the West Coast. I'd spent the previous four years in Georgetown, until Drea told me to flee. She had been my mentor, my lover, my sugar mommy, my idol. She represented everything I wanted to be. Then, at age thirty-nine, at the height of her career, she fell apart. Some publicists burn out. She went nova.

"Get out of Washington," she told me. "I want you out of this game. If I ever find you working here, I'll do everything I can to destroy your career."

She had said this out of love, not anger. She simply wanted to save my soul. Consumer and entertainment PR were kindergarten compared to the lobbyist arena. I saw some of the tricks Drea pulled. I saw what they did to people. What they did to her. When she told me to run, I ran. To this day I've kept far out of political affairs. I don't even vote.

Pushing me out west was one of the best things she ever did for me. L.A. suited me. I loved the weather. I enjoyed the people (in small doses). And I cherished the space. The city did not lack for elbow room. I had my own three-bedroom duplex in the heart of Brentwood for the measly cost of twenty-two hundred a month. One bedroom was a dusty mini-gym. The other was a dusty office (I do everything by laptop now). The master bedroom wasn't dusty, but it certainly wasn't used to company.

Another great thing Drea had done for me was teach me how to properly screw. Prior to her, I was doing everything wrong. This was news to me. In my four years at Cornell, I had partnered with women who were either too young to know, too polite to say, or too drunk to care. Meanwhile, I was busy making up for all the sex I didn't have in high school. Drea was thirty-five when she took me under her wing and sheets. By that age, she knew exactly what she was doing, and what she wanted done to her. I learned much.

But I couldn't shake the feeling that I was still a mediocre lover. I never got the sense that I had moved the earth, rocked my partner's world, or even had my own world rocked. Usually, sex with me ended like the Fairmont Keoki project: a B+ effort. Maybe my expectations were too high. Maybe most guys were so-so in the sack. Or maybe I simply thought too much.

With Miranda there was no question. The sex was bad. It wasn't really her fault, or my fault. It was the people we brought into bed with us. The living ghosts of Jim and Gracie hovered nearby the whole time. The only thing more distracting and less erotic would be having my dead parents walk in.

When we finished (at least the "me" part of "we"), Miranda broke down. I held her in my arms as she sobbed, but all I could think about was Drea. With the exception of height (Drea was almost six feet tall), she and Miranda were extremely similar. They were both strong-willed, well composed, and very masculine about their emotions. This was the first time I'd ever seen Miranda cut loose with tears. It was uncomfortable for me. I never asked for this kind of access. And I never claimed to have the skills or resources to help her out of her emotional pit.

"What's wrong with me, Scott? What the fuck's wrong with me?"

I merely held her and stared at the stucco ceiling. She had already asked me that question in Honolulu. I didn't lie. I truly didn't think there was anything wrong with her, except her taste in men.

4
JEREMY SHARPE

The last time I decided to seek an outside life was in December 1997. At the time *Titanic* was causing millions of damp-eyed women to wonder if their own men would die of hypothermia for them. Gracie, as always, was ahead of the curve. Her heart had already gone on. It was my mother's sudden departure that really shook me up.

On December 15, a ruptured cerebral aneurysm caused her to stroke out in her sleep. She was sixty-four. Prior to that, she'd been perfectly healthy. At least physically. When my father lost his yearlong battle with cancer, most of my mother died with him. She spent the last four years of her life reading, writing, waiting. Over Thanksgiving dinner, a mere three weeks before her death, she told me that her biggest nightmare was gathering dust for forty more years in some decrepit nursing home.

From that perspective, I was almost relieved for her. But from now on I'd only be sharing my turkeys with friends. I certainly didn't lack for them (friends, not turkeys), but only if you went by the local definition. Los Angeles, appropriately enough, was the land of the fair-weather friend. Some of the people in my Rolodex required great weather in order to remain amicable. If the temperature ever went below fifty degrees, we'd probably all eat each other. This was more of a career effect than anything else.

After my mother's funeral, I decided to look for camaraderie outside the media world. I'd had enough of the border collies. It was time to get to know some sheep. Unfortunately, I was soon reminded that most sheep were incredibly stupid, especially in Los Angeles.

My snobby solution was Mensa, the high-IQ society. In order to get into this renowned club I had to take a fun but challenging series of tests. They only accepted those at the top 2 percent of the national IQ scale. I barely squeaked in with a 135. That made me one of the dumber new members to join. Cool.

Most outsiders picture Mensans as big-domed nerds who sit around speaking Esperanto and plotting world domination. That isn't entirely accurate. With the exception of a few annual theme gatherings, Mensa is mostly a network of special-interest groups (SIGs). There was a skiing SIG, a writers' SIG, a Christian SIG, even a target-shooting SIG, which was no doubt safer than being around stupid people with guns.

The funniest group—a spin-off, actually—was the International Society for Philosophical Enquiry, otherwise known as the Super High IQ Society. To get in, you had to retest and rank in the top 0.1 percent of IQ scores (151 on the Stanford-Binet scale, 172 on Cattell). I doubt they skied, prayed, or fired weapons any differently than the rest of us smart folk, but I suppose there's a vain appeal in belonging to an organization where one can kick back and make fun of those idiots at Mensa.

Out of all the factions, I was only interested in the Young M's. I saw their posting in the local Mensa newsletter (*L.A. Mentary*) and decided to drop in on their weekly game night at a Hollywood coffeehouse. On the way over, it occurred to me that "young" was a somewhat vague term. The last thing I wanted to do was walk in on a bunch of child prodigies playing Risk in German. I was quite relieved when I spotted the assortment of twenty-somethings gathered in the back. They were indeed smart and pleasant people. Sadly, they were also—as Douglas Adams would say—aggressively uninteresting.

The only exception was Ira.

If there was ever a Super-Duper High IQ Society that only the top minds from the Super High IQ Society could qualify for, Ira would be one of them. And I'm equally sure that within thirty minutes, the other two members would want to see him mauled by a bear. It's not that he lacked social skills. He just ignored them. He was an asshole savant, with the mind of da Vinci and the temperament of da Vinci after spending six hours in line at the Department of Motor Vehicles.

Worse, his foul disposition had a way of sneaking up on people, masked as it was by a deceptively jovial appearance. He was a large, shaggy-haired man, a cross between Jeff Daniels from *Dumb & Dumber* and comedy writer Bruce Vilanch. Simply put, he looked like a fun guy to be around. He did indeed have a robust sense of humor, but it usually left people in the wrong kind of tears. His tongue was a chain saw. He was the evil clown.

Classic example: Ira at the pharmacy. Late one evening he picked up his prescription allergy medication, signed for it, and then paid by credit card. The cute young clerk was supposed to check his billing signature against the handwriting on the back of his card. Instead, she checked it against the name he'd just scribbled on the pharmacy slip. Most of us would smirk at the innocent mistake and assume she was simply at the end of a long and tiresome day. Not Ira. He glared at her like she'd just taken a dump on his shoe.

"I can't believe you just . . . Do you even realize what you did? You took a signature I made five seconds ago and compared it to a signature I made ten seconds ago. Let me ask you, what in God's name were you hoping to verify? That I'm the same person who signed both receipts? I am. I haven't moved. I haven't even left your field of vision. Or are you just concerned that, in the five seconds between signatures, I was possessed by some demonic entity that was out to defraud both MasterCard and Sav-on? I really have to wonder if you're fit to hand out lifesaving remedies to people. For all I know, you just gave me estrogen pills. Don't they screen people here? What's the qualification standard? As long as you don't drool on your shirt, you're in? Jesus. I hope you accidentally gave me Zoloft, because frankly, people like you depress the hell out of me."

By that point, the clerk was sniffling, crying. Her burly manager had caught the tail end of the cutdown and was fixing to pound Ira into chutney. Wisely, he fled.

Poor Ira. Yeah yeah, what about the poor clerk? Look, she was young and pretty. She probably went home and cried to her boyfriend, who held her, stroked her hair, told her she was beautiful, and then screwed her raw. Ira had no such solace.

I can only assume it was a desire for human connection that had brought him to that Young M event in the first place. Still, it took just one game of Pictionary to clear out the room. The Mensans were too polite to tell him to take his art critiques and shove them up his alimentary. They simply found excuses to go home early, no doubt praying for his absence at the next gathering.

They got their wish. In fact, neither of us went back. That night Ira and I stayed behind and talked until 3:00 A.M. I may be no beauty, but he's no beast. Once he realized he couldn't push me away, he retracted his quills. The thing about Ira was that he loved people as an entity. He was a chaos mathematician, a brilliant one. By the time he was twenty, he had five published papers. When I met him, he was twenty-seven and widely considered to be the wünderprick of his field.

Soon after graduate school, he began working his way through each of the Big Six (now Big Four) accounting firms as a top-level market analyst. The drill was always the same. He went out of his way to earn the contempt of his bosses and peers, but because his work was so revolutionary, they labored to put up with him. It never lasted. Inevitably, the commoners would unite to gather their torches and run him out of the village. By the time I met him, he had already been chased out of Deloitte & Touche and Arthur Andersen and was repeating the process at Ernst & Young. He lasted only five months there, followed by equally brief and adversarial stints at KPMG and Price Waterhouse.

The real tragedy was that he got painfully depressed every time he was banished. After the Price Waterhouse fallout, in which a manager actually throttled him, he visited my apartment for the first time. I had invited him over on several occasions, but he preferred to meet in public, as if I were a potential rapist. I didn't question it. I was just surprised when I came home one day to find him literally crying at my doorstep.

"I feel like I was born without something," he told me. "Something everyone else has. I just can't bullshit people. I can't ask them how their weekend was when I really don't care. I can't tell them that I like their outfit when I really don't notice. And when they do something to screw up a project, *my* project, I can't just sit back and say, 'Hey, good work.' I just wasn't built that way. And they all hate me for it. They hate me. What's wrong with people? When did it become such a handicap to be honest?"

Once he was hired at Coopers & Lybrand, the last of the Big Six, he swore to amend his ways. He wouldn't just survive there; he'd make friends. He was half successful. I assume Ira's attempts at jocularity seemed eerily forced and a little unholy. But turning off the chain saw certainly brought his QScore out of the red.

Unfortunately, the work situation soon exploded again, for circumstantial reasons. In July 1998, Coopers & Lybrand merged with Price Waterhouse, taking the unwieldy new name of PricewaterhouseCoopers. Ira was forced to reunite with several of his old nemeses, including the manager who had choked him. Since the oldco C&L people were still relatively unhateful toward Ira, the two merging factions came to a wise solution: make him telecommute. Honestly, I don't know why they didn't think of it before. This led to Ira discovering his next true love: the *Ishtar*.

That's where I went late this morning, right after dropping off Miranda at the Claremont. After the sex, which we had both agreed was terrible, we simply held each other all night and talked. That made up for everything. If I had known the postcoital communion would be so pleasant, I would have suggested we skip the coitus altogether and spoon. To most men, that probably sounds as lame as drinking nonalcoholic beer at a game of touch football. Untrue. It was that kind of intimacy I had missed more than sex. Her skin was smooth and warm. Her small fingers ran back and forth across my wrist. We spoke in tones so soft that the specters of Gracie and Jim took the hint and left. For all intents and purposes, it was the first time we'd ever truly been alone with each other.

"I think lifelong monogamy may be one of those myths that the human race is slowly catching on to," she told me shortly before dawn. "I mean in these complex times, it's really cocky and presumptuous to assume that two people will continue evolving along the same path for the rest of their natural lives. One might go faster than the other. One might go in a different direction. Or both of them might keep spiraling around each other, up and down, up and down, like a dysfunctional double helix. You know what I'm saying?"

I held her from behind, listening, enjoying.

"Conservatives keep freaking out about how more and more couples are getting divorced sooner. You know what I say? Good. That means more people are being honest with each other when it's time to move on. I mean what's the big deal? With one out of two couples getting divorced, there's not much to be ashamed of. Fifty percent of companies fail within the first five years, even in a good economy. The bottom line is that things change. People grow apart. Shit, why deny it? What's the alternative? Hating each other? Cheating on each other? What's the point? So we can justify all the flatware we got at our wedding? That's bullshit. Don't you think?"

After a few seconds of silence, she laughed and checked my wrist for a pulse.

"I'm still here," I said. "Just listening."

"Am I even making sense?"

"Yeah. Definitely. Your statistics are a little off, though."

"What, about the companies?"

"Well, that too. But I was mostly referring to the divorce rate. Everyone throws that figure around all the time, but it's just a media myth."

"How do you know?"

"Because I know the people who started it. They're an independent research group in Boston. Twelve years ago, they were hired by a Christian organization to get some hard numbers they could use. They said, 'We don't care how you get them, just get them.' So the researchers spent six months raiding the public records of a hundred and fifty counties, tallying the number of approved marriage licenses and divorce papers signed in 1987. They discovered exactly half as many divorces."

"So? That's one out of two."

"No it's not. They were counting the divorces from *all* married couples, not just the ones who got married in 1987. Look, let's say there are ten million married couples in those counties. One hundred thousand of them got married in 1987. Fifty thousand of them got divorced in 1987. Guess what? That's fifty thousand out of ten million, not a hundred thousand. It was totally faulty reasoning, but the Christian group went all Chicken Little to the press anyway. Nobody ever stopped to question it."

Miranda rolled over and eyed me, in full skeptical journalist mode. "Scott, are you trying to tell me that the divorce rate is actually one half of one percent?"

"No. That's just the same mistake reversed. My point is that you can't compare one year's results to the whole pool. You have to take it year by year."

"But in 1987 it was fifty percent."

"In 1987 there were half as many divorces as there were weddings. In those counties."

"But if that statistic matches up every year, then the divorce rate will still be fifty percent!"

"Yes, but that's a very big 'if' for such a small sample. Look at the stock market in 1987. One bad day turned it into a *very* abnormal year. Hell, if I only used this week as a sample, I could say that I have sex with a married woman at least once a week."

She stared at me, stunned, and then turned the other way.

I looked over her shoulder. "Oh no. Did I upset you again?"

"I'm not upset," she said, befuddled. "I'm just . . . I'll put it this way, Scott. You know just what to say to make a girl feel numb. Is it okay if I check my messages?"

She reached over me to use my phone, resting on top of my chest. I felt like apologizing, but I didn't know why. I got the painful notion that there were fifty better ways I could have handled the conversation but I couldn't think of one that wasn't trite or saccharine. I thought I was showing her respect by not subjecting her to any romantic clichés. I knew Miranda was strictly anti-sentiment. Then again, so was Gracie, until the day it suddenly occurred to her that if she stayed with me, she'd be numbed out of existence.

Later in the morning, outside the hotel, Miranda and I sat in awkward silence. She kissed me good-bye from the passenger seat. Not an eternal good-bye, of course, but it told me what I wanted to hear. The show was over. Brigadoon officially went back to being a grass field.

"You're still an ass," she said, getting out. "Get your car fixed."

"Have fun exploiting the carnage."

With a half-smile, she entered the hotel. It was 11:30. Over the past two days, I'd gotten a total of five hours' sleep. And yet I felt fine. I was content.

———

At 12:15, I reached Marina del Rey, where Ira greeted me from the dock of his floating home and sanctum. He looked like a proud slob in his untucked button-down shirt and black jeans. He carried a huge binder filled with data. He wasn't big on self-maintenance, but he always kept his numbers pretty.

"Don't even tell me to change," he said without greeting me. "If this guy's going to write me off just because he doesn't like my wardrobe—"

"Relax. He won't care. He'll just think you're too brilliant to be stylish."

"I don't even know why I have to go."

"Because it's your project. I'm just helping you sell it."

He locked up the yacht. The *Ishtar* was a 1984 Gibson Executive, fifty feet long. Fiberglass hull. Twin 350 HP Crusader engines with a cruising speed of twenty-two knots. Flush-mounted exterior deck and 385 square feet of living space, including full galley, salon, and two tiny staterooms. He had bought it two years before, for a little under $75K. The seller claimed to have purchased it straight from Warren Beatty, who apparently had a sense of humor about his previous flops. I checked the story. It was crap. Warren may have a self-effacing wit, but he was never a yachtsman. Ira didn't care. He just wanted respite from loud neighbors and evil landlords. He went through apartments like he went through jobs.

Half an hour later, we arrived at Lulu's, a casual eatery on Beverly Boulevard. We had a lunch date with Keith Ullman. He was extremely late, of course. In Los Angeles, tardiness was treated as a sign of status and chic. Not only was it standard not to offer an explanation, it was considered rude to ask. I reminded Ira several times to hold his tongue when Keith, the prospective client, finally did arrive.

"So what's the name of this thing again?" he asked after fifteen minutes of idle industry banter.

"Move My Cheese," I replied, sending Keith into a fit of puzzled laughter. He was a stylish, silver-haired player, part of Hollywood's old guard. He held a diploma from the Robert Evans school of reminiscing and name-dropping. His favorite story, told ad nauseam, was how he had personally led Universal's effort to make *Jaws* the very first summer blockbuster to premiere nationwide. Oh, he met resistance from everyone, especially Dick Zanuck, blah blah blah. There was simply no way to turn off his audio commentary.

As a silent partner in this fledgling venture, I had advised Ira to act interested and to never ever disparage Spielberg in front of Keith. They were *landsmen* and (according to Keith) good friends. Ira, however, had harbored a mad-on for Spielberg ever since Jeff Goldblum's "offensively simplistic and incorrect" portrayal of a chaotician in *Jurassic Park*. Whatever. All I cared about was selling Keith on Move My Cheese, a virtual paradigm that could revolutionize the entire movie industry. And that wasn't just hype.

"Explain to me again how it works," said Keith, through a mouthful of Chinese chicken salad.

Ira looked to me. His explanation usually caused massive bleeding from the ears.

"It's simple data-fusion software," I told him. "You plug all your movies in to a calendar. All your competitor's movies. You add the number of screens, and presto. The Cheese chews it up and spits out the projected box-office totals for everything."

Of course, it wasn't really that simple. Keith was understandably skeptical. "Come on . . ."

"We've been testing it all through the year 2000. It has eighty-nine percent accuracy in predicting first-weekend grosses, and eighty-one percent accuracy for final domestic."

"But not international," said Keith.

"No," said Ira, annoyed. "It doesn't give you a blow job either."

Keith laughed, assuming the joke was inclusive. "Then what the hell am I doing here?"

I opened Ira's binder to an earmarked page. "Look, while everyone predicted that *X-Men* would open between twenty-eight and thirty-one million, our forecast said fifty-four-point-five. It opened at fifty-five-point-one. Was it exact? No. But compared to everyone else, that's like throwing a key in the keyhole."

"We were also the only ones who said that *Perfect Storm* would overtake *The Patriot* by a two-to-one margin," Ira added.

"That's right. Not only that, but if Sony had this software, they would have known to bow *The Patriot* over Thanksgiving weekend instead of Fourth of July. According to our projections it would have replaced *The Grinch* as the holiday moneymaker. It would have closed at two-thirty-five."

"But how can you be sure?"

"We're only eighty-nine percent sure," I stressed. "But that's still more than the NRG can give you."

The National Research Group, the child of a Dutch media conglomerate, was the current prognosticator of choice for all the major studios. Their methods were ridiculously archaic. Three times a week they phoned a sample of four hundred people and bothered them with intrusive questions: How old are you? What's your skin color? What's your income? Have you heard of *Battlefield: Earth*? Okay. Do you think you're, um, planning on seeing it in theaters? Why not?

What the pollsters who steer this country don't want you to know is that phone surveys, by their very nature, suck. They rely on the feedback of two kinds of people: those who enjoy talking to telemarketers and those who enjoy lying to telemarketers. Neither group speaks well for the rest of us. To give the NRG credit, their system was created solely to measure audience awareness of upcoming films. But the studio suits, nervous about where to blow their last-minute ad budget, began using those four hundred participants/liars to project box-office numbers, a practice even the NRG didn't endorse. "Hey, guys, if you're going to use our data for that, can we at least raise the sample to a thousand liars?" Nope. Costs too much. Just do that voodoo that you do so well. The results were usually in the ballpark, if you include the parking lot, but the methods were piss poor when it came to predicting the tastes of kids, genre nerds, and African Americans.

For each future release, Move My Cheese employed over two hundred different variables, everything from box-office grosses of all the actors' previous works to the number of cleavage shots used in trailers. But the real genius was in the calendar program, which factored in considerations like holiday trends, TV schedules, even local weather patterns. It retrieved much of this information off the Internet, automatically adjusting its math to fit vicissitudes. The NRG was a crude Magic 8-ball. The Cheese was just magic.

Of course it wasn't without problems. For starters, there was an extraordinary amount of data entry involved, not to mention educational guesswork. In the hands of Ira, it was a precise instrument. In the hands of a sloppy marketing intern, it would be no better than tea leaves. It would require at least two weeks for Ira to train the MGM staff to properly use his Ouija. That part worried me the most. The software, like Ira, tended to be user-hostile.

Still, the numbers were hard to ignore. Keith was so impressed with Ira's professed accuracy rate that he was willing to pay seventy-five hundred dollars for a limited trial run. In two weeks Ira would visit their Santa Monica studio and give them a true taste of the Cheese. Our meeting was officially a success, and my part in the project was over for now.

We threw in fifteen more minutes of obligatory shop talk, then I paid for lunch. As the three of us left the restaurant, Keith took my arm.

"Listen, Scott, do you have time to take a ride with me?"

"Sure. You want to drop me off in Marina del Rey?"

"No problem."

I gave Ira the keys to my car and told him I'd meet him at the *Ishtar*. Although I didn't show it, I was excited. Keith wouldn't have taken me aside like this if he didn't have PR work for me. And since his wife, Hayley, was a vice president at my old firm, Tate & Associates, that meant the work was too covert for them. I loved covert projects. They always paid big, always under the table. And as ominous as they sounded, most of them were actually nice and simple. Drama-free.

"This goddamn school shooting," he muttered, tapping his cigarette out the window of his BMW Z8. "As if the coming strikes weren't bad enough. Selfishly, though, I thank my lucky stars that it's more rap-related than film-related. But it's still gonna hurt *Hannibal* when it opens next Friday. The movie's not exactly an after-school special. If you read the book, you know."

"I know." I hadn't read the book. Just the reviews.

"Man, that little girl picked a hell of a time to go postal."

No kidding. I looked beyond Keith to the sprawling CBS Television City complex. Late one night Gracie and I had bribed a guard to let us sneak onto the set of *The Price Is Right.* I just wanted to look around. The sex was her idea. She climbed up onstage, got undressed, and told me to come on down.

"The whole entertainment industry's gonna catch hell for this," said Keith. "Soon it'll be easier to market tobacco products than R-rated films."

"People still smoke, though."

He laughed and held up his cigarette. "This I'm addicted to. I don't know anybody who had a fit to see *The Mod Squad.*"

I smiled. Keith turned left on Fairfax. The infamous Melrose High was just a few blocks north of us. I could feel it. A big black hole, sucking in all the conversational air. For over a year it had been the same way with O. J. Simpson's house, a mere shuffle from my apartment.

Keith took a deep drag off his cigarette. "Scott, you know that everything I'm about to say is in complete confidence."

"Of course."

"Good. There's an interesting opportunity for you. An urgent one. That was sort of the real reason I wanted to meet with you so quickly. No disrespect to your Cheese thing."

That only made me tingle. "No. That's fine. Sounds like quite a jam."

"It's not my jam, thank God. It's a job my wife came across. She would have called you herself but she doesn't want this coming within a mile of Tate. This is a complete mercenary effort. You get caught, you're on your own."

I loved movie people. "What kind of job?"

"It's a de-publicity effort. The story's already written, and it needs to be unwritten. The problem is that you've got to work fast, because it's coming out soon. Probably sooner than *Hannibal.*"

"Care to give me details?"

"You ever heard of a guy named Jeremy Sharpe?"

"No."

"Neither did I. Listen, all you need to know is that he's a very important man who needs a hero right now. You save his ass, and you're in the catbird seat. We're talking an easy six figures and a lot of gratitude from a lot of big names. You interested?"

Jesus. Yes. "Depends. I assume this is short-term, right?"

"The shortest of terms. This'll keep you busy while you have it, though. So clear your schedule."

No problem. I had already cleared it for the Fairmont Keoki project. If this hadn't come along, I would have had to start making cold calls again. This worked out wonderfully.

"I'm interested so far. What's the next step?"

He handed me a hotel business card. L'Ermitage. A swank luxury pad on the outskirts of Beverly Hills. A room number was scribbled on the back.

"Be there at eight tonight. They'll fill you in on the rest."

"You don't have any more information? I usually like to prepare so I don't say anything dumb."

"Don't worry. My wife already sold you to them. All you need to do is show up and say yes."

Hayley Jane Trudeau was the last of the old guard at Tate & Associates. In 1998 a London ad agency acquired the firm and put it through a huge turnover, kind of like *The Poseidon Adventure*. Many jobs were lost. A small band of survivors, including myself and Hayley, made it to safety. Under the incompetent new regime, the job quickly began to suck, kind of like *Beyond the Poseidon Adventure*. I quit and went freelance. Hayley threw me some crisis work now and then.

"So, Scott, can I tell them you're coming?"

Fun fact about me: the less bait you put on the hook, the greater the chance I'll bite. I tried not to be predictable, but damn it. I fell for it every time. Hayley knew that, of course.

"I'll be there."

Keith threw his cigarette out the window before getting on the 10 West. "Good. I just finished my household chore for the day. Can I ask you a question now?"

"Sure."

"Why the hell is it called Move My Cheese?"

If you don't already know, it's not worth explaining. Trust me. I wanted to call it What If . . . ? That was the name of an ongoing series that Marvel Comics ran in the eighties and nineties. It was a great concept. Each issue they took a different superhero and threw in a speculative twist. What if Spider-Man's uncle had lived? What if Captain America had never been unfrozen? What if Magneto had formed the X-Men? It allowed writers to experiment with classic characters without messing up decades of continuity. Unfortunately, Ira didn't appreciate the connection. Like I said, it was his baby.

Keith dropped me off at the Marina at 3:15. My dented car was already back. I didn't know when the hell I'd be able to go to a body shop. At the moment I didn't care. I just wanted a sneak peek at what I had tentatively signed up for.

I went aboard the *Ishtar*. A yacht wasn't the best place for a home office. Ira's workstation took up half the galley. His printer sat on top of his microwave. Wires ran everywhere, and Ira worked in the middle of it all, a fat techno-spider. He loved it, but it wasn't very friendly for all his visitors, namely me.

"So that went well," he said, in lieu of hello. "What did he want with you?"

"PR stuff."

"Specifically?"

"I don't know yet. You ever heard of Jeremy Sharpe?"

"No."

"Well, look him up."

I could always share proprietary knowledge with Ira. He'd never given me a compliment in his life but he would saw off his own legs before double-crossing me. He spun his chair and launched Netscape on his souped-up Dell.

"So you just accepted a job without knowing what it entails."

"I didn't accept anything yet." I looked over his shoulder. "I think it's Sharpe with an 'E.' "

"Doesn't matter." He punched it into Google. The list came up. There were only ten items on the page, but they were merely the first of 1,912 hits. You may be wondering how a media-savvy fellow like myself had never heard of this man, who merited so many mentions plus a score of dedicated fan sites. The answer was right there in the titles of those digital shrines. Jeremy Sharpe was just an alter ego. A not-so-secret identity. To his legions of acolytes, he was simply the rapper known as Hunta.

"Shit."

"Shit indeed," said Ira. "It was nice knowing you."

Ira did know me. He knew there was no way in hell I'd turn down a challenge like this. But that didn't mean I had to be happy about it. If my life were a computer adventure game, this would be the part where I saved. That way if I screwed up or died, I could just come back to this very place and time and try a different approach, like walking away.

Convenient, right? Too bad my game didn't have that feature. All I had—all I have now—is hindsight and a whole lot of regret. I can't go back. But sometimes, just to piss myself off, I play a few rounds of What If . . . ?

TWO

RAP

It had burst forth from the chest of disco. The New York City dance clubs, the quintessential social scene of the seventies, phased out cheesy cover bands in favor of the vinyl-spinning disc jockey. Thanks to the invention of the mixer, club DJs were free to creatively fade, scratch and shift to their heart's content. The reggae "dub" style of Jamaican mixmasters gradually introduced a signature prominence of beat over melody. Then came the art of the toast, in which eurhythmic DJs worked up the crowd by shouting to their own groove. Finally, they delegated the microphone duties to an accomplice called the MC. And thus the rapper was born.

Of course that's just an oversimplified breakdown from a white guy with Web access. I had to look this stuff up, even though I was only a hop, skip, and bridge away from this whole cultural genesis while it was happening. What can I say? The street revolution never made its way to my cul-de-sac. In fact, my cracker white ass didn't get its first peep of the hip or the hop until a fine-looking Deborah Harry (you know, Blondie) got the fabulous Fab 5 Freddy to put the rap in her famous "Rapture."

Sad? Perhaps. But I at least caught the tail end of hip-hop's commercial fertilization. It was in 1984 that a young MTV served me my first full platter of rap, the music video for Run-DMC's "Rock Box." Suddenly the business that began with a seven-inch single from the Sugar Hill Gang became a chart-topping, Adidas-plugging, Aerosmith-reviving crossover bonanza. It was Run's brother, Russell Simmons, who cofounded Def Jam Records, rap's first commercial empire. And in 1986 *Yo! MTV Raps*—hosted by the same Fab 5 Freddy—began channeling a steady infusion of urban groove into the homes and hearts of those who could afford basic cable.

Mostly what we got was the sanitized, glamorized version of the genre. Call it hip-pop. Nobody considered MC Hammer a particularly dangerous influence on our nation's youth, unless one had a fear of parachute pants. Vanilla Ice was only bad in a musical sense. And Will Smith, the Fresh Prince himself, was a media darling even to parents who just didn't understand him. Those were the salad days, when a rapper could throw his hands in the air and wave them like he just didn't care.

But things done changed. Once heavy metal music went the way of the Go-Go's, the middle- and upper-class youth of America lost their chief means of alarming their elders. Meanwhile, old-school purists became increasingly dismayed by the vacuous Top 40 "crap rap" that turned an artistic revolution into a corporate cash cow. By the early 1990s, MC Hammer had become a cartoon version of himself, a glittery Stepin Fetchit who danced his way through Kentucky Fried Chicken ads while drugs, crime, and police brutality continued to decimate the boys in the 'hood. Just as the economic downturn of the seventies and the heroin invasion brought about the hip-hop movement in the first place, it was the Reagan era and crack that created a mass demand and supply of hard-core gangsta rap.

So much has been written and said about this genre, from so many ignorant sources, that I'm reluctant to add myself to the mix. The word "gangsta" itself is a flimsy label, as overused and misapplied as "feminist" or "politically correct." Unlike those, however, gangsta rap is one of those rare scapegoats enjoyed by all. Dan Quayle said it had no place in our society. Newt Gingrich openly encouraged advertisers to pull their spots from radio stations that played it. Even waffling übercentrist Bill Clinton got props from the soccer moms when he condemned Sister Souljah for her seemingly anti-whitey comments in *The Washington Post*.

Truth be told, I was more than happy to keep my distance, to remain quietly uninformed and nonjudgmental. But with a simple two-word inscription on a mini-videocassette, Annabelle Shane threw the issue onto the nation's frontmost burner, right along with Jeremy Sharpe, aka Hunta. I had four hours to learn everything I could about the original Bitch Fiend himself. So much for that comfortable space I had put between myself and America's war with the hip-hop nation. I guess I just picked my side, yo.

From the March 2000 issue of *The Source:* the Magazine of Hip-Hop Music, Culture & Politics:

HOLLA IF YOU HEAR HIM

With no public beefs, no criminal record, not even a tattoo, Hunta's the new stainless star of South Central. But can this former 2Pac protégé take the Thug out of Life and still sell albums?

BY ED FREEZE

"Man, look at this," he says, pointing to the wall of his alma mater, Crenshaw High School. The tan brick surface is covered in gang graffiti, territorial tags from the Rollin 30s, Rollin 40s, Rollin 60s, and on and on. But that doesn't bother him. He's not even looking at the RIP tribute to all the students who were shot and killed over the summer. The one scrawl that gets his attention is a two-word, three-foot declaration of idolatry: 2PAC LIVES.

"They should kill that shit, man. I'm saying love the brother, but let him rest. That shit ain't true."

Hunta would know. He was there that infamous night of September 7, 1996, when his mentor Tupac Shakur was gunned down at a Las Vegas intersection following the Mike Tyson/Bruce Seldon fight. Hunta was 30 feet behind Marion "Suge" Knight's rented black BMW 750 when it got sprayed with bullets. Unlike his friend Yusef Fula, Hunta never talked about what he saw that night. Unlike Yusef, Hunta is currently alive and well. He still doesn't talk about it. It's not fear, he says. Just respect.

That's something he will talk about. Respect. Hunta grew up in this area, in a Section 8 housing project ten blocks away from "Da Shaw." Today he's returned at the request of his favorite teacher, Anita Moultrie, to talk to her students about his experiences both in and out of the 'hood. At the ripe young age of 22, Hunta has already survived two brothers, several friends, and countless stray bullets, all by-products of a gangland culture. He even survived a few brushes with fame, including the Death Row/Bad Boy war of 1996. Despite all that, his biggest battle now is surviving a perceived lack of street credibility, a respect he thinks he's due.

He has a point.

On the other hand, look at him. In contrast to the Crenshaw High walls, Hunta is completely unmarked by slogans or drawings. His ink-free muscular arms practically shine as much as his jewelry.

"My father was the Reverend," he says. "He told me 'Boy, you ain't no billboard. You gotta love your skin the way God made it.' I didn't always agree but I respected it, you know? This is my dad. He made me."

And made him well. When it came to looks, God was clearly on Hunta's side. With his large almond-shaped eyes, sharp-angled face, and Soloflex body, he looks more like a cover model than a real Compton City G. Of course, Tupac had the exact same problem. How to be gritty when you're so goddamned pretty. The great Makaveli's solution, hands down, was to overcompensate. He lived and died the thug life so loudly that even the most rap-ignorant Americans got a taste of his notoriety.

Hunta, meanwhile, doesn't even have a speeding ticket to brag about. In an industry where bad is better, will the market make room for a gangsta rapper without a rap sheet?

"I never claimed to be gangsta," he says defensively. "I ain't frontin' like I busted niggas or shot a cop, you know what I'm saying? But I grew up on these streets. I seen things. I lost people. I got a right to put it to words."

He was born Jeremy Sharpe on May 15, 1977, in Jackson, Mississippi. When he was two, his 28-year-old mother, Leticia, was bludgeoned to death on the way home from her job as a night nurse. Nobody was ever charged with the murder, but Raymond Sharpe—aka the Reverend—had no doubt it was race-related. He moved Jeremy and his two older brothers, Ray Jr. and Malcolm, all the way here to South Central.

"After living in the Deep South, that gang shit didn't scare the Reverend," he says. "First day here, he went right up to the local 60s [Crips] and said, 'Look, my young brothers, you got them guns but I got God on my side. You keep your guns away from me and my boys, and I'll see if I can keep God off your sorry ass. We got a deal?' The Rev's got them killer eyes, man. He scared the shit out of them niggas."

He admits that for his father, it was a two-way battle. "That gangsta life just pulls in you in. In this area, if you ain't a Cuz, you just some bitch. The Rev tried to keep us all out of trouble, you know, but it wasn't easy for him."

Or entirely successful. In 1990, at age 16, Malcolm was shot in the head during a battle with a rival Crip faction. He died after eight months in a coma. Two years later, his brother Ray—then a 24-year-old postal clerk—was killed in an altercation with local police after being pulled over on a suspected DUI. The two officers (one of whom was black) were suspended but eventually exonerated, mostly due to the fact that Ray's blood alcohol was indeed twice the legal limit.

As with the murder of Tupac, Hunta refuses to discuss the details of the incident, although he made his feelings toward the LAPD quite clear when he guest-rapped on L-Ron's hit single "Law Ain't Protectin' Dick": "Treatin' us niggas as a form of pollution / Seein' execution as the final solution / Well, bitch, put this on your APB / Hunta ain't playin' that, see / Took out Ray / DOA / Y'all ain't gettin' me the same way."

"You know like most black people, I got mad hate for the police but I ain't falling into their trap. I ain't gonna become just another young nigga in jail or in the ground. My way of saying 'fuck you' to the system is growing old, living free, and having lots of kids. I promised that to the Rev. I'm his last boy. I promised him my only weapon would be my talent."

It's a weapon well honed. While he was enrolled at Crenshaw High's gifted program—one of the few all-minority accelerated programs in the nation—Jeremy's speaking and writing skills won him several awards in poetry competitions. Anyone who's seen him at the mike can certainly understand why. His commanding bass voice and his bouncy energy remind many of Tupac himself.

It was at a 1996 freestyling competition that an 18-year-old Jeremy—then going by the name MC Rage—caught the attention of the late Yusef Fula, who was part of Tupac's backup band, the Outlawz Immortals. This led to an introduction, and later a friendship with 'Pac himself.

"Best day of my life was meeting him after a competition," says Hunta.

"I didn't even know he was in the crowd. After I finished he came up to me and was like 'Yo, man. That shit is tight!' I was trippin' from that. I mean this was Tupac! You know what I'm saying? Just watching him in action, man . . . He was always comin' up with rhymes. He could just bang that shit out. You couldn't stop him."

Hunta catches his poor choice of words and grows silent. He spent a good deal of time with Tupac during the last few months of his life, appearing as an extra in two of his videos. Soon enough, Hunta earned himself an introduction to notorious Death Row Records mogul Suge Knight.

"That was scary. I won't lie. You know like everyone I heard things about Suge. Like how he beat the shit out of these two niggas just 'cause they was using his phone. But I met him twice and both times he was real good to me. The first time he put his big hand on my back and was like, 'My boy Pac says you got talent. Man, you gotta sign with tha Row.' I mean, shit. When a big nigga like Suge gives you respect, man, you just know you hit it. He was Don Corleone. Everyone around him wanted to please him."

He laughs. "Sure as hell ain't nobody wanted to make him mad."

It was after he signed with Death Row that he rechristened himself as Hunta, an acronym for Helping Us Niggas Take Action.

"I dropped the MC Rage tag, mostly 'cause they already had the Lady of Rage on the label. And I wanted a fresh start anyway. They loved it. It all started happenin'."

He gets somber again. Everyone knows about the Las Vegas tragedy that occurred the following month. The murder that lasted six days. What's also well known is that shortly after Tupac's death, Suge was sentenced to nine years on a probation violation stemming from an assault that occurred at the MGM Grand just hours before the shooting. Once Suge went away (he's up for parole in April 2001), a litany of investigations and civil suits—including one from Tupac's own mother—buried Death Row under a mountain of red tape. Hunta's career stalled before it even started.

"It wasn't a good time for me," he admits, "but it ended up good. The Judge found me."

Byron "Judge" Rampton, 49, is the founder and president of Mean World Records, an independent label whose rap acts include hot artists L-Ron, X/S, and Hitchy. After getting Hunta's demo tape from a former

Death Row executive, the cherubic mini-mogul quickly bought out the rapper's contract and put him back in the studio.

"He was way too talented to be floating in limbo," the Judge later tells me from his spacious Century City office. "Hunta had a fresh voice that was amazingly real. After Tupac and Biggie went down, we needed that kind of honesty again."

Hunta's debut album, *Huntaway*, will be released on March 14 through Mean World and distributed by Interscope. So far the promotional campaign has been extensive, but it's still hard to put your name out there when rivals like Jay-Z, DMX, Eminem, Puff Daddy, even fellow newcomers like Drama and Shyne, are hogging up the headlines with their criminal troubles. Is Hunta worried?

"Look, whatever shit happens happens. If folks don't wanna hear me because they don't think I'm hard, fuck 'em. I ain't gonna take a bullet or do time just to sell albums."

The Judge was also quick to dismiss concerns. "With all due respect, it's you folks in the media who still thrive on that stuff, not the fans. To the kids out there, it all comes down to talent. Just hear the music."

That's exactly what I did. After listening to an advance copy of *Huntaway*, I could understand why the Judge wasn't worried. First of all, the album is fly. With the exception of a few ill-chosen samples—most notably a bizarre urbanized remix of Heart's "Barracuda"—the songs are original, fast-paced, undeniably mesmerizing blends of hardcore and R&B.

More important (commercially speaking), Hunta makes up in sex what he lacks in violence. In the hyper-libidinous vein of Master P and Too $hort, his songs are full of misogyny and cheap kicks. Tracks from his upcoming album include "Keep Ya Head Down," a satirical ode to fellatio; "Chocolate Ho-Ho," a lusty account of a ménage à trois; and "Bitch Fiend," a disturbingly explicit tale about a man who secretly videotapes his sexual exploits with women and then shows them to his friends.

Although the content isn't shocking by today's rap standards, one might argue that this is hardly a reemergence of "keeping it real." When I bring this up to Hunta, he grins and shrugs.

"It's real to me. I may have never shot a nigga but I've gotten play. I mean I love the ladies. And the ladies love me. Why should I hide it?"

The bell rings at Crenshaw High. As if we're stuck in a flashback, it's time for Hunta to get to class. As he crosses the Quad, the grassy courtyard in the center of campus, he attracts a trio of lovely, bare-midriffed girls. With his raw good looks, not to mention the "bling-bling" of his diamond-cross necklace, he clearly conveys his status as a player. Still, they don't recognize him.

"Who you s'posed to be?" one calls out to him.

Hunta lowers his shades. His smile alone is able to convert all three young women into fans, a promising sign of things to come. "I'm s'posed to be me." ∎

5

SUBTEXT

The story was out of Annabelle's hands. Now that the media had a full day to dress up the event, it was purely a network affair.

The *CBS Evening News* ran a glossy four-minute eulogy of Annabelle Shane: honor student, beloved daughter, tragic symbol of a generation gone out of control. Over at ABC, Peter Jennings took a more macroscopic look at the carnage. What's happening in our nation's schools? How did they become so violent? More important, how can you tell if your child is on the edge? NBC picked the fruit off its own tree when it focused on the post-Melrose panic that's infected the country. Over 600 high schools sent their kids home early today. Another 250 were closed entirely. Attendance rates in all remaining classes, kindergarten and up, were at their lowest since Columbine, the *Titanic* of school shootings. Once again, parents were afraid to drop their kids off at school. As well they should be. According to Ira, the chances of their offspring dying in an auto accident on the way to school were over nine hundred times greater than the odds of being shot by a classmate. The chances of their dying at home were only two hundred times greater. Despite all that, the L.A. *Times* ran a poignant piece on the rise in home-schooling: it might just save your child's life.

The one calm voice in the storm was Miranda, who spent eight hundred words highlighting the brief lives of the four students murdered by Annabelle. Yes, murdered. Once you read between her lines, it was obvious that Miranda was sick of all the double-standard knee-jerk empathy we adopted for our underage killers. *Hey, assholes! This bitch took innocent lives!*

Yes, but were they *all* innocent? As usual, it was CNN that had the time to bite into the underripe portion of the story, namely Bryan Edison and his merry band of Bitch Fiends. For today the network was content to simply get the questions out there. The L.A. County sheriff's office refused to comment on that part of the investigation but at least confirmed that there *was* an investigation. You've got to hand it to the folks at AOL–Time Warner–Turner. They sure knew how to foreshadow. They even threw in a few dozen mentions of Hunta, marking him up as next week's grillhouse special.

It took considerable effort to make myself late for the meeting. I ended up circling the Beverly Center for half an hour before making the final turn onto Burton Way. I arrived at L'Ermitage at 8:15. There weren't any quote-hungry reporters waiting outside, which meant someone had done a good job misleading the press. No doubt there was a gaggle of newsfolk holding a camera-light vigil outside the gates of Casa de Hunta, in Silverlake. I pitied his mailman.

In the elevator I took a deep breath and gathered myself. Confronted by the clear scope of the project, not to mention my inexperience with the rap world, I couldn't shake that "first day of school" feeling. That was fine as long as I didn't show it. Being a celebrity's crisis manager is like being the emperor's new tailor. You have to earn his absolute confidence if you want him to wear the air you crafted. Still, I wished I had come into the situation knowing more. I'd spent the whole afternoon researching Hunta. Most of what I'd read was spoon-fed crap created by people like me: puff pieces full of sound and fury, signifying nothing.

I knocked on the door to Suite 511, which opened to a square-headed, bear-sized bodyguard. I could have used his stretched black T-shirt as a hammock.

"You Scott Singer?"

"Only if you're happy to see him."

He smirked politely, as if he'd never heard that joke before. "ID?"

I showed him my driver's license.

"Lift your arms, please."

He patted me down, just in case I was a pistol-packing publicist.

"Since we're getting to know each other better," I said, "what's your name?"

"Just call me Big Bank."

Too many bon mots entered my caffeinated mind, all of them in danger of being poorly received. I felt the primal need to prove to this excessively large man that he didn't scare me, which pretty much proved that he did.

"What's that in your shirt pocket?"

"Just my Palm Pilot," I said, showing him. "Can't leave home without it."

The best bodyguards made upward of five hundred dollars a day. Those were the ones who knew how to protect their clients from extortion as well as physical threats. For all Big Bank knew, I was carrying a digital recording device disguised as a Palm Pilot. I turned it on for him.

He nodded. "All right. You're cool. Come on in."

Another satisfied customer. There was a neat little spy shop on Olympic Boulevard that an associate of mine turned me on to. Some of their gadgets were so fancy that you'd half expect Q to come out of the back room and demonstrate them for you. My handy toy—$850 after tax—was a digital recording device disguised as a Palm Pilot. It captured seventy minutes of audio on a removable chip the size of an airmail stamp ($92 each). Even better, it had a "Boss" button that displayed a snapshot of a Palm OS desktop, allowing me to trick the sharper tools in the shed, like Big Bank. As soon as I demonstrated it for him, it began recording.

Extortion was not the game. It was merely self-protection. So far I'd never been forced to use a recording, or even threaten to use it. Nobody had ever thrown me to the wolves before. Of course, nobody had ever broken my leg, either. That didn't make it unbreakable. I preferred to be cautious.

With a polite smile, I followed Big Bank into the $1,200-a-night suite. Immediately I was hit with the competing smells of marijuana and Thai food, both of which were laid out on the huge glass coffee table in the main room. Over a dozen people, some of them not even old enough to buy the liquor in their hands, filled the couches and watched MSNBC on mute while rap music played in the background.

Everyone was partying it up until I stepped out from behind the great wall of Big Bank. They simmered down and eyed me, this white corporate flack straight outta Brentwood. My inner Dale Carnegie, 2001 edition, told me to avoid the instinctual "I'm down with your people/some of my best friends are black" smile. With a curt nod, I simply advertised my utter lack of concern over their opinion of me. A few of them dutifully nodded back. Likewise.

The oldest-looking man in the group (my age, actually) put down his chicken satay and rose to greet me. He was tall, husky, and extremely dapper. With his four-hundred-dollar slacks, fancy silk bow tie, and designer black suspenders, he struck me more as a lawyer than a record executive. Turns out he was both.

He shook my hand. "Mr. Singer. Hi. I'm Doug Modine, executive vice president and attorney for Mean World Records. Glad you could come."

For a man built like James Earl Jones, he talked like Don Cheadle. "Thanks. Call me Scott."

"Sure. Just give me a few seconds to check on Maxina and the others."

"Wait. Maxina Howard?"

"Yeah," he answered, surprised. "You know her?"

"I know of her. I didn't know she was here."

"God, yes. She's our guardian angel. Hang out for a minute, okay?"

Doug disappeared into one of the bedrooms, leaving me, Big Bank, and a very quiet entourage.

"So," I said, with forced flippancy, "anything good in the news?"

Most of them indulged me with a soft grin. I scanned the men in the posse twice just to confirm that none of them was actually Hunta himself. I still wasn't entirely positive. All I'd seen of him so far were low-res, highly stylized photos on fan-created websites.

"So you a big-shot PR man," said a particularly fetching young woman in a micro-thin halter top.

"Not as big as Maxina Howard."

"What kinda shit you do?" asked another.

"Oh, all kinds of shit."

"Like?"

"Well, did you hear about the affair Tom Hanks had with that teenage prostitute?"

"No."

"Damn right," I replied immodestly.

They were all stunned. "Are you messing around with us?"

"Well, it wasn't Tom Hanks. If I told you who it really was, I'd be breaking client privilege. But it's someone just as big."

They all dived after my tasty nugget, shouting theories over each other. In truth, it was a C-list sitcom actor who had reached his zenith in the early eighties. He was afraid the scandal would destroy his chances for a comeback. It probably would've helped.

"So where were you when Jesse Jackson needed you?" asked one of the guys, to laughter.

"That one was a lost cause, I'm afraid. The Republicans knew about his mistress for years. They were just saving it up for the right time."

"What was that?"

"January nineteenth. The day before he was supposed to lead the Shadow Inauguration against George W. Bush. Took the wind right out of the whole protest."

They stopped laughing. Even Big Bank got disturbed. "Man, that's fucked up."

I shrugged. "What can I say? Bullets don't work anymore. Now they just kill with information."

Doug peeked out of the master bedroom. "Scott? Come on in."

"Okay. Great."

I got up and looked around at the group, who all shared a moment of silence for the buzz I killed.

"Don't worry, guys," I said, upbeat. "They're not getting your boy the same way. Not if I have anything to say about it."

That lit them back up. One of them held a fist to me as I approached the bedroom. You go, man. Never leave them depressed, always impressed. I was pretty confident now that none of them was Hunta.

For those of us who worked backstage in the great American drama, it was impossible not to have heard of Maxina Howard. Her Atlanta firm, Dandridge Associates, was the emergency PR resource for almost every major African American organization in the country. When the NAACP needed some extra power in their bullhorn, they called her. When the Nation of Islam got stuck in yet another foot-in-mouth media jam, they called her. When Bill Cosby got hit up by his alleged secret daughter, ditto. In the court of public opinion, she was an invisible defense attorney, sometimes a prosecutor. People who wish she'd never been born include Marge Schott, Mark Fuhrman, John Ashcroft, the executive board of Texaco, and every publicist for Denny's.

Only once was I set against her, although we never directly crossed swords. Four years ago, a young filmmaker shot a feature-length documentary about Nigerian playwright Ken Saro-Wiwa, who, on behalf of the persecuted Ogoni people, became a vocal critic of the country's military dictatorship and was hanged for it in 1995. This was all well and good, except the film made a very incriminating case against Shell Corporation, whose close involvement with the oppressive junta allowed them to keep pumping out three hundred million dollars a year in Nigerian crude. The documentary included interviews with former security-force members who claimed that Shell executives specifically urged them to silence anti-drilling upstarts as quickly and efficiently as possible. As you can imagine, Shell did not want this film reigniting a boycott frenzy.

At the time I worked for Tate & Associates, which worked for Shell. I spent two weeks quietly erasing Maxina's pencil lines. This took pathetically little effort. Killing the story in the mainstream press was like convincing Burger King not to add steamed beets to their menu. I was impressed that Maxina got as far as she did. The documentary received a fair amount of play on PBS, the network of elite liberal geriatrics, and the issue crossed the armrests of a few Sunday-morning talk shows. Otherwise, it got buried until the usual rigmarole. I wasn't sure if Maxina knew of my small role in the situation. I certainly wouldn't bring it up if she didn't.

Doug led me into the lavish main bedroom, where Maxina waited. She kicked her short legs up onto the emperor-sized bed and waved to us as she continued her cell-phone conversation.

"You're not listening to me. Listen. I don't want you to come across as some kind of conspirator. Try to appeal to his sense of . . . I know. I know. I understand that. But nobody likes to think of themselves as an opportunist. Take the high ground. If he has any self-respect, he'll try to find a compromise. It doesn't matter as long as you get him to release that footage, okay? That's all I'm asking."

She was a heavy woman, at least 250 pounds. I'd never seen her picture before. I was expecting someone much more upscale. With her close-cropped hair, discount blouse, and owl-rimmed glasses, she looked more like a PTA mom than an A-list socialite. Still, there was no denying it when you saw her razor-sharp eyes: she was a player. She shaped this culture as much as any top-notch celebrity or politician. She definitely deserved my respect.

Maxina casually sized me up. She probably already knew what cereal I ate. "I understand that," she said into the phone. "Just do your best. And do it now. I'll call you later."

She disconnected. "Scott Singer," she chimed musically. "Née Scott Schulherr. Why did you change your name?"

"The focus group liked it better."

She smiled along. "See that, Doug? First rule of PR. Always lie entertainingly. Help me up."

Doug took her wrist and helped her out of bed. She grunted in pain, then glanced at me. "It's not because I'm fat, Scott. I've had a bad back since I was a size six, and it's only gotten worse. That's why I don't travel anymore. As you can see, I made an exception for this."

"Understandably," I said, stifling a yawn.

"Nothing understandable about it. I made it clear to Jeremy from the start. I don't like his music. As a self-respecting woman who grew up on love and Motown, I'm *offended* by his music. But I also made it clear to C. DeLores Tucker and every other moral watchdog who dangled a check in front of me that I will not help their scapegoat crusade. I've got two sons of my own and I take full responsibility for their upbringing. They know that if I ever hear them calling a woman a bitch, I will cloud up and rain all over them."

Doug and I smiled. Maxina took my arm. She was at least sixteen inches shorter than me, but her potent stare made me want to shrink down to her vantage.

She gestured to the bathroom door. "I know you've been kept in the dark, Scott, so let me start illuminating. My client is in that bathroom. Your client is standing right here in front of you. Now you and I are going to be working on two very different projects, but you still report to me. Are we clear?"

"As seltzer."

"Good. Now before you think I'm an egomaniac, I'll also make it clear that you can say whatever you want to me. Tell me I'm wrong. Tell me I'm crazy. Tell me I'm stupid. But when we're around Jeremy and Simba, we speak in one voice. Mine. Clear?"

"Got it." Simba?

She shot me a penetrating smirk. "Oh, you're one of the sharp ones. You're a raptor. Hayley Jane was right on about you."

"She's a good woman."

"Hasn't steered me wrong yet. Now let's get you up to speed."

"Hold it," said Doug, grabbing his briefcase from the bed. "Before we go in there, I'd like you to sign some nondisclosure agreements."

"Forget it," Maxina told him. "You know damn well we can't sue him for messing up a secret mission. Just like he knows damn well that I have the power to cut the legs off his career if he ever double-crosses us. Why don't we just all accept that and avoid a paper trail?"

My stomach sank. I had much to learn from Maxina. And much to fear. She was right. She had enough contacts and credibility in the media industry to make me persona non grata. On the plus side, she made a careful distinction between messing up and double-crossing them. She'd tolerate a little of the former and none of the latter.

"Come on," she said. "While they're still in hot water."

As soon as I stepped into the Roman-style bathroom, I was hit by ninety degrees of moist air, the heavy scent of bath oil, and the sight of a gorgeous young family in the giant tub. The three of them—man, woman, and infant—were almost surreal in their unblemished perfection, as if they were chiseled from marble. Ordinarily, I would feel intrusive walking into such an intimate scene, but somehow seeing them naked was no less awkward than looking at art.

With a grand gesture, Maxina presented me. "Jeremy, Simba, this is Scott Singer. Put your trust in this man. He can spin straw into gold."

"Let's hope so," said the woman, extending a wet hand. "I'm Simba Shange. The dutiful wife."

She had the darkest skin of anyone I'd ever met, the color of walnut. Although her name and her features were both exotic, her dialect was as American as mine. I had no idea what her story was, but I could research her later. My immediate goal was to avoid ogling. When isolated from the family picture, she was a glistening feast for the eyes. Everything about her was long and sculpted: her wet hair, her lithe arms, her flat stomach, even her protruding toes. Fortunately, my lascivious peepers were still a little snowblind from Keoki Atoll.

With a warm, chaste smile, I greeted her. "A pleasure. Who's the little one?"

"This is Latisha," she said, squeezing her daughter. "She'll be one next month. That's right, sweetie. Your first birthday. Say hi to the tall man."

The girl was adorable and somewhat scared of me. In lieu of waving, she shyly bit her fingers. It intrigued me that her ears were already pierced, decorated with fat gold studs. I wasn't a father, but I questioned the wisdom of puncturing your kid before she learned how to say "ow."

Throughout all of this, the star of the show kept his eyes on the wall

TV, currently tuned to NBC. He only gave me a cursory glance. I, on the other hand, couldn't help but scrutinize. The man had the face of a model, the body of a superhero, and . . . honestly, I didn't look everywhere. I didn't *have* to look. Jeremy Sharpe had enough sexual confidence to make me cower in the corner of my mind. Even while sitting in a tub watching *Providence,* he radiated more manly eros than twelve of me ever could. I got the dark sense that if he had taken Miranda to my bed last night, she'd still be there right now: still naked, still gasping, and now utterly convinced that she'd wasted years of her sex life on effete and cerebral white men.

"So, you the hired assassin," he said, still watching TV.

"Sorry. I don't kill people. Just scandals."

He finally looked at me. "Yeah? Well what you do when a person *is* the scandal?"

Maxina shut off the TV, then sat down on the closed toilet. "All right. Enough of that. Time's short. Scott, take a load off."

For lack of space, I had to sit on the edge of the tub. This wasn't the best room for a kickoff meeting.

With a slap of her thighs, Maxina began. She focused on me. "Okay. I assume you already know most of what we're dealing with here. Before yesterday Hunta was a rapper on the rise. Now he's the gangsta who inspired a rape which inspired a school shooting."

"That's bullshit."

"We're not talking facts here, Jeremy. We're talking press coverage. This Bitch Fiend subplot is going to hatch wide open and take center stage over the killings. Annabelle, God rest her troubled soul, basically gave the authorities a paint-by-numbers account of what's been going on at that school."

"What's been going on at that school?" I asked.

"Pretty much what everyone's guessed," said Doug. "Bunch of boys used hidden cameras to videotape their sexual encounters. Then they watched it with each other on weekends. It's not a competition, like that Spur Posse shit. It's just a club."

"*Just* a club?" asked Simba.

"You know what I mean."

I yawned. Fortunately, the only one who noticed was Latisha, who yawned back.

"I assume all these guys have trashed their home movies by now," I said.

Maxina shook her head. "Not all of them. Bryan Edison wasn't exactly alive enough to run home and burn his own collection. This morning the police got a warrant and seized everything in his bedroom. According to our source in the Bitch Fiends—"

"I told you, stop calling them that," snapped Hunta, looking down at the water.

"And I told *you,* you better get used to it, because it's not going away. Anyway, our source confirmed the worst: that Annabelle's on one of those sex tapes. Reportedly, she was having such a bad time that even Bryan's fellow Fiends got scared when they saw it. They strongly suggested he ditch the evidence."

"Are we sure he didn't?"

"Pretty sure," she said. "It seems Bryan was a big fan of his own movie. He thought it'd be easier just to intimidate Annabelle. To threaten her into staying quiet. You can see how well that worked out."

Simba scoffed, "As far as I'm concerned, he got what he deserved. And I hope the rest of them get their sorry asses thrown in jail."

"Yeah. That's just what they saying about me," added Hunta.

"You better get used to that, too, my dear. Because believe me, they haven't even begun."

Maxina certainly wasn't much of a sugarcoater. Personally, I would have assured him that criminal charges would never be filed against him in this situation. Even in a civil suit, the burden of proof would be monstrous. I kept silent. Maybe she was toughening him up for an eventual press conference.

She kept illuminating me. "Here's Problem A, Scott. In addition to the name connection, this little stag film of Bryan's apparently has a familiar soundtrack."

"You're kidding."

"We wish," sighed Doug. "He was playing 'Bitch Fiend' in the background. For him, it was more than a name. It was a personal anthem. That's very bad for us."

Hunta pounded the water, splashing my leg. "What 'us'? It's bad for *me*! I'm the one they coming after! A white boy rapes her! He's dead! So now they stringing me up in his place!"

Simba shielded Latisha. "Jer . . ."

He gathered himself, then rubbed his baby's head. "Look, y'all gotta find a way to kill that tape."

"It won't ever—"

"It doesn't matter," said Maxina, overriding me. "I told you. The tape will never hit the airwaves. The news of the tape, however, is going to be busting out all over. By Tuesday at the very latest. There's no way in hell we can stop it. All we can hope to do is pull your ass out of this fire."

She turned back to me. "Our main defense is that 'Bitch Fiend' is a morality tale. Both the song and the video are simply a story where Hunta plays a character."

"A pathetic character!" he yelled. "That's the whole point of it! This nigga's so weak and so down on himself that he has to stick his jimmy in a different woman each night so he can feel like a man. He's addicted to it, like a crack fiend. Get it? He can't love no one. He even tapes and watches his own sex because he's like a spectator in his own life. It was some deep shit, man! I was using subtext!"

Simba eyed me with dark curiosity. "Does that surprise you? That it was a think piece instead of the usual tits-and-ass number?"

Yes. "No. But then I don't speak for the moral crusaders. Sadly, they don't tend to see the difference between portraying something and endorsing it."

"Unless you a white artist," Hunta growled. "Nobody went after Clapton when that motherfucka said he shot the sheriff."

Nobody went after Marley either, but this wasn't the time to nitpick.

"Is there anyplace on record where you explain the lyrics?" I asked.

"I always explain where my words are coming from! But they always take that shit out! If I say we black people can't keep shootin' each other, they only play the part where I say, 'Keep shootin' each other.' "

"In answer to your question, yes," said Doug. "Last year Jeremy did an interview for BET where he defended the point of 'Bitch Fiend.' Maxina's people are working to procure the footage."

I guessed as much. The real stumper was what the hell they needed me for.

Reading my thought balloon, Maxina tossed me a canny grin. "Scott, you need to know this stuff but you don't need to worry about it. This is my part of the project. I've got a staff of thirty working around the clock. We brought you in for Problem B. It's very important, very delicate, and it might get a little dirt on your hands. Are you okay with that?"

"Depends. I'm fine at digging dirt, but I'm not so good at throwing it. Especially at clean people."

"This bitch ain't clean," Hunta muttered.

A crisp, tense air wafted into the bathroom. Most of it circulated around Simba, who could have frozen the whole tub.

"Okay," said Maxina, getting up. "The dry folks can take it from here."

Simba rolled her eyes. "It's all right. I'm not made of glass."

"No, but this toilet is. So unless you get a nice big couch in here, I'm moving this meeting to a more comfortable room. Besides, I'm getting tired of looking at your skinny body."

Reluctantly, Simba nodded. "All right. Get out of here."

Doug and I got up. As I moved toward the door, Hunta grabbed my pants leg with his dripping right hand. "Yo. Hold up. What's your name again?"

"Scott. Scott Singer."

"Well, Scott, Scott Singer, let me tell you something. Ever since the movies / Ho's try to do me / If they can't screw me / They find a way to sue me."

"Nice," I lied, scanning my inner rap dictionary. "Was that a freestyle?"

He chuckled. "Naw, man. They ain't even my words. They were Tupac's. Just remember them, all right? I don't want it happening to me what happened to him."

"It won't," I said, assuming he was making a figurative reference to the drive-by ambush that had killed his mentor. Turns out I was wrong. I really had a lot more research to do.

L'Ermitage was just a hop away from San Vicente Boulevard. So was my apartment. However, the ride home wasn't as simple as one would think. The Beverly Hills San Vicente had nothing to do with the San Vicente in Brentwood. They were connected only by name. Connecting them physically would require bisecting UCLA and a major golf course. Nobody wanted that.

Once again, I was forced to ride the ever prevalent Wilshire Boulevard, the one street that linked both San Vicentes. I hated taking Wilshire through Beverly Hills. A dense array of traffic lights turned a two-mile stretch into a twelve-minute series of angry spurts. To make matters worse, I was now forever bound to equate Wilshire with the secret menace of deaf drivers. I still had to take my car in for an estimate, but that wouldn't happen anytime in the next twenty-four hours. I had a lot of thinking to do. When Maxina said I *might* get a little dirt on my hands, she meant definitely. And when she referred to a *little* dirt, she meant just enough to bury someone.

"There was an incident," Doug said after he, Maxina, and I reconvened in the bedroom. Simba's icy turn had already clued me in to the nature of Problem B, and the nature of my problem-to-be.

"Her name is Lisa Glassman. She was a production assistant for Mean World who started with us last summer. We put her under Kevin Haggerty, the producer on Hunta's second album."

I nodded. Get to the damn incident already.

"Since September she'd been working closely with Jeremy and Kevin, doing really great work. She's young. She's pretty. And it was clear that she . . . Look, I won't mince words. Jeremy enjoys women. And vice versa. His marriage with Simba is very . . ."

"Clintonesque," said Maxina with obvious derision.

"Sort of. Anyway, they managed to finish a rough master of the new album right before our label's Christmas party, so they had double reason to celebrate. At the party . . . I don't know. Things got out of hand. People were drinking, smoking, having a good time. All of a sudden, the following Monday, Lisa quits and tells me and the Judge that she's going to press charges against us. Against Jeremy."

"So why hasn't she yet?"

"We've been negotiating with her all through January," he said. "Trying to come to some sort of compromise. Look, this is nothing more than extortion, Scott, plain and simple. I know Jeremy. He's a good man. He goes to church every week. He reveres his father, spoils his daughter . . . He may not be the most faithful husband, but he's never forced himself on a woman in his life. He's never had to."

Maxina rolled her eyes.

"Well, if she's extorting him," I asked, "why were you willing to negotiate with her? What else does she have on him besides an accusation?"

"She's a woman and he's a rapper. What else does she need?"

"Legally? Quite a bit."

"If this were just a legal issue, Scott, I wouldn't be worried. You're a publicist. You know the stakes involved. Jeremy has his whole career ahead of him. Not just in music, but acting. He's got the looks and the talent to become a huge crossover hit, maybe even the next Will Smith. The problem is that the studios won't touch him if he has all this dark smoke around him, even if he's proven innocent. We all agreed that it would be cheaper and safer to keep Lisa quiet."

"But now," Maxina segued.

"But now all this Melrose shit has happened. She's got us over a barrel. Forget negotiating. She's going Anita Hill on us. Her lawyer could file as early as next week. Once that happens, Jeremy's screwed. And we're screwed. We'll be like a cash machine to every woman who ever brushed hands with him."

Maxina seemed less than *verklempt* over Mean World's financial plight. Although she had understated it earlier, artistic free expression was a fierce crusade with her. When President Reagan insinuated that "obscene" music didn't deserve constitutional protection, she went postal. When the state of Oregon made it illegal for retail stores to display ads or even photos containing rapper Ice Cube, she went ballistic. And there's no word violent enough to describe her reaction when they started arresting record-store executives for selling 2 Live Crew's explicit albums.

Once again, it seemed, the recording industry needed her rage. Within the last decade, sanctimonious lawmakers had gotten smarter in their attempts to suppress the material they found objectionable. The way around those First Amendment whiners, they knew, was to implement severe marketing and trade restrictions on all naughty stuff. It's not censorship, they say. Just keeping it out of the hands of kids (and everyone else). The password was "financial disincentive." Sure, you have the *right* to release an NC-17 film. We just won't let you advertise it or show it in 95 percent of the nation's venues. Sure, you have the *freedom* to put out a stickered album. We're just going to pressure the major music retailers like Wal-Mart to stop carrying it. For the media giants of the world, it all came down to a simple decision: the Wite-Out or the red ink. Not much of a f****** choice now, is it?

And there was more correction fluid coming. Riding the wave of fear and blame that came about from Columbine, senators such as Joe Lieberman and John McCain had been able to open the door to even tighter reform. Now the Melrose situation could very well blow it off its hinges.

"The bottom line," said Maxina, "is that we've got to get Hunta and his music out of this whole equation. We've got to lift him up above it. But we won't have a shot in hell of doing that if Lisa Glassman gets to tell her story."

"Her *fictional* story," Doug added.

"That's the key, Scott. We can't afford her a moment of credibility. We have to stack the deck before she even plays her first card. Now Doug is doing everything he can to stall her lawsuit, but you're still on a seriously tight schedule. You've got to strike hard and fast. Are we painting a clear picture here?"

"Like El Greco." I did not like this.

They both smiled. Doug opened his briefcase and retrieved a thin manila folder. "We hired a private investigator to look into Lisa's background. This is all we have on her. I won't lie. She's pretty clean. You're going to have to get crafty."

As soon as the file touched my hands, I was officially sucked into the maelstrom that Annabelle started. The one Hayley wouldn't come within a mile of. It was easy to see why. After all the *Sturm und Drang,* it turned out Hunta was right. All they needed was an assassin.

Personal smear campaigns were not to be taken lightly. Drea taught me that. She had the skill and the power to drop mountains on people. With a few phone calls she could make someone, anyone, so radioactive that even their pets wouldn't come near them. It was one of the worst things you could do to a fellow human being. Just ask Richard Jewell, the poor Atlanta security guard who became the chief suspect in the 1996 Olympic Park bombing. Knowing damn well he was innocent, the FBI flacks used him as media chum to lure the hungry press away from their real investigation. A necessary evil? Perhaps. But believe it or not, most publicists have souls. Most of us find it difficult to justify those means even for noble ends. Amazingly, I was no exception.

Neither was Maxina. She had all the resources to handle Lisa in-house. She just didn't have the stomach for it. As a "self-respecting woman who grew up on love and Motown," she would clearly eat her young before raining knives on a fellow sister, especially one who may have indeed been wronged, no matter what Doug says. For Maxina, there was only one course of action: close her eyes, summon a demon, and convince herself that it was all for the greater good.

Apparently I was the first name she found in the Yellow Pages, under "Demons."

The day I truly became a free man was the day I stopped caring about the world's impression of me. Like everyone else, I was raised to seek affirmation and avoid contempt. Unfortunately, the quest to be liked by everyone triggered an undue amount of stress, anger, and acquiescence in my life. By the time I left college, I realized I'd never be happy unless I undid a lifetime of conformist conditioning.

Thus, I reversed my directives. I shunned affirmation and craved contempt. I sought arguments from argumentative people. I encouraged judgment from judgmental people. I went out of my way to trigger all kinds of scorn from anyone who was willing to give it, and there was never a shortage of volunteers. It wasn't the easiest phase of my life. In fact, there were dozens of nights I cried myself to sleep. But like the most determined bodybuilders, I stuck to my regimen and eventually began to see results. Eventually, I became a human fortress, impervious to even the most subtle and penetrating forms of disdain. At long last, my mind became a peaceful, self-sufficient entity. Life got easier from there.

But my defenses occasionally sputtered, especially when I was tired. That night, in the master bedroom of Suite 511, I suffered a hull breach. I couldn't help but reconstruct the conversation between Maxina and Hayley, at least the encapsulated version:

MAXINA: Hey, girlfriend. I'm in a big fix, and I need someone evil. I don't just mean right-wing evil. I mean head-spinning, fork-tongued, baby-eating evil. Know anyone?

HAYLEY: Do I ever!

It wasn't Maxina who bothered me. She only had my client list to judge me from. Glock. Philip Morris. Monsanto. Shell. Of course she knew about Shell. Who was I kidding? For a social crusader like her, my résumé might as well come with a pentagram. She knew my work but she didn't know me.

Hayley, however, was the plastic knife in my back. We had fought side by side fifty hours a week for four years. Many a time we dozed next to each other on her office couch following a twenty-hour phone blitz. True, she was more of the East Coast, old-school style of publicist, but never once did she complain about my gangsta methods. At least not to my face.

Fine. Whatever. I let it all out through a wide yawn. I may have been feeling a little sore, but I sure as hell wasn't going to show it.

"All right," I sighed. "No doubt you'll want to know what my game plan is. And soon."

"Smart man," said Maxina. "Come back here tomorrow. Six o'clock. Bring two game plans. Or at least one good one."

"Tomorrow at six," I said, heading for the door.

Doug was confused. "Uh, Scott? Don't you want to talk about money?"

"That's okay," I said. "You can pay me in goat's blood."

For the first time, I heard Maxina laugh. Heartily. It was to her credit that she took it so well. In no uncertain terms, I'd just given her the verbal finger.

I was ready to fall asleep at the wheel. After two nights of travel and one night of adultery, my circadian rhythm had hit its fermata. With each infuriating red light, it only got worse.

So did my mood. You would have seen it on my face if you had driven past me on Wilshire. With my guard down, all the fears and insecurities I kept buried in the back of my mind came creeping forward. I could see them, oozing around the edges of my vision. I could hear them buzzing in my ears. They were so happy to be noticed again. *It seems like it's been ages, Scott! We have so much to catch up on!*

I drove faster. This was what happened when I pushed myself too hard. I probably shouldn't have taken this job.

Probably?

Oh, don't start, you. I spent most of my life as a slave to doubt, looking at myself through other people's eyes. Why? Why should I care?

Because, my boy, those opinions you claim to be so impervious to are looking more the same each day. A motif, if you will.

Right. Right. I'm a heartless bastard. A supervillain. A card-carrying member of the Brotherhood of Evil Flacks. News flash, buddy. Even if a million people see me as Pol Pot, it doesn't mean they're right. A million people also believe that everything they see on the news is real. A million people believe that the divorce rate is 50 percent. A million women believe that all rappers are rapists, and a million rappers believe that all women are bitches. So tell me, O tar of the soul, O former master, what the hell is your point?

No point. Just curious why everyone tends to see you as such a soulless prick. That's all.

"I don't know," I blurted. "I guess nobody loves a publicist."

And then that was it. No more questions. This discussion was over. If those dark little voices wanted to chat among themselves, they had my blessing. But I was out of the loop. Out of earshot. As far as my deepest, darkest thoughts were concerned, I was a deaf driver, stuck on Wilshire, inching his goddamn way home.

6

MEAN WORLD CHRISTMAS

I didn't know it at the time, but on the night I met Hunta, he was celebrating his eighth anniversary of being an only child.

Maybe "celebrating" isn't the right word. At 11:00 P.M. on February 2, 1993, Ray Sharpe was driving his '86 Pontiac Bonneville down Lincoln Boulevard in Venice when he saw the flashing lights of the police cruiser in his rearview mirror. He pulled over. The two confronting officers told him they could hear his goddamn music from a mile away. They would have let the issue drop then and there, but Ray became irrational and belligerent. After failing two sobriety tests, he made the unwise decision to flee to his car. One of the officers fired a shot into his leg. It wasn't meant to kill him, but it was Ray's bad luck that he tripped and smashed his head against the passenger window. The glass merely cracked. His neck shattered completely.

The music he had been blasting that night was from Tupac Shakur's second solo album, *Strictly 4 My N.I.G.G.A.Z.*, which had come out in stores the day before. Similarly, just eight months prior to Ray's death, a nineteen-year-old Texan named Ronald Ray Howard had been playing Tupac's first album, *2Pacalypse Now,* from his tape deck when he was pulled over by a state trooper. Only this time the officer was the one killed. At the trial, the defense attorney placed the blame squarely on Tupac, whose anti-cop lyrics *clearly* incited Ronald Ray to violence. The jury didn't buy it. Neither did the civil court when the officer's widow sued Tupac for the same reason.

But that wasn't the end of Tupac's troubles. Seven months later, he was hit with another wrongful-death suit, this one from the parents of a six-year-old boy who was killed in the crossfire between Tupac's crew and some old Marin City gang rivals. Tupac's label, Interscope Records, settled out of court for a little under half a million. Nine months after that, he was arrested for trying to club a fellow MC who had upstaged him at a Michigan State concert. He pleaded down to a misdemeanor and served ten days in jail. Five months after *that,* he was charged in the nonfatal shooting of two off-duty Atlanta police officers. He claimed that he and his posse were simply coming to the aid of a black motorist the officers had been harassing. His defense—and his lyrics—were later substantiated by mounting evidence of racism on the part of the two cops, one of whom wrote in his report that the "niggers came by and did a drive-by shooting." The charges against Tupac were dropped.

And then came his Waterloo, three weeks later, in the form of a nineteen-year-old woman named Ayanna Jackson. In November 1993 she cried rape. Everyone listened, so much so that when Tupac's third album, *Me Against the World,* premiered at the top of the Billboard charts in 1995, he became the first recording artist in history to enjoy a number one debut from inside a prison cell.

Well, maybe "enjoy" isn't the right word.

I don't want it happening to me, said Hunta, *what happened to him.*

For my own well-being, I should have caught up on sleep, but I was simply too keyed up. By 9:00 A.M. on Saturday, I was back in my car, driving aimlessly around Los Angeles, hoping to jump-start my sputtering brain. I needed to understand the woman I was suddenly up against. And to understand Lisa Glassman, I needed to understand what really happened to her the night of Friday, December 15, when she celebrated a very Mean World Christmas.

Doug Modine was no stranger to the fine art of ass-covering. Right after Lisa had tendered her angry resignation, he solicited written statements from nearly two dozen people who had attended the party. These weren't sworn depositions. Doug just wanted to get the story down while the facts were still fresh. He put it all in the file.

For the gala, Mean World had rented out one of the grand ballrooms at Le Meridien, a posh hotel on the eastern end of Beverly Hills. Between the staff, the talent, and all their friends and families, there were more than two hundred people present for the buffet.

After dinner Byron "Judge" Rampton spoiled all the kids with gifts, mostly of the PlayStation2 variety. The employees got generous checks.

The artists got car keys. Despite the fact that music sales were stagnating for the first time in two decades, 2000 had been damn good to Mean World. Things were festive. So festive, in fact, that by 9:30 all the mothers in the room got the heads-up from Doug. Very soon this party would not be suitable for children.

Although the alcohol consumption had started with dinner, nighttime was the right time for all the homeys in the house to break out the bud. You know what I'm talking about. The bammer, the brown, the buddha, the cheeba, the chronic, the dank, the doobage, the hash, the herb, the homegrown, the ill, the indo, the method, the sess, the sake, the shit, the skunk, the stress, the tabacci, the wacky. Marijuana. What can I say? California knows how to party. For the boys at the label, it wasn't enough to crack another 40 and smoke some kill. They were also determined to put the "ho" in "ho ho ho."

So in came the ladies. Dashers and dancers, prancers and vixens. What started out as an evening of reindeer games devolved into one big stag party. You won't hear me casting judgment. After Keoki Atoll, that'd be the pot calling the kettle bitch.

At the same time, I can spare some empathy for Lisa.

Born and raised in Oakland. Accepted, full scholarship, into the San Francisco High School for the Performing Arts. Graduated magna cum laude. Accepted, full scholarship, into UC Santa Barbara. Graduated summa cum laude, with a BA in African American studies and a BFA in Music Theory. Card-carrying member of the ACLU, DNC, Black Women's Caucus, and (for God's sake) Mensa. Has published poetry in numerous anthologies and has written a bunch of articles for *LA Weekly,* covering the hip-hop scene. She'll be twenty-six in July.

This was no bitch.

As a smart and skillful young woman, Lisa must have had a hard time breathing in all that secondhand smut. Lord only knew what rationale she used to fuel her polite smile. Boys will be boys? All's fair in rap and war? Ain't nothing but a gangsta party? Or maybe she went for the straightforward reasoning whenever she watched those half-dressed hoochies shake their thang. *That is not me. I am not all black women. I can only speak for myself and, speaking for myself, I declare that is not me. I am nobody's bitch.*

I didn't know. I didn't pretend to know. All I had was the testimony of others. The witnesses all seemed to agree that Lisa was having a bad time to begin with. All throughout the night she threw loaded glances at

Hunta, enough to trigger a loud spat between him and Simba. No one was particularly alarmed by the squabble. *It wasn't a big deal,* one source quipped. *They only fight when they're married.*

At 9:50 Simba took Latisha and left. Hunta didn't go after them. Instead he smoked some blunts (pot-filled cigars, for the uninitiated) and got obnoxious. He felt up Felisha, the label's very own platinum-selling R&B mulatto sex princess, which ignited a heated argument between Hunta and Felisha's husband, fellow rapper X/S. The fight was broken up by the Judge, which led to Round 12 of the battle over the title of Hunta's upcoming second album. Hunta wanted to call it *Love Is Real.* The Judge thought that was way too sappy, and too easy to misread as *Love Israel.* Ever the mediator, Doug stepped in and proposed *Luv Iz Real,* which both men hated equally. The issue remained unresolved.

Hunta eventually settled down. With Lisa. They retreated to a remote couch and had, as witnesses describe it, a quiet but serious-looking conversation, complete with lots of touching. At 10:30, Hunta and Lisa set off for quieter pastures. Everybody saw them leave together.

An hour later, Lisa came back. Alone.

Everyone agreed in no uncertain terms that she seemed perfectly fine. Her hair. Her clothes. Her demeanor. All was jake. She spent another ten minutes talking to her immediate boss, producer Kevin Haggerty. All work-related stuff, according to him, although he admitted in his statement that he was too stoned to do anything but nod. At a quarter to midnight, she gave Kevin a kiss on the cheek, wished him and his family a great holiday, and left. Ipso facto.

Wrongo. It occurred to me during my aimless drive that these accounts were a little too consistent and time-accurate, especially for a bunch of people baked out of their muffins. I had gone through my own marijuana phase in college. After two joints I became chronologically challenged. Every time I opened my mouth to say something, I got the nervous sense that I'd been droning on forever. "You know, the other day I—JESUS! How long have I been talking? I'm so sorry! I don't usually ramble like—JESUS! I'm doing it again!"

Maybe the folks at Mean World held their ganja better than I did. Maybe Lisa wore a huge clock on her back. Or maybe Doug had embellished the stories, which meant there were facts worth hiding.

At 10:00 A.M. I parked the car in front of a mattress store on Santa Monica Boulevard and called Doug. In L.A. the pay phones were merely decorative nostalgia. Nobody actually used them. From the way passing drivers looked at me, I might as well have been wearing a porkpie hat and riding a penny-farthing bicycle. Like everyone else, of course, I owned a cell phone. I just didn't want to show up on any of Mean World's phone logs, should the very worst happen.

Doug sounded half asleep. "Hello?"

"Doug, it's Scott. I didn't wake you, did I?"

"A little. Are you using a pay phone?"

"Yeah. Listen, I've been reading these statements. I've got a bit of a problem."

"What's up?"

"Well, I don't mean to sound like a TV lawyer, but I can't help you if you're going to lie to me."

That woke him up. "Whoa. Wait. What do you mean?"

"I read the reports. You overdid it. Now what are you not telling me?"

"Everything you need to know is in that file."

"I need to know the whole story. You gave me the Blockbuster version."

"Look, unless you're writing her biography, that's more than enough to—"

"Doug, we don't have time to wrestle. What are you not telling me?"

Short pause, then a sigh. "You know, I really wish you'd signed those nondisclosure agreements."

Lawyers. "I understand your concern, but I've never screwed over a client in my life. If you don't want to believe that, fine. At least believe Maxina when she said she could cut the legs off my career. And believe that I believe it. Okay?"

"I believe it." He laughed, then followed it with a yawn. "Look, you know the expression: if you repeat a lie enough, it becomes the truth. I just made people write it out because I wanted them to get familiar with the slightly altered version. Just in case."

"It's a smart plan. So what changed from the original?"

"There's only one significant difference." Pause. Sigh. "She left upset. Really upset. But it's not what you think."

"Then tell me."

He carefully measured his words. "She was into Jer. Heavily. It started out as a very good working relationship. Not to belittle Kevin but Lisa was the real force behind the album. She's got serious talent as a producer. Dr. Dre talent. Creatively, she and Jer fed off each other. The tracks they cut together are absolutely incredible. Really deep, innovative stuff. Nothing like his first album, forgive me for saying. The problem is that, look, when you spend that much time together, when you connect on such a creative level . . . it affects you. It affected her. Even if she wouldn't admit it, it was clear to everyone else that she wanted to be the next Mrs. Sharpe."

"Did she notice the first one was still around?"

"Yes. It was hard to miss her. But Jer and Simba have the kind of relationship that always seems like it's circling the drain, you know what I mean? They fight all the time. He threatens divorce. She threatens child custody. Then after they've screamed themselves blue, they cry, hug, and have sex in the nearest available bed. It's a never-ending drama with them. They'll never leave each other."

"I guess Lisa didn't see it that way."

"No. And Jer didn't help. That's his other problem. He's a sweet-talker. When he's high and when he's mad at Simba, he becomes Barry White to whoever smiles at him first. That night at the party, Lisa made her move at just the right time. Whatever words of romance she threw at him, he gave right back with interest. It's just the way he operates. Now do you see where this is going?"

"Upstairs," I said.

"Right. Room 1215. They got it on. When it was over he thanked her for the sex and then called Simba for his nightly apology. Naturally, Lisa didn't take it well."

"I'd imagine."

"Hey, I felt bad for her. We all did. It was cruel for him to use her like that. But everything that happened was entirely consensual. This doesn't come anywhere near the realm of sexual abuse. You agree?"

"Wholeheartedly."

"Okay then. The problem is that it's her word against his. You know, the irony is that if Jeremy really was a Bitch Fiend, he would have filmed the whole thing and we'd have hard evidence against her."

"Wouldn't that have been nice?" I flipped through the file. "I also notice she has absolutely no history of crying wolf."

"At the moment, no."

I chuckled darkly. "Sorry. That old trick doesn't work anymore, my friend. It'll only backfire."

He didn't chuckle back. "Then I can only hope, my friend, that you come up with something better. Any more questions?"

"One. Where's Hunta's statement?"

"You just heard it."

"Okay. But I have to ask. What you just gave me, is it the original version or a slightly altered one?"

Doug frosted over. "Scott, if you don't want to believe me, that's fine. But you seem like a smart man, so just follow your logic. There were over three dozen fine-looking women at that party who would have fucked Jeremy for the price of a smile. If Lisa had said no, he would have gone straight to one of them. Or two of them. Or three of them. It's just that easy. That's the world he lives in. It's nice, but the downside is that he doesn't get the benefit of the doubt, even from the people on his own team."

"Doug, I'm not forming any opinions. I just need to know what's going on in Lisa's head."

Now he chuckled. "Thoughts of revenge and a whole lot of dollar signs. That's all that matters. I'll see you at six."

He hung up. I couldn't blame him for getting testy. He was right. As far as presumed guilt went, young black rappers had it worse than anyone. They were like flypaper to even the most frivolous charges. As the label's head lawyer, Doug had to deal with that crap eight days a week.

At the same time, he wasn't giving Lisa enough credit. If this had just been about greed, she would have simply raised her asking price instead of stopping the negotiations. And if this was just revenge, well, I think Annabelle Shane conveniently took care of that for her.

This was something more. This was a woman who lived, loved, and breathed a style of music that wasn't exactly known for loving women back. She spent her life forgiving it. Defending it. Even improving it. And in the end it dissed her and dismissed her like she was just another bitch.

Lisa Glassman wanted respect.

Now I knew. And now I had less than eight hours to figure out how to keep her from getting it.

The thinking wasn't going well, so I made stops for errands. I went back to my favorite West L.A. spy shop and bought an untraceable mobile phone. The phone itself was nothing fancy. The seller, however, was quite unique in that he took cash and asked for no ID. I now had four thousand minutes of anonymous call time. For a few hundred dollars more, I could have gotten the Drug Dealer Special. It had a microchip inside that made it virtually impossible for the feds to monitor or track by location. I politely declined. Nothing like a little perspective to make me feel better about my own line of work.

I kept driving, but I wasn't getting any ideas. Stacking the deck against Lisa was impossible if she was holding all the cards. Even the dreaded smear campaign wasn't a viable option. You couldn't just pull dirt out of thin air. You had to take an actual smudge from the person's past and turn it into an oil spill. Lisa was spotless, and there was nothing the news loved more than a spotless victim.

That was the other problem. As far as the press was concerned, it was always more interesting to favor the accuser over the accused, especially when the accused is a celebrity, and *especially* when he's a celebrity in the middle of another hot controversy. The slightest allegation from another woman, any woman, would make Lisa's case ten times stronger. There would be no shortage of former bedroom buddies willing to hang Hunta out to dry in exchange for a few minutes in the spotlight. And short of a flat-out retraction, nothing would erase the stains from their accusations.

Shit.

I made my next errand a comic-book run. Since I was near Culver City, I stopped at Comics Ink, a small but friendly store that was short on back issues but always well stocked in recent releases. I was a sucker for the Marvel mutant titles. When I started collecting back in the early 1980s, there was only one monthly X-Men comic: *The Uncanny X-Men*. In 1985 it spun off into *The New Mutants,* a team of junior X-Men, and then *X-Factor,* a team of senior X-Men. Seeing substantial profits thanks to fools like me, Marvel Comics X-ploded the franchise to a ridiculous X-tent. Currently gracing the stands were *Uncanny X-Men, Ultimate X-Men, X-Men Forever, X-Men Unlimited, X-Men: The Hidden Years, X-Force, X-Man, Mutant X, Generation X,* and plain old adjectiveless *X-Men,* which would soon be rechristened as *New X-Men* and then joined by *X-Treme X-Men.* The fact that I could keep track of all this usually made me wonder how I ever got laid at all.

There were over three dozen fine-looking women at that party who would have fucked Jeremy for the price of a smile.

There was an idea stuck in the back of my mind, like a caraway seed. It was maddening, because I could feel the shape of it, enough to know that it was something good. There was a solution. There was a way to thwart Lisa's attack without even having to draw blood. I just couldn't shake it loose.

I bought my comics, stopped for a California Roll, and then continued to amble about town. The clock was down to five and a half hours, and my teasingly brilliant idea was only getting more elusive.

There was something in Tupac's rape case, something I needed to know. I drove straight home and got back on the laptop. Thanks to Nexis and a scandal-hungry media, I had access to a ton of articles that detailed Ayanna Jackson's accusations against the great but controversial artist known as Tupac Amaru Shakur.

She'd met him at Nell's, a downtown New York nightclub. They dirty-danced. They kissed. She fellated him right there on the dance floor, according to Tupac and his character witnesses. Frankly, that part smelled a little like spin to me, the kind of discrediting tactic a desperate and uncreative lawyer would use. Then again, I wasn't part of that world. I didn't personally know any women that friendly, but it wasn't hard to believe that a man who looked and rapped like Tupac did.

What was established is that they had sex later that night in his hotel room. That ended fine. The trouble happened four days later, when she returned to pick up some of her belongings. Still mutually fond of each other, they went back in the bedroom. She gave him a massage. They started kissing. And then three of Tupac's crew entered and turned it into a party.

"Don't worry," Tupac reportedly said to her. "These are my brothers and they ain't gonna hurt you. We do everything together."

Proving his point, they fondled her, tore off her underwear, and sodomized her. At some point during all this, Tupac left to chill on the couch in the other room. His version was that she didn't say a word in protest. Her version was that she said plenty, including the golden word "no." She certainly had some choice phrases afterward, when she cried and screamed at Tupac: "How could you do this to me? I came here to see you! I can't believe you did this to me!"

Tupac's response, per Ayanna: "I don't got time for this shit! Get this bitch out of here!"

Whether he said it or not, she was clearly looking for vengeance. Within hours, the police, the press, and Tupac's publicist were in the hotel lobby, along with Ayanna. She incriminated Tupac and his man-

ager, Charles "Man Man" Fuller. Both were cuffed and led away to police cars.

En route, Tupac held his head up high to the paparazzi crowd.

"I'm young, black . . . I'm making money and they can't stop me," he
declared. "They can't find a way to make me dirty, and I'm clean."

Not according to the jury, who saw Tupac as the serpent in this tale.
Although he and Fuller beat the rape and sodomy charges, they were
convicted on three counts each of first-degree sexual abuse. The third
accomplice pleaded down to a misdemeanor, and the fourth was never
charged.

Tupac was sentenced to four and a half years at Rikers Island. He
ended up serving eleven and a half months, until he was sprung on a
$1.4 million bond posted by Suge Knight. Thus began Tupac's infamous
stint with Death Row Records, not to mention the last year of his life.

All along he proclaimed his own innocence, maintaining—like
Hunta—that this was a setup. Shortly before the verdict, he was interviewed by *Vibe* journalist Kevin Powell. "It was all right with that police
thing [in Atlanta]," he said. "But this rape shit . . . it kills me. 'Cuz that
ain't me."

"I love black women," he told Powell. "It has made me love them
more because there are black women who ain't trippin' off this. But it's
made me feel real about what I said in the beginning. There are sisters
and there's bitches."

It's obvious which category he put Ayanna in. After that interview
was published, she defended herself in a letter to *Vibe*. Her closing:
"Tupac knows exactly what he did to me. I admit I did not make the wis-
est decisions, but I did not deserve to be gang-raped."

Fade out. Credits. Seven and a half years later, there I was, deeply
rooted in her side of the tale. With just a tiny sliver of the truth, simplified and amplified for my reading enjoyment, I had no trouble believing
her. It would have taken a mountain of direct conflicting evidence to tip
my scales in Tupac's favor. Was it biased on my part? Sure. Was it fair?
Nope. But it was a natural reaction. Like everyone else, I'd been condi-
tioned to assume the worst of people, particularly those who had the
nerve to obtain more money, power, and sex than me.

Hunta was screwed.

Even though I bought Doug's version of the story, or at least rented
it, there was no mountain or molehill I could build to get all the jour-

nalists, obstructionists, and watercooler cynics to side with Hunta. I realized this at 2:00 P.M., four hours before my scheduled meeting. My brilliant but elusive idea managed to flee the country and change its name.

I was screwed. In lieu of wowing Maxina and the others with a magic-bullet solution, I would have to settle for presenting multiple catastrophe plans, the PR equivalent of assuming crash position. Anyone can hire a bastard. They'd specifically ordered a devious bastard. This would not help my career.

The sound of the apartment buzzer pulled me back into the present. I pressed the intercom button by the door. "Yeah?"

No answer. All I could hear was the crackle and hum of the speaker, the tinny sounds of traffic.

"Hello?"

Nothing. Whatever. But right as I sat back down at the coffee table . . . BZZZT.

"Jesus." Once again, I rose and pressed the talk button. "Who is it?"

Once again, no answer.

"Look, if you're hoping to be buzzed in, you'll have to give me a little more to go on, okay?"

After a few more seconds of nothing, I went back to the laptop. I got so desperate I started to consider the ramifications of using the truth. So Hunta's a philanderer. An adulterer. So what? So are half the politicians who have spoken out against rap. Maybe I should propose a "glass houses" attack against every senator who burns Hunta in effigy.

No. Who was I kidding? Clinton's affair, at least with Monica, was beyond consensual. And still they roasted him in the public rotisserie. Even chief griller Henry Hyde was able to admit to his own past infidelities and keep on basting.

BZZZT.

"Goddamn it!" I didn't have time for this. I hustled straight past the intercom, out of my apartment, and all the way down the hall. A petite woman watched me through the glass of the front door. From a distance, I thought it was Miranda, until I saw her short hair and hoop earrings.

Jean Spelling. The web designer/deaf driver whose SUV rode up my poor Saturn's tailpipe. She looked much different in broad daylight. A little older, a lot cuter, and much WASPier. Maybe it was her sky-blue eyes. Her button nose. Or her respectful but ass-end-of-fashion Target blouse that seemed to scream "church."

I joined her on the front steps. She was alone and noticeably twitchy. With a sheepish grimace, she handed me her Handspring Visor. Its small color screen was filled with text.

HI SCOTT. I'M REALLY SORRY TO INVADE YOUR LIFE (AGAIN). I WAS WONDERING IF MY DAUGHTER STOPPED BY HERE ANYTIME IN THE LAST 24 HOURS.

I glanced back up at her. Without her kid around to sarcastically translate, was I supposed to talk or write back to her? I flipped a mental coin, which landed on "write."

Wrong. She held my wrist, shook her head, then took back her handheld. She was a Jedi master with the stylus. I couldn't believe how well she could use that thing. Anyone who's ever tried a pen-based PDA knows how easy it is to GRTZXL up whatever it is you want to write. Not Jean. She wrote as quickly and accurately as I typed.

IT'S OK. I CAN READ LIPS. JUST NOT ON A DARK STREET AT 3AM. :)

Her real face didn't quite match the smiley. She was at the end of her wits.

"I haven't seen her," I said, in a slow and loud drawl usually reserved for idiots. "I don't . . . Why do you think she would come here?"

Jean let out a hesitant sigh before answering.

NOT TO EMBARRASS YOU BUT I THINK MY KID HAS A LITTLE BIT OF A CRUSH ON YOU. SHE THOUGHT YOU WERE REALLY COOL, ESPECIALLY WHEN SHE FOUND OUT YOU WERE A PUBLICIST. SHE'S INTO ALL THAT MEDIA STUFF.

"No. Sorry. I don't know how she would find me. I don't even know how *you* found me. My address isn't on my card."

I must have looked away while saying it. She touched my cheek and pointed me back in her direction, shrugging. *Repeat, please.*

"How did you find me?"

Ah. She wrote quickly: YOUR BUSINESS CARD.

"It doesn't have my address on it."

I PLUGGED YOUR PHONE # INTO A REVERSE DIRECTORY. I LEARNED THAT TRICK FROM MADISON. THAT GIRL COULD USE THE INTERNET TO FIND HER SOCKS.

"That is pretty clever."

With a cute but unstable smile, she scribbled more onto her handheld.

SHE'S TOO CLEVER FOR HER OWN GOOD. (BTW, YOU DON'T HAVE TO TALK EXTRA LOUD OR SLOW AROUND ME. AS LONG AS YOU LOOK AT ME STRAIGHT ON, I CAN KEEP UP)

I was mortified. This seemed like such basic stuff. "Uh, has she been missing a long time, or . . . ?"

She shook her head.

SINCE LAST NIGHT. SHE DOES THIS A LOT. USUALLY SHE RUNS OFF TO THE AIRPORT. DON'T ASK. THAT'S WHERE I PICKED HER UP FROM ON THURSDAY, RIGHT BEFORE I [wince] RAN INTO YOU.

Before I could answer, she cleared the screen and wrote some more.
HAVE YOU GOTTEN AN ESTIMATE YET?

"No. I haven't had time."
I'M SO SORRY. I SWEAR I'LL PAY FOR EVERYTHING.

"I know. It's all right."

She ran her hand through her dark hair. Once again I noticed her beautifully simple wedding ring, which I'd originally thought was silver. In the light of day, it looked more like white gold.

LOOK, IF YOU SEE MADISON, CAN YOU PLEASE E-MAIL ME AS SOON AS POSSIBLE? IT GOES STRAIGHT TO MY PAGER. YOU STILL HAVE MY CARD?

"I'm pretty sure I do."

With a shrug, she gave me another one. ORIGINAL X WEB DESIGN. I had almost forgotten this was MRVL GRL. She probably spent as much money on X-Men books as I did.

"Look, good luck with Madison. I hope it all works out."

She gave me a spirited grin, but the facade quickly collapsed. In the middle of writing her response, her hand got shaky, and she was forced to stop. She bit her lower lip and turned away.

Before I could say anything, she held her other palm up to me. In layman's sign language, it meant "talk to the hand," but there was a soft grace to her movement that said so much more. *No token gestures, Scott. You don't have to react on my behalf. I didn't come here fishing for sympathy, and to be honest, it would only make me feel worse. Just bear with me.*

Maybe I read too much into it. It was a simple motion. But I remembered being amazed by how much information she and Madison managed to trade with so few gestures. It was fascinating. I was such a nut for research that I wanted to go straight to the Web and give myself a crash course in sign language. Unfortunately I was under the gun with Hunta.

There were over three dozen fine-looking women at that party who would have fucked Jeremy for the price of a smile.

There it was again. My rogue idea, the one I'd been chasing all over the city. With a mere flip of her hand, Jean had managed to stop it in its tracks. Don't ask me how my mind works. I was just glad to see it working again. I'd finally caught up with my muse. And she had a hell of a song for me.

Wiping her wet cheeks, Jean took a deep breath, rolled her eyes at herself, then let out a tired sigh.

SO! GOT ANY KIDS OF YOUR OWN?

Absently, I shook my head.

SMART OF YOU. THE KEY WORD IS "KARMA." ALL THE CRAP WE PUT OUR PARENTS THROUGH AS TEENAGERS . . . IT COMES BACK. TRUST ME.

I smiled. I liked this woman. And I felt bad for her. But at the same time I desperately wanted to run inside and work out my new equations.

Perceptively, she wrapped it up. THANKS FOR BEING SO PATIENT WITH ME. YOU'RE A GOOD MAN, SCOTT.

"I . . . You're welcome. Good luck finding her. If I see her, I'll let you know."

She squeezed my arm and, with her moist blue eyes, bathed me in a look of gratitude usually reserved for living organ donors. It was inflated and mostly unjustified. But I certainly didn't mind being mistaken as an angel for once. It made a nice counterweight to last night's snit.

Jean went back to her SUV. As she drove off, she gave me a final wave and apology. In her mind, I probably rued the day we ever crossed paths. In reality, her unannounced visit was the best thing that could have happened for me, Hunta, and the entire music industry. It wasn't hard to find the irony in that.

At 5:45, I left for my second meeting at L'Ermitage. Maxina had instructed me to bring two ideas, or at least one really good one. I had a really good one.

But, "good" is a subjective term. The XFL, which was debuting right at that very moment, seemed like a good idea to many. After all, nobody ever went broke underestimating the taste of the American public. At least until the XFL. Who knew? Spokespeople for the soon-to-be defunct football league would attribute the poor ratings to all the Melrose-fueled hypersensitivity. In other words, they'll blame the blame.

Some ideas were just plain bad from the start. Earlier that day, in Lake Mary, Florida, a twelve-year-old named Thomas Hitz doused his hand in bug spray and lit it on fire. Seeing his error in judgment, he tried to put his hand out on his cotton T-shirt, also a mistake. By the time he jumped into his swimming pool, his only smart move, he had second- and third-degree burns all over his hand and chest.

Thomas and his parents would go on to blame MTV's *Jackass* for the incident. They weren't the first. The week before, a Connecticut boy named Jason Lind poured gasoline on his legs and lit himself up, hoping to imitate the same televised stunt that had inspired Thomas (even though the show's host, Johnny Knoxville, repeatedly stressed that he was wearing a flame-retardant suit). On behalf of the Linds, Senator Joe Lieberman was quick to further publicize *Jackass* by calling for its cancellation. In actuality, four times as many kids (eight) were injured by real-live jackasses each month, and much more directly. From strictly a numbers point of view, donkeys were the more prevalent threat to our nation's youth. Either Senator Joe didn't know, or he was afraid to go after his party's totem animal. Politics.

Alas, it's a strange world. A strange nation. In the end, though, everything balanced. For every overreaction, there was an equal and opposite action. Hunta was destined to bear the brunt of America's latest outcry. There was no way to stop it or even slow it down. Same went for Lisa. I was so busy worrying about how to destroy her or discredit her when all I had to do was upstage her. If she wanted to cry rape, I'd simply have to find another woman to cry it louder. And sooner.

7

MAKAVELI, MADISON

"Is this some kind of joke?"

That was Byron "Judge" Rampton: former car salesman, former VP of Columbia Records, founder and president of Mean World Records. If Buddha were black, impeccably dressed, and determined to show off his wealth through the bling-bling of expensive ornaments, he'd look just like the Judge. He eyed me from one of the many couches in the living room of L'Ermitage Suite 511. He insisted on being here for the meeting, even though I didn't need him for what I had planned.

"You want to save Jeremy from one slanderous charge by hitting him with another."

That was Doug, sitting next to the Judge. Once again he looked ready for the courtroom in his Fruit of Islam wear. Didn't someone tell him, it was Saturday?

"No," I assured him. "I want to save him from one slanderous charge by *missing* him with another. That's the key difference."

I paced around the room, high on caffeine and inspiration. The entourage was gone. My audience consisted of six people, six and a half if you included baby Latisha. Even she seemed incredulous.

"The name of the game is 'full public exoneration,' " I told them. "Lisa herself is not the threat. Her impending civil suit is not the threat. It's the media we need to worry about. It's their theater. Their show. And they will cast Hunta in whatever light it takes to keep things interesting. This is sweeps month. The networks won't care where their story comes from as long as it's dramatic. So I say let's preempt Lisa's drama with ours. At least that way we have control over how it develops and, more important, how it ends."

"But why that?" asked Simba from another couch. "Why swap one fake rape for another?"

"Because if we go with any other story, there's nothing to stop the press from placing Lisa's allegation on top, like a cherry on a sundae. They don't cancel each other out."

"Neither do two rapes."

That was Maxina, on the third couch. She was clearly in a motherly mood, judging from the way she rocked Latisha in her beefy arms.

I smiled. "You're right. Two different accusations only serve to strengthen each other. But two of the *same* accusation? Uh-uh. Then you've got a problem."

Behind Simba's couch, a shirtless and sweaty Hunta hung from a portable chin-up bar. When the meeting began, he'd been in the middle of an impressively long set of lifts. Now he was too stunned to do anything but dangle.

"There were a lot of other women at that Christmas party," I continued. "If we get just one of them to beat Lisa to the press with the exact same charge and the exact same story, down to the minute, then Lisa will be jammed forever. She'll be nullified. What's she going to say? 'No, Hunta didn't sexually abuse that woman that night. He was too busy sexually abusing me'? Nobody would take her seriously. She'd be a copycat. A shameless opportunist. She'd barely get a mention."

Big Bank, the last person in on the conspiracy, stood next to Hunta. He chewed on my idea. "But if we use our own woman, what's to stop Lisa from joining in and saying Jer messed her up some other night?"

"Nothing. She could do it. So could fifty other women. But as far as the press is concerned, it's not who's right, it's who's first. If we get there first, our woman will be the tent pole. She'll be the one the reporters rally around. And once she goes down, everyone goes down with her. It's like fruit from a poisonous tree. That's why it's really important that we work fast and get our decoy out there first."

Big Bank nodded in amazement. I also caught the sun rising on Doug's face. Two down.

Simba remained firmly rooted in skepticism. She looked damn good in clothes, even though there was more cotton to be found in Advil bottles than in her white baby T.

"I don't understand," she said. "You're going to have one of these dancing skanks come forward, frame Jeremy, and then what? Admit it was all a lie?"

"Yes, but not hers. That's the best part. She'll tell the world she was offered a lot of money by some unnamed source, some shadow conspirator with an anti-rap objective. The press will eat it up. They'll do a total 180 and go after all the people who were going after Hunta. How's that for payback?"

I turned to Hunta, still hanging. "Not only will this silence Lisa, not only will this turn you from monster to martyr, but this'll weatherproof you against all future accusations. For the rest of your life, you'll have the benefit of the doubt. You'll have *precedent*."

His expression morphed from disbelief to abject wonder. Dare he dream?

Maxina, naturally, wasn't as easy to sway. "That's very ambitious, Scott. A few problems, though. First off, if this woman—this patsy of yours—admits she made it up, that's a straight guilty plea for fraud and extortion. She could get up to thirty years in prison. Are you planning on mentioning this when you hire your actress? Or are you just going to let her find out the hard way?"

I shot her a crooked grin. Uh-uh. Not tonight, toots. My shields were at full capacity.

"Nobody's going up the river. Not if we pick our actress carefully. We need someone sympathetic and telegenic. Someone with a dramatic reason to need the money. Sick mother. Sick child. Brother in dutch with the mob. Anything, as long as the audience understands why she lied for cash. Plus, if she comes forward on her own, if she makes the moral choice and decides she won't slander a fellow human being for *any* dollar amount, forget it. She'll come out of this with a slap on the wrist and a book deal."

Maxina still wouldn't budge. "You can't say that for sure. Manipulating the media is one thing. Manipulating the legal system is quite another. I'm not saying your plan isn't clever. It is. But when it comes to gambling with the lives of innocent people, it has to be foolproof."

Hunta finally dropped back to the ground. "Besides, what's to stop this woman from giving us up if the police start putting the heat on her and shit?"

"She wouldn't even have to know we were involved," Doug replied, inspired. "As far as she'll be concerned, there *was* a white conspiracy behind it."

"Well, that's not exactly—"

The Judge cut me off. "But what if somebody else gets to her? Somebody who offers her more money not to absolve Jeremy? I mean we're putting a lot of power in this woman's hands."

"That's why I'm going to record my initial conversations with her," I stressed. "If she goes rogue on us, we'll simply leak a tape that exposes the plot to frame Hunta, but not the plot to absolve him. Either way, she gets outed and we've got our asses covered."

Speaking of covered asses, my so-called Palm Pilot was once again capturing the moment from the warmth of my shirt pocket. The sound chip was going into my safe the second I got home.

Maxina shook her head. "I don't like it. There are too many things that could go wrong. Even if your girl comes forward and says she lied, what's to stop people from thinking that Jeremy's guilty anyway? That someone paid her off or threatened her into saying it never happened?"

Hunta nodded along. "Right. Yeah. I don't wanna be the next O.J."

I counted off fingers to him. "Okay, one: you won't be fleeing in any Broncos. Two: there's much more motive to frame you, a hot young rapper, than him, a washed-up football star. And three: if Nicole Brown Simpson suddenly showed up in front of the cameras and confessed that she faked her own death to screw the Juice, I think we'd all be changing our tune about him. You agree?"

I was hot tonight. That yanked Hunta, Simba, and the Judge well onto my side. Four little, five little, six little Indians.

And then there was one. Maxina crossed her arms, locked in dissent. "Scott, if there's one thing I learned in my many years in the field, it's that the press always finds a way to make the black man the bad guy. It's what they do."

"What they do," I countered, "is sell our eyeballs to their advertisers. Black. White. It's all green to them. As soon as our stand-in spills the beans, the media's one burning question will be 'Who framed Hunta?' It's a fresh new angle. A hip-hop political thriller. Believe me, they'll ride that wave as far as they can take it."

"Uh-huh. And what if it takes them right to you?"

Touché. I didn't have time to finish that part of the equation. I knew I'd be the one playing the cigarette-smoking man, the guy with the trench coat and the briefcase full of cash. And once our ringer let the cat out of the bag, there would certainly be an investigation. To make matters worse, there had to be a second voice on that insurance tape. Also yours truly.

"I won't lie," I said. "It's a huge risk. But the risk is all on my part. Even if I told the truth under heat lamps, nobody would buy it. It's just too crazy to think that Hunta hired someone to frame himself."

"There's a reason for that," he muttered.

"So what would you do?" asked Big Bank.

"Get a good lawyer. Implicate the government. Fake my own death. I don't know. There'll be plenty of time to work out the contingencies. The important thing is that this will work."

Simba scratched her chin. "I don't know, Scott. This still sounds risky. For all of us."

Doug stood up. "Listen, I think it's definitely worth considering. But I'd like to talk to the Judge and Maxina alone for a few minutes, if that's all right."

"Hold on," snapped Hunta. "This is my life we're messing with. When do I get my say?"

The Judge switched to paternal mode. "The final decision's yours, Jeremy. We just need to decide if we want to recommend it to you."

"Just hang tight," Maxina told him. "We'll be back."

Maxina returned Latisha to her mother. In grim silence, she, Doug, and the Judge marched into the master bedroom and closed the door. I got the silly mental image of the three of them sharing the bathtub. There'd be room for about a cup of water.

For now it was just me and the obscenely chiseled half of the party. I sat down on a couch.

"So," I quipped, "I think they went for it."

Hunta kissed his daughter's head, toweled off, and then dropped down next to me. Big Bank threw him a hand-rolled cigarette and a lighter. As soon as he lit up, my nose confirmed that the tabacci was a little wacky.

"They didn't want me in on this meeting in the first place," he said, taking a drag. "I said fuck that. It's my life. I got a right to hear this for myself."

"And now that you have?"

"Now that I have, I'm glad you ain't working for the other side," he said with a laugh. "You one slick motherfucker."

I grinned. "I don't do this every day."

"So how do you know it'll work?" asked Simba.

"I can't guarantee that everything will be perfect again, but I know that if we get to the cameras first, Lisa will be stopped dead in her tracks."

Hunta nodded, impressed. "It's a crazy plan, but I'm starting to like it."

"Listen, I don't want to mislead you. It won't be a walk in the park. There'd be at least a week, maybe two, in between our woman's accusation and her confession. During that time, you're not going to like being you."

"Why so long?"

"Because you've still got that Melrose cloud over you. If we play this right, our actress won't just draw all the bad air away from Lisa, but from Annabelle too. That'll take some time."

"Yeah but—"

"Trust me, the more they fry you, the more crow they'll eat when we pull the rug out from under them. It's to your extreme benefit."

"Yeah but the Grammys are coming up. I don't want this shit hanging over me at the Grammys."

"Oh. I didn't know you were up for one."

"He's not," said Simba. "But he's scheduled to perform a number with L-Ron. At least for now."

He squeezed my arm, blowing thick smoke through his nostrils. "Look, man, I've been dreaming about doing the Grammys since I was a little kid. I got family. I got friends watching. This is everything I worked for. If you can clear all this shit before then—"

"When are the Grammys again?"

"February twenty-first," said Big Bank.

I waved my hand. Pshaw. "That's three weeks from now. By then the whole country will be kissing your ass, apologizing for ever doubting you."

He patted my back, grinning. "You just became my white knight."

"Let's see what the others say. But I'll tell you this, guys: if we move forward with my idea, we can't just keep it under our hats. We have to keep it under our scalps. That means nobody else hears about this. Not even your family. For every Michael Jackson, there's a LaToya."

Big Bank nodded. "We know how to keep a secret."

"That's all I needed to hear."

Hunta grinned thoughtfully. "You know, 'Pac would've really been into your shit."

I laughed. "Me? Why?"

"When he was doing his time, he got into Machiavelli. I mean, really got into him. He must've read *The Prince* like a thousand times. He loved all that scheming and plotting business. He cut his last album under the name Makaveli."

"Really," I said. "You know, a lot of historians believe that Machiavelli faked his own death."

"Yeah," said Hunta, intrigued. "I know. That's where 'Pac got the idea."

"Wow. I thought that was just an urban legend."

Hunta got solemn. "Oh, he didn't do it. He just talked about it. The only reason he was out of jail was 'cause Suge bailed him out while the lawyers appealed the rape verdict and all that. If they lost, he would've had to go back. 'Pac didn't want that. No way. If that happened, he probably would've done it. Faked a murder. Got a new face and shit. Ain't no way he was going back."

He took another long drag off his joint. "But he didn't do it. I know that for sure. I seen him get hit. I seen him in the coma. And I seen him dead."

"Sorry."

"Yeah, so am I. But he lived the last year of his life like he knew it was the last year of his life, you know what I'm sayin'? When it came to livin' large, he was King Kong, man. It ain't the amount of time, it's what you do with it. The man changed a lot of lives. Changed mine."

"But they never caught his killers."

"The police? No."

Big Bank got wary. "Jer . . ."

"What? I don't know shit about it. I'm just speculating, is all. Ain't no way Suge would've let them killers keep walking around, all notorious and big."

Simba rolled her eyes. "Baby, shut up and keep smoking."

Hunta shrugged at me. Suddenly, I got hit with that "second day of school" feeling. Maybe it was all the conspiracy thinking, or the marijuana smoke I was reluctantly inhaling. Either way, I knew I still had a lot to learn, way too much for me to be acting this confident.

Doug opened the bedroom door. "Scott?"

Just like yesterday, Maxina leaned back on the emperor-sized bed. The Judge sat on the other side. Doug closed the door behind me and motioned to the chair. From Maxina's face, it was obvious which way the troika split.

"Against my advice," she began, "the Judge and Doug have agreed that your plan is the best course of action. I, however, am not a big fan of human sacrifice."

"You just haven't tried it, then."

Maxina wasn't amused. "Scott, I need to get back to my part of the project, so I'm simply going to say my piece and leave. I think that some cures are worse than the disease. Apparently, I'm in the minority, but it's not my dime. I'm going to step back and let you do your thing. If your little scheme achieves everything you say it will, you'll be our secret savior. And I'll be right there with the best of them, whispering your praises. But if you destroy an innocent woman in the process, I will be your bane. Your karma. Your comeuppance. You understand me? Whoever this girl is, I'm not going to let you use her and throw her away like Kleenex. I want you to do everything in your power to protect her."

"That was my plan from the beginning." And may I remind you that I'm doing this to avoid destroying Lisa Glassman? Give me some credit, woman.

I had to hand it to Maxina, though. She was one of the few people who could see past my granite expression, straight on through to my surface thoughts. In very clear images, I told her she had me all wrong. With equal silent precision, she told me to prove it.

"All right. Looks like we all have a lot of work to do. Someone help me up, please."

Once again, Doug assisted her, all the way to the door.

"The minute the news breaks about the 'Bitch Fiend' tape," she informed me, "the race is on. You'll need to have your show ready to launch by Wednesday at the very latest."

"We'll be ready by Tuesday."

"Good man," she said with cautionary emphasis. She gave her good-byes and left.

Doug closed the door behind her and settled down in her sunken place. "Despite what she thinks, the Judge and I agree that your plan is brilliant."

"If it works," the Judge added.

"If it works," Doug echoed. "What do you need from us?"

"The lowdown on every woman who attended that Christmas party. Strike the ones who've worked with you anytime since then. Strike the ones who are married or close to married. Strike the ones who are known or rumored to be super-promiscuous. And definitely strike the ones who are known or rumored to have had sex with Hunta. Hopefully, that leaves a few."

"More than a few," said Doug. "If they worked for us even once, we've got a whole file on them."

"Perfect. I'd like to see those files as soon as possible."

"Fine. We can fax you what we—"

"No. Just keep the papers at your place, and we'll review them tomorrow. The earlier the better. I want enough time to pick three good candidates and run a background check on each of them."

The two men traded satisfied grins, as if they were working with the legendary Jackal.

"Anything else, Scott?"

"Yes," I added, wishing I had a cigarette to pad their false impression. "I think it's time we talked about money."

Between all the plotting, scheming, and fee-wrangling, I had very little time to process the personal ramifications of my proposal. I knew whatever solution I came up with would be deceptive, even underhanded. That was just the nature of the business. But it had finally hit me that my frame-within-a-frame, my secondhand smoke screen, went way beyond the definition of "publicity stunt." I was orchestrating massive fraud. Before Hunta, my worst-case scenario always stopped at a civil suit. Now it kept right on going, all the way to jail time. That was a lot of risk for $160,000 and a rapper I'd never even heard of before Thursday.

Ira felt compelled to offer his blind advice: "Walk away. It's not worth it."

We sat on the deck of the *Ishtar,* eating take-out Chinese food and watching the calm black waters of the Pacific. It looked so peaceful out there in the open sea. I wanted to hoist the anchor and ride off into the night, just to enjoy some real quiet for a change. Of course, I'd have to get rid of Ira.

"Seriously. It's futile. Whenever a white kid goes on a killing spree, someone has to take the blame. Remember Columbine? The politicians went after Marilyn Manson, despite the fact that the killers didn't even like his music. The only thing that saved him in the end was obsolescence. I mean, who cares about an androgynous Goth freak when you've got all these bad-ass gangstas running around, singing about their bitches and AKs? So unless something even scarier than rap comes along, I'd say your man is hosed."

I didn't tell Ira anything about Lisa Glassman or my remedy to her. I wasn't sure why I kept my mouth shut. After all, I trusted him fifty times more than the people already in on the joke. Out of all of them, I was worried the most about Hunta himself. I got the nervous sense that once the heat got high—or he did—he was liable to spill everything.

"Annabelle Shane wasn't white," I corrected.

"What?"

"She was half-black, half-Thai. There wasn't a drop of white in her."

Ira took another forkful of lo mein. "She looked white. And she was middle class. That's all that matters. You're pissing in a hurricane."

I checked my watch. After thirty-two minutes with Ira, I was already starting to appreciate places like "elsewhere." Really, he wasn't a bad guy, if you took him in fun-sized doses.

"I'm serious," he said. "It's not worth the grief. Besides, it's not like you're hard up for money."

"How do you know?"

"Because you don't exactly live the wild life."

"No, but I do have a whole mess of dwindling tech stocks."

He nearly spit out his food. "Still? I told you! I warned you to get your money out!"

It's true. He did. Three years ago. This was the same guy who treated Y2K like an Extinction-Level Event. He took all his cash out of the banks, loaded up the boat with Ensure, and made damn certain he was at least a hundred miles off the mainland when the computers hit the big double zero. He even asked me if I wanted to join him on his safe getaway. No thanks. Even if society did crumble, I saw being stuck at sea with Ira as one of those post-apocalyptic futures where the living envied the dead. He ended up riding his ark alone, until he got bored enough to come back.

But he was right. I wasn't hard up for money. In truth, only a minuscule portion of my nest egg was wrapped up in investments, and not because of Ira's portent. I still remembered the painful lessons of October 19, 1987, the day the Dow tripped and fell a mile. On that awful

Black Monday, I lost $7,200 of my hard-earned savings, everything I'd squirreled away since college. I didn't exactly bawl over my bad fortune, but I did hurl some pissy words up God's way. In retrospect I probably shouldn't have taken it so personally. That was a bad day for a lot of people.

One notable exception was Jean Spelling, then known as Jean McKnight. That was the day her own investment finally paid off. It had taken nine long months of hard work and mood swings, but it was worth it. While everyone else cried over their losses, she ended the day with a six-pound, nine-ounce gain. She named it Madison.

Madison told me the story herself, thirteen and a half years later, from my very own couch.

"I think it cursed me somehow," she professed, with a rising inflection that made her statements sound like questions. "You know, being born on Black Monday. All my life, I've been like a business jinx. When my mom and dad were still married, they put all their money into this ASL school that folded within a year. Then my mom married my stepfather, and they started this company that sold these special movie-theater seats that let deaf people see captions. That went bust. Now he does captions for live TV events and even that's not going well. And don't get me started on my mom's so-called web design business. Sometimes I really think it's me. I've got this black-cat thing going on."

I sat across the room from her, listening, nodding, and covertly e-mailing her mother from my laptop. *Jean. Your daughter is here. I'm going to try to stall her as long as I can. Please come soon.*

I had returned from the *Ishtar* at 9:30, only to find Madison waiting outside my apartment door. This was my first good look at her. In brighter light, I could see that she had inherited her mother's sharp blue eyes, her perfect bone structure, and her tendency to drop by unannounced. It was also clear from her rumpled clothes and unwashed golden hair that she had yet to make her way home.

"Aren't you going to ask me how I found you?"

That was the first thing she said to me, in the hallway. I already knew the answer. My instant reaction was to play dumb. If Madison knew her mother was one step ahead of her, she might flee for an even less obvious hiding place. I decided my good deed for the year would be to capture this stray cat myself.

"Actually, I was going to ask *why* you found me."

"I used a reverse directory," she bragged. "It used to be that only the cops and phone companies had them. Now they're all over the Web."

"That's pretty clever. How did you get here?"

"SuperShuttle. I also did some research on you. I found a lot of your old press releases. They're really good. You write them just like articles."

"Journalists are busy people. They can use all the help they can get."

"Yeah, but I love how you bury the things you're selling into the story itself. I mean you're really subtle. I want to learn how to do that."

I leaned against the wall. "Madison—"

"Hey. You remembered my name."

"I'm good with names."

"I'm not. I'm only good with faces."

"Madison, what's going on?"

She lost her smile. Now she looked as frazzled and desperate as Jean. "Can I come in?"

"Does your mother know you're here?" No. That's why she's here.

"No. That's why I'm here."

"Look, I don't want to get involved in some sort of domestic thing."

"It's nothing tragic," she said. "It's not like she beats me or anything. It's just really . . . Look, can I just come in? I promise I won't stay long."

After a quality pause, I let her in. Obviously, I didn't want to seem too eager, lest she get suspicious. But it was all a Method act. The real Scott wasn't in the mood for live family drama. He was looking forward to watching HBO until he fell asleep.

As soon as I closed the door behind us, I had a horrible thought. What if, for some malicious reason, she decided to cry rape? I'd be just as screwed as Hunta. It wasn't too crazy to think about. After all, she clearly wasn't a model of teenage stability, if such a model existed. Even worse, she could turn Jean against me with a few mere hand signals. *Oh, it was terrible, Mother! He kept me prisoner here! When you showed up, I screamed and banged against the window! But you just couldn't hear me!*

Problem B: Lisa Glassman's file was all over the coffee table. Before Madison had time to sit down, I gathered up the papers.

"Do you want anything to drink? I've got water, milk, apple juice."

"Apple juice is fine."

"Okay." I still had Jean's business card in my back pocket. As soon as I slipped into the kitchenette, I pulled it out and memorized her e-mail address. It wasn't hard for an old X-Fan. Her user name was Phoenix.

After giving Madison the last of my juice, I sat across from her and turned on my laptop. "Sorry. I just need to check my stocks."

"It's Saturday."

"I invest in the Nikkei market. They go six days a week. They should be closing right about now."

That lie had more holes than a tuna net. Fortunately, it just triggered the story of Madison's Black Monday juju, which gave me enough time to send the message. Relieved, I closed the laptop and leaned back in my seat. We stared at each other.

"So. Madison Spelling."

"Madison McKnight."

"Why Madison?"

She curled up on the couch. She was a skinny little thing. Her thighs were thinner than Hunta's arms. But her face was wide and uniquely captivating.

"I don't know. I think it was my grandmother's name. I hate it. Too many syllables, and I hate 'Maddy' even more. Of course my parents don't know that. I mean about the syllables."

"Oh. So your dad's also . . ."

"Deaf? Yeah. So's his wife and their daughter. My stepdad isn't. He's a coda like me."

"Coda?"

"Child of Deaf Adults."

"Oh. I wasn't even sure a deaf couple could have a hearing child."

She scratched her nose. "Neither of my parents were born deaf. It was just something that happened to them, like a scar or a broken arm. It's not the kind of thing that gets passed on."

I shook my head at myself. "Right. I should have realized that."

"But even if both parents are born deaf, there's still only a twenty-five percent chance that the kid's born deaf, too."

"Wow. I didn't know that. That's really interesting."

"Not really."

Her tense posture was sign enough for me to move on from the whole deaf/family thing, but I couldn't seem to swing us toward a new topic.

To my relief, Madison grabbed a new thread. "So you're a publicist."

"That I am."

"Tell me about it."

"What would you like to know?"

"You don't work for a company or anything, right? You're totally freelance."

"Have gun, will travel."

She smiled. "That is so cool. That's like my dream life. Hey, you need an intern?"

Before I could say anything, she qualified herself. "Look, I'm smart. I'm media-savvy. I can find anything on the Web. And I really want to learn this stuff. You could be my mentor."

"Oh wow. God. I don't know. . . ."

"Come on. Why not? It'd be great for both of us. I'd come over after school and on weekends. I'd do all your filing. Answer phones. Office stuff. You wouldn't even have to pay me. Just teach me."

As soon as she mentioned school, it finally hit me that her situation wasn't as dire as I'd been led to believe. Here I was, guarding her like she was about to sprint off to Zurich, when all along she had every intention of going home. I guess she just needed to get away for a bit and torture her mother in the process. Jean called it karma but I didn't think any nonabusive parent deserved that kind of treatment.

"I don't think so, Madison. I'm sorry."

"Why not?"

"Well, first of all, I'm out of the house a lot—"

"So? I'm thirteen. It's not like I'm going to choke on a toy while you're gone."

I laughed. "I don't have any toys. What I do have are a lot of sensitive documents—"

"I'll sign any gag agreement you want. You can even give me the one they use for *Survivor,* where I have to pay you like ten million dollars if I open my mouth."

Yeah, that would work. PUBLICIST SUES TEENAGE GIRL FOR GOSSIP. DEMANDS $10 MILLION FROM DEAF MOTHER.

She wouldn't relent. "Look, I really want to learn about this stuff. Everywhere I go, I'm hit by all this . . . I don't know. I don't even know what to call it."

"Corporate conditioning," I offered.

She snapped her fingers. "Yeah! Exactly! On TV, in movies, in magazines. I can feel it but I can't see it. I mean I know it's there. And I know there's like this whole psychological world behind all of it but nobody's able to tell me anything. My friends are all slaves to it. My teachers tell me I shouldn't worry about it. And my parents? Please. My stepdad's the world's most boring man and I don't even know where to begin with my mother. She reads comic books and fantasy novels all day and then goes online to argue about them with nerds who are *my* age! She's barely even an earthling! But you're different. You're like the total insider. I want to learn what you know. I want to see what they're doing to me."

It took a huge effort to hide how impressed I was. It wasn't every day I came across a thirteen-year-old girl who'd prefer *Utne Reader* over *Tiger-Beat*. Gracie would have loved her.

I sat back, eyeing her. "Are you familiar with the expression 'Ignorance is bliss'?"

"Yes. I'm also familiar with the fact that bliss is bullshit."

"That's pretty cynical, don't you think?"

She shrugged. "I'm a total cynic. I admit it."

"Don't be. Cynics make the worst publicists. Skeptics, on the other hand, make the best ones."

"What's the difference?"

"Let me put it this way. If I told you that George W. Bush has a 160 IQ, would you believe me?"

"Uh, no."

"Okay. What if I told you he has an 85 IQ and that the White House has spent millions of dollars keeping that information quiet? Would you believe me?"

"Probably."

"That's the difference between a cynic and a skeptic. Cynics blindly accept any information that confirms their lack of faith in humanity. Skeptics question everything, even the bad news. Cynics are easy for the media to control. Skeptics aren't."

She leaned forward in wide-eyed wonder. I didn't want to enjoy this. Really.

"So how do I become a skeptic?"

"It's not easy. You've got over thirteen years of that corporate conditioning in you. The U.S. is only six percent of the world's population, and yet we consume fifty-seven percent of the world's advertising. And nobody on earth is peddled to more than the American teenager. By the time I was eighteen, I was practically a nihilist."

"Well how did you change?"

Drea. "Reading. Watching. Listening. Keeping an open mind. If you want a peek behind the curtain, here. Let me show you something."

From my bookshelf, I pulled a few recent issues of *Brandweek*. I hunkered down next to her on the couch, flipping through pages.

"This is one of our trade magazines. This is where we get to loosen up and be ourselves. See, behind your back, we don't call you customers, we call you 'targets.' We don't provide services, we 'perpetuate campaigns.' And this is where the media advertises to the advertisers by selling them people. Look at this. 'The Learning Network: We Have Mothers Coming Out of Our Ears.' 'Tripod Delivers Gen-X.' Oh, here we go. MTV. 'Buy This 24-Year-Old and Get All His Friends Absolutely Free.' That's the practice of targeting audience leaders. In other words, you get the cool kids to follow your orders so the less cool kids will follow theirs. Trickle-down advertising. Tobacco companies do it too."

She could only gape as I thumbed through ad after ad. "Wow."

"Oh, it gets better. Here's one for the Cartoon Network. 'Today's kids influence over a hundred and thirty billion of their parents' spending annually. That makes these little consumers big business.' Very, very true. It's the kids even younger than you who drive the industry now."

"And this is the kind of stuff you do?"

"No. What I do is worse. Look, here's a company that sells digital ad space for elevators."

She closed the magazine. "Hold it. Hold it!"

"I'm sorry. Too much, too fast?"

"Yes. No! I just . . ." Yup. Too much. Too fast. She fought to put her questions in some kind of order but she was overwhelmed. Giving up, she mimed a pistol to her head, pulled the trigger, and collapsed with her tongue out.

"That's the problem," I said. "This is no place for cynics. That's why our industry, especially mine, has a high burnout rate."

"So how do you survive?"

"By keeping perspective. I mean, it's silly to believe that all the people who work for the Cartoon Network are evil. Or MTV. Or even Philip Morris. Believe me, they don't run over kittens for fun. They play tennis. And they're not after your heart or soul. They want your designated spending money, just like the butcher, the baker, and the candlestick maker. The system's not perfect. Usually it's underhanded. But when you're dealing with people who have eight zillion choices, you have to get clever or you just won't survive. That's what a free market is all about. Make sense?"

I was her new god. "Scott, I want to learn this."

"The thing is, you have to be sure. Because once you get that X-ray vision, you can't turn it off. You're going to see the business angle behind everything. And I mean everything. Not just your TV, movies, and magazines. I'm talking about your news, sports, and weather. That's my playing field. And once you know what I know, you won't be able to enjoy any of it the same way ever again. It'll be like having flies in your soup every meal of the day. Do you think you'd be able to handle that?"

"Yes."

"Are you sure? Because it's not too late to take the blue pill."

"I'm sure!"

"And if you worked for me, I would need absolute secrecy from you."

"I promise."

"I'm serious. If you ever betray my trust, I'll kill your career before it even starts. You'll spend the rest of your life working at Hot Dog on a Stick."

"I promise!"

She meant it, too. You couldn't fake that kind of intensity. I eyed her one last time.

"Okay, then."

"So I can work for you?"

"I don't know," I said, reading *Brandweek*. "You'll have to ask your mother when she gets here."

Madison's first lesson under my tutelage: don't trust anything anyone says, especially about the Japanese stock exchange. Once I clued her in on the gag, her expression chilled so fast, I could practically see her breath.

"I always come back," she informed me matter-of-factly. "My mom knows that. I don't know why she freaks out every time."

"Because she worries about you. It's not safe out there."

"It is at the airport."

"Why do you go to the airport?"

"Because it's safe. Because it's always open. Because I like it there."

"But what do you do there?"

"I watch people. I'm a total people-watcher. Sometimes I talk to them. I always make up different stories. Like this one time, I convinced this old couple that I was flying to Seattle to donate a kidney to my brother. They bought me dinner."

I grinned, even though I knew I shouldn't encourage her. "It's still a bad thing to do to your mother. Don't do it anymore."

She shot me a piqued glare. My godlike status had disappeared sometime during the debriefing.

"You know she's married, right?"

"Yes, I know she's married. What? You think I'm trying to score with your mother?"

"You wouldn't be the first."

I flipped through my newspaper. "Relax. I'm not big on adultery."

"Just be careful. She has a way of pulling guys in."

"You two have issues. Leave me out of it."

"I'm serious. You know how I ruin businesses? Well, she's the same way with men. She did it to my dad. She's doing it to my stepfather. I'm just trying to stop you from being next."

With a sigh, I put down the paper. "Madison, I'll be honest. You're starting to give me second thoughts about this whole thing—"

She shot up her palms. "Wait! Scott! I'm sorry! You're right! You're totally right! I was just being stupid!"

"You're not stupid. I just think you have a lot going on right now—"

"Look, I'm really tired. That's the last time I'll bother you with my personal crap ever again. I swear to God. I could have a tumor and you won't hear about it."

Fighting a grin, I scrutinized her. "I don't mind health issues. It's just your home life I'm trying to avoid."

"So am I," she said weakly. "This'll work out great."

At 10:30, Jean reached my door. Reflexively, I moved to the intercom, then caught myself.

"You can just buzz her in," Madison told me with forced neutrality. "She keeps trying the knob until it opens."

That made sense, but when it came to all things Jean-related, the kid had no credibility with me. I decided to play it safe and fetch her myself.

Outside, Jean was practically bouncing in relief. Her text was already written out for me.

THANK YOU! THANK YOU! THANK YOU! I WAS GOING CRAZY!!

"It's all right. She's fine."

I led Jean into the apartment. The reunion was not touching. Madison barely looked up from her magazine. Jean's face turned stern and dark. It didn't take an interpreter to read her orders. *Get. In. The. Car.*

Madison held up the magazine. "Can I borrow this?"

"Keep it."

With demonstrated pomp, she shook my hand. "I look forward to working with you."

"I told you. That's up to your mother."

Catching that, Jean looked at me. *Excuse me?* Once Madison left for the car, I explained it all, stressing about twenty times that it was entirely at Jean's discretion.

She was more amazed than anything else. She barely knew what to write.

SCOTT, YOU JUST WENT FROM BEING ABNORMALLY DECENT TO DISTURBINGLY SAINTLIKE. WHY WOULD YOU DO THIS?

A fair question. The answer I gave her was that I could use someone to do Web research for me. This was true. Once the shit hit the fan with Hunta, Madison could save me hours by keeping a beat on the Internet news sites, summing up the general tack. She was more than qualified. The more sensitive reason, which I also explained, was that a new outlet for Madison just might be the call of the day. She wasn't exactly a French-club kind of girl. This could do her some serious good.

But those were still surface thoughts. The deepest answer, which I didn't share, was that it felt nice. I tried to avoid vanity at all costs, but it was just so damn nice to be looked at the way Madison and Jean looked at me. These were two people I had a perfect record with. If my life ever got put on trial, I would now have two character witnesses to counteract all the Deb Ishams who'd line up to testify against me, all the Iras and Mirandas who wouldn't commit beyond labeling me "a not too terrible guy." And being a great believer in third-party endorsements, wouldn't it be nice if Jean shoved her handheld right in Maxina's face, screaming through all-caps: HEY LADY! YOU'VE GOT HIM ALL WRONG!

As nice as they felt, these feelings worried me. Affirmation was a drug I kicked a long time ago. I didn't want to get hooked again. On the other hand, I had the strong hunch I'd need external reinforcement in the very near future, when I'd be pushing an innocent young woman into the fiery mouth of the Great American Bitch.

8
HARMONY

To anyone who knew her, there were three indisputable truths about Kelly Corwin: the girl was dark, the girl was gorgeous, and sweet Jesus, the girl could *sing*.

Back in 1996 rap was at its peak of profitability, but these were also the golden days for reigning sexy pop divas. At seventeen, Kelly wanted nothing more than to become one of them. She knew she couldn't do it from the genial suburbs of Richmond, Virginia. Nope. Hollywood was the place she ought to be. So she loaded up her car and moved to Southern Cali. Palms, that is. Crappy area. Not the safest.

But fate was ridiculously kind to her. After one audition, she got a job as the regular chanteuse at a Venice Beach coffeehouse. After two performances, she found representation with a high-powered talent manager who just happened to be in the audience. He believed in her so much, he paid out of his own pocket to put her in a high-end recording studio. After three weeks, she had a completed demo tape boasting a fine selection of rhythmic croons, all of which Kelly had composed herself.

Her karma stopped at the front door of the music labels. While being shopped around to every major outfit, she got the same baffling rejection over and over again. She's incredible. She's original. She's daring. We love her. But I'm afraid she's just not for us. Best of luck in the future.

Kelly didn't get it. She had the face, the bod, the pipes, the whole package. And yet she kept hitting the same invisible wall. What the hell was the problem?

Finally, a brave promotions executive just came out and said it: it was the skin. Kelly was simply too black, even for black audiences. Look, a few years ago exotic was in, but now, as far as fuckable singers go, the buying public likes a little cream in their coffee. We didn't make it that way, but there it is. Best of luck in the future.

Desperate times, desperate measures. If she couldn't shake the "exotic" label, her last-ditch effort was to ride it all the way. Soon after her eighteenth birthday, Kelly—who had never been to Africa in her life—changed her name to Simba K. Shange, an awkward mix of Zulu and Swahili that aurally translated to "the lioness who walked like a lion." On the aesthetic advice of her manager, she eventually dropped the "K," but in Swahili, "ke" was a feminine suffix. So not only was she left with an inappropriately masculine moniker, but she was now officially "the lion who walked like a lion." To a native Kenyan, the name would sound as nutty as Bucky McDeerhop. Her manager quickly reminded her how very little her future success rode on the approval of native Kenyans.

Using the same demo tape, Simba got a record deal with one of the very labels that had rejected Kelly Corwin. The songs were rerecorded with a world-beat flair, and by December 1998 the album was on the shelves of record stores everywhere. Well, the East and West Coast. Actually, Seattle and New York. But it was well received by the scholarly Afrocentric population of both cities, even if they were perplexed by her name.

In the end, the album tanked. The label went bankrupt. Her manager moved on to lighter pastures. And Simba settled for life in the background, earning a semi-decent living as a studio backup singer. On the plus side, she got to work with some interesting talent. One of them she married.

While her husband had more than three dozen fan sites devoted to him, somewhere in the corner of the Internet there was a single typo-ridden Web page that lovingly chronicled the all too brief career of the artist formerly known as Kelly Corwin.

I had discovered it at 7:30 A.M., on the gray Sunday morning of February 4. Already I knew I was in for one of those existential off days, the kind where you wake up a little bit wrong and don't completely reacclimate yourself to reality. In my dreams, I'd spent the night with Simba. Nothing carnal. It was more Lifetime than Cinemax. Actually, it seemed like a reenactment of Thursday night's adultery, with Simba playing the part of Miranda. We were curled up in my bed. She was talking. I was listening. But after her long diatribe about something (I couldn't remember what), I interrupted her with a question that—in the dream—had been nagging me for some time. "What do you *do*?"

That was when I woke up. Poorly. I still had my dream goggles on, so much so that it wouldn't have surprised me to find Simba in the kitchen, in my shirt, cooking eggs for two. Sometime over the course of my shower, I found my way back to this plane of existence, but I still wanted to get her story.

Obviously, I felt bad for her, to be held back by such a narrow mindset in this day and age. On the other hand, I knew that—like it or not—she was about to get plucked out of limbo, and soon. I wasn't sure which way things would turn for Hunta and his stand-in accuser, but Simba "Rodham" Shange would come out of the shitstorm smelling like a garden. Hell, it might just resurrect her career, even if her husband's dies on the vine. Wouldn't that be a Hollywood twist?

But I was getting ahead of myself. The scandal still needed its Monica. She'd be the star of the show, and I needed to find the perfect actress to fill the part. I was like Botticelli in search of his Venus. Of course, unlike the great master, I had roughly forty-eight hours to find the woman, talk her out of her clothes, and get her onto the clamshell.

I was still a little spacey when I arrived at Doug Modine's house in Hollywood. On the way over, I had been honked at on two separate occasions for not noticing the light turn green. Both times my attention had been captured by nearby billboards. The first one was an embarrassingly lascivious ad for the Beeper King, in which four provocatively dressed young women touched each other while surrounding a giant pager. I couldn't decide if it was a deceptively clever ploy to tap in to the "so uncool it's cool" chic, or just a genuinely pathetic effort by a decrepit old adman who should have retired with Nixon. Most likely the latter.

The second billboard, however, was pure elegance. On behalf of a major bank chain, a thirtysomething redhead stared back at me and said, in a classy serif font, I WORK FOR MY MONEY. I EXPECT MY MONEY TO WORK FOR ME. While the copy would never win any awards, the art director deserved a trophy just for his choice of model. The woman was upscale but accessible. Beautiful but not intimidatingly so. Smart-looking but not arrogant. And that pleasant but soulful look on her face . . . perfect. In a split second, I wanted to trust her, meet her, take her out to dinner, fuck her, get her number, and then switch to her bank, the one that seemed to make her so content. To get all of that from a simple photo was astounding. I never claimed to be immune to good advertising; I just had a deeper appreciation for the sublime ingredients behind it. I could have studied her for hours. Unfortunately, the man in the Bentley behind me didn't share my sentiment.

Ninety minutes later, I plummeted deep into the photograph of another woman. That was my very first glimpse of Harmony.

The secret Patsy Selection Committee, as no one ever called it, met in the living room of Doug's bohemian bachelor home. Until I got there, I had assumed the panel would simply be me and Doug, but the Judge and Simba were already there. The Judge insisted he was crucial to the process because he had extensive knowledge of virtually everyone who worked for his label. Simba was there to firmly represent Hunta's best interests, a not-so-subtle finger-shake at the people handling this crisis.

Almost instantly, I was reminded—for the millionth time—why I was so much more effective as a solo operative. Working by committee was about as productive as building with wet cement. They had each come into this meeting with a strong candidate in mind. For the next forty-five minutes, they squabbled over the inadequacies of each other's selections. Turns out all three leads were terrible. The Judge's favorite video vamp, Giselle Thomas, had been hit with three different restraining orders from three different men. Simba's choice, Monique Plana, had partied it up with Hunta's posse several times since Christmas. And Doug's proposed *j'accuser*, whose name I forgot the moment I heard it, was notorious for fellating every male recording act from Aaron Neville to ZZ Top. Doug seemed almost hurt by the news.

This was going nowhere. I tuned the others out and leafed through the spilled assortment of employee files on Doug's coffee table. All I could think about was the redhead on the billboard. There were just some people out there who were blessed with a magical face, the kind that could encode volumes of thought and feeling into a single expression. My mother was one of them. Jodie Foster also comes to mind. Gracie only had an enchanted smirk, but when she used it, the Mona Lisa seemed about as mysterious and captivating as bean dip. I suppose I could have added Jean to the list. She had the face of a silent film star, but that might have been a link of convenience, her being silent and all.

For my purposes, several of the ladies in Doug's files were perfectly qualified to play the role I was casting. And for the media's purposes, they would rally around any woman prettier than Paula Jones, especially when she said such explosive things like "Yes, Hunta sexually abused me," "No, I'm not a lying opportunist," "Okay, yes, I'm a lying opportunist, but some shady white man offered me a lot of money to say that Hunta sexually abused me." In the end, though, the press was only as strong as their sponsors, the sponsors were only as strong as their audience, and for the audience's purposes, they needed a woman who gave good face. A face that could divert them from their unfulfilling lives. A face they could believe in, even when it admitted to lying.

By that token, it was kismet that I came upon the face and file of Harmony Prince.

"I got it," I said, four seconds after laying eyes on her photo. "I found her."

The photograph itself was crud: a faded two-by-three Polaroid with rumpled edges and a coffee stain on the lower right corner. Unlike the other Mean World booty-shakers, Harmony didn't have a professional head shot in her file. She didn't have representation from any of the prime booty-shaker talent agencies. All she had was a handwritten application and a casual photo taken during some low-rent picnic event. With her elbows on the table and her chin on her fists, she gave the camera a tight, weather-beaten smile that brimmed with effortless sincerity. But it was the touch of sadness in her eyes—the undeniable hint of hard-earned wisdom—that cut through every one of my prickly defenses. She was painfully real, and instantly compelling.

I was sure it was just her well-toned body and light cocoa skin that had paved the way for her part-time gig as hip-hop eye candy. What a shame that such a terrific face was being wasted as background filler, as extra flesh in some rapper's video harem.

That needed to change, quick. With my help, Harmony Prince could be forever yanked out of the scenery and into the annals of cultural history. In my hands, she would be molded and forged into a weapon of mass distraction.

Doug peeked over my shoulder. "Who'd you find?"

"This one," I said, holding up the file. "Harmony Prince."

As soon as I said her name out loud, I knew it was a winner. Not only was it mnemonically friendly, it rolled off the tongue like a sonnet. I hadn't heard a name that catchy since Tawana Brawley.

And yet all three of my associates were forced to take pause as they scanned their memory banks.

" 'Chocolate Ho-Ho,' " said Simba finally.

"Right. Right," said Doug, looking through her file. "The girl in the second set."

"Is that one of Hunta's videos?" I asked.

"Yeah. We shot it in Glendale last April. About a month before 'Bitch Fiend.' "

"Oh, I remember her now," the Judge added. "The quiet one."

"Good," I said. "Now before I get my hopes up, are you sure she was at the Christmas party?"

"Apparently so," Doug replied. With a little embarrassment, he held up a pay stub.

I nodded knowingly. "Ah. And just to clear things up, she was hired to dance."

"Of course. If she was a hooker, she wouldn't have a W2 with us."

Well, there were people hired to dance, and then there were people hired to "dance." Know what I mean? But it wasn't worth pressing the issue. All would be revealed in the background check.

"So tell me everything you know about her," I said. "Does she have a drug problem? Criminal problem? *Any* disqualifiers?"

The Judge shook his head. "Nothing I've heard of. She was really quiet."

"I don't think she has any kids," said Simba. "We had a little day-care thing set up at that video shoot. I don't remember seeing her there."

"She's not one of our regulars," said Doug. "But we fish from the same pool as Aftermath, Dre's label. She might have done some work for them."

"That's okay. I'll find out. But my last big question for now is how did she and . . . At the video shoot, how did she get along with Jeremy?"

"You mean did they fuck?" Simba laughed, then looked to the Judge. "I don't know. Did they?"

"I don't know," he replied indignantly. "It's not my job to keep tabs on that stuff."

"Well, maybe someone should."

I closed Harmony's file, then isolated it. "All right. We seem to have one good candidate here. But I don't want to stop until I have at least three names for the private investigator. Who's next?"

The rest of the session was just a cautious formality to me. I knew I'd found my catch in Harmony. Of course only an idiot was 100 percent sure of anything. That's why God invented vetting. After another half hour of useless committee blather, I decided to get a jump start on the process. I slipped away to Doug's bedroom and made the first call from my new anonymous cell phone.

Most private investigators come from a law-enforcement background. Eddie Sangiacomo, a wiry, middle-aged ferret of a man, came from the clergy. The story of how he abandoned his calling and became a free-lance gumshoe was surprisingly dull, at least the way he told it. But he was still a power Catholic at heart and treated his business like the con-fessional. Once the name "Harmony Prince" came back to him from every corner of the news, no earthly agent could get him to cough up the fact that I had something to do with it. I gave him Harmony's social se-curity number, wished him well, and sent him on the hunt.

During the call, my gaze had been captured by a series of snapshots that ran all around the inside frame of Doug's dresser mirror. They were all of the same beautiful baby boy: eating, sleeping, bathing, what have you. Although there was no chronological order to the pictures, the sub-ject seemed to stop aging at around four. Maybe I was still lost in deep photoanalysis mode, but the meticulous shrinelike nature of the collec-tion led me to believe that the child was no longer among the living. I've noticed that dead people, especially children, have this retroactively ghostly quality in all their old photos, as if they were haunting in ad-vance.

But then again, maybe he was still alive and Doug just got the ass end of a custody agreement. Who knew? Everyone had their backstory, some more interesting than others. To this day, I never got Doug's tale. He didn't seem like the kind to open up, and I certainly wasn't the kind to pry. At least openly.

"I didn't know you had an album," I had said to Simba while driving. Of course that was a lie. I'd known since 7:30 that morning. As with Doug, I didn't feel any particular need to inquire unless it was brought up. That afternoon, on the way back to Wilshire Boulevard, it was brought up.

Thirty minutes earlier, the committee had nailed down its third and final candidate and called it a wrap. Before I could leave, Simba asked if I was going west and, if so, could I give her a ride to her cousin's house in Beverly Hills. She had come with the Judge. She didn't want to go back with him. The first thing she did upon entering my car was explain why.

"He's a fat, lecherous fuck," she told me, lighting her millionth cigarette for the day. Her daughter's absence allowed her to revert to her natural state as a smokestack. "He's always putting his big clammy hands on my leg. Or my arm. Or my back. And then he gives me this smile that makes me want to take a shower. The worst part is that ever since Thursday he's been stepping it up, only this time he's doing it under the pretense of consoling me. 'It's all right, babe. Everything's gonna be all right.' "

She shuddered. I grinned in empathy. I must have still had some dream residue on me, because I felt a heightened but artificial sense of intimacy with her, like I had already explored the dark skin beneath her tight leather pants and midriff-baring tank top. It was a dirty sensation that I took little pleasure in.

"I don't trust him," she added. "Him or Doug. If they could sacrifice Jeremy to save Mean World's precious relationship with Interscope, they would. And if they could somehow find a way to make money off this shit at our expense, they wouldn't hesitate. Not for a second."

"Well, at least you have absolutely no doubts about me," I teased.

Simba laughed and covered her face. "Oh shit. Am I that obvious?"

"No. It just stands to reason."

"True. But we like you, though. Jeremy's totally fascinated by you. Whenever he talks about you now, he just calls you Slick."

"Really," I said ambivalently.

"Hey, be flattered. When a black man gives you a nickname, it's a sign of respect. Unless it's a girlish nickname, which Slick isn't." With a low chuckle, she put on her best machismo. "Besides, there are some names that are just too white to come out of a nigga's mouth, know what I'm sayin'? Like *Scott*. Who wants to say *Scott*? A nigga don't sound hard when he say shit like 'Yo, motherfucka. Where Scott at?' "

Smirking, I shook my head.

"Doesn't mean we trust you all the way, though," she added.

"I'd be surprised if you did."

"The thing that makes us feel good about you is that you seem to be in it for the challenge more than anything else. Like you're determined, just for pride's sake, to haul Jeremy's ass out of the fire."

"And get everyone to kiss it afterward," I added with pride.

She laughed and touched my arm. "Okay. So we were right about you. I just hope you can get one of these stupid girls to play along."

"I will."

Her smile deflated over the next two blocks. "There are just too many of them, Scott. There are too many sisters out there waiting for the chance to degrade themselves. For money, attention, revenge. Whatever. It's just sad."

"I don't think it's limited to sisters."

"No, but they've cornered the market. I mean everyone shits on rappers for being so sexist, but how can they *not* be when all they see are these mindless chickenhead hos just lining up to be humiliated like—" She cut herself off with a wave of the hand. "Whatever. You probably think I'm like the biggest hypocrite in the world for going all feminist on you."

"Of course not. Why would I think that?"

"Why? Because I keep standing by my husband even though he fucks everything that lets him. Look, I'm not a street bitch. I wasn't raised to put up with that kind of shit. But ever since I got involved in the music industry . . . Let's just say I'm glad one of us in this car still has pride."

She grew silent again. I hoped she wouldn't continue on what was becoming a deeply personal monologue. There was a set limit to what I wanted to learn about her, and I could feel her stepping over the comfort line.

"I don't enjoy being cheated on," she continued, "but it's the kind of thing I stopped taking personally. I mean, I've known from day one that this is his shit, not mine. I could be the goddess of love herself, and he'd still mack on other women. That whole player image thing is such a deep part of him, because of the way he grew up. In South Central, if you're a nigga and you're not wearing colors, you might as well be a woman. And if you're crazy enough to be a gifted student, getting love from the teachers and scoring all A's like Jeremy did, you might as well be a *white* woman. He got shit from all sides, especially when he didn't have his brothers around to protect him anymore. Can you imagine growing up like that?"

"Nope."

"Me neither. So this is how he fights back. This is how he proves himself to all the men who put him down. He becomes a hard-rhyming, pumped-up 'playa.' He throws his dick and his money around like there's no tomorrow. Of course the problem, another problem, is that right now he's all dick and no money. Don't let that hotel fool you. We're down to nothing. We already blew the advance on the second album, which wasn't much to begin with. Now we only get whatever the Judge feels like fronting us. Even if the album goes triple platinum, we'll probably still end up being in debt to Mean World."

"Sorry."

"Yeah. It really sucks. I think I liked it better when it was just white people screwing us over."

She glanced out the back window. "Oh shit. You had to turn left back there. I'm sorry."

"No problem."

As I made a U-turn, Simba stared at the endless grid of well-kept houses.

"I had my own thing going on," she said in a quieter tone. "I had my own plans. My own album. But now all I am is the wife of some rapper. The *cheated-on* wife of some rapper. That wasn't part of my dream, Scott. This isn't the way I wanted people talking about me."

That was when I said—disingenuously—that I didn't know she had an album. Sure, I could have used my inside knowledge and pretended that her fame had preceded her, but that just wasn't me. Out of the many flavors of bastard out there, I couldn't bear to be a patronizing one.

For the next few minutes she gave me a first-person account of the miseducation of Simba Shange. What wasn't mentioned on her one adoring fan page was that her manager at the time had also been her lover. The man was twice her age and, when all was said and done, left her for his next big discovery. I'd tell you her name—trust me, you know it—but I've already had enough legal troubles to last me a lifetime. Suffice to say she made it further than Simba. Further than Hunta, even.

"I'm tired of being angry about it," she told me. "I'm tired of being mad at where I ended up. And I'm definitely tired of being angry at Jeremy. He's not . . . He really isn't a bad man, Scott. And as much as I bitch about him, as much as he fucked around with Lisa, he never laid an angry finger on her. He's never laid an angry finger on anyone. If there's anything I know for sure, it's that."

"I believe it."

She turned to me and put her hand on my leg, a strange reminder of a night that never happened. "Then promise me you'll do what's best for us. I know we're not the ones paying your bill, but I can tell you know right from wrong. So no matter what the Judge or Doug or even Maxina says to you, promise me you'll do what's right for me and Jeremy."

Softly, she squeezed my thigh. Ah, there it was. The hook. All throughout the car ride, I'd been nagged by the vague sense that she was angling for something. For a disturbing moment I thought she was going to hit me up for a loan. But as soon as she touched my leg, she confirmed my first instinct. It was nothing more than a loyalty play. All she wanted to do was charm some extra allegiance out of me, just to play safe.

I was disappointed. More so, I was insulted. I didn't mind being her sounding board. In fact, I was starting to like her. But did she really think a few rounds of flirting would turn me into her lovestruck champion? How stupid. How amateur. How utterly base. Suddenly, I got the flipside image of her relationship with the Judge. Lord knew how much she had to touch and caress him in order to squeeze out the latest stipend. Maybe she did more than that. I didn't want to know.

All I knew was that I wasn't as easy to tease. She had underestimated me by miles. My dark and petty id wanted to play her back, to push and see how far she'd go to curry my favor. But I wasn't that kind of bastard, either. Besides, the situation was sordid enough. I played it chaste and oblivious.

"Simba, I can't guarantee success, but I promise you I'll do everything in my power to get you and Jeremy out of this mess in one piece. My real goal is to get you both out of this mess better than when you came in. That's extra-credit work. That's the real challenge. And I'm only making that effort because I like you guys."

No, I'm not above playing fake. In this case, all I had to do was tell her what she wanted to hear. It worked. She squeezed me one last time and then moved out of my personal space.

"Just keep going down this road," she said, grinning. "We're almost there."

———

Okay, I might have overreacted to that whole scene. I might have read too much into her actions. Being an insanely beautiful woman (or man,

I suppose) is like a having an extra muscle. Sometimes it's used on purpose, for good or for evil, and sometimes it's just reflexive. Simba, for understandable reasons, clearly felt helpless in the grand scheme of things. Maybe she had to stretch that muscle just to convince herself she was doing something.

Ordinarily, I would have realized this right away and not taken her actions personally. I could have saved myself a good twenty minutes of smoldering indignation, filled with grumbling thoughts about the world, the entertainment industry, even black people. No, I'm not above racial generalizations, either. But only in my weaker moments. Like I said, I was having an off day.

Thank God again for Harmony Prince.

By the time I finished my follow-up phone call with Eddie Sangiacomo, I had forgotten all my petty grievances. That was Harmony's real power. It wasn't enough for her to be blessed with a face you could fall into. She was also cursed with a backstory that—even in its driest form—made Anne Frank look like a spoiled JAP.

"Jesus Christ, Scott. Where did you find this woman?"

He had called at me at five o'clock. Ever since I'd gotten home, I had little to do but read e-mail and wait. I was tempted to do my own research on Harmony, but alas, the cyber pathways Eddie traveled went much further than mine. With just a social security number, he could piece together an entire life through stored records, both public and private. The vast majority of this information could be obtained easily, legally. As for the rest of it . . . let's just say a good PI has a lot of file clerks for friends.

I suppose I should have told him right off the bat that Harmony was young, black, and not exactly a member of the gold-card elite. But he found that out soon enough by digging up her birth certificate. When you're an investigator and your target is a kid from the 'hood, there are three smart sources to tap: the hospitals, the police stations, and the courthouses. Of all three, only the courts were closed today, but the Lexis database picked up the slack by leading Eddie to a whole slew of family-court dockets.

As with all cases surrounding minors, the records were sealed, but Eddie was able to crack them open wide enough to get the name Sherry Greenleaf. She was a county social worker who played a supporting role in many of Harmony's family crises.

By the time I had dropped Simba off at her cousin's house, Eddie was at the door of Sherry's home in Culver City. Although he had brought three hundred reimbursable dollars of incentive in his pocket, it turned out Sherry was willing to talk for free. In fact, by the time she was done she had sacrificed two hours of her life and about a thousand Kleenex.

Harmony Miesha Prince was born on January 21, 1982, in the nearby town of Inglewood. Her mother, Aasha Harris, was a fifteen-year-old orphan and ward of the county at the time. The father, Franklin Prince, was the thirty-eight-year-old patriarch of Aasha's current foster family. Quite the scandal. When Harmony was two months old, Aasha and Franklin took their love child and fled upstate to Modesto to live happily ever after. It didn't last. Within six months, Franklin left Aasha for someone even younger. Still a minor, she had little choice but to take Harmony back to Inglewood and throw herself at the mercy of Social Services. They put her in a group home for young mothers.

That didn't last, either. Aasha eventually moved in with her new beau, a twenty-eight-year-old mechanic named Umberto Ortiz. Although his eye didn't wander as far as Franklin's, his parenting skills left a lot to be desired. In April 1984 a neighbor caught him whipping Harmony with an extension cord. That led to Umberto's arrest and Harmony's first appearance in family court. She was two.

Once Umberto was out of the picture, Aasha moved on to John M. Jackson, a forty-two-year-old music producer with an unruly Afro and a shepherding role in the brief forgettable career of the eighties funk band Picadilly (you might remember them from such cheesy tunes as "Watch Me Watch You" and "Phone Call"). Although not a millionaire, John did get Aasha and Harmony out of Inglewood and into a lovely three-bedroom house in West Hollywood.

And here their troubles began.

For both Harmony and Aasha, the years 1985 to 1993 were a nightmarish string of abuse at the hands of Jackson. At the age of five, Harmony was sent to the ER for numerous fractures and contusions caused by a ball-peen hammer. When she was seven, she and her mother were treated for second-degree scald burns. The next year Aasha nearly died from multiple stabbings with a corkscrew. Each time the assaults were blamed on freak mishaps or anonymous attackers. Each time the social workers were left wary but helpless.

It all came to a tragic head in December 1993, when eleven-year-old Harmony was hospitalized for internal distress that was soon revealed to be—are you ready for this?—a miscarriage.

I know what it's like to be sexually abused, I pictured Harmony telling the press. *I was taught to stay quiet about it. To let him get away with it. Well, I will not be quiet about this one. And I will not let Hunta get away with it!*

With the help of Sherry Greenleaf, Aasha and Harmony fled to Inglewood yet again and took refuge in a women's shelter. But without a decent source of income, Aasha could no longer afford the twelve dollars a night the shelter charged. She and Harmony soon moved into the Dominguez Hills apartment of Kenneth Prince: Franklin's son, Harmony's biological half brother, and Aasha's former (and obviously forgiving) foster brother. Before long, he and Aasha became lovers, and she became pregnant with her second child. This new addition to the family would be, like Kenneth, Harmony's biological half sibling. Confused? Don't worry. Things are about to get terribly simple.

On June 17, 1994, at 11:15 A.M., John M. Jackson used an aluminum bat to break into the apartment and skull of Kenneth Prince. A hysterical Aasha tried to stop him, but a firm swing to her own temple instantly ended her life and the one inside of her. She was twenty-seven.

Four hours later, Harmony came home from her last day of school and discovered the bodies on the floor. She was a year younger than Madison.

"Jesus Christ." That was my first reaction. In fact, that was my only reaction throughout the entire tale. And Eddie wasn't exactly the best narrator. His delivery was embarrassingly flat, and his nasal, squeaky voice made him sound like Dustin Hoffman doing a bad impression of Andy Rooney, or vice versa. But Harmony's story transcended the telling.

John M. Jackson was caught, convicted, and sentenced to three consecutive life terms. This all happened with lightning speed and little fanfare. Domestic crimes, especially among the minority masses, were never big news to begin with. Even if a reporter had wanted to glom on to the human-tragedy angle of young Harmony's plight, it would have been crushed under the wheels of O.J.'s big white Bronco, which made its historic run across every channel the day Harmony became an orphan.

Well, half orphan. But Franklin Prince was nowhere to be found, so

Harmony became a ward of the county, like her mother before her. For the next four years, she bounced her way through a dozen foster and group homes. Some of them were straight out of Dickens. At one home, the girls weren't allowed to use electricity after 6:00 P.M. At another, Harmony was locked in her unventilated room all summer. And at another, Harmony was sent to the emergency room after a drugged-out roommate attacked her with a knife. She had to get thirty-two stitches on her left arm.

Despite all of this, she went on to become a model student. At fifteen, she made the local news by winning first prize at a regional poetry competition. This brought her to the attention of Jay McMahon and Sheila Yorn, a pair of freelance documentarians who were itching to shoot a multi-part series about Southern California black kids, re: their struggle to overcome adversity. For the next two months, Harmony gave them over a hundred hours of footage: interviews with her, interviews about her, follow-arounds, you name it. Her story was so compelling that four of the other eight subjects were dropped from the lineup, and the remaining three were relegated to supporting roles. On seeing the rough cut of the first episode, PBS began negotiations to air the whole series. Suddenly our tragic heroine was about to become the biggest thing to hit public television since Barney.

And then, tragically, it all fell apart. Sometime during final editing, Jay and Sheila hit a major skid in their twelve-year romance and split up. Worse, they waged a long and vicious battle over the rights to the unfinished documentary. By the time I'd gotten wind of this, nearly four years later, the tapes were still trapped within the legal chalk circle, with both parties still refusing to let go. My plans would only make things worse for them. That footage was about to become white-hot property.

But I could imagine poor Harmony's anguish. The documentary was going to be her claim to fame, her day in the sun, her backstage pass into the hearts, minds, and checkbooks of the guilty white elite. Sorry, toots. It's back to the scenery for you. But hey, you came real close. Don't lose hope. Best of luck in the future.

If there wasn't already enough evidence to prove the existence of God through His inexplicable beef against Harmony Prince, here comes the final kicker. On December 18, 1998, just halfway through her junior year, she was hit by a speeding LAPD cruiser.

Harmony had just stepped into the crosswalk at La Cienega and

Arbor Vitae when the cop car, in pursuit of absolutely no one, turned a sharp corner and rammed her. Had the driving officer been even less attentive, Harmony would have been rendered to pieces. As it was, the policeman spotted her with just enough time to skid into her at thirty-five miles an hour. In the span of a second, she was thrown into the windshield, flipped over the siren, and then spiked down to the ground like a touchdown ball. Her body rolled twenty feet before coming to a complete stop.

Obviously this was California's problem. The incident caused a major row between the city of Los Angeles, which was financially liable for the LAPD, and the county of Los Angeles, which was financially responsible for Harmony. Eddie had to sift through two hundred digital pages of bureaucratic hair-pulling just to find out what happened to her.

From a physical perspective, she was extraordinarily lucky. Her limbs had nothing but perfectly clean breaks and fractures, and her spine was left in mint condition. In fact, she didn't seem to have any permanent damage at all, if you didn't count her brain.

After three days in a coma, she emerged with all her memories intact but left behind her ability to read, write, and speak. It took thirteen months of rehabilitation in a Watts convalescent home to bring her back to 90 percent of her old self. By then she was no longer a minor, and thus no longer California's problem. Worse, at 90 percent functionality, she didn't qualify for any state disability benefits. Had she the mind or the will to hire even a crappy lawyer, she probably would have scored a high-five-figure settlement from the government, possibly more. But all she got was $212 of "good luck" money and a few references for private group homes.

Thus, on January 25, 2000, Harmony Prince was set free into the world, left to God's good graces. Fortunately, God seemed to be done with her.

I guess that made it my turn.

Life has not been good to me, I pictured a tearful Harmony telling the press. *I know that's no excuse for what I did. And I can't apologize enough for what I put Jeremy and his family through. But in the end, I was tired. I was tired of doing everything the hard way. And when that white man offered me money to tell a lie, I did it. I was tired. I was weak. I was wrong. And I am sorry. I'm sorry for everything.*

I took out the photo, the cruddy little Polaroid that had captivated me earlier that day. There was no doubt left. She was the one. She was my Venus. And I knew the only way I could move forward without my nagging conscience tripping me up was if I convinced myself, once and for all, that Harmony Prince would finish this tale better off than when she started; that when she told the world she was sorry, it'd be just another happy lie. Just the latest in a long string of words—my words—coming out of her mouth.

9

TAXI DANCER

"You were right. I was wrong. Your plan is ingenious. I see it now."

Those words came directly from the mouth of the great Maxina Howard. They had to travel through five miles of fiber optics, but they reached their intended source. Pinch me, Simba. I may be dreaming again.

At 9:00 P.M. on Sunday, I called Maxina at her hotel. My main goal was to tell her all about Harmony, but I also wanted to give her mad props for the *Dateline NBC* coup. Ever since Thursday, she had been chipping away at BET's video archivists, trying to get a copy of last year's "106 & Park" clip, in which special guest Hunta described "Bitch Fiend" as a morality tale. Not only did Maxina succeed in shaking the footage loose, but she managed to get it to NBC's midtown Manhattan office right under the wire. That may seem like no big deal to the average person, but then the average person can't fathom the great corporate gorge Maxina had to jump. You see, BET was the recent three-billion-dollar acquisition of media giant Viacom. Viacom owned CBS. CBS ran *60 Minutes*. And *60 Minutes* wanted a lock on that video, even though they weren't sure if they were going to use it. Even if they did, Maxina knew they wouldn't include the all-important caption indicating when the clip originally aired. That would have given their fourteen million viewers the false but dramatic impression that Hunta had been making his comments recently, in response to the Melrose shooting.

Obviously *Dateline* wasn't a bastion of journalistic integrity, either, but their producers were comparatively easy to bend. Once Maxina miraculously got the video across enemy lines, she strong-armed Jim

Donnell—whose wife I'd recently boned—into running the clip with a date stamp. So at 8:20 P.M. (7:20 CMT), eight million viewers got to hear Hunta's defense *and* know that it was made several months before Annabelle Shane's bloody rampage. In other words, it wasn't just desperate knee-jerk spin. Given what was coming, Hunta needed every morsel of credibility he could get.

Maxina's feat took a level of skill and clout that few mortals possessed. It still may not seem like great shakes to you, but to me it was like watching Superman stop a runaway train. I was in awe of this woman, which made her praise all the more sweet. Here it is again:

"You were right. I was wrong. Your plan is ingenious. I see it now."

I'd spent twenty minutes filling her in on Harmony's cataclysmic history. Compared to Eddie, I was the far better storyteller, but the material alone would be enough to send Toni Morrison into a blue funk.

"My God . . ."

Maxina had two ways to go from there. She could have fallen into a fit of simplistic, hackneyed *Parade*-magazine-style morality and insisted I keep my sleazy white-devil mitts off of poor Harmony, who'd clearly been through enough. Or she could have looked beyond all the weltschmerz and examined the situation on a more intrinsic level.

Props again, Maxina, for picking Choice B. From the beginning she'd believed my plan would serve its function, but only at the cost of an innocent young woman. Her concerns were actually quite valid. But Harmony was the battery that would last and last and last. In a land that thrived on high drama, political correctness, and sweet-young-victim chic, she made Elián González look like a tapeworm in a fat man's ass. Even when the jig was up, she would not only remain impervious to media and political scorn, but to prosecution.

"They'd never touch her," Maxina said. "You were right. Even if she admitted to fraud, the law would never touch her."

And only because the law felt bad about running her over. In their endless quest to heal their tattered public image, the LAPD was forced to err fifty miles this side of caution when it came to high-profile black people. And considering that the city mowed her down in a crosswalk, bandaged her skull, and sent her on her merry way without so much as a fruit basket, it was obvious that any public figure who called for Harmony's head would soon have his own handed back to him by the liberal furies. In short, Harmony would become the ultimate L.A. paradox: a red-hot celebrity sensation who couldn't get arrested in this town.

"She has no criminal record," I stressed while pacing my living room carpet. "No history of substance abuse. No children, legitimate or otherwise. She's never applied for any kind of government aid. And if that's not enough to make her a conservative's wet dream, the poem she wrote? The one that won first prize in the regional competition? It was all about abstinence."

"Unbelievable."

That was when I told Maxina the best part. Not only did Harmony come standard-equipped with a great face and a monstrous past, but she was also available with a documentary feature. One hundred hours of raw footage just waiting to be cooked, sliced, and tossed, hibachi-style, into the open mouths of hungry news directors. Granted, it was a bit of a side quest to hack through the legal red tape of Jay McMahon and Sheila Yorn's creative-property dispute, but if anyone could do it . . .

"I'll do it," said Maxina, just as I'd hoped. "This is incredible. Absolutely incredible. Tell me, Scott. Were you amazingly brilliant in discovering this woman, or just amazingly lucky?"

"I'll never tell."

"Well, I'll certainly say this . . ."

I was right. She was wrong. My plan was ingenious. She saw it now. Don't worry, that's the last time you'll hear it. For the most part, that was the last time I'd hear it.

"No. No. No!" the Judge barked from atop his porcelain throne. "That is a dangerous idea! That is a *shitty* idea! I'm not going to let it happen that way!"

After talking to Maxina, I had phoned Doug to fill him in on the latest. He insisted we conference in the Judge, who was currently hanging with the wife and kids at their home in Pacific Palisades. I could tell from the succession of background sounds—a television, a radio, a juicer—that the Judge was working his way through the house. By the time I finished my second rendition of Harmony's tale, the noises were gone, and his "Jesus Christ" had the padded, echoey lilt that could only come from a man on the crapper.

It wasn't Harmony herself that made the Judge nervous. After getting the whole story, he and Doug were in hearty agreement that she was the perfect foil to Lisa Glassman, maybe even the perfect foil to Annabelle Shane. It was my proposed method of hiring and managing her that caused the argument.

"I think what the Judge is trying to say, Scott—"

"I know what you're both trying to say."

Simply put, they didn't want Harmony to know who she was really working for. As far as she was concerned, I really would be a member of the political anti-rap conspiracy. On the plus side, she'd have plausible deniability when the shit hit the fan, and thus could never implicate Mean World when put under the heat lamps. On the minus side . . .

"It would never work," I said. "This entire plan hinges on one thing: Harmony's confession. It has to be made in just the right way at just the right time. Now how can I get her to do that if she thinks I'm working against Hunta?"

"You *manipulate* a goddamn confession out of her," the Judge yelled. "That's what we hired you to do! Manipulate!"

"Maybe you can pretend to have a change of heart yourself," Doug suggested. "That way you could sort of, you know, switch sides together."

I must have died and gone to Screenwriter's Hell. Suddenly I was trapped in a bubbling lava pit with uncreative executives and their awful script notes.

"Guys," I said in a forcibly even tone, "in order for Harmony to do what we want her to do, she and I need a relationship based on trust. That means I plan on lying to her very sparingly, if at all."

"But—"

"Look, I don't have time to argue with you. And I don't have the patience to deal with your micromanagement. Either let me do my job, or I walk right now."

"Scott, come on." That was Doug. The Judge's response, I imagine, was all excretory.

"Look, my ass will be hanging out there in the wind right alongside yours. Now given that, don't you think I will do everything in my power to make sure Harmony doesn't screw us all over?"

"We don't doubt your intentions." Doug again.

"Okay, well then you doubt my abilities. If that's the case, why did you even hire me?"

"We didn't," the Judge growled. "Maxina did."

"Good. Then call her. Because she knows exactly what I have planned, down to the very last detail. And she likes it. She likes it a lot. So if you have issues, bother her. Just let me do my goddamn job!"

I hung up for dramatic emphasis. I wasn't really mad. In fact, I could totally understand their point. But sometimes I had to play the prima-donna card just to reinforce the notion that I was a black belt at this, which of course I wasn't. There was an occasional downside to not hav-ing a defensive ego. For starters, it was much harder to convince myself that I knew exactly what I was doing. I mean, objectively, how could I say for sure that this whole thing would work? I've never built a ma-chine this big before, much less run one. This was massive.

Thankfully, so was Maxina. Her strong new endorsement of my plan would be more than enough to get the Judge and Doug off my back.

She and I had held a lengthy discussion about the best way to gain Harmony's trust. We both knew I had my work cut out for me, being a slick white man and all. We agreed that the only way around it was to play it 100 percent sincere. No wide-screen pretty pictures. No paper-thin platitudes. I'd treat her like a trusted member of the team instead of expendable hired booty. And the only way to achieve that dynamic was to do exactly the opposite of what the Judge wanted. I'd tell Harmony everything, even the things she didn't need to know, even the things she didn't want to hear.

(With one or two creative omissions.)

In the meantime, I was anxious to move forward. Doug called back a half hour later to give me the official green light. By that point I was al-ready in my car, on the town, and out in search of Harmony.

As you can imagine, it's not easy to engineer a grand-scale media hoax. For starters, what do you wear? Obviously a suit wouldn't do much to combat the "corporate wolf" aura a guy like me emitted. And yet, over-compensating in the other direction would only make me look like a wolf in cheap clothing.

The middle ground solution was to go business casual, like I always did. Button-down black Gap shirt. Loose-fit khaki slacks. My oldest and second-least-expensive pair of boat shoes. But what about the face and hair? After all, I was about to be seen. If I could be seen, I could be iden-tified.

Screw it. I'd just go as myself. Aside from my height, I was pretty nondescript, or so I've been told. One of Gracie's old college friends was a police sketch artist. He said I had such a unique lack of distinguishing features that if I ever robbed a liquor store, I wouldn't even need a mask.

Although he meant it as a casual barb, I took it well, considering the source. He had a terminally unrequited crush on Gracie and, might I add, a nose you could see from space.

There were two other factors that played well in my favor. First, Harmony was—unbeknownst to Harmony—living her last few days of anonymity, which meant that people had yet to notice or care about the strange men she talked to. Second, and more important, her regular job allowed her to converse with all the strange men she wanted. In fact, it was encouraged.

In addition to digging up Harmony's past, Eddie Sangiacomo had given me a little dirt on her present. She had an address in Venice Beach, but she didn't live there alone. The phone, gas, electricity, and cable bills were each registered to a different man. The lease itself was signed to a woman named Tracy Wood. That was quite a lot of inhabitants for a nine-hundred-dollar-a-month apartment. Before I left home, I tried calling Harmony but ended up getting one of her male roommates. The rap music on the other end of the line was so loud that I had a hard time telling the speaker apart from the song.

" 'Lo?"

"Hi. I'm looking for Harmony Prince."

"Who dis?" he yelled.

"I work for Mean World Records. Is Harmony around?"

"*Who* dis?"

I had to raise my voice to compete. "My name is Scott. I work at Mean World Records. We've talked with Harmony before. Is she around?"

He turned down the music. He took a wary pause, then a few bites of some crunchy legume. "She ain't here, man."

"Do you know where I can find her? It's really important that I get in touch with her."

"What you want with her?"

"I'm sorry, what's your name?"

He paused again. "McB."

"Mick Bee. I like it. You a rapper?"

"Hey, man. Why you wanna know about me now?"

"Just curious. You've got a strong voice. And we're always looking for new talent. By the way, I assume you saw Harmony in Hunta's video for 'Chocolate Ho-Ho.' "

He laughed. "Yeah, man. The second time. The first time I sneezed."

I grinned along. "I know. I know. That's why I want to get in touch with her. We've got a video coming up, and we want to put her in it. And I don't mean put her in the background, man. She's going to be a key player."

"No shit?"

"No shit. But it's important that I find her tonight. Extremely important. You feel me?"

After a moment's thought, he caved. "She working now."

"Where?"

"The Flower Club."

Whoa. That wasn't part of Eddie's profile. I suppose it was too much to hope that it was just a fun place for gardeners.

"Uh, where is it? Downtown?"

"Downtown," he said. "On Sixth and Flower. Shit, wait. Seventh. Yeah, Seventh."

"That's okay. I'll look it up. You know what time she usually gets off?"

"I dunno. She usually get home 'round one or two. Hey, you really work for Mean World?"

"Yeah. Why wouldn't I?"

" 'Cause, I don't know, you sound white. Really white. No offense."

"It's all right. I get that a lot."

"Just understand that we all look out for Harmony here, you know what I'm sayin'? You fuck with her, we fuck with you. We clear?"

"We clear," I said, oddly touched by his concern. "But trust me. She'll be glad you took this call."

"Well, go find her then."

That was the idea. But this Flower Club thing made me nervous. My grand design would hit a major skid if our sweet little angel turned out to be a stripper by night.

Before going downtown, I had to stop and make a cash withdrawal, a moderately fat one. I needed some kind of financial incentive to get Harmony to even listen to me.

"Don't make it too high," Maxina had warned. "If it's too high, she'll start to question the level of risk involved in earning that much money. She won't trust you."

That, and she could be tempted to take the payment and run. I knew all this. The more pressing concern was that I had only seventy-four dollars on me. That was when I remembered Ira's Y2K stash, which he now called his earthquake fund. Whatever. It was ten thousand dollars worth of twenties just taking up space in his safe. Perfect. En route to Marina del Rey, I called and asked him if I could borrow fifteen hundred of it.

Initially, he was hesitant to take some of the stuffing out of his disaster cushion, but by the time I got to the *Ishtar*, the money was waiting for me on the dining tray.

"What's the matter?" I teased. "Too scared to open the safe when I'm around?"

"I don't recall being entrusted with your combination."

Touché. Decked out for comfort in his ratty blue robe, he sat in his leather command chair and clicked away at his PC. He seemed to be building some kind of virtual house. I wanted to inquire, but I knew that would trigger a painfully elaborate software demonstration. The important thing was that he enjoyed it.

"So what shady business are you conducting now?" he asked, still focused on his LCD.

I pocketed the cash. "How do you know this is for business?"

"Because your social life isn't that exciting."

The fact that he could say that while putting up digital drywall was an irony that escaped him.

"Actually, I'm off to the Flower Club," I replied cattily. "To see the strippers."

I was hoping that would faze him. He didn't even bat an eye.

"It's not a strip club," he informed me. "It's a hostess club."

"How do you know?"

"Because I've heard of it."

"What's the difference between a stripper and a hostess?"

"Hostesses don't strip. They're simply paid to look nice and sit with dirty old men on dirty old couches. From what I'm told, there's groping involved."

"Terrific."

"Yeah, well, that's what you get."

"For what?"

"I don't know," he said, adding stucco. "For whatever it is you're up to."

A brief history of the hostess club, courtesy of the Internet:

Shortly after World War I, a sweeping wave of moral reform washed away America's bordellos and red-light districts. This put a lot of prostitutes out of work. A few intrepid bar owners—unaware that the bell was about to toll for them—hired many of these ladies as hostesses. Their new task was comparatively chaste: to lure men out onto the dance floor, hold them tight, and squeeze lots of drinks out of them. Eventually, these bars became known as closed dance halls, because admission was now restricted to men. The only women to be found inside were the ones who worked there. And their job, as always, was to work the men.

Once Prohibition hit, those same bar owners stopped being subtle and just made the women the business. Instead of paying through drinks, customers would now purchase tickets to dance (read: bump, grind, and grope) with a hostess of their choice. These ladies were soon referred to as "nickel-hoppers" and "dime-a-dance girls." That may sound marginally sleazy but these were quite respectable establishments at the time. All the men wore suits. The women wore long dresses. It was like a big senior prom, except for all those nickels and dimes changing hands.

It was here in Los Angeles, the land of sexual enterprise, that the dance ticket was phased out for a more sophisticated punch-card system. So instead of charging by the song, the women were metered out on a clock. This led to their newest and most common moniker: the taxi dancer.

All right, now things were getting a little sleazy. I mean, women renting themselves out by the hour? Sounds awfully familiar. And yet as strange as it may seem, these hostess clubs weren't just flimsy covers for prostitution rings. Don't get me wrong. I'm sure a lot of paid sex did indeed transpire, covertly, in the bathrooms and dark corners of the establishments. But for the most part, the taxi dancers had a lock on one thing: the lending out of warmth and intimacy. You want to get laid, go see a hooker. You want to get *touched,* through slow dance or deep conversation, go see a hostess.

In 1932, Chicago scholar Paul Cressey tried to get to the bottom of this phenomenon in his book, *The Taxi-Dance Hall: A Sociological Study in Commercialized Recreation and City Life*. He saw the men who frequented the joints as a different creature than the standard, straight-out whore-monger. He wrote: "Many of the romantically inclined patrons crave affection and feminine society to such an extent that they accept willingly the illusion of romance offered in the taxi-dance hall."

Cressey blamed the industrialization and urbanization of modern culture for creating wave after wave of these detached, lonely men. And he naturally faulted unrestrained capitalism for enabling the development of such a cheap love substitute.

Despite his fears, hostess clubs never quite took off as a franchise. After all, prostitution did offer more bang for your buck. And strip clubs lifted the cumbersome chore of having to imagine the dancers naked. Plus, once America got thrown into the freewheeling sixties, forget about it. Subtle touching was out. Hard fucking was in. By the end of the sexual revolution, there were less than fifty hostess clubs left in the United States. Today there are about a dozen, divvied up equally between downtown L.A. and the nearby City of Industry. In these explicit times, it would seem that the hostess club was neck and neck with the Hawaiian monk seal in the race to extinction.

Personally, I found it difficult to care about the plight of the taxi dancer. My only concern that night was liberating one of them.

On a late Sunday night, the Convention Center area of downtown Los Angeles probably wasn't the best place to walk around with $1,574 in cash, but it was such a desolate wasteland that there weren't even any shady figures to avoid.

The Flower Club was nestled inside a four-story industrial complex that looked from the outside like an ancient textile plant. If it weren't for the faint but penetrating bass of R&B dance music, I might have questioned my Yahoo! map directions. I had to climb two flights of mildew-ridden steps before reaching the door to a red velvet anteroom.

A bullnecked Anglo bruiser greeted me from his chair by the entrance. He wore a business-quality blazer over his wife-beater T-shirt.

"Hi. Are you new to the Flower Club?"

"I am."

"Welcome then. Are you familiar with how things work in a place like this?"

"I am not."

"Okay then. Here's the deal. There's a six-dollar cover charge, but there's no drink minimum. We don't serve alcohol. If you want to dance with one of our hostesses, the rate is twenty-four dollars an hour, or forty cents a minute. There's a ten-minute minimum per hostess. Tipping is expected. It's a common courtesy to match the hourly. We accept all major credit cards and ATM check cards, but there's a twenty-four-dollar minimum on those. And if you do use a card, it'll only say 'McNulty Video Productions' on your statement. What am I missing?"

I was tempted to say "me," but I let him finish his spiel.

"Oh, these girls have the right to refuse service to anyone. You're allowed to touch them but you are not allowed to *touch* them. I'll assume you know the difference. Any lewd behavior is prohibited by law and will get you ejected. By me. Our hostesses are not allowed to leave the premises with customers, even if their shift is up, so don't bother asking. We're open until three. And finally, have fun. My name is Chip."

"Hi, Chip." I wanted to leave. I considered staking out Harmony's apartment until she got home, but that probably wouldn't make the best first impression either.

The hell with it. If this was the lowest point of the whole endeavor, I'd be fortunate. I paid the cover charge, took my last relatively clean breath, and stepped into the smoke.

From the moment my eyes adjusted to the dim lights and haze, I realized that my mental image of the typical sex club was seriously off. Thanks again, Hollywood. I'd seen a lot of late-night crime thrillers in my time, and virtually all of them went out of their way to include some kind of den-of-iniquity scene. You know what I'm talking about. Champagne bottles, high rollers in Italian suits, giggling sluts in gold lamé, and usually some sort of pool and/or hot tub to allow for further gratuitous skin displays.

Granted, I wasn't expecting anything that upscale, but the air at Club Flower was just pitiful. It had the social awkwardness of a bar mitzvah party, with most of the "boys" standing quietly at the nonalcoholic bar while the "girls" sat on the other side of the room, looking bored as hell on their Naugahyde couches. The only real mingling happened on the dance floor, and that wasn't pretty either. Paunchy white men in their forties rubbed and pressed against skeezy, barely legal gals in halter tops and micro-minis, all to the funky eighties beat of Chaka Khan's "Ain't Nobody."

I did not want to be here one second longer than I had to. The problem was locating Harmony. It wouldn't be easy to identify her in the smoke and darkness. The only way to get a semi-decent vantage was to sit at the bar with all the oglers. I took an open stool between two Asian businessmen.

Within seconds, the man to the right of me got up and approached a diminutive Latina in a frilly, lacy underwear-as-outerwear outfit. She was probably just a fetus when Madonna invented the look. Although I couldn't hear them, it was clear from the girl's slightly bewildered expression that one or both of them had a limited command of English. Wisely, they connected through mock sign language. *You, me, dance now.* Fair enough. The girl retrieved a punch card from a large mounted wall rack and fed it into the clock. Ka-CHUNK. The meter was running. They joined the grind of dirty dancers. Within seconds, his hands were on her ass and she was singing sweet music in his ear.

What a pathetic place, I thought. What pathetic men. All of them. Whatever they were in reality—fighters or sailors or bowlegged tailors— they looked like idiots by subscribing to this paper-thin charade. I wasn't one to extol the benefits of brothels, but at least there the client pays to scratch a physical itch. Here the men were simply buying the attentions of a pretty young thing, paying a woman to go against her natural judgment and actually give them the time of day. How sad. How degrading. Just sitting here among them, I could feel the blue-book value of my entire existence go down by hundreds.

"You might want to be careful with that disapproving look," said a man two seats over from me. "People might think you're a cop."

He was in his early-autumn years, husky, and dressed in denim from collar to cuffs. With his flowing white hair and beard, his kind and wizened face, he kind of looked like God, at least the Memphis version.

"Sorry. I didn't know I was broadcasting it."

"You're not. I'm just observant." He took the empty seat next to me and extended his hand. "Dave, from Richmond."

I shook it. "Dave, from Brentwood."

Clearly there were no true Daves in this conversation. We shared a brief, knowing grin and then moved on with the pleasantries.

"You think this is bad," he said, "you should try going to a place like Club Starlight. There they keep the women in this big windowed room. You're not allowed to approach them. When you see a girl you like, you point to her in the window and the matron goes to get her for you. It's like a pet shop. I didn't like it. Wasn't very conducive to a social atmosphere."

"Doesn't sound like it."

"Yeah. This place is better. My absolute favorite was Club Flamingo, but damn it, they closed it down to make way for the Staples Center."

I scanned the faces of the many couched girls. Only a small percentage was black, which made my task easier. But those faces were so heavily dolled up that any one of them could have been Harmony. All I had to go by was that low-quality Polaroid.

"So I guess you're a longtime customer," I said, still searching.

"Here? No. This is only my second or third time. But I've been going to places like this for thirty years now. Every time I'm in town."

"And without inferring judgment, Dave, may I ask what it is you like so much about places like this?"

To his credit, he merely smiled. "There are a lot of answers I could give you, Dave. Most of them would take an hour. And all of them, I imagine, would gloriously fail in converting your viewpoint to one that matches mine."

I liked this guy. He had the sharp, knowing quality of a man who's seen enough bullshit in his life and had no urge to add to the pile. It wouldn't have surprised me if he was cut from the same vocational cloth as me and Maxina.

He took a puff of his expensive cigar and then shrugged. "But I'll give you a few small pieces of the puzzle anyway. What you do with them is up to you. I've been married. Twice. My first wife broke my heart. My second wife broke my heart and took my wallet. I should also add that when you factor in legal costs, wife number two ended up costing me more than what they charge here. But in both cases, the love they claimed to have for me was nothing more than an illusion, intentional or not. Wife number two: intentional. Wife number one: not. Am I losing you already?"

"No. Not at all."

That was my fault. As he talked, I studied every young black hostess who entered my field of vision.

"Now, I refuse to blame an entire gender for my bad experiences," he continued. "I'm too smart and self-aware for that. If anything, I blame myself. But the problem is that I'm also too smart and self-aware to jump back on that proverbial horse and trust my heart to another woman. And why should I? Out of fear of dying alone? Please. Save that one for insecure people. Out of the pain of *being* alone? That one's more valid. I love affection and I love intimate conversation. Oftentimes, I find them better than sex. And you'd be surprised by some of the smart and soulful women you find here, Dave. These are gals who've been through a lot. Even the young ones."

He didn't have to tell me. The one I was looking for had enough drama to fill a miniseries.

"I appreciate these girls," he said. "And when I find the right one, I get the same kind of pleasure from their company that I did from my two ex-wives, when things were good. And when things aren't good? Either one of us is free to clock out at any time. No theatrics. No pain. No lawyers. Why should I give my soul to another human being when I can just portion it out? On my schedule. On my terms. To whomever I choose. See, I'm renting myself out to these women as much as they're renting themselves out to me. It doesn't get more mutual than that."

Over Dave's shoulder, the door to the ladies' room opened, and a young black woman stepped into the lounge. She wore a tiny black spaghetti-strap dress, which was conservative compared to her coworkers'. Although her face was marred by layers of garish cosmetics, I still managed to recognize it.

"It may seem like a cold transaction," said Dave. "It may even seem like another illusion. But you know what? And this is the thing that very few people ever understand—"

"I have to go," I said with a compunctious shrug. "I'm very sorry, Dave."

Again, he only smiled. He looked to the woman, then me.

"You didn't come here for the usual reasons, did you?"

"Afraid not."

"Well, I won't pry. Go to her."

"Thank you. It really was nice talking to you."

"I believe you. But if you want some unsolicited parting advice, my friend, tread carefully. Just because she's half as old and half as smart as you doesn't mean she can't hurt you."

I had to stifle a laugh. For all his observational skills, "Dave" thought I was in love. My excitement and anxiety must have created a remarkable facsimile.

I left him behind and approached her. She had stopped to fish for something in her little black purse, but soon gave up looking. As she started for the couches, I caught her by the purse strap.

"Excuse me. Wait. Hi."

She eyed me warily. "Hi."

"If you don't mind me asking . . . what's your name?"

"Danesha."

Smart. I guess there was something about this place that brought out the pseudonym in everybody.

"Danesha," I said. "That's a very pretty name. Do you mind if I just call you Harmony?"

This was how I officially crashed the world of the lovely young Harmony Prince. I could have been more delicate, I suppose, but I didn't want to start our relationship out on a game. I didn't see the need and I didn't have the time.

"Who, uh, who are you?"

"My name is Scott. Scott Singer. You and I have a lot to talk about."

She stared at me for a few long moments. Maybe it was the nature of her job. Or the sincerity of my smile. Or maybe it was just the fact that she'd seen enough monsters in her life to know that I was comparatively benign. Whatever it was, she grabbed the hook before I even had to add bait.

"Hold on," she said, disturbed and intrigued.

She grabbed a punch card from the wall rack and fed it into the slot. Ka-CHUNK. The meter was running. Now we were both on a clock.

10

SERENADE

Technically our relationship did start out on a game.

"My first job," I said while lining up my shot at the 1-ball, "was with a Republican polling firm in Bethesda, Maryland. I started out as a phone jockey, sitting in a warehouse with a hundred other pimply-faced peons, calling people in the middle of dinner to ask them what they thought about Ed Meese. I was your age, and I was perfectly miserable."

From the other side of the decrepit pool table, Harmony watched me break. It was just the two of us here in the so-called fun room. Every so often, a gangly old security man buzzed by just to keep the fun level acceptable. From the telling stains on the worn red felt near the left side pocket, I had to wonder what they considered unacceptable.

By the end of the break, the purple 4-ball had become a casualty.

"Guess I'm solids," I said.

Expressionless, she batted her cue stick from hand to hand. Her relaxed stance was encouraging. She could see I wasn't fixing to add more stains to the table.

I targeted the 1-ball again. "Anyway, in a job like that, I realized the only thing worse than being miserable was being complacent. I watched the people around me, one by one, get sucked into the drone life. I could see the light go out inside of them. I didn't want to be next. So I decided right then and there that I would either become a spectacular success at what I was doing, or a spectacular failure. Shit."

As soon as I hit the cue ball, I knew its trip would end with a scratch. I took the ball out of the pocket and placed it by Harmony. "Don't hold back."

She gave me a shy metallic grin. "Okay."

Her orthodontry was one of several revisions to the mental image I had constructed from the Polaroid. For starters, she was tiny. Even with her shoes on, the woman barely topped five feet and ninety pounds. But that was just an in-person issue. The cameras would never reveal her small stature unless she was scaled against a guy like me.

What bothered me more was her face. Sure, it was round and pretty, with pleasant cheekbones and alluring hazel eyes, but the deep, soulful sheen that made her photo leap out at me was completely absent. Was the photo a fluke? Or was I catching her at a bad time now? I figured it didn't matter. As far as the histrionic media cared, Harmony offered more than enough victim appeal, not to mention sex appeal. She confirmed the latter the moment she leaned forward to line up her shot.

"You can keep talking," she said. "It don't mess up my game."

Mentally, I winced. I knew the street grammar would cost her a point or two on the credibility scale. If only I had more time to play Henry Higgins.

"Long story short," I continued, "I wound up sticking out in a good way."

She sank the 12. "How?"

"I rephrased the questions to help get the results my bosses were looking for. For example, when there was a Republican politician at issue, I'd ask people how they'd rate their 'approval.' When it was a Democrat, I'd ask how they'd grade their 'performance.' It made a difference. Today that kind of stuff is a no-brainer. I mean they've got question-loading down to an art form. But back then it was enough to impress the boys upstairs. Within four months I was promoted to associate research consultant. The pay wasn't much better, but at least it got me away from the phones."

Harmony made a skillful bank shot, pocketing the 9. "You still a Republican?"

"I was never a Republican. I just worked for them. And I haven't done that since the late eighties."

"So who you work for now?"

"Lots of people. In lots of different places. Occasionally I work in the music business."

She let out a quick, knowing smirk before eliminating the 10-ball. "Me too."

"I know," I admitted.

"Yeah? What else you know about me?"

"Not as much as you think."

She paused her game to give me the stern eye. "You ain't been following me and shit, have you?"

"No. I'm not a stalker. I didn't even know you existed until about twelve hours ago."

"What happened twelve hours ago?"

"I discovered your file."

"My file? Where?"

"Mean World."

"You work for Mean World?"

"At the moment. You can keep playing, you know. It doesn't mess up my talking."

Harmony didn't see the humor. "What do you want with me?"

"Keep playing. I'll keep talking."

I watched as she reluctantly got back to the game. For a woman with brain damage, she sure seemed to be running on all cylinders.

She overshot her cue. Circling the table, I took my time finding the best angle.

"You worked with Hunta on the video for 'Chocolate Ho-Ho,' right?"

She shrugged it off. "Yeah. Me and like a thousand other women."

"What did you think of him?"

"He was all right, I guess. He was gone most of the time. I mean, you know." She took a hit from an imaginary joint. "Gone."

"But he wasn't rude to you or anything."

"No. We never even talked."

"And did you like working for Mean World? I mean, did anyone there ever give you a hard time?"

She kept her cautious gaze on me, even as I used an impressive bit of backspin to sink the 5.

"Why you want to know about all that?"

I smiled. "Just curious."

"You really work for Mean World?"

"Yeah. Why wouldn't I?"

She raised an eyebrow. *Are you kidding?*

"I never said I rapped for them."

"I still ain't never seen a white man working there."

"What can I say? They're getting progressive."

I made my shot for the 3. An indentation in the table caused the cue ball to make a wild turn, setting off an unfortunate chain of events that ended with the premature sinking of the 8-ball.

"I guess I lose," I said.

"Yeah, but that wasn't fair."

"When are things ever fair?"

At last I got the look from her. *That* look. The one that hinted at a world of pain, a lifetime of hard knocks. She was in there after all, under all the bad lighting and makeup. Thank God.

Nervously, she bounced the cue ball around the table. "So . . . what now? We play again?"

I approached her. "Got any room in that little purse of yours?"

"Why?"

With the subtle grace of a veteran briber, I slipped her a five-hundred-dollar roll of twenties. She looked down at her hand like I'd just spit a diamond into it.

"What . . . what's this for?"

"That's for starters. Do you have a car here?"

"No. I take the bus."

"Good. Let me drive you home and I'll give you another thousand dollars. It's just me talking and you listening. Nothing more. I promise."

I doubted I was the first customer to try to negotiate an outside acquaintance with Harmony, but her stupefied look made me wonder if I'd gone too high on the up-front. I didn't want to seem desperate or insane.

"I . . . I can't," she said. "They don't let us leave with customers."

"When's your shift up?"

"Soon."

"All right. When you get off, come outside and look for a black Saturn sedan with a dented trunk. That'll be me. If you show up, great. If not, keep the five hundred and have a good life. I promise I'll never bother you again."

Good. Better. I could already see her mental alert fall from red to orange. After scanning for witnesses, she stashed the money in her hanging purse. No doubt her mind was still working feverishly to figure out the catch, starting with the usual suspects.

"Just talking," she confirmed.

"Just talking."

"Because I ain't like most of these other girls, okay? I don't do that shit. Not with you. Not with Hunta. Not with nobody but the man I marry."

"We're just talking."

She stared me down (or in this case, up) for a good long time.

"Okay."

"Okay," I echoed. "Now how do I clock out of here?"

Despite the fact that I was standing in the dingy stairwell of an industrial complex in the heart of downtown Los Angeles, my first breath outside the Flower Club was the sweetest air I'd ever tasted. I felt I'd played a good game with Harmony, figuratively speaking, but the whole taxi-dancer experience had left me thoroughly unclean.

It wasn't like me to be so uptight and judgmental. Ordinarily I was a social Libertarian. Whatever floats your boat, as long it doesn't sink anyone else's. But something in there set off a trip wire inside of me. Perhaps it was "Dave's" valiant but ultimately sad attempt to rationalize the hiring out of intimacy. Or the warped, love-stained pool table that forever ruined the game of 8-ball for me. Or maybe, just maybe, it was the way I'd used hard cash to lure Harmony toward a series of drastic, life-changing events she couldn't possibly prepare for. I had my suspicions, but whatever it was, it filled me with the overwhelming desire to do something admirable.

That led me to think about Jean and Madison.

Already I saw a bad pattern in the making. I couldn't keep running to them for free karma refills every time I crossed the moral comfort barrier. Then again, on closer inspection, it seemed they were the ones who kept bringing the refills to me.

"Well?"

"Well what?"

"You got my mother's approval like six hours ago. So am I working for you or not?"

Right before I'd left for the Flower Club (via the *Ishtar*), Madison had called me. I could only imagine the dramatic debates that had gone on in the Spelling/McKnight household over the last twenty-four hours. First Madison does her umpteenth disappearing act, and now she has a standing job offer from a strange man who by all rights should be subjecting Jean to the full fury of Allstate instead of making standing job offers. Who the hell is this guy? What's his angle? What's a poor tormented mother to do?

Indeed, six hours before, Jean had sent me a heartfelt e-mail. Although it was nice to see her with her all-caps off, I was daunted by the sheer amount of text she'd thrown my way. I was used to taking her in palm-sized doses.

Scott,

I know I already thanked you a million times for everything but please accept thanks number million and one. I'd be lying if I said I wasn't a little hesitant about your taking on my daughter. My first concern is whether or not Madison's responsible enough to handle a job. My second concern is whether or not you're tough enough to handle Madison! :) As you may have noticed by now, the kid's a handful.

On the other hand I can't remember her being so excited about anything. You wouldn't believe the promises I got her to make in exchange for letting her work for you. As soon as my husband and I left the bargaining table, we high-fived each other like crazy. When it comes to Madison, we don't get leverage very often. We liked it.

So given all that, if you're still cool with bringing her in, I'm ready to give the green light. But I do have a few provisions: 1) she works only on weekdays, after school of course, until I pick her up at six; 2) any bad behavior on her part (equal but not limited to acts of tantrum, insubordination and/or sass mouth) gets reported to me posthaste for immediate parenting, and finally, 3) this is an UNPAID internship. I mean it, mister. If anything, I should be paying you (see: your mechanic).

Oh, and since I will be using this job of hers as incentive to keep her in line, you may want to anticipate her occasional absence due to grounding.

```
That's about it. I have the urge to add some mushy sentiment about
what an uncommonly kind person you are, but you strike me as a man
with a low-mush threshold. So just accept thanks #1,000,002 and
let me know when you'd like my daughter to start.


Best regards,
Jean


P.S.—Kudos on not being a registered sex offender.
```

The only time I laughed was at the very end. The rest of her message was the clear reflection of a woman who got off on being cute. But I admired her for having the smarts to run a check on me, plus the honesty to admit it.

Now I just had to decide whether or not I was really going through with this.

"It's not a matter of *if* you're going to work for me," I told Madison. "It's a matter of *when*."

"Meaning what?"

"Meaning I've got a lot on my plate right now."

"Oh," she said dryly. "I can see why you wouldn't want help then."

"Sarcastic little thing, aren't you?"

"Let me help!"

"I will. I promise. I just need to get organized, okay? As soon as I'm ready—"

"How soon?"

"Very soon. Very, very soon."

"I'm available tomorrow."

"I might not be."

She sighed. "Are you sure this isn't just some extended blowoff?"

That was quite possible. "It's not. I promise."

"Because if it is—"

"It's not. I will let you know when I'm ready. I mean it."

That seemed to sate her. "Okay. Sorry I got pushy."

"Don't be. In my line of work, that's the only way to get things done."

"Good," she said with a charm way beyond her years. "In that case I'll call you tomorrow."

The twenty-five minutes I waited for Harmony were hands down the most stressful part of the job yet. What if she's not coming? Did I put enough bait on the hook? Too much? Would I have to start from scratch with one of the two vastly inferior backup candidates? And what if I couldn't get them?

I had parked across the street from the building and then turned off the ignition. Working under the lampposts, I loaded a new seventy-minute sound chip into my Palm Pilot audio recorder and tested it out. It was in fine working order. One less thing to worry about.

After doing some fidgety cleanup work inside the car, I discovered Jean's business card, the one she had handed me right after the accident. In lieu of a phone contact was her two-way pager number. Just for a diversion, I embarked upon the quest to send her a message from my cell phone. It was easy enough to find the text-messaging function. The challenge was typing with a numeric keypad. Press "2" once for "A," twice for "B," three times for "C," et cetera. With all the gaffes and mis-strokes, it took me fifteen minutes to key in the following:

RECEIVED YOUR E-MAIL. YOUR PROVISIONS ARE FINE. TELL MADISON SHE
CAN START TOMORROW IF SHE WANTS. THANKS. SCOTT SINGER.

And off it went. I wasn't going to question my decision. For the foreseeable future, I was determined to reserve all my jitters for Harmony.

Soon after midnight, she exited the building. She had changed out of her little black dress and into a casual denim jacket and jeans. Her short hair, which had been moussed into a large and unwieldy construct, was now clean and slicked back. She looked totally different. With her make-up gone, I could see the kindness in her pretty young features. She had the type of face that TV producers craved, especially when they were looking to add a little nonthreatening color to an otherwise homogenous show. How the hell could somebody go through everything she'd been through and still manage to look so wholesome?

She spotted me and started across the street. As I unlocked the door, I activated the Palm Pilot recorder and placed it atop the loose pens and nickels in the center storage well. I may have been floating on excitement and good-natured optimism, Harmony-wise, but I was still a realist. I knew how crucial it was to capture her voice. It was the only insurance we'd have if she ever went rogue on us.

I'll trust you, Maxina had said earlier in the evening, *to make sure it never comes to that.*

Harmony entered and, after a brief hesitation, closed the door.

"Thanks for coming," I said.

"No problem," she replied timidly.

"Look, before I even start the car, I just want to confirm the fact that I'm taking you straight home. And all we're doing between now and then is having a conversation. Okay?"

"Okay."

"Good." I turned the key. "But just to prepare you, you should know that the whole thing's going to end with a job offer."

That raised her interest, of course, but didn't lower her guard. She still had trouble getting her suspicions out of the gutter.

"What kind of job?"

"Acting."

"What kind of acting?"

"Don't worry. It's for a network show."

"Which network?"

I smiled at her. "All of them. Buckle up."

And off we went.

———

"Okay, let me just give you the overview for a moment. It's no secret that all the media in this country are controlled by corporations. Big corporations. In fact it's six giant multinationals that pretty much run the whole show. They don't advertise that a lot, because they don't want us making a big deal out of it. You know how we get when big business starts to look a little too big, like Microsoft. Who needs that kind of hassle? Still, you have your typical reactionaries who freak out and say that by controlling the airwaves, these few conglomerates are controlling us, the little people.

"I, for one, can tell you that's bullshit. All of these companies—News Corp, Viacom, Disney—they lose money on ninety percent of the things they push on us. For every hit there are nine misses. And why? Because we *do* have free will. Not only that, but we're pretty goddamn fickle about where we put our valuable attention. So what you have in each of these six companies are thousands of executives and specialists and analysts scrambling to get a better understanding of the mass

American psyche. I give them credit for trying but let's face it. It's like washing cars on the freeway."

I had no idea how much of this Harmony was processing. She watched me the whole time, nodding, listening, and most likely wondering when the hell I'd get to the part that involved her. My fault for trying to impress her.

"So once in a while a public drama comes along that causes everyone to stop and look. It fixates us, for whatever reasons. O. J. Simpson. Jon-Benet Ramsey. Elián González. Columbine. The networks didn't engineer these events. They just happened. And when they do, man, are they lucrative. I mean for everyone. Viewer and subscription ratings go up, which means ad sales go up. Experts and pundits get to speak their minds and plug their books. Even the nonprofits profit. Every time a relevant activist group puts their two cents in, they get thousands back in donations. It's all part of the fun and games of a modern free market. Are you still with me?"

She nodded.

"All right. So here we are again. With Melrose. It's a lot like Columbine, except this time the shooter was cuter."

"And white," she groused.

"Actually, the Columbine shooters were white. And Annabelle Shane wasn't. But the important thing is that the Melrose tragedy is a goldmine of human interest. Mostly because it's rap-related."

"They haven't proved that for sure."

"They will. Very soon. Trust me. This one is going to progress to a full-fledged indictment of the music and entertainment industry. As far as the media folks are concerned, it's the perfect storm. Black versus white. Parents versus kids. Washington versus Hollywood. Nobody's going to let this one go. And everyone with an agenda, noble or otherwise, is going to throw their own hat in the ring. In fact, there's only one guy who doesn't want be a part of this mess, and he's trapped right in the middle."

"Hunta."

"That's right. That's why they hired me. My job is to get him out of that ring alive. Now I can't kill this story. Nobody can. But what I can try to do is steer it in a different direction, toward a much more favorable outcome. It's kind of like one of those old Looney Tunes, where the Road Runner paints a fake new curve in the road and leads the Coyote into a brick wall."

At last I got her to chuckle. Too bad she wouldn't be doing much of that for the cameras. She had a gorgeous laugh.

"There's only one way for me to accomplish my goal. I have to give the people something even more exotic than what's been going on already. If they've got a horse, I've got to give them a zebra. If they've got a twelve-car pileup, I've got to give them a plane crash. Now I think I've got the story to top all stories, but what I don't have is a compelling lead."

Finally I connected the big picture to her. She stopped smiling. "Wait. Me?"

"As far as I'm concerned, you're perfect for the part."

"That's crazy. I ain't . . . I don't do that acting stuff."

"That'll only help your credibility."

"But I don't get it. What do you want me to say? What am I supposed to do?"

All at once, a series of glaring doubts caught up to me with a vengeance. This was too much to spring on her, too soon. I'd assumed my enthusiasm for the plan would be infectious. I'd assumed Harmony would jump at any opportunity to escape her current hapless existence. Even worse, I'd assumed she'd take my crash course in media literacy as a sign of good faith instead of the mark of a soulless prick. But what if I was wrong on all counts? Suddenly I felt like a student who crammed for the wrong test.

"Do me a favor," I said, with considerably less aplomb. "Open the glove compartment."

She did, and immediately gawked at the standout item: a fat stack of bills.

"That's your thousand," I told her. "Your listening fee."

"Why you giving it to me now?"

I took an extended breath. "Because this is the part where you earn it."

Sometime during the next twenty minutes, the sound chip in my recorder became a dangerous and valuable item. It was both a weapon and a shield. There were a good two minutes of dialogue that, when properly isolated, would provide us with one hell of a net should Harmony ever betray us.

Getting that was the easy part. Getting Harmony in tune with my grand design was the more difficult and pressing concern.

She rested against the passenger side of my car, smoking a cigarette under the clear black sky. The car itself rested in a parking lot off Lincoln Boulevard, right in front of a sleeping strip mall. Hunta's brother, Ray, had died somewhere in this vicinity. For all I knew, it was right where we were standing.

It was my idea to pull over. I wanted to give Harmony time to regroup and weigh the issues. With the cigarette dangling from her mouth, she pulled a generic pill bottle from her purse and poured herself three chalky-white tablets. This was the second time I watched her dry-gulp a trio of painkillers.

After giving her a few minutes of solitude, I leaned against the car, inches away from her. We gazed at the dark Thai eatery in front of us.

"Look on the bright side," I offered. "At least now you know I'm not just some guy trying to fuck you."

She coughed out a quick laugh, then covered her mouth. At the very least, my bombshell had cracked away her timid exterior. I was starting to get a nice glimpse of Inner Harmony.

"This the craziest shit I ever heard in my life."

"Tell me which part worries you the most and I'll see if I can clarify."

"Which part? All of it! You want me to yell 'rape' against a man who never even touched me . . ."

"We don't really want to call it rape."

"With no evidence . . ."

"You won't need evidence."

"And then fry his ass for no good reason . . ."

"You'll have a very good reason."

". . . just so I can save him."

"Right."

She blew smoke at the pavement. "Right. Meanwhile I spend the rest of my life in jail."

"You won't go to jail. You won't even be arrested."

"How can you know for sure?"

"Because I know your background. I know you've been put through the wringer more times than anyone has a right to be. Run over by cops. Screwed over by bureaucrats. And all that family trauma. Jesus Christ, honey, life owes you. You know it. I know it. And once everyone knows it, it'll be political suicide for anyone to do anything short of hugging you."

That didn't help her state of mind. "Who . . . who told you all that stuff about me?"

"It's all on record. It's all out there for anyone willing to dig. Harmony, look, I am truly sorry for all the crap you've had to suffer through. But if you go along with my plan, that crap is exactly what's going to save you in the end. When you retract your story, everyone will understand what motivated you to lie. They'll forgive you for it. And most important, they'll admire you for eventually coming clean and undoing it. This is the stuff TV was made for."

"This is my life!"

"Right. And?"

"And I don't want it out there like that! I don't want people talking about me, feeling sorry for me and shit."

"Sure you do."

"No I don't!"

I shrugged. "Well, at one point you did."

"Excuse me?"

"Jay McMahon and Sheila Yorn. Remember them?"

From her stunned gape, you'd think I was levitating.

"Goddamn. Do you know everything about me?"

"I know you spent over a hundred hours in front of the camera for them. Sharing your life. Not to be cynical but I don't think you did it just to advance their careers. You did it for you. You did it in the hopes that it would get you on the air, make you a cause célèbre, and open up some bright new doors. It was a solid plan. Really. It's a shame it didn't work out."

She aimed her sour glare at her feet. "Yeah, well, what makes you think you'll do any better?"

"Because I have better skills, better resources, and better circumstances to work with. I'm not just going for PBS here. I'm putting you everywhere. I'm going to make you a household name. I can't guarantee complete happiness. Everyone knows that fame is a mixed bag. But I'll get you there. And I promise you this: you'll never have to spend another day as background booty in some rap video or hostess club."

Inevitably, I had to hit her where she worked. I had to rely on the hunch that she wanted to get out of that awful place as much as I had. And worse, I had to prey on that one sliver of hope left inside of her: that God would balance her uncommonly dark past with an uncommonly bright future.

She took a long, shaky drag off the cigarette. "How do I know if you for real or not?"

"Are you questioning my existence or my credibility?"

"I'm questioning *you*."

"I don't know what to tell you," I said. "All I know is that I've got a plan. Yeah, it carries risk. For you, me, and a lot of people. But I did manage to talk Hunta into it, if that says anything."

"See, how do I even know that? For all I know, you never even met the man."

"I met him twice. He likes me. He even calls me Slick."

"Prove it."

"Tomorrow."

"What's tomorrow?"

"Tomorrow's the day I take you to see him. If you're up for it."

That didn't help her state of mind, either. She was clearly looking for an out, some irrefutable sign that this was all bullshit. Then she could go on her way without ever having to wonder if she missed her one true shot at something better.

"Listen, Harmony, you're scared to trust me and I don't blame you. You want my advice? Don't."

"Don't trust you."

"Not until you're ready. I don't need your absolute confidence just yet. All I need to know tonight is whether or not you'll meet me again tomorrow. And you don't even have to decide that until I get you home. So just hold off. Take a deep breath. Think about it. Do you want to keep going, or do you want to stay here a little while longer?"

Whether she knew it or not, she was beginning to believe in me. And whether she wanted to or not, she was beginning to like me. As for me, I was way beyond sold. I was ready to shout her name from the rooftops.

She took one last smoky breath and then stomped her cigarette. "Let's keep going."

Except for her directions, the rest of the ride was dead silent. At 1:15, I reached her apartment complex, a seedy-looking building that made me think of the pool table at the Flower Club.

I stopped the car, but she didn't get out. She looked like she was about to ask me something, then let out a nervous laugh.

"What?"

"I forgot your name," she admitted with some embarrassment. "I know you told it to me, back at the club. But I don't remember it."

"It's Scott."

"Okay. Scott. Can I ask you something?"

"Anything."

"Why'd you pick me? Out of all the women out there you could've used for this thing, why me? Is it 'cause I'm easy to feel bad for?"

"No. I picked your photo before I knew a single thing about you."

"Why?"

"I don't know. There was just something about your face. It sang to me."

After a long pause, she tittered again. "You sure you ain't some guy trying to fuck me?"

I smiled along. "If I am, I really need to work on my foreplay."

She covered her grin with her hand but it soon disappeared on its own. She lowered her head.

"I never asked anyone to feel sorry for me, you know."

"I know."

"I mean I'm not the kind of person who asks for stuff just because, you know, I been through some bad things."

"I get that sense," I told her.

"But that doesn't mean I want more bad things happening to me, you understand what I'm sayin'?"

"This will only lead to good things. That's what *I'm* saying."

She glanced at her front door. "Yeah, that's just what Jay and Sheila said, too. And that didn't turn out to be anything."

I sighed. "Harmony, I wish I could say just the right thing to put your mind at ease. I really do. But it's late. You're tired. And I'm officially out of new things to tell you."

"Just promise me."

I waited for a rider to that, but it didn't seem like one was coming. "Promise you what?"

She was still working out the verbiage, as if I were one of those cruel genies who always granted wishes in the most literal, ironic sense.

"Promise me that when this is all over, that when everything's said and done, I won't hate you."

Although awkwardly phrased, her request was almost brilliant in its wide-ranging simplicity. It pretty much covered all bases.

"Harmony, I can't control whether or not you hate me. All I can promise is that I'll never give you a reason to. You're going to have to accept that, plus my heartfelt conviction that when this is all over, when everything's said and done, you'll be glad you met me."

That was it. There was nothing left to add. Her hard disk was full. She spent her last few watts on a skeptical half-grin.

"I see why they call you Slick."

She grabbed her purse, opened the door, and then stared ahead for several seconds. "I got to get my braces tightened tomorrow. At ten."

"Okay."

"After that, I'm free."

I smiled. "Okay."

I kept smiling all the way home. I couldn't stop. A wide, shit-eating grin usually reserved for lovelorn schoolboys. This wasn't love, despite what "Dave" may have thought. This wasn't even infatuation, despite my urge to sing Harmony's name. Although I had meant every word of what I said, and would fight to the end to protect her, the ugly truth was that she was still just a vehicle to me. She was just a potent way for me to get to *her*. The Bitch. That fickle and elusive model/goddess who stretched and writhed atop an entire nation and beyond, endlessly bored with our petty little offerings. Annabelle had managed to get her to look this way, and then conveniently left the scene. Now it was my turn. No cheesy love notes this time. This was a full-blown serenade. I couldn't wait. I couldn't wait.

Upon returning home, my phone emitted a series of beeps. The small LED informed me that I had one new text message. It seemed the curious Ms. Spelling was something of a night owl. I scrolled through her words.

SCOTT. GOT YOUR NOTE. MADISON'S COMING TOMORROW AT 3. GET A GOOD NIGHT'S SLEEP, MY FRIEND, THEN BUCKLE UP. YOU'RE IN FOR ONE HELL OF A RIDE.

Yeah. Weren't we all?

THREE
NOISE

I'm a shameless man living in shameless times, but the blood of my vocational ancestors runs through me. The seeds of my profession were planted centuries ago, by men with the ingenuity and nerve to manipulate thousands. In fact, it was Benjamin Franklin, the father of electricity, who secretly discovered a different source of power: the media hoax.

In 1732, at age twenty-seven, Franklin published his maiden edition of *Poor Richard's Almanac*. In order to generate buzz for his new endeavor, he used astrological hooey to predict the exact date and time that Mr. Titan Leeds—Franklin's number one competitor in the almanac market—would die of natural causes. Naturally Mr. Leeds was quite smug, ten months later, when his prescribed expiration date came and went without so much as a headache. Like Franklin cared. The next edition of *Poor Richard's* included a heartfelt obituary for the dear Titan Leeds, plus a warning to readers that any future written statements from the deceased, re: his not being deceased, were purely the work of profit-seeking forgers. Franklin's head game was unprecedented for its time, and quite successful. Despite Leeds's repeated and furious insistence that he was still alive, sales of his almanac dropped consistently each year, all the way to his actual death in 1739. Once the final edition of Leeds's work was published, Franklin openly thanked the forgers for giving up the ghost.

In 1835, Richard Adams Locke, a cheeky young reporter for the *New York Sun,* used astronomy instead of astrology to trick the masses. Trading in on the name of Sir John Herschel, a renowned British stargazer, Locke invented the tale of a giant new telescope that revealed the existence of unicorns and bat-winged people on the moon. His continuing chronicle of Herschel's "discoveries" was so successful that competing papers ran sensational confirmations of the story, just to get a contact sales high. Eventually Locke's own big mouth did him in, but nobody seemed to mind being duped. Even Herschel himself took it with good humor, months later, when the story finally caught up to him at his observatory in South Africa. The only one left grumbling in his absinthe was Edgar Allan Poe, whose own attempt at a moon-related hoax was eclipsed by the *Sun.*

Not all fabrications were driven by numbers. In 1874, Joseph Clarke, a writer for the *New York Herald,* was so incensed by the cruel treatment of zoo animals that he vented his rage through a five-column fib. The animals have staged a mass escape! he declared. Two hundred beasts are running amok through the streets! People are being eaten by lions! Gored by rhinos! Trampled by hippos!

Word spread fast. All over town, screaming citizens boarded up their windows and huddled with their guns. Some even jumped into the river in hopes that the crisis was limited to land creatures. The most amazing part is that Clarke admitted in the last paragraph of the article that the whole thing was a gag. Apparently, no one read that far.

But when it comes to mass deception, nobody—and I mean nobody—holds a candle to William Randolph Hearst.

The son of an obscenely wealthy California senator, Hearst used his family fortune to become a newspaper magnate. His endless lust for sensationalism, plus his obsessive competition with rival Joseph Pulitzer (no angel himself), caused him to sink his numerous papers into new depths of putrescence. But I'll give the man credit. Like no one before him, Hearst understood the winning elements of a good public drama. Moreover, he knew how to slip his personal agendas inside each tasty little distraction.

In 1897 one such agenda was the liberation of Cuba from Spain. It infuriated Hearst that the United States wasn't intervening on our neighbor's behalf. He tried for months to drum up public outrage through blood-curdling tales—mostly exaggerations and fabrications—of Spanish cruelty. This time his readers weren't biting. They knew that outrage would lead to pressure, pressure would lead to war, and nobody wanted war. Nobody but Hearst.

That was when he learned of Evangelina Cosio y Cisneros, the lovely nineteen-year-old daughter of an elite Cuban family who was arrested on suspicion of aiding revolutionaries and sentenced to twenty years in a Moroccan prison. Bad news for her. Good news for Hearst. If anyone knew the marketing power of a tragic young hottie, it was him.

Quicker than you could say "Rosebud," he made her a national crusade. He devoted over 375 columns of text to his "Cuban girl martyr" and dispatched two hundred reporters to gather fifteen thousand signatures in a petition to free her. True to form, the public became engrossed in the plight of poor Evangelina, who had only fought to defend her virtue from a lecherous Spanish colonel and was now due to be sent to a North African penal colony filled with murderers, thieves, and ravishers, all of whom would compromise her virtue on a daily basis.

[Actually, she was arrested for seducing/distracting a prison guard during the escape of three rebels, and furthermore, it was unconfirmed that any sentence had been passed down on her at all.]

Despite Hearst's best efforts, Evangelina continued to languish in a Cuban holding cell. The story began to die from lack of development until suddenly, bang! EVANGELINE ESCAPES PRISON! Hearst's papers broadcast the amazing tale of Charles Duval, a stalwart man who, with little more than a chivalrous heart and a sturdy ladder, daringly rescued the pretty young maiden from her impending fate and smuggled her out of Cuba by disguising her as a boy.

[Actually, "Charles Duval" was none other than Hearst's trusted reporter, Karl Decker. And his daring rescue consisted of bribing every guard and his cousin. But the part about the boy disguise was true.]

Hearst couldn't have been happier with the outcome. Evangelina was hailed as a hero upon her arrival in New York, where an extravagant hundred-thousand-person rally (funded by you-know-who) was held at Madison Square Garden. Later, she traveled to Washington, met President McKinley, and addressed Congress about Spanish oppression in her homeland. It wasn't until her testimony that the government authorized the deployment of a thousand troops to Cuba, plus one battleship. That battleship was the U.S.S. *Maine,* which eventually exploded and sank in the port of Havana. After that, armed conflict was a no-brainer. America was all set for the Spanish-American War, furnished by none other than William Randolph Hearst.

It wasn't the first time a pretty face had launched a thousand ships, and it wasn't the last time a compelling young girl would be used to lure

Congress toward military action. A group of Washington publicists pulled a similar trick in 1990. If you want that story, just go on the Web and search for "Gulf War" and "Nayirah." You'll get quite a tale.

I wasn't part of that particular endeavor, but I knew one of the perpetrators quite well. In fact, I adored her. She was ruthless, brilliant, sexy and utterly unstoppable. Or so I thought at the time. That was the job that took her down. That was the gig that destroyed her from the inside out.

But all of that is history. Ancient history. My thoughts were aimed at the future. I was about to add a bold new chapter to the Big Book of Media Tricks. Nobody had ever attempted a two-layer deception like mine before. Nobody had ever dared to fake a hoax. But that's just to my knowledge. After all, the best tricks are the ones that don't make the Big Book at all. The best gags are the ones that, even centuries later, we have yet to catch on to.

11
SECRET NAME

On Monday morning, Annabelle Shane was laid to rest. The media presence at her funeral was paltry: two photographers, one from AP, the other from Reuters. They captured her burial through telephoto lenses and then quietly slipped away. Sometime over the weekend, the collective shock at her killing spree had worn off. The public eye was now officially fixed on the abominable Bitch Fiends.

Not that Annabelle minded. That was her plan all along. She didn't want to be the show, just the opening act. She didn't care if everyone loved her or not. She just wanted them to hate Bryan Edison.

Believe me, sweetheart, they're working on it. His funeral, by contrast, was a blue-ticket event. News crews from every major network waited patiently at a distance, like a murder of crows. Once the procession let out, they squawked their rapid-fire questions, one atop the other, in the vain hunt for a quote, a bite, anything airable. The press was just gathering filler, of course. They knew the next big plot point would be coming from the L.A. County sheriff's office. Most of them even knew, from tales told out of school, what that next plot point would be. But journalists still had a few standards left. They wouldn't report on the Bryan/Annabelle sex tape until it became an official police rumor.

Either way, Bryan's name was in for a solid trampling. Whether the odium was accurate or not, few would know and few would care. I, however, was a devil's advocate by nature. Maybe he never molested Annabelle. Maybe he was simply a colossal jerk who had wooed her into sex, filmed it, and then replayed it for all his fellow Fiends. Maybe the humiliation of that was enough to send her over the edge. Or maybe he really was a vile monster.

Sadly, none of this would ever be explored. To the public, the content of the forthcoming videotape would be overshadowed by its soundtrack. To the media, Bryan Edison was just a bridge to greater controversies. He was simply the next and last stop on the road to Hunta.

I woke up at 8:30, much later than planned. I had a crazy list of things to do before picking up Harmony, not the least of which was house-cleaning. Starting today, there would be an intern in my home every day, for at least three hours. Never mind the vacuum. My sole mission was to gather up all the dirty laundry, literal and otherwise. Any financial records. Any personal records. Any loose credit cards. Anything with my social security number on it. Shit, man, anything that a highly resourceful adolescent girl could use against me if she ever got pissed. It all went into the safe.

Then there were the files of Lisa Glassman and her substitute, Harmony Prince. This was the one job where I could really use Madison's help, and yet bringing some kid I barely knew into the conspiracy was about as smart as humping a beehive. The solution was limited disclosure. Madison was strictly on a need-to-know basis. And she didn't ever need to know about my connection to these two ladies. Into the safe they went.

After rendering my apartment inviolable, I conference-called Doug and Maxina and filled them in on the Harmony situation. Naturally they were both pleased with my success, not just in getting her but getting her on tape. And naturally, they each wanted a copy right away. Thus I replayed the useful portion of last night's conversation into the mikes of two minicassette recorders. It was a pathetically low-tech solution, I'll admit, but the crackly quality of the secondhand audio added an air of authenticity. That, and it obscured my voice. I was all in favor of that.

By the time I had fulfilled my basic human needs, it was already a quarter after ten. Before leaving home, I looked around one last time, trying to determine if there was anything else worth hiding. I was puzzled by my own anxiety. Just last week, an investigative reporter spent the entire night here. That didn't bother me. Why was I getting all worked up now?

Because, my friend, last week you weren't planning to con an entire nation. And I'm not talking nude chicks and monk seals, bucko. You're playing in the majors now.

That would probably explain it. To drive the point home, I made another run to the spy shop and traded in my current untraceable cell phone for the Drug Dealer Special. It was brick red and as bulky as a cordless, but the shopkeeper assured me it was the ultimate stealth device. It couldn't be hacked, tracked, cloned, or zoned (whatever that meant). You could even use it to threaten the president. I didn't think my plan would extend that far, but I could certainly use a phone that the press couldn't tap in to. In fact, I could use two.

At eleven o'clock I arrived at the UCLA Center for the Health Sciences, home of the dental school. It worked a lot like barber college. In order to get her free braces, all Harmony had to do was let some shaky neo-orthodon test his mettle on her teeth. I had to admire her resolve. I wouldn't trust my pearly whites to someone who only recently stopped living in a dorm.

But apparently they did right by her. She beamed a shiny smile as she emerged from the building, fifteen minutes later. She had just learned that this was her last tightening. The braces were coming off in May, four months sooner than expected.

"It's so good," she told me. "It's like early parole for my mouth. I can't wait."

I smiled at her as she buckled her seat belt. "That's great. You look very nice, by the way."

She lowered her head. "Thank you."

Harmony was dressed to impress, with a red one-shoulder top, wide-leg leather pants, and numerous sparkly adornments. Unless she had a crush on one of the dental students, she was all dolled up for Hunta and company. That was a good sign that she was at least a little bit ready to move forward with us.

I backed out of the parking space. "This shouldn't take long. I'll have you home by two."

She gazed out her window. "Okay."

"Still nervous?"

"Wouldn't you be?"

"Absolutely. Tell me what I can do to help."

She fingered the metal on her upper cuspids. "I don't know. I guess I need more explanation. I been up almost all night thinking about this . . ."

"But not talking about it."

She emitted a dark chuckle. "No. Don't worry. I didn't tell none of my roommates. I couldn't explain it even if I wanted to. I can't even explain it to myself."

"What are you stuck on?"

"Lots of things."

"For instance?"

"For instance, what if people don't believe me?"

"What, that Hunta sexually abused you?"

"Yeah."

I grinned. "Not a problem. The cards are stacked in our favor. All we need to do is convince the media of two things: that Hunta had the opportunity to abuse you, and that his people are scared shitless about what you might say."

"How you gonna prove he had the opportunity?"

"Well, first there's your pay stub, which proves you were at the Christmas party. Then there's a hotel receipt, signed in Hunta's name, which proves he got a room that night. The rest we'll fill in with witnesses and pictures."

"Pictures?"

"Not of the incident itself. Just of you and Hunta standing together before this whole thing happened. It'll help establish a prior connection, and it'll give the press something to use."

She was baffled. "There ain't no pictures of me and him."

"I know. That's why I'm taking you to see him."

"So you can take pictures."

"Uh-huh."

"From last year."

"You got it."

Perplexed, Harmony lit a cigarette and then opened her window. "This shit's too much for me."

"I know. I keep dumping a lot on you. I'm sorry. If I had the time to ease you into it, I would. All I can say is keep asking me questions and try not to let the whole thing scare you. You're in good hands."

She emitted a wry grin. "You know, I hate to say this but the nicer you are to me, the more scared I get."

"Well, in that case, screw you."

Harmony laughed. "See? That's what I'm talking about. You being all sweet and funny. And you seem like you being straight with me, but . . . I don't know. I guess I just seen too many movies, that's all. I keep waiting for the part where things get ugly."

Of course she was. And from everything just said, it was clear that I was only making it worse. I was trying too hard to earn her trust, to prove what a genuinely swell guy I was. By overdoing it, I was only reinforcing her suspicion that I was being disingenuous, even when I wasn't. In the media world, we call this the Al Gore Effect. The corrective course was to play down the fairy-godmother bit and start cozying up to her cynicism. Modern-day advertising was built on this foundation.

"You want to know why you're really tripping?"

Harmony smirked, with a hint of mocking humor. "Why am I really tripping?"

"Because no matter how much I comfort you, no matter what I promise, you know that in the end, my job is to help Hunta. Not you."

Her eyes lit up. "Yes! See? That's exactly what it is!"

"Right. Of course. He's the one paying me. I never hid that. What, you think I'm doing this because I'm a rap fan?"

She shook her head, amused but not relieved.

"I'm getting paid a lot of money to save his ass," I said. "If I don't deliver, I'll probably never see a dime. So yeah, that makes me his loyal soldier. That's great for him but I can see why it raises troubling issues for you."

"That's right."

"Like what's to stop me from sacrificing you in order to save him?"

"Right . . ."

The poor thing. My new tack was throwing her for a loop. But I was going somewhere with this.

"If you want the answer to that one," I teased, "then touch my face."

"Excuse me?"

"Just poke it, real quick. Wherever you want."

She hesitated, confused.

"It's okay. I don't have anything contagious."

After another brief pause, she reached over and gently prodded my cheek.

"Okay," I said. "Now tell me. Does it feel like I'm wearing a mask?"

"No."

"Right. That means you know what I really look like."

Shifting in my seat, I retrieved my wallet and threw it on her lap. "My license is in there. Take it. Study it. Then you won't just know my face, you'll know my full name and address."

She opened my wallet, but only gave my ID a cursory glance.

"I may be loyal," I added, "but not enough to go to jail for him. I won't have my life destroyed over some stupid media stunt. The problem is that you've got an invisible lasso around me now. So if you go down, all you'd have to do is give it a tug and . . . yoink. I go down with you."

"Unless you take me out." She was only half kidding.

"I'm just a publicist, hon. Forget the moral argument. If you die by any means, there'll be a cloud of suspicion hanging over me and my clients for the rest of our natural lives. We don't want that. Trust me. The cheapest, easiest, safest way to keep you quiet is to keep you happy. Just think about it."

At last, she could see me through the darkness. She took my advice and retreated inside her own head, checking my equations.

By the time we exited the UCLA campus, she came back for more numbers.

"How much?" she asked.

"How much what?"

"How much you making from all this?"

"You really want to know? Because I'll tell you."

"Tell me."

I smiled modestly. "A hundred and sixty thousand."

"JESUS!"

"Tell me about it."

"JESUS!"

"I know."

"You always make that much?!"

"Nope."

"Goddamn!"

She was quiet again. Her next response was so obvious, I could have counted down to it. Three . . . two . . . one.

"How much will I make?"

"That's hard to tell, since your money won't be coming from us.

There'll be the exclusive interview deal you'll squeeze from one of the networks. The book deal. Movie rights . . ."

"Give me a ballpark."

"I can't. I just know it'll be more than what I'm making. A lot more."

"Holy shit."

"Yeah. You'll come out okay."

"And even if I admit to lying and all that, they'll still want my story?"

"Especially if you admit to lying. Because then everyone's going to be focused on this sinister conspiracy you ended up foiling. We'll even get you some bodyguards to make it look like your life is in danger for speaking out. It'll be exciting stuff. After that, they'll pay through the nose to hear your side of things."

"And Hunta will be all clear and shit," she said, utterly amazed.

"That's the plan."

Harmony's eyes were wide open now. The look of marvel on her face filled me with warm satisfaction, like I had just gotten all the Christmas lights to work.

"You thought this whole thing up yourself?"

"Pretty much."

"Wow," she said, with a chuckle, "I just . . ."

Her sudden amusement snowballed into an uncontrollable fit of giggles. Silly, desperate, incredulous laughter. I smiled along but I was hopelessly locked outside on this one.

Eventually, she slowed down enough for a winded moan. She pressed the side of her mouth. "Ow."

"You all right?"

"Yeah. It's always sore like this for a few days."

We kept silent as we cut through Westwood. Her cigarette had been burning between her fingers, unsmoked, for over two minutes now. She finally just threw it away.

"Hey, you ever listen to anything by Wu-Tang?"

"Can't say I'm familiar with his work."

She laughed. "Actually, it's a group. You ever hear of the Five Percent Nation?"

"We're talking religion now. Not music."

"Right. Good. So you heard of them."

"Yeah. They're an offshoot of the Nation of Islam. Right?"

She batted my shoulder. "Right. Very good. I'm impressed, Scott."

Sadly, I learned that from watching *Oz*. "Why do you bring them up?"

"Well, they believe the people of the world are split up three ways, okay? Five percent are the righteous teachers who preach the truth to the masses, like Wu-Tang or Common. Eighty-five percent of the people are the masses. You know, the ignorant and dumb who need to be saved. That would probably be me."

That didn't seem to bother her. She smiled wider. "And then there's the last ten percent. Some call them the white devils but they don't all got to be white. They got the knowledge and the power but they use it to dick around that eighty-five percent. They twist the truth to abuse and confuse the masses."

"Hey, that sounds like me."

She giggled again, touching my arm. "Baby, that *is* you!"

"So that's why you're laughing."

"No. I'm laughing because I ain't never had one on my side before!"

She fell into another hysterical giggle fit, one so flimsy that a stiff breeze could have knocked it over and sent her to tears.

"I like it," she said, wiping her eyes. "God help me. I like it."

We all knew that Hunta's hideout would inevitably be uncovered, but few expected it to happen so soon. News vans camped all along Burton Way, guarding every exit from L'Ermitage. Rather than sneak Hunta to another hotel, the Judge simply rented out the two other rooms in the wing and then hired extra muscle to guard it like a compound. It was a wise decision. The trick for me was smuggling Harmony up to Suite 511 without having her (our) picture taken.

This morning Doug had given me the drill. As I approach the hotel, call him. Then drive down to the second level of the garage. Wait for Big Bank. Follow him to the maintenance hallway. Finally, take the service elevator up to the fifth floor. By then it should be clear of any stragglers.

With each step of the process, Harmony wound herself up tighter and tighter, to the point where she practically creaked. Who could blame her? I had lured her into the woods, and now she was starting to realize how truly lost she was. The appearance of large, scary creatures like Big Bank didn't help.

As Doug promised, the fifth floor was all secure. As Big Bank opened the door to Hunta's suite, I gently pulled Harmony aside.

"Hey. I want to ask you how you're doing, but that's probably a silly question."

"I'm scared out of my mind," she said.

"I know. The thing is, this is it. This is pretty much your last chance to back out without causing us damage. If you truly feel you can't handle it, I'll take you home right now. No guilt. No questions. No problem. But if you do—"

"I'm ready."

"You're sure now?"

"I'm sure. But if you keep talking, I might not be."

That tickled Big Bank. I threw them both a shrug. "Fair enough."

She took my arm. "Wait. Just . . . just stick by me, okay? Don't leave me alone with anyone."

"I'm not letting you out of my sight."

With that, she was ready. But she didn't let go of my arm until we had crossed the threshold together.

The only time Harmony had ever been inside a fancy hotel before, ironically, was the Mean World Christmas party. And even then she hadn't ventured inside any of the majestic rooms, although that story would change. Thus, Suite 511 was quite an assault on her working-class senses. She didn't gawk, but she drank in the opulence with such intensity that the curtains almost swayed toward her.

I, on the other hand, was surprised by the excess of people. Our secret operation had begun with a core group of seven. Now there were over twice as many strangers in the room, all young black professionals in dynamic, East Coast business wear. Clearly this was Maxina's posse, not Hunta's.

Most of the furniture had been cleared to make way for an ad hoc production studio, currently in session. As Big Bank led us deeper into the suite, I could see some round, familiar faces padding the crowd of flacks: the Judge, Doug, and Maxina herself. They stood scattered among the cameras and lights, all aimed at the lovely young family on the sofa.

At long last, Hunta was speaking out about the Bitch Fiends.

"I know I got a responsibility," he declared, looking respectably dapper in his white silk shirt. "I mean as an artist. And I take it very seriously, you know what I'm saying? I never hurt a woman in my life. I never forced a woman into sex. And I never, ever told anyone they should do that stuff. Never said it. Never wrote it. Never rapped it."

That was good. Very good. Next to him, Simba held Latisha in her bare arms, nodding along. That wasn't so good. Her supportive expression was hopelessly overdone, which meant she was pissed about something. If I were in charge of this production, I would have stopped filming immediately to address the issue. I also would have handed Latisha her crawling papers. No offense to the baby, but her mere presence in the shot was transparently political, not to mention desperate.

Harmony and I sat on a desk, well off to the side of the cameras. The Judge was the first to notice us. He looked at me like I just brought a match into a gas-filled room.

"What are they doing?" Harmony whispered up to me.

"They're shooting his exclusive interview."

"For who?"

"For whoever wants it the most."

Across from them, outside camera range, a mousy young woman read from her clipboard: "Simba, how did you interpret the song when you first heard it?"

Simba crossed her legs studiously. "I didn't hear it. I read the words before they were ever recorded. I think that's the key difference. If you read the lyrics, you'll see my husband's only telling a story. Not only that, but he condemns the main character in the very last verse. I mean it's right there."

Harmony leaned in to me again. "Who's the woman asking questions?"

"She's just a press agent. She won't be in the final cut. Whoever gets the tape will eventually loop in their own person."

"What?"

"I'll explain later."

Some members of the crew began to look our way. Admittedly, Harmony and I made quite the elephant in the corner. Surely by now they had all been briefed on the tall white man and his devious white plan. And that pretty young thing with him? My word. She's awfully small for an A-bomb.

Doug saw us and held up a courteous finger. One more minute, please.

"Try it again," Maxina told Simba. "You came off a little too combative. And uncross your legs."

Simba rolled her eyes and uncrossed her legs. "Can I get the question again?"

The associate scanned her clipboard. "How did you interpret the song when you first heard it?"

Simba repeated her answer almost verbatim. I could see the hints of frustration on Maxina's stoic face. Her underlings were simply bored.

Harmony shifted uncomfortably. "They keep looking at us."

"They know who we are."

"How? We ain't done nothing yet."

"Yeah," I whispered, "but they know what we're about to do."

I assumed she had never held any real weight before, that she'd never made ripples just by entering a room. I couldn't tell if she was enjoying her first small taste of power or not. Her fresh young face, which was normally quite expressive, went fully opaque as she processed the implications.

But to my pleasure, she was soon breathing good humor into my ear.

"You know you the only white man here."

"I know. Why do you think I gave you my wallet?"

She let out a loud laugh, then covered her mouth. Now everyone looked at us.

"Sorry," I said. "My fault."

Hunta shielded his eyes from the light. "Yo, is that Slick?"

"All right," said Maxina, crossing into the shot. "We're not getting anywhere. Let's take a breather."

Simba shot to her feet. "Thank God. These goddamn lights are frying my baby."

Her husband sniffed. "She ain't the one complaining. You are."

"Then why don't you do this fucking thing alone, okay?"

Now Latisha was complaining. Simba carried her crying child through the crowd, furiously brushing away any hand that tried to calm or subdue her. "Expect me to sit and nod my head like some black Barbara Bush. This is bullshit. Why don't I just bake some goddamn cookies while I'm at it? Hi, Scott."

I waved to her as she passed. Simba and Harmony traded glances. For a moment I feared the fiery Ms. Shange would say something I'd have to fix. Fortunately, she kept going, all the way out the door.

Sighing, Maxina cleaned her glasses on her untucked blouse and then worked her way toward us. "Well, if it isn't L.A.'s answer to Sidney Falco. And this must be the lovely young Harmony Prince."

I stood up. "Harmony, this is Maxina Howard. She's in charge of the whole effort."

Harmony turned to me, thrown. "I thought you were."

Maxina raised an eyebrow. Oh, come on. It's not like I had time to whip up an org chart.

"No," I corrected, "I'm just in charge of the part that involves you."

"You're in good hands," Maxina added graciously. "Mr. Singer here has one of the craftiest minds in the business."

She then leaned forward and gave Harmony some lighthearted sidespeak. "And although he'd never admit it, the man's got a heart in there, too."

Harmony grinned. "I believe it."

"Good. In that case, I'll leave you two to work while I see what I can do about poor Simba." She donned her glasses. "What do you think, Scott? Leave the baby out next time?"

"You read my mind."

She winked at Harmony. "He's never been one for the front-door approach."

Maxina could be pretty damn sly herself. I knew she wouldn't try to undermine my influence with Harmony, but she was such a Zen master of subtext that she could talk about the weather and still slip a message through. And with Harmony, the message was clear: *I've got a handle on this man, even if you don't. Listen to him, but put your trust in me.*

Once Maxina left, I shot Doug an impatient look. He nodded, then addressed the troops.

"Okay. Listen, everyone. While we break from filming, we're going to take some pictures of Jeremy and . . . well, I guess I should formally introduce her. Folks, this is Harmony Prince."

Some of the publicists greeted her as if she just stepped into an A.A. meeting. Others actually applauded, as if she were about to go up in the space shuttle. As for Harmony, she might as well have left the planet already. This was too bizarre.

"You'll get used to it," I said.

"I don't think so."

"Let's just shoot these photos so we can get you out of here."

The workers were already setting up the cameras and backgrounds. Some of them stopped to introduce themselves. Doug took a moment to shower Harmony in words of comfort and goodwill. The Judge kept his distance, but only because he was enmeshed in a tense phone call. He snapped and hissed into his cellular all the way out of the suite.

Throughout all of this, Hunta simply stewed from his spot on the interview couch. Who could fault him for his pissy mood? He was being forced to stay sober just so he could defend himself for the way his song was misread. His wife was giving him shit. And now he had to sit and watch while everyone in the room kissed up to the woman who was about to falsely accuse him of sex crimes, just to stop another woman from doing the same. He was only twenty-three years old, goddamn it. He had superbly managed to follow his mentor's success without re-peating any of his mistakes. Yet now he was in for an avalanche of perse-cution the likes of which Tupac had never seen.

In spite of everything, he was amazingly level. Before anyone had to ask, he stood up and moved on to the next set piece, where Harmony was already waiting. He pulled a pack of smokes from his back pocket and quietly offered her one. Nervously, she obliged.

"So," he said, lighting up for both of them, "I guess you and me about to have a history together."

The next ninety minutes were spent catching up on old times. Our goal was to take a set of pictures from three different eras: three months ago, seven months ago, and ten months ago. Per my instructions, all of these so-called candids were to be completely nonsuggestive. Just Hunta and Harmony sitting around, friendly but not too friendly. Together but never alone together. I made sure the backgrounds were peppered with faceless extras, whoever was available in the room. The key here was subtlety. Let the media draw their own conclusions.

For each period, Hunta and Harmony had to endure a thorough array of hair, makeup, and wardrobe adjustments to reflect their ap-pearance at the time. Poor Harmony spent at least fifty of those ninety minutes sequestered in one of the bedrooms, getting worked over by Maxina's crew. Her first ensemble was the one she'd worn for the "Chocolate Ho-Ho" shoot: a frilly bikini top and a leather miniskirt so short I could have used it for a cummerbund. Her makeup job was even trashier than the one she had sported last night at the Flower Club. A strip of white film was taped over her teeth to hide her braces. I couldn't read her face under all those obstructions. Was she mortified at doing this, or was I mortified for her?

There are just too many of them, Simba had said to me, twenty-four hours ago. *There are too many sisters out there waiting for the chance to degrade themselves.*

I was too open-minded to put the blame entirely on the sisters, and I was too focused to succumb to another attack of progressive guilt, like the one I'd suffered at Keoki Atoll. Besides, my goal wasn't cheap exploitation this time. Just the opposite. Upon viewing the digital thumbnails of the first few shots, I was delighted to see that Harmony's wholesome humanity had broken through the makeup and made it all the way to the cameras. Even in full vamp mode, she broadcast her depth. She was more than a mere sister. She was *somebody's* sister. Somebody's daughter.

For the second round of photos—purportedly taken at Mean World's fun-filled, rape-free Fourth of July bash—Harmony was dressed more respectably in a short summer dress. By then the Judge had returned from his lengthy phone call. He wasn't pleased. I assumed (correctly, it turns out) that his problem had to do with Interscope. I also assumed (incorrectly, it would seem) that he'd refrain from making his problem my problem.

I was talking to Big Bank, enlisting him in a very special mission, when I saw the trouble out of the corner of my eye. The Judge had finally seen fit to introduce himself to Harmony, but he wasn't being cordial about it. He held her arm with one hand and pointed in her face with the other. Her tense posture told me the rest.

"HEY!"

The last time I had expressed anger at the Judge, it was just for show. A silly ruse designed to get him off my back. This one, I admit, was more natural in origin.

I raced across the room. "What the hell are you doing?"

The Judge let go of her, surprised. "I'm just talking to her."

"Bullshit! You were threatening her!"

Everyone stopped to observe the exchange. I was too occupied to study their reactions. I imagined at least Hunta and Big Bank were darkly amused.

The Judge wasn't. "Watch your tone with me."

"Watch your tone with her."

Doug chimed in. "Guys . . ."

"I was just telling her how important—"

"You were threatening her. If you do it one more time, I will bring this whole operation to a screeching halt, you understand me? I don't care where we are in the process. I'll stop it and I'll take her away."

If this were Suge Knight, I'd already be hanging from the balcony. The Judge, however, was a smaller man in a bigger jam. He was forced to settle for raging indignation.

"Who the hell do you think you are?!"

"Who the hell do you think *she* is?! She's your messiah! She's the one who's going to part the sea and lead you all to safety! Who am I? I'm the one responsible for her. And I'm telling you right now, you either treat her right or you'll wish you had a snorkel real fast. I am dead serious."

Technically, I wasn't. My wits (and my wit) came back moments after going away. By then the only smart option was to fake the rest of my fury. Otherwise I'd be undermining my own authority.

Of course, the Judge was unable to back down for the very same reason. Fortunately, he had Doug.

"Okay!" yelled the lawyer, stepping between us. "Look, I think it was all a misunderstanding. Let's all cool down and take a breather. Guys?"

That was my cue to back off. "If it was a misunderstanding, I apologize. If it wasn't, then I said what I had to say. You doing all right?"

The question was aimed at Harmony, who stood immobile the whole time. If anything, I owed the Judge a hearty handshake. Our spat triggered a whole slew of beneficial side effects, not the least of which was Harmony's strong new trust in me. Our relationship started out as a house of cards, became a tower of toothpicks, and was now a construct of pure reinforced steel, stretching all the way to the sky.

"I'm okay," she assured me, nonetheless stepping away from the Judge.

"It's all right. We're almost out of here."

Although I hadn't noticed, Maxina had come back into the room sometime during the melee. She stared at me with a mystified smile, no doubt questioning the authenticity of my outburst. I figured she'd want to talk to me, but first I had to finish business with Big Bank.

With a glib look, he shook his head at me. "The only white man in the room and he's making threats."

"You impressed?"

"A little."

"So does that mean you'll do it?"

He shrugged. "Sure."

"Good. You start tomorrow."

Big Bank's assignment was a sliver of work compared to Harmony's, and virtually no risk. But I needed someone smart and trustworthy for the job. Now I got him. Another beneficial effect.

"You don't want to turn around right now," said Maxina as I reached her at the door.

"The Judge still mad?"

"He's not used to being told off."

"He could have ruined everything."

"Byron's a good man, Scott. He's just under a lot of pressure."

"I get that. Really. But if he wants me to help, he needs to back off and let me do my thing."

She took a long moment to pleasantly study me.

"Yes?"

"I'm just astounded," she mused, "by how much you take after Drea."

Jesus. That one hit me from right field. I couldn't even mask my surprise. "You knew her?"

"Still do."

"I . . . Wow. I had no idea."

"Small world. Small business."

Too small. The connection disturbed me, as Maxina knew it would. Damn it. This fat, short-legged woman ran circles around me. She wasn't playing me for fun. She had very strategic reasons for keeping me off balance. Unlike the Judge, Maxina knew damn well who the real threat to the operation was. Once the ball got rolling, there would be over a dozen ways for me to hijack Harmony for personal profit. All of them sank Hunta. Most of them would take Mean World down with him. A few would even rupture the hull of Maxina's firm. I certainly had the shrewd mind to pull off a devastating double cross. But did I have the nerve?

Unfortunately, there was nothing I could say or do to kill her concern. I'd just have to get used to her dorsal fin around me. But at least she knew now that whichever way I went, Harmony would be riding shotgun, a willing accomplice instead of a hopeless dupe. That probably wasn't much comfort.

Maxina watched her pose with Hunta. "Your girl's a real find, Scott."

"She's wonderful."

"You two certainly seem to have hit it off."

"We have. The best part is that I haven't told her a single lie."

"I see. And how many truths have you actively withheld?"

With a soft grin, I mentally cursed her out. "Just two. Here's one of them."

I handed her a microcassette from my shirt pocket. She examined it.

"Is this the whole conversation, or just the insurance part?"

"The insurance part."

"Can I have a copy of the whole conversation?"

"Of course," I replied, venting a thin jet of steam. "I can rush-messenger a copy the second I get home."

"No hurry, no hurry. Just curious."

I didn't tell Maxina about the fifteen-minute gap in the tape, the part where Harmony and I talked outside the car. That should make her real curious.

She pocketed the cassette. "So what's the other creative omission?"

"Lisa Glassman."

That was a judgment call on my part. The hardest thing Harmony would ever have to do was confess to her adoring public that she'd misled them. I figured if she knew about Lisa, it would be all too easy to convince herself that Hunta really was a sexual aggressor. And if she thought that about Hunta, then why save him? Why sacrifice her sweetheart status to deliver an absolution he doesn't deserve? Harmony would have plenty of motivation to skip out on her mea culpa. I didn't want to add more.

Maxina mulled it over. "Hmm. I don't know if I would have played it that way. But I'll trust you."

The photo shoot was wrapping up. Hunta was still on his best behavior. He joked around with Harmony. Teasing her. Charming her. Separating her from the role she was about to play. I couldn't have asked for more. Despite his marital shortcomings, he seemed like a pretty decent guy. And despite Maxina's fears, I was steadfastly determined to save his public image. Even more, I was obsessed with getting the job done right. Maybe I did take after Drea.

"So how is she?" I finally inquired.

"She's good," Maxina replied. "At first she was happy to be out of the game. Now she's just happy."

After failing to get a reaction, she looked to me. "Isn't that nice?"

"What? Yeah. Of course. That's fantastic."

Like a child, I was being coy. I was just playing my own round of silly games. In truth, the news had warmed my heart. I just didn't want to admit I had one.

We finished at 1:30. It was a very productive meeting. I had introduced Harmony to her new co-conspirators, met with all the people I wanted to meet with, and come away with a Zip disk full of maximum-quality JPEG photographs. Fifteen minutes later, she and I were safely smuggled out of the hotel. By then we were both starving. I took her to an upscale Chinese restaurant at the Beverly Center.

"You sure it ain't bad for us to be seen together like this?" she asked.

"No. Not yet."

"But it will be, I guess."

Yes. Soon. Although I hesitated to tell her, tomorrow was probably the last day she'd ever see me. After that I'd be nothing but a voice in her ear, an invisible guide on her journey through the Ten Percent Nation. I figured we might as well enjoy the face time while we had it.

Our appetizer arrived, but instead of eating, Harmony rested her chin on her fists and gave me a warm smile. Just like her Polaroid.

"By the way, thank you."

"For what?"

"For sticking up for me the way you did. He *was* threatening me, you know."

I speared a dumpling. "Yeah. I'm sorry about that. The Judge isn't very familiar with how these things work."

"He said that if I ever betray Hunta or Mean World, he'll ruin my life."

"He won't," I told her through a full mouth. "I won't let him."

"I know."

"But Hunta seemed to be treating you well, right?"

She finally dug in. "Yeah. He was great to me. He kept asking me about the police. He heard what happened to me and was all tripping from it, like 'Yo, I can't believe those motherfuckers ran you down, woman.' I told him it was an accident but he wasn't hearing that. He said there ain't no accidents with the LAPD."

"What do you think?"

Harmony laughed. "I don't know. I never believed in any of that conspiracy shit before. But then you came along."

I smiled. "Just don't get carried away with that kind of thinking. It'll drive you nuts."

"No. Don't worry. I got the opposite problem. I don't think anything happens for a reason. I don't even believe in God no more. I think we all just here doing our shit, trying to find success for ourselves, and that's that."

"Yeah? So where would you like to find success?"

"What do you mean?"

"I mean what's your big dream? You looking to carve your way through the music industry?"

She giggled. "Why you think that?"

"I don't know. With a name like Harmony . . ."

"Nope. Can't sing. Can't play nothing. But I can dance. And I guess I can look good doing it, so, you know, videos. That's as far as it goes, though."

"Okay. So then what's your real ambition?"

She took a quick sip of water. "It don't matter."

"Oh, come on."

With a jaded half-smile, she rummaged through her purse. "You know, I answered all these questions for Jay and Sheila."

"And nobody's asked since?"

"No," she said, retrieving her pill bottle. "It's a very white question."

I laughed. Now my curiosity was really piqued. I figured a good eight seconds of expectant silence should shake her tongue loose.

It took twelve. She popped her pills, then rolled her eyes. "Children's books, okay?"

"Ah," I said. "You want to write."

"And draw."

"You good at it?"

She shrugged uncomfortably. "I don't know. I used to be. I'm out of practice now."

"I see. So what's your message?"

"What do you mean?"

"Children's books always have some kind of moral or message encoded into the story. They always teach something. You know, don't take candy from strangers. Never judge a person by his shoe size."

Harmony shook her head at me, bemused.

"What? Another white question?"

She looked around covertly. "If I tell you what I had in mind—"

"I'm not going to steal it."

"I know you ain't gonna steal it. I just think you gonna laugh."

"I won't laugh."

"Forget it," she said, picking up her glass. "You just gonna have to guess for yourself."

"Abstinence."

She almost choked on her water. Coughing, she wiped her mouth. "Jesus!"

"Was I right?"

"Yes! Did you just guess that?"

"I put two and two together."

She eyed me in astonishment. "That shit's more than two and two. You freak me out, man. I think you was one of them government super-babies or something."

"What I can't figure out is how you plan to sell abstinence to a bunch of toddlers."

Her humor slowly drained away, enough to make me feel horrible for all the things I knew about her. My God, she had miscarried her stepfather's baby at age eleven. That was hard enough to fathom when she was just a face in a file. Now she was right here in front of me. I desperately wanted out of this thread, but there was nothing I could say without openly backpedaling.

"I was gonna do what you do," she told me in a low tone. "I was gonna go around through the back door. Sneak it in there. You don't got to talk about sex. You just . . ."

With a tired sigh, she leaned back in her seat. "It's kind of like a fairy tale, this story I have in mind. You sure you wanna hear it?"

"Only if you want to tell me."

"I don't mind telling you. It's just that I ain't so good at explaining it sometimes. It starts like . . . okay. In the story there's this country, all right?"

"All right."

"And in this country, every woman has a secret name. There's the name they was born with, and a secret name they pick for themselves. They ain't supposed to give that name to anyone except the man they fall in love with and marry. You see what I'm getting at here."

"Yeah. I do. That's pretty clever."

"Well, that's the setup. That ain't the story. See, in that country, that's the way things are *supposed* to work, but it don't work like that anymore. Now the women are giving up their secret names to every man that asks for it, to the point where it ain't even a big thing these days. But there's this one woman who decides not to do that. She ain't a princess or nothing. She's just this country girl who says no to one too many guys. And she starts to get a reputation for it. Her friends think she's crazy, and the men . . . well, you know how men are. Once the word gets out, folks from all over come to see her. Princes and barons and dukes and all that. They're all convinced that they the ones who can get her to give up her secret name. They offer her diamonds and rubies and castles. Some of them even offer to marry her, like in the old days. But she still don't give it up, because by this point she knows how famous she is, and she know that none of them are trying to get her secret name for any of the right reasons."

I nodded. "Okay. So what happens?"

"Well, this traveling man comes along. Just some drifter guy. He didn't even come to town for this girl. He was just working his way through. But the minute he sees the girl, without even knowing what she's famous for, he makes a promise to her that no one else does. He promises to ask her everything *but* her secret name. He says he'll take her all over the world with him, asking everything about her, learning everything about her. It don't matter how long it takes, or how many questions he has to ask, he promises not to ask her secret name until that's the very last thing he don't know about her."

"I assume she takes him up on his offer."

"Well, yeah. Of course. The way I see it, they end up crossing the planet ten times before he finally runs out of things to ask her. And by then she ain't even famous anymore. Nobody else cares about her secret name. Except this guy. But by then she knows he's the real deal. So she finally tells him and . . . you know. It's all really sweet. And it's all really cheesy. It's a kid's book."

I shook my head. "No, don't sell yourself short. That's really smart. That's a really clever idea."

She bit into another dumpling. "Well, I still got to draw the thing."

"Then draw it already. I think it's great. I think it could be really successful."

"And you ain't just saying that?"

I lowered my fork. "Sweetheart, haven't I convinced you by now that *I'm* the real deal?"

Harmony laughed. "No."

"Well, then I'll just have to keep trying. In the meantime . . ." I raised my water glass. "A casual toast."

With a soft smile, she lifted her own glass. "To what?"

"To success."

"I hear that."

We tinked glasses, drank our water, and got back to our food.

Over Harmony's shoulder, I noticed a small flock of people gathering in the bar, all looking up at the hanging television set. I couldn't hear it, but I could see a press conference on-screen, garnished by a big, bold BREAKING NEWS overlay.

Unless a plane had crashed, it was safe for me to assume that the dam finally broke with the Bitch Fiend sex tape. By late afternoon, the nation would be flooded with all-new speculations and implications. By dinnertime, the parents and critics and pundits and cynics would finally unite in their most delicious conviction: that Annabelle Shane was a victim of rap.

"Oh boy," I said. "Here we go."

Harmony turned around. "Here we go with what?"

I thought about Lisa Glassman. I never met the woman and she never met me, but we were now officially locked in a frantic race to get to the media first. God help us if she won.

"Here we go with you," I said, before taking a good long drink.

12

IT'S ON

On Tuesday, the first shot was fired.

At 8:30 A.M., a lanky young courier named Mick (not his real name) stepped into the vast antiseptic clerk's office of the Los Angeles Superior Court Building, Central District, and joined one of the many lines. Once he advanced close enough to the service wall, he caught the knowing eye of Jimmie (not her real name), who waved him over to an empty window.

After exchanging their innocuous friendly greeting, Mick presented a stack of papers for filing. Among those in the pile: Judicial Form CH-100, "Petition for Injunction Prohibiting Harassment"; Judicial Form CH-110, "Response to Petition for Injunction Prohibiting Harassment"; and Judicial Form 982(a)(5.1), "Notice of Entry of Dismissal and Proof of Service."

Now a normal clerk would question the completeness of this package. It would be like filing a birth certificate, marriage certificate, and death certificate all at once for the same person. Fortunately, Jimmie wasn't a normal clerk. Once Mick presented a different stack of papers (the smaller, greener kind), Jimmie put her stamp on each and every form. It wasn't a normal stamp either. Like Marty McFly's famous De-Lorean, it was meticulously calibrated to go back in time.

Thus, officially, the first shot was fired on Thursday, January 4, a full four weeks ago. That was when Harmony Prince filed for a temporary restraining order against Jeremy Sharpe. So much for their retroactive friendship. It just hit a retroactive skid.

"Publicity is . . ."

On Monday, while the news of the Bitch Fiend sex tape continued to break over the nation's collective head, I stretched out on my couch and bounced a tennis ball off the ceiling. Like a therapist, Madison watched me from the easy chair, notepad in hand. Her long blond hair was tied back in a ponytail. She wore a man's oxford, tucked into pressed black slacks. She was adorable. You'd think this was her first day at Charles Schwab.

"Okay. Let me ask you this. How many planets are there in our solar system?"

"Nine," she said, humoring me.

"How do you know?"

"I don't know for sure. It's just what I've been taught."

"But you heard it from more than one source, right?"

"Right."

"How do you know?"

She tilted her head. "What do you mean?"

"You got it from your teachers. Where did they get it from? Probably their textbooks. Where did the textbooks get it from? Probably other textbooks. This information has been passed on and on since . . . shit, maybe Galileo started it. I don't know. I'm not accusing him of lying. All I'm saying is that there's a big sky out there. When's the last time anyone checked for themselves?"

The ball bounced off the arm of the couch and rolled away. I looked to Madison. I wasn't exactly blowing her mind.

I sat up and grabbed the remote. "All right. Let's bring this back to earth."

"What are we doing?"

"You are going to watch the news," I told her, "and I am going to ruin it for you."

On Tuesday, the first hint was dropped.

Andy Cronin returned from lunch to find a thin white envelope on his office chair. It had been delivered via messenger from an unidentified source. He sat down and examined the contents.

Nestled between two pieces of card stock was a single sheet of inkjet paper. Printed on the paper was a slightly pixelated photo of a handsome young black man who by now was easy to recognize. From an ornate living room, he innocuously smiled with some pretty little cupcake. Her head had been circled in red marker.

It wasn't until Andy shook the envelope that a slip of paper the size of a bookmark fluttered down to his desk. The typeface was big and bold.

Andy. This woman's name is Harmony Prince. She's about to become very important. If you hurry maybe you'll get to her first. Good luck.

It was the opinion of more than one person that Andy and I were cloned from the same German DNA. We were both six and a half feet tall, quietly brainy, emotionally distant, and annoyingly pragmatic. Unlike me, Andy was a journalist with the Associated Press. Unlike Miranda, Andy had no pretense of a higher purpose. He knew he was being fed by someone with an agenda, most likely nefarious. He didn't care. If it had to do with Hunta, it was worth looking into.

On the back of the slip were two phone numbers: one for Jay McMahon, the other for Sheila Yorn. I figured at least one of them would be willing to tell Andy all about this mystery woman. Of course, neither would admit to sending the envelope, since they hadn't. Nor would they explain why Harmony Prince was about to become very important, since they couldn't. Like everyone else, they'd have to read about it in the paper. Even Andy. In truth, he wasn't meant to get to Harmony first. But if he played his cards right, he'd have her whole dramatic backstory ready, right when the Bitch demanded it.

"My main function," I told Madison, "is to influence the news. Their main function is to catch the collective eye of a demographically desirable audience and hold it there long enough to show them the advertisements. The only way to support my function is to support their function. And the only way to do that is to understand how they operate."

She sat next to me on the couch, taking copious notes. I grabbed her notebook and chucked it.

"Hey."

"Don't write," I said. "Just watch. What do you see on TV?"

"The local news."

"What are they covering right now?"

"I don't know. You keep talking over them."

I muted the television. "Don't listen. Just watch. What do you see?"

"A photo of that guy from Melrose. What's his name? The Bitch Fiend."

"Bryan Edison," I said.

"Right. Him."

"And who are they showing now?" I asked.

"Annabelle Shane. I am so sick of hearing about her. Did you know at my school—"

"Whoa, whoa. Wait. Shut up. Did you notice any difference between the way they were just shown?"

She gently grimaced. "Uh, I guess not."

"When they flashed that picture of Bryan, it was an extreme close-up. Enough to see the pores on his nose. He wasn't smiling. And there was some weird darkness around the edges, making him look even more sinister. With Annabelle, it was just the opposite. The shot they used of her was bright and smiley and a little bit blurry, giving her this distant and angelic quality. And if you think that's a fluke, wait and watch."

I flipped to another local newscast. Within seconds, images of Bryan and Annabelle were presented again. Different photos. Same motif.

"You see?"

She saw. "Jesus."

"Yup. It used to be old-school journalists who produced and edited the news. Now they've all been replaced by these Gen X vid kids. They work cheap, they work fast, and they know all the great film-school techniques to spice up the drama."

Madison took the remote out of my hand and did her own surfing. "Damn. I can't believe I never noticed this before."

"It's almost impossible to catch on your own, especially with the sound on."

"Huh. That's probably why my mom never watches TV."

I thought about it. "Oh yeah. That's right. I guess she would see stuff like this all the time. That's kind of cool."

"My mother's the polar opposite of cool. Wait! There it is again! Holy shit! Does everyone do this?"

"Everyone who wants to stay in business."

"But why does it work?"

I shrugged. "If I knew that, I'd be in advertising."

"Come on."

"It's human nature. We like a good distraction. The more extreme, the better. Not only that, but most of us are so overwhelmed by the complexities of modern existence that we're secretly relieved when the newscasts squeeze reality into a familiar storytelling construct. Don't just give us information. Tell us a tale. Who's the victim? Who's the villain? How does it end? What's the moral? Of course if it's presented *too* dramatically, we can't accept it as reality anymore and we turn away. That's why they have to be subtle. It's really not easy to please us."

From her end of the couch, Madison beamed me a goofy smile.

"What?"

"Will you be my daddy?"

"Shut up."

She went back to the TV, which now gave us a five-second music-video clip of a do-ragged Hunta at his most sexually menacing. Even I got scared of him.

"Wow," she said. "I caught that one. You know, it's kind of funny that the news is the only place you can see or hear 'Bitch Fiend' now. It's like contraband everywhere else."

"I've never heard the song."

"It's lame. It's just Hunta strutting around, bragging about his big dick and all the different bitches he's bagged. It only got popular because it has a good beat and the video shows lots of skin. I can't believe it would corrupt or inspire anybody."

"That's the debate," I said.

"What do you think?"

"I think the press is going to screw Hunta into the ground."

"So if you were his publicist, what would you do?"

"If I were his publicist," I replied, "I'd start screwing back."

On Tuesday, we made some noise.

As the sun set over the Pacific, Gail Steiner speed-walked the perimeter of the Griffith Park Observatory. She had returned to her beat at the *Los Angeles Times* last week, after eight months of maternity leave. Nobody could picture this rocket of a woman doing the domestic thing. She'd probably spent the whole time buzzing furiously around the house, scorching the walls with her afterburn. Well, now it was her husband's turn to be the latchkey parent. She was back out in the open sky, doing what she loved.

Eventually, she pegged her new contact. It was hard to miss him. Rocket-of-a-Woman, meet Tank-of-a-Man.

"Calvin?" she asked.

He paused before answering. "Yup."

"Hi. I'm Gail. It's great to meet you. How you holding up?"

"Could be better."

"I know. Listen, like I said on the phone, you have nothing to worry about. I would go to jail before giving up your name. You're totally safe with me. Okay?"

That was essentially what I had told him, but Big Bank was more afraid of the rumors. If any of his compadres caught him leaking to the press, his reputation would be ruined. I had assured him the odds of that happening were as slim as he wasn't.

"And by the way," she lied, "you're doing a good thing by talking to me."

"Doesn't feel that way."

"I know. It's never easy. But if Hunta's doing something wrong—"

"Not something," he corrected. "Someone."

Surely, Gail was beginning to realize the jackpot she had won. Too bad I couldn't take credit for it. I would have had a chit with her the size of Ohio.

"Calvin," she said, slowly reaching into her purse or jacket, "I just want you to know before we even begin that I'm going to be recording this. Nobody's going to hear this tape but me. Ever. I promise. Is that okay?"

"Yeah. I guess."

Of course Big Bank had been recording from the moment she arrived. His tape would be heard by several of us, including Hunta. Big Bank had insisted on it. There was already a big cloud of mistrust inside this operation, most of it centered over me. Wisely, he wanted to keep his own skies clear.

"All right," said Gail. "It's on. You ready?"

"Yeah."

"So what's the story?"

"You want a story? I'll tell you a story. It's all about a woman."

On tape, I could practically hear Gail smile. "What's her name?"

———

Your name is Harmony Prince, and these are the facts as you recall them. On Saturday, March 11, 2000, you attended an open dance audition sponsored by Mean World Records. You succeeded in landing a small role in one of their videos ("Chocolate Ho-Ho").

On April 5 and April 6, you participated in the video shoot at a production studio in Glendale. This was when you first met Jeremy Sharpe, aka Hunta. He didn't seem to take any special interest in you until he noticed the scar on your right thigh. When he asked you how you got it, you told him of your fateful "run-in" with the Los Angeles Police. From that point he seemed *very* interested in you. He conversed with you as much as his schedule allowed. At the end of the second day, you and he exchanged phone numbers. He promised he would use you for his upcoming video ("Bitch Fiend"), but the shoot came and went without you even knowing.

But at least you made it into Mean World's database of fine young things. At least once a month you received a mailed invitation for some sort of bash. You ended up attending two of them: a Fourth of July barbecue and a November tenth gala to celebrate *Huntaway* going platinum. Both shindigs were held at the swank estate of Byron "Judge" Rampton. Both times you spent at least an hour talking to Jeremy. You were never completely alone with him; nor did he ever try to get you alone. At the November tenth event, you did notice he spent a lot of time touching you, but you didn't take it as an overt sexual gesture, especially since he was stoned out of his mind and touching everyone.

Then came the Christmas party.

This time you weren't invited, you were hired. On December 11, Marjorie Bunce, the Mean World publicist/event planner, offered you four hundred dollars to grace the label with your presence. The terms were simple. Put on sexy hip-hop elf-wear (to be provided). Dance from ten to midnight. Mingle from midnight to two. Then stay or leave as you see fit. At a hundred dollars an hour, the job was a holiday miracle. You would have done it for the buffet.

On Friday, December 15, your roommate Daryl "B-Nasté" Lynch dropped you off at Le Meridien Hotel at 9:20 P.M. Upon checking in with Ms. Bunce, you joined your fellow dancers in the designated changing room. By 9:50 you and the rest of the elves were assembled in two-by-two formation by the main door to the ballroom.

Five minutes later, you got your entrance cue. You recall passing Simba Shange, Hunta's wife, who was making an unmistakably furious exit. Already things seemed off with this party. You've seen inebriated people, of course. You've even seen inebriated Mean World people. But tonight the revelers seemed really out of control. Chairs were being thrown. Bottles broken. Women groped.

Jeremy was hardly above the fray. From your dancing spot, you watched him cup the breast of R&B sensation Felisha, immediately triggering a brawl with her husband. By the time you looked back, he was arguing with the Judge. You'd never seen him so crazy before. You figured it had something to do with Simba. Still, for the first time, you hoped he wouldn't notice or approach you.

At 10:20, he did both. Fortunately, all he had for you was a wide neon grin. You relaxed. You even smiled when he held you by the hips and danced with you for a minute or two. Once the song ended, he asked you to come sit with him on a nearby couch.

You can't, you told him. You're supposed to dance until midnight.

He waved it off. "Naw, fuck that shit. Nobody care. Come on."

You can't. . . .

"Come on, Harmony. I ain't seen you in months. Come talk to me."

Actually, it had only been a month. But you were flattered that even in his state, he remembered your name and wanted to catch up with you. You figured it'd be okay to desert your post for one of the label's top artists. You joined him on the couch, well in view of at least a dozen others.

For Jeremy, catching up was a one-way street. Over the next fifteen minutes, he buried you under a mountain of personal angst. His father still didn't respect him, despite his success. His wife resented him *because* of his success. His friends kept using him for his money. The Judge kept confusing him *out* of his money. And his critics kept bashing him, either for trying too hard to sound like Tupac or for not trying hard enough. He was being hit from all sides and nobody understood him.

All along, you listened and nodded like the well-trained hostess you were, increasingly aware of the strong hands moving up and down your arms, then your legs. Admittedly, you didn't mind. For five nights a week, you were hit up, talked up, felt up by toads. By every comparative standard, Jeremy was a prince. He was all sweet and sad and funny, and damn, the way he looked at you. The way he *looked*! Jesus. You're only human. By the time he said "Let's get out of here," at 10:30, you were under his spell.

It wasn't until he returned from the concierge desk, hotel key in hand, that you came to your senses. You knew what he wanted. How the hell were you going to tell him? How the hell could you—a fawning, near-naked, cheap-flesh party elf—explain to this man that you were saving yourself for marriage?

That was your dilemma as you quietly rode up the elevator, as he kissed your neck and whispered into your ear that he hasn't stopped thinking about you since the day he met you (which was crap, of course, but such wonderful crap). As soon as the elevator opened, you wanted to run, but still you followed him, all the way to the door of Room 1215.

At last, you cracked. You can't, you told him. You can't do what he wants you to do. In broken, clumsy phrases, you explained the whole abstinence thing. He was more stunned than anything else.

"Hold up. Wait. You saying you a virgin?"

No. You never said that.

"So this a religious thing."

You never said that either, but it was easier just to nod your head and go for the simple story. You looked away. You cried. You apologized for being so stupid. But then his hand clasped your shoulder, and he gently turned you around. Suddenly he was more sober than you'd ever seen him before.

"Hey, it's all cool," he assured you. "It ain't about that."

You wiped your eyes. Really?

"I swear," he said. "I just wanted to, you know, be with you. There are lots of ways I can be with you. Shit, we could lie down and talk. I don't care. Right now I just want to be with someone who ain't using me or judging me. Look, just hide out with me. Just for a little while. Please?"

Once again he managed to extinguish all your fears. Right there in the hallway, he held you close and stroked your hair. As you nuzzled against his strong chest, you thought you'd found a true prince indeed. You teased yourself with a sudden crazy vision of the future, one in which he leaves that shrew wife of his, marries you, and takes you all around the world. You compiled a list of things you *would* do with him in that hotel room, being the sweet guy he is and looking the way he does. Jesus. You're only human.

At 10:45, in Room 1215, you and Jeremy kissed. You kicked off your pointy elf shoes. You fell into the bed. You began to walk him through your list. It was a good list.

Unfortunately, it wasn't enough for Jeremy. He was still drunk. Still stoned. Still strong. As soon as you felt what he was doing—

"Stop. Please."

On Tuesday, it became official: I wasn't going to heaven.

At 11:00 A.M., I pulled the car over on Ocean Park Boulevard, in

Santa Monica. In the course of ninety minutes, I had taken Harmony from her apartment in Venice, past the downtown L.A. skyline, through the wide and airy streets of Pasadena, and then all the way back to the shore. The real journey was happening inside the car, as I walked her through a dark and stormy narrative. For the most part, she listened well. It wasn't until the last few details that she turned to face the window. She didn't make a sound. I didn't even know she was crying until she asked me to stop.

"I didn't mean stop the car," she said, wiping her nose. "I just meant stop talking."

"You want me to keep driving?"

"Yeah."

I put us back on the road. I didn't want to coach her in public for this very reason. There was simply no way I could feed her her story without opening up old wounds.

Still, this was a bold new low for me. At that moment I was able to float outside my body, through the fourth wall, and into the seated audience that was watching the movie version of this. I could look around and see the bitter expressions they leveled up at the big-screen me. I was the asshole. I was the villain of the story. And no matter what I did or said, no matter what my intentions were, the audience wouldn't be happy until I got my comeuppance, hopefully at Harmony's hands.

"I'm sorry," I said, and left it at that.

Eventually, she swapped her Kleenex for a Pall Mall, then punched in my car's cigarette lighter. By the time it popped back out, she had regained herself.

"He didn't do none of that shit," she said, lighting up.

"I know."

"He didn't even know who the hell I was. He walked right by me. A couple times. Went straight to the couch with some other woman."

I knew that too.

"I can't tell what's crazier," she added. "The fact that you're doing this to him or the fact that he's *paying* you to do this to him."

At the moment, I was more concerned with what I was doing to her. As soon as the coast was clear, I made a sharp U-turn.

Harmony clutched her door handle. "Whoa. What you doing?"

Distracting you. "Taking you to the airport."

"Why?"

"Because this is hard work. We need a vacation. You and I need to get out of this goddamn city."

She laughed smoke at me. "Shut up."

"I'm serious. I'll pay for the whole thing. Where do you want to go? Paris? London? Rome?"

"You're crazy."

"Why am I crazy?"

"For starters, what makes you think I want to go anywhere with you?"

"All right," I said with feigned umbrage. "If that's the way you feel about it, we'll take separate trips. I'm going to Madrid. What's your pleasure?"

"Forget it."

"Come on. If you could go anywhere, where would it be?"

"I don't know."

"Fine," I declared. "I'll just give you my American Express card. You can go wherever you want. Just make sure to come back by the twelfth."

Harmony crossed her arms and eyed me.

I caught her gaze. "What?"

"You ain't serious about this."

"No."

She rolled her eyes. "I figured you was just teasing me."

"Hey, the only thing I'm teasing you with is your future."

"My future," she parroted skeptically.

"Your near future. When this is all over and you get your advance money from the book deal, the movie rights, and all that, you're going to go to LAX. You're going to buy a whole book of plane tickets, and then you're going to hit every corner of the world. How does that sound?"

I was sure it sounded great, but judging from her dour expression, Harmony wasn't in the mood for the soft sell. I toned down my zest.

"Look, I don't expect you to believe me, hon, but there will be a point when this whole crazy whirlwind comes and goes and you'll see that you're still standing. You're going to see all these great opportunities you've never had before, just lying at your feet. And that's when you'll realize that all this hard work, all this drama, all this time with me, was actually worth it. I promise.

"Until then," I added with a shrug, "I don't know. If it helps, just try to picture the world. Because I'm going to put you all over it. Even if I have to drive you myself."

If I affected her, she didn't show it. She continued to stare out the window between wisps of her own smoke. After a few miles of silence, I brought us onto the 405 South.

"We still going to the airport?" she asked.

"If you want to, sure."

"Actually, I wouldn't mind. I never been there. I lived in Inglewood almost my whole life and I ain't never been to the airport."

"Your wish is my command."

Out of the corner of my eye, I could see her loosen up. I shouldn't baby her so much. She was strong. Much stronger than me. If I had suffered even a fraction of her ordeals, I'd be broken china. Useless. No wonder the audience liked her better. *I* liked her better.

She threw out her cigarette, grabbed a new one, then punched in my lighter. By the time it popped back out, she was ready to work.

"So after the Christmas party," she said, lighting up, "what did I do?"

"Obviously, she wouldn't go to the police," I had surmised sixteen hours earlier. "Not after what they put her through."

From the driver's seat, Doug concurred. "That's good. I think people will buy that."

If they ever handed out awards for grand-scale media hoaxes (call them the Shammys), and I won for the Harmony Prince story, the very first person I'd thank at the podium would be Doug Modine. He picked up the slack everywhere I dropped it. I had spent so much energy casting, courting, and grooming Harmony that I had barely spent an ounce of thought on who we'd get to play her lawyer.

Once again Doug came through. On Monday evening he picked me up at home and drove to our 7:30 meeting at 3345 Wilshire, in the heart of the Koreatown district. There on the eleventh floor, nestled between an Asian banking firm and a nonprofit housing organization, was the law office of A. Richard Lever.

"You're going to like this guy," Doug assured me. "He's a real pistol."

"As long as he fires on our command."

When it came to celebrity lawsuits, Alonso Lever was the rare kind of attack dog who was all bite and no bark. Over the past six years, he had shepherded over one hundred civil actions against the rich and infamous. Palimony. Paternity. Assault. Abuse. Harassment. You name the claim, he had the claimant. And he chose his plaintiffs well. They were virtually all pretty young black and Hispanic women from the wrong side of the tracks and the right side of the law. They were unimpeachable, especially compared to those scurrilous rappers and athletes who threw their id around like wrecking balls.

Alonso only played with stacked decks, and it served him well. Out of those hundred or so cases, he only had to step into the courtroom twice. His vein was to go for the quick money. His clients loved the nearly instant cash results. His opponents loved the all-encompassing gag orders that came with each settlement. No wonder I'd never heard of him. He rarely left a mess to clean up. His deals were always win-win, or at least win-manage.

After the millennium, however, his reputation as a potent celebrity juicer began to slide. Word got out among his opponents that he was settling way too quickly, taking whatever number you threw at him and then calling it a day. Doug had found this out for himself early last year, when one of Alonso's disenfranchised clients sued Mean World rapper Hitchy (then known as Hit-G) for defaming her in one of his songs.

"I knew he would never let it go to trial," Doug explained on the ride over. "So already I had the upper hand. But when I offered sixty thousand, he made the most perfunctory attempt to raise it and then caved. I thought he was kidding at first. I mean, I could have handed him a check right then and there for two hundred grand."

"Didn't he consult his client first?"

"Of course," he said. "But like most of his plaintiffs, she had a ninth-grade education and a home in the projects. She didn't know any better. He should have."

"Sounds like he's all burnt out. How old is he?"

"Thirty-five. Just like us."

"Wow," I said, chuckling. "I like this guy already."

Alonso had a soft spot for me as well.

"In my days," he declared with the eloquence of a man at the pulpit, "I have met some mad geniuses, and I have met some reckless fools. But I must say that you, Mr. Singer, are the very first person I would characterize as a reckless genius, and I mean that as a compliment."

"Call me whatever you want," I responded. "Call me a mad fool. Just don't call me Mr. Singer. I have an intern, and even she doesn't call me that."

With droll humor, he raised his palms. "Hey, whatever your intern calls you in private is not my business."

He was a tall, thin reed of a man, with narrow shoulders, small eyes, and thick-rimmed glasses. He had a majestic presence, to be sure, but there was an underlying goofiness to him. He was Malcolm X by way of Urkel. Strangely, the dichotomy worked on him. He came off as strong but personable. Media-wise, he'd go together with Harmony like chicken and dumplings.

Alonso's staff was gone for the evening. It was just the three of us in his expansive office, which seemed to have been assembled straight from the official Law Firm Starter Kit: black leather couches, polished marble floors, copperplate text engravings. He even had a token brass scale of justice on his desk. I fidgeted with it during the first half hour of the meeting, which was all legal finery and foofaraw. Doug had dropped Alonso in a sea of nondisclosure agreements, and Alonso took his own sweet time getting back to shore. Maxina would have rolled her eyes with me. We both knew that in a dirty game like this, a secrecy clause was about as reliable as a fishnet condom. But if it made the lawyers feel better, fine.

Then it was my turn to play. It took twenty minutes to walk Alonso through my elaborate maze. He was enthralled at every turn. Soon after he praised my reckless ingenuity (and joked that I was having inappropriate relations with Madison), he sat on the edge of his desk and let out a ponderous exhale.

"For the moment, gentlemen, let us attack the scenario as if this woman had approached me on her own. Now when, exactly, would this be?"

"The third week of December," I answered. "Say the twentieth."

Alonso nodded and scribbled into last year's calendar. "All right. Obviously I would take her case on contingency, without hesitation, but I wouldn't make my move until after the holidays. The first thing I'd do in January is submit a CH-100 for a temporary civil restraining order. Just as an icebreaker. I prefer to file on a Thursday so the defendant gets served on a Friday and worries about it all weekend."

"Okay," Doug replied. "That's good. I would have to submit a CH-110 response, with declaration, and then move to postpone the hearing."

"Relax," said Alonso. "There wouldn't be any hearing. My next step would be to call you after the weekend and offer to withdraw the TRO in exchange for a quick, quiet face-to-face."

Now things were getting fun. I sat back and watched as the lawyers continued their volley.

"Naturally, I'd accept that," said Doug, a little wary. "But I'd try to push that meeting back, too."

"I would only give you until the Friday the twelfth. I assume you'd meet me then."

Doug nodded. "Of course. But I wouldn't exactly bring the check-book."

"Of course not. Not yet, anyway. But if I found my client a truly compelling presence—"

"She is," I added.

"—I'd bring her to this meeting and have her tell you her story her-self. Just to give you a sense of how she'd look on *Dateline.*"

Now it was Doug's turn to act smarmy. "That wouldn't faze me. I'd just bring in Jeremy's wife to impeach the testimony. Just to give you a sense of how she'd look in court."

Ooh, good move. Alonso chewed on that one.

"Hmm. You didn't tell me the defendant was married. I assume then that his wife is quite . . ."

"She is," I added.

Doug agreed. "She looks better, speaks better, plays better. If she painted Harmony as a gold-digging stalker, any jury would buy it."

"That's debatable. And also moot. You would never let it go to trial."

"I would before you would. No offense, Alonso, but you do have a reputation."

Alonso didn't seem offended at all, but he was stymied.

"What we have here, Scott, is a small conundrum. At this point my next move would be to leak the hints of the story to a reporter."

I shook my head. "Can't do that."

He sighed. "I figured. Backdating paperwork is easy. Backdating a press leak is not. It would seem then that my hands are somewhat tied."

I stood up. "Look, we have some flexibility here. Is it unrealistic to say that the two of you continued playing chicken for the next couple of weeks, all the way to February?"

The lawyers traded glances. Alonso shrugged. "I suppose not. If he puts up a decent stonewall."

Doug nodded. "Right. Let's assume I did."

"But why the delay?" Alonso asked me. "Why February?"

"Check the news lately?"

Now he got it. "Ahhh. The Melrose tragedy. Right. Yes. How stupid of me." He simpered at Doug. "No offense, but I *would* have your fat ass in a sling, wouldn't I?"

The counsel prepared their back-and-forth paperwork, an easy but time-consuming process. I passed away the hours on Alonso's jurassic PC, typing up the first draft of our official new continuity. Naturally it was an unpleasant task to dream up the details of the incident in Room 1215. Believe me, if I could truly rewrite history, I'd erase all the terrible traumas from Harmony's life instead of keying in a new one. The story was a slap in the face to Hunta as well. But in the end, it was just a story. It never happened. And as sure as the main characters knew it, both villain and victim, the world would know too. Eventually.

By the stroke of midnight, the whole legal minidrama had been collected into one big messenger envelope. Poor Doug was tired and sweat-stained. The jacket and bow tie had come off hours ago, and his sleeves were rolled up to his elbows. Alonso, by odd contrast, never once compromised his crisp three-piece ensemble. He looked unnaturally fresh and spry for a man who had pulled a double workday.

"Well," he said, kicking back in his chair, "I certainly look forward to meeting this young lady."

"Tomorrow afternoon," I told him, "I'm handing her off to you."

He chuckled. "That must make you as nervous as a new mother."

It did, and then some. But unlike the Judge, I issued my threats with diplomacy.

"Ordinarily it would, Alonso, but the nice thing about this operation is that we've established a system of checks and balances. I've got Maxina Howard looking over my shoulder, keeping me honest—"

"And I've got you," he surmised.

"You've got me *and* Maxina," I corrected.

Bemused, he fingered his scale of justice. "Well, that's certainly a check. I don't know if I'd call it a balance. Especially with one of her weight. Figuratively speaking."

"Yes," I offered, "but look at the flip side. You know her reputation. You know she takes care of her own. When this is over, she'll put that considerable weight behind you. And so will I."

He took off his glasses and rubbed his eyes. "Scott, I appreciate the consideration you've shown me so far. You could have just as easily played me for a chump, sending Harmony to my office like a poison pill. But you didn't. You were straight with me. So let's not start kidding each other now. You know as well as I do that when our ingenue confesses, my reputation will go from a slow decline to a mad plummet, and there's nothing anyone can do to stop it. To the teeming masses, I'll either be a foolish patsy or a race-traitor servant of the 'vast white conspiracy.' Considering the demographics of my client base, I might as well shut the doors when this is over. As a matter of fact, that's exactly what I'm going to do."

Enjoying our surprise, he rummaged through his lower desk drawer.

"Since you were nice enough to let me in on your joke," he announced, "I'll let you in on mine."

With that, he dropped a fat stack of papers on the desk. Doug and I leaned forward and examined the top sheet. In the center of the page were three short lines of Courier text.

```
GODSEND
a novel
by Alonso Lever
```

"It's no secret that my heart has left my practice," he told us. "This is where it went. For three years, I've nurtured and developed this manuscript. Writing it has been the greatest experience of my life. No, actually, finishing it was the greatest experience of my life. Selling it, however, has been a stygian nightmare. Through an agent, I've submitted a draft to virtually every publishing house, both large and small. Each time I was damned with excessive praise. Each time I was shunned with extreme encouragement. So unless I'm suffering from an acute delusion of quality, I can only assume the book is failing to sell for reasons of marketability."

"What kind of novel is it?" asked Doug, failing to hide his fear of a long answer.

"It's a futuristic love story, with a spiritual bent." Alonso turned to me. "Please take this copy, Scott. I think you of all people would appreciate the premise."

Politely, I took the bundle. I hadn't read a novel in years, but I was curious enough to put his book on my skim list. I peeked at the top right corner of the last page. Christ, the thing was 464 pages. No wonder he couldn't sell it.

He stood up. "Anyway, let me share my vision of a more immediate future. I pretend to be Harmony's lawyer. I follow your every cue to the letter. Once she confesses, I close my firm in disgust. I then negotiate a deal to write a tell-all account of my experiences as an unwitting accomplice in the mass deceit of the decade. I'll hold out, of course, until a publisher gets hungry enough to offer me a two-book deal. After that, I sit back and enjoy my long-awaited career transition. I've been thinking about this future all evening, gentlemen. It makes me smile. The real question: does it make you smile?"

It made me beam. Doug was a little less tickled but Alonso assured him that the tell-all would tell nothing. Of course it wouldn't. What did Alonso care as long as *Godsend* got published? He had everything to gain by cooperating with us. Too bad I didn't have a novel of my own to offer up as collateral. Maybe then Maxina wouldn't be so wary of me. But at least we wouldn't be losing sleep over Alonso. I told him that as long as he didn't mention me or malign Harmony in his first-person canard, he had my full support.

At long last, our business was concluded. This was the second night in a row I had toiled into the wee hours. I was on the verge of cognitive collapse. Doug was already flatline.

But Alonso showed no signs of slowing down as he walked us to the elevator bank. "Well, my friends, I must say I'm excited to be part of the show."

After pressing the call button for us, he leaned against the wall and gazed down at his expensive Italian shoes.

"I'm not proud," he added. "But I am excited."

Up until the 1920s, the Bennett Rancho was little more than a bazillion acres of wheat and barley. Then Charles Lindbergh started using it as a landing strip on his pioneering journeys. The owners thought that was kind of neat. In 1927 they leased out a big chunk of their field to the city of Los Angeles, which turned it into a municipal airport. They named it Mines Field, after William Mines, the real estate agent who brokered the deal. Lord knows how that happened, but it wasn't fated to last. Eventually it became known as Los Angeles International Airport, or LAX.

There are millions of people whose experience of L.A. is limited solely to the airport, and yet many of them use their layover to not just support the claim that they've been to Los Angeles but to personally confirm some or all of the negative stereotypes associated with the city. Well, if you're one of those people, I've got news for you. You've been to Inglewood. Congrats. And the gang violence, road rage, mudslides, earthquakes, smog congestion, and phony attitudes you witnessed from your plastic seat in United Terminal 7 were most likely a product of your jet-lagged mind. Except maybe the phony attitudes. For that, we're very sorry. They're always so fake down there in Inglewood.

Harmony was a notable exception. Not only was she a refreshingly genuine person, but she truly did spy with her very own eye most of the above-listed enormities. She had every reason to complain about Los Angeles. She had every reason to complain, period. One of the many things I liked about Harmony was the fact that she didn't.

"So what do you think?" I asked.

She laughed. "I think it's just like the LAX I seen on TV. I wasn't expecting much more."

We dined at an overpriced wood-paneled franchise restaurant/bar in Terminal 2. By now I was way behind on the coaching I wanted to do, but screw it. I could finish the job by phone. There were only a few hours left for me to see her live, uncut, and unscripted.

"There's this girl who works for me now," I told her. "Whenever she wants to get away from her mother, she finds her way here."

"You got an employee?"

"I've got an intern."

"I didn't even know you had an office."

"I don't. She works out of my apartment."

Harmony raised her eyebrows suggestively. "I see . . ."

"You know, that's the second time I've mentioned her to someone, and the second time I've gotten that joke. I'm not Bill Clinton, okay? This girl is thirteen."

"Thirteen?"

"Yes, but I'm not Roman Polanski either. There is absolutely nothing sordid going on. See, this is the problem with living in a tabloid culture. We see everything as a scandal in the making."

"That's funny, coming from you."

"You think that," I said, lowering my voice, "but what I'm creating here is an anti-scandal. This is a bomb that's going to defuse itself. If anything, it should teach the cynics and moral mouths of this country not to be so quick to judge."

"So that's your message with this thing?"

"No. My message is 'stop kicking my client.' "

For some reason, that tickled her funny bone. She just couldn't stop chuckling. Once the waiter came by with our food, she looked down and giggled into her fist.

I grinned at her. "It's not *that* funny."

"I know. I know . . ."

Once the waiter left, Harmony sobered up and got to her meal. She had decided to "keep it light" with a Cobb salad. I didn't want to tell her but she'd probably have to eat a ham steak the size of a Michelin in order to get the same number of calories as that thing.

Even as she ate, she had aftershocks of chuckles. I marveled at her.

"Harmony, I've got to tell you. You are not the person I expected to find when I looked up your background."

She immediately lost her humor. "What do you mean by that?"

"It's not an insult. I'm giving you praise here."

"I believe you. I just don't know what you mean by it."

"What I'm saying is that for someone with your life story, you're a hell of a lot sunnier than I expected you to be. I mean I'll be honest. If I went through all the awful things you went through, I'd have a chip on my shoulder the size of a Lexus. I'd be an angry, bitter, hateful psycho. And I don't mean a standard, mutter-to-myself-on-the-street kind of psycho. I mean I'd be building a death ray."

Harmony stared at me with dark intrigue. "Okay . . ."

"Let me ask you a question I know the interviewers will ask. How have you managed to cope so well?"

After a moment of quiet reflection, she gulped a forkful of blue cheese. "Shit. I guess I'll have to come up with something."

"You must have some idea."

"I think I know. I just don't think it's gonna play well."

"Then run it by me first. What do you think I'm here for?"

She took a deep, halting breath. "Okay. When I got hit by that police car, it was a bad thing. But in some ways it was also a good thing. Getting my head knocked in like that. I know that sounds messed up but ever since the accident, because of my brain damage . . . I mean I still got all my memories and shit. But ever since the accident, they seem like they all outside me. It's like none of that stuff ever happened to me personally, you understand what I'm saying? To me, it was all just like some movie I watched from the very front row."

"Wow."

She shrugged. "Sometimes I wish I had a stronger memory, especially of my mother. And then sometimes, when it comes to the bad stuff, just remembering the movie is enough to set me off. Like this morning. That's pretty rare though. At the end of the day . . . I don't know. I don't know how I'd be if I didn't have that distance. Maybe I'd be just as messed up as you expected me to be. I can't say. I just know that the police car hitting me turned out to be a good thing. Except for all the headaches."

I sat in silence, parsing her circuitous new data. Ever since she flashed me her first loaded look, I'd known how perfect she was for the role I was casting. But now I felt a strange sense of artistic possessiveness. Suddenly I was afraid to share her with the world, for fear they wouldn't get her right. I certainly had new qualms about sharing her with the media, with their quick cuts and dynamic framing techniques. Damn those lazy fucks. Those lowbrows and philistines. They'd flatten her many layers. They'd take this swan and cram her into a duck-shaped hole. Worse, they'd force me to help.

"So what do you think?" she asked. "Is that gonna play well on TV?"

"I think *you're* going to play well on TV. But we'll definitely have to work on trimming your answers."

"You're the boss."

"I'm not the boss," I stressed. "If anything, you and I are partners on this."

Harmony shrugged before getting back to her mega-fat salad. "Boss. Partner. Whatever. You the one with the freaky super-brain."

On Tuesday, my freaky super-brain wondered if Lisa Glassman was abstinent.

Excluding our lunch break at the airport, I had driven Harmony around for six hours and 149 miles. At 3:20 we made our final stop in Koreatown, just around the corner from Alonso's building. I turned off the ignition and looked at my passenger.

"Well, good luck. Hope it all goes okay."

She laughed. "Thanks."

"Actually, if you reach under your seat, you should find a small cardboard box."

She did, and she did. "What's this? A parting gift?"

"It's something you'll need."

Inside the box, snuggled in its plastic tray, was a brick-red wireless phone, plus accessories. I had hidden a pressed stack of seventy-five twenties beneath the tray. That was the parting gift. She wouldn't find it until she got home.

"This for me?"

"That's for you. That thing cost me five C-notes, so treat it well."

"Five hundred dollars?"

"It's worth it. It's got a special chip in it that . . . I don't know how it works. All I know is that nobody will be able to pick up our conversations. But listen, it's only going to work with me, because I've got the exact same kind of phone. The call has to be secure on both ends."

She kept flipping it over in her hands. "I never had one of these before."

"This is how we're going to communicate from now on. So don't lose it. Don't lend it out. And always remember to keep the battery charged. That's very important."

She put the phone back in the box. "Shit, man. This is starting to feel real."

"Hey. Look at me."

She turned to me. She was back to being the quiet and awkward Harmony I had chatted up at the Flower Club. We'd come such a long way in just forty hours. And yet all I'd really done was bring her from one game of dirty pool to another.

"I am going to be with you every step of the journey. I'll be all around you, like a guardian angel, keeping you out of harm's way. You won't be able to see me, but you'll hear me. You and I are going to talk a million times a day. You think you have brain damage now, just wait until you're done with that thing. We'll be lucky to have four neurons left between us."

She wasn't as amused by that as I was. "You just gonna call me or can I also call you?"

"You better. If you have any concerns, I want to be the first and only person you talk to. You have any problems, you stub your toe, I want you to call me. Any time of the day or night, as often as you like. I'll always be reachable."

"What's your number?"

"I already programmed it into memory. It's under 'Slick.' "

Now she laughed. "You're too much."

"Actually, I'm not enough. That's why we'll both appreciate Alonso. He's a nice guy. And he'll take care of everything I can't."

"If you say so."

He better. "He will. And he's waiting for you, so . . ."

"Yeah."

Despite that, she didn't budge. I wasn't sure if she was scared to move forward or sad to leave me behind. I assumed it was both. I hoped it was just the latter. I think it's time to admit that with Harmony, my defenses were thin, my foothold was weak. She could move me, to good or bad places. But somehow I'd managed to tell myself that given the weight of this assignment, anyone in Harmony's role would have the same emotional leverage over me. I reminded myself that for all the good things about her, she was still just a nineteen-year-old kid with a cracked skull.

"You know what I noticed about you, Scott?"

"What did you notice about me?"

"You never really touch anyone. I mean most people when they talk, they like hold an arm or pat a back. Hell, even Hunta did that shit with me yesterday and he knows what I'm about to do to him. And when I was crying today . . . I don't know. I ain't criticizing you. I think that's just a part of being you. All I'm saying is I noticed. That's all."

I didn't take it as criticism at all. I held my left hand up to her, as if I were making a pledge. Catching my drift, she pressed her right palm to mine and then closed her grip. Her hand was tiny, like a child's. And dark. Never in my life had I seen such dark fingers contrasted against the back of my hand. It was fascinating to look at, like a complex variation of the yin-yang.

I tightened my grip. "This is your last day of being anonymous. Tomorrow there are going to be a lot of people whispering your name. By Thursday you're going to hear it from every direction. By Friday you'll need a hat and glasses to go to the store. And by Monday you won't be able to go to the store."

Demurely, she looked down at her knees but squeezed my hand harder.

"You and I are going to conquer the world," I said. "You better be ready."

"You better be with me."

"I won't let you down."

"You better not."

It would be all too easy for the audience to make a big deal about the brief and feather-light kiss that Harmony and I shared. It would be all too convenient to pan the camera, add a soundtrack, and frame our exchange in some broad romantic context. It would also be a mistake. This wasn't romance, despite the appearance. This wasn't even attraction, in a physical sense. This was all energy. We were two ends of the same battery, positive and negative, bound together in a symbiotic quest for power and glory. When our hands clasped tight, we were simply sealing the casing. When our lips touched, we were only sharing the spark of ambition. It was electric, dynamic, and utterly fantastic. We might as well have been kissing the Bitch.

The whole transaction, three seconds at best, was neither hot or cold. It was merely sweet. It was one of the sweetest moments of my adult life. How it looked to others, how it played in the theater, was not my concern.

Still blushing, Harmony undid her seat belt and opened the door. "I'm gonna miss this car," she joked.

"I'm going to miss the smell of smoke in here," I teased back. "Someday."

With a mischievous sneer, she pulled a cigarette from her shirt pocket and stashed it behind my right ear. She stepped outside.

"He's on the eleventh floor," I reminded her. "Alonso Lever."

She closed the door and peeked in through the window. "I know."

As she turned around, I called after her. "Hey!"

With a roll of her neck, Harmony indulged me with a final glance. "You holla?"

She smirked. "I holla."

With that, she walked away for good. I tossed the cigarette, raised the window, and then dialed Alonso from my own new cellular.

"She's on her way up right now."

"Excellent," he declared. "I can't wait. And have no fear. My staff and I will treat her like royalty."

"Just be up front with her, okay? She's going to hear enough bullshit. She won't need more."

"I'll be her oasis of honesty."

"Okay. Good. But at the same time, don't refer to her final move as a confession. It'll only freak her out. Just call it a retraction. Or better yet, it's 'clearing Hunta's name.' I know I'm splitting hairs—"

"I'm a lawyer, my friend. I've split finer hairs than that."

"I'm sure. Now tonight or tomorrow, you should be getting a call from Gail Steiner from the L.A. *Times*. And probably Andy Cronin from the Associated—"

"We went over this already. It's all under control."

I pressed my temple. "I know. I'm sorry. I'm just being anal."

"Scott, you've done a man's job. You designed and built this machine in record time. But a body can only work so much. Go home. Take a nice hot bath. You deserve it."

Holy shit. He was right. After four days of running around like a maniac, I had finally finished off my massive task list. I had dotted every "I," crossed every "T," planted every seed. Now I had absolutely nothing to do but stare at the ground and wait for sprouts.

"Just be good to her, Alonso."

"Go home."

I should. It was already 3:30. By the time I'd get back to Brentwood, Madison will have been waiting outside my door for almost an hour. I didn't have much of a choice, but all the same, she wouldn't take the abandonment well. Congratulations, Slick. You just fucked your intern.

I sped home, spending most of the drive thinking about Harmony. She had kissed me in the way a woman would kiss the plastic surgeon who was about to make her beautiful. And the surgeon? Well, if he loved his job as much as I loved mine, maybe he was just as grateful. Maybe he was simply kissing the woman who was about to become his greatest work. His landmark achievement.

His death ray?

Screw that. I had finally earned some real downtime. I wasn't going to waste it on self-analysis. Besides, I was already late for my next drama. I didn't mind dealing with it. Truth be told, I could use the distraction.

13

STORIES FOR KIDS

The first time I had returned home from Alonso Lever's office, on Monday night, it was 1:10 A.M. I was hysterically tired. On the ride back, I had read aloud excerpts from *Godsend,* the futuristic love story with a spiritual bent. Doug and I were lost in a fit of red-faced guffaws, like a pair of stoned teenagers. Doug was laughing at the prose, which, like the author, was brimming with vainglorious eloquence. I, on the other hand, was simply laughing at Doug's laugh: a high-pitched, whistle-throated wheeze that could have come straight from the mouth of a cartoon dog. It was a silly trip, and I was thankful when it ended.

A normal person would have gone straight to the toothbrush, then to bed. Or even just straight to bed. But I have this thing about e-mail. It's a sick compulsion with me, as inexplicable as it is incurable. I knew that if I didn't scratch the itch, my laptop would moan at me all night. So on it went.

I had only one new item. The message was short, cute, and increasingly bizarre. Like the author.

Dear Scott,

I'm not sure if you're familiar with the term "pod person," so I'll explain. A pod person is a humanoid replica produced by an alien plantform (or pod, if you will), designed to replace the man or woman on which it was copied. Although physically indistinguishable from the original body-snatched human, these

pod people are recognizable by their sudden cheerful attitude,
tireless energy, and extremely goal-oriented behavior.

Now, as much as I appreciate the fine work you did on "Madison"
(i.e., the smiling, the helpfulness, the use of complete multiword
sentences), I can't help but wonder what your sinister plans for
the world are. Okay, you're a publicist. What exactly does that
mean? What are you about? What's your job? What's HER job?

Naturally I tried asking the pod girl myself, but she claims to be
under an extremely restrictive verbal confidentiality agreement
(typical alien response). So if you could paint me a picture in
broad strokes, without spilling any client secrets, I'd be much
appreciative. I was going to send my husband over there to shake
some answers out of you, but I was afraid he'd come back all
clean-cut and smiling.

Oddly,
Jean

PS—I might send him anyway. You do replace husbands, right?

Silly woman. And silly Madison. I had yet to give her a shred of confidential information. What I had given her, apparently, was an excuse
to be vague and secretive with her mother. I would definitely send
Jean a broad-strokes overview as soon as I had the time and the brain-
power.

In the meantime, I figured one flippant note deserved another:

>you're a publicist. What exactly does that mean? What are you
>about?

I'm the best there is at what I do, but what I do isn't very nice.

Evenly,
Scott

(yes, we replace husbands)

That should make her eyes pop, and not because it was strange and cryptic but because she'd know exactly what I was talking about. This was MRVL GRL, a flamboyant X-Men reader if there ever was one. I, however, was more of a closet case. Now, with one classic Wolverine quote, I'd just outed myself.

Before I could even close out of my e-mail application, a new message chimed in. Jesus. Not only was Jean an odd creature, she was an odd creature of the night.

Thank you for your order. Your new item will be arriving shortly.

I assumed that meant she was about to gift me with comic books. She probably wouldn't stop until she paid off her debt of gratitude. Very unnecessary. If that was the scheme, I'd have to nip it in the bud. Tomorrow. Sleep in bed now. Nip in bud tomorrow.

———

The second time I had returned from Alonso's office, on Tuesday afternoon, I found Madison crouched outside my door, waiting for me. And waiting. And waiting. I had a lot of time to anticipate her reaction. I wagered an even split between super-hot fury and ice-cold silence.

Amazingly, she was tepid. "Hey."

"I am so sorry," I gushed, "I was in a meeting on the other side of town—"

"It's okay."

"It's never going to happen again."

"Scott, it's okay. I figured you were running late."

Right. I wished I could relax, but I could see the scale of the tempest she was holding back. Although her hair was down today, she was once again dressed to the nines. Stylish black blouse. Professional gray skirt. High-heeled shoes. She must have raided her mother's closet. She also must have gotten a good deal of shit from her classmates. How upsetting it must have been to see all that thought and effort waste away in an empty hallway. Yet even now she fought to proclaim her maturity. I figured the best thing I could do, for both of us, was reinforce the facade.

"You've got thick skin," I commended as I unlocked my apartment door. "I like that. When I was thirteen, I took everything personally. Even when the Falklands were invaded. I just knew it had something to do with my acne."

All Madison could offer was a quivering half-smile. She was trying so damn hard to defuse herself, but she was losing the battle. The poor kid.

"Come in," I said.

With her jaw clenched tight, she marched in ahead of me.

"Do you want anything to drink?" I asked. "Apple juice?"

She plopped down at the far end of my couch, dropped her book bag, and hunched forward. We both knew that if she opened her mouth now, it'd all come spilling out.

"Madison, I am really sorry."

She waved me off. *No! Wrong way! Go back!* Good point. I wasn't helping with my pity. I opted to give her some space and let her work it out herself, but by the time I retreated to the kitchenette, I could hear her quick, wet breaths.

Shit. This was the second time today I made someone cry. My duller instincts told me to sit down next to her. To pat her back or something. Anything. Then again, she was clearly embarrassed by her own reaction. She was only mad at herself. So why baby her and make it worse? Why rub her back like she was a four-year-old who just skinned her knee?

You know what I noticed about you, Scott? You never really touch anyone.

I hadn't noticed it myself until Harmony brought it up. At the time I took it as flattery, considering that it meant *"Please touch me."* But now I saw the flip side to her observation. I saw a glimpse of Gracie toward the end of our relationship. The look in her eyes that screamed *I need more from you!* even as her mouth was telling me that everything was fine. So I had trusted the wrong source. What did she expect from me? What did Harmony expect from me, now that I was forced to keep my distance?

And, more urgently, what did Madison expect?

After a few tense moments, I reentered the living room and faced her from the easy chair.

"I'm sorry," she said through a curtain of hanging hair.

"I'm the one who screwed up."

"No. I'm sorry for this," she said, sniffing. "I'm just being stupid."

"You're not being stupid."

"Yes I am. I was just . . . I thought I did something yesterday to disappoint you. Or piss you off."

"Of course not. Madison—"

"No, I know I didn't. I know *now*. But while I was waiting . . . God,

I do this. I do this all the time. I just fill my head with these black thoughts, even when I know they're bullshit."

"Well," I stated lamely, "that either makes you an insecure adult or a normal teenager."

She finally looked up at me. "See, that's exactly why I didn't want to lose it in front of you! Everybody's tiptoeing around us all the time now, like we're all just Annabelle Shanes waiting to happen! I didn't . . . The last thing I want is to freak you out."

I couldn't help but chuckle at this wonderful young girl. The way her explosive mind worked. This was Gracie's field, not mine. She was the Jane Goodall of the teen market. She spent hours each day watching them in their natural habitat, absorbing their lingo, tracking their spending habits. It was more than a job to her; it was a lifelong riddle she was determined to crack. Personally, I didn't get her fascination, in the same way I didn't get cat people. But that was long before Madison ever scratched at my door.

She crossed her arms and looked down at her knees. "Thanks for laughing at me."

"No, hon. It's not you. I swear. I feel for you. It's just . . ." I laughed again. "I can only imagine what they're putting you through at school."

Moaning, she shook her head. "You have no idea. We have special assemblies ten times a day. They've posted armed guards on one side of the hallway and emergency psychologists on the other. And a girl can't even reach into her bag for an Altoid without twelve people ducking."

Now I really laughed. Madison fought her own grin.

"It's not funny," she said, tossing a couch pillow. "It's your fault!"

"Me? What did I do?"

"You work with the media, and they're the ones who make us all crazy with these end-of-the-world panic stories!"

"Well, that's hardly my fault. That's hardly even their fault. We had mass hysteria long before we had mass media. You think television was to blame for the Salem witch hunts?"

"Yes."

"See, now you're just being silly."

With a weak laugh, she rubbed her eyes with her sleeve. I jumped to the kitchen and retrieved a box of tissues. This time I hunkered down next to her.

"You're the only person in my life who makes sense," she told me, sniffling. "Everyone else is scrambling around like they don't have a clue. Like they don't know how to manage. But you're totally above all that. You seem to have a handle on everything."

"If that were true, sweetheart, I wouldn't have kept you waiting so long."

"I don't care about that, Scott. As long as you don't . . . Just have faith in me, okay? I promise I won't go psycho on you. I won't disappoint you. Ever."

See, Gracie, I'm not made of ice and granite. Notice, Maxina, how I open the gate and let another precious young woman into my give-a-shit zone. And take a good hard look, Harmony, as I lean forward and gently poke her in the shoulder. I didn't know any sign language, so I had to make up my own phrases. With a smile and a jab, I told her I wouldn't worry if she didn't.

Madison got the message. She crunched up her tissue and slapped her thighs. "Okay! This ends the dramatic portion of our afternoon."

"Good," I said, opening the laptop. "Because orientation's over. It's time to put you to work."

Yesterday, Madison had asked me what I'd do if I were Hunta's publicist. It was a perfect opportunity to bring her into the fold (the outer fold, at least) but I had let that ship sail. Today, I confessed. Okay, I *was* Hunta's publicist. But I was just one of many crisis managers involved. I was a mere cog in Maxina Howard's giant machine. Mostly an information-gatherer, really. Nothing too exciting.

Still, from Madison's wide-open gape, I might as well have been Batman. For all she expected, I was just another schmuck pushing Lysol on the nation's vast subconscious. And she would have been happy with that. But now she just learned that I was playing a defensive role in the nation's hottest hot-button topic. And she was helping! Holy hambone! She might as well have been Robin!

"Oh my God. This is amazing. So what kind of stuff are you working on?"

In response, I rattled off a list of Maxina's action items instead of mine. First and foremost was the heat-and-serve "interview" with Hunta, which would be airing tonight at ten on CBS. Then of course was the organized celebrity support effort. There would be a big tug-of-war between Washington and Hollywood over creative content issues.

The more people pulling for our side, the better. Finally, we were prepared to get slappy with every "think of the children" activist who hit below the belt. They were already coming out of the woodwork. Maxina had her hands full, all right.

"Yeah, but what kind of stuff are you personally doing?"

I couldn't tell her about my collusion with Harmony, not because I didn't trust her but simply because that part of the job came with a moral burden. She was in eighth grade, damn it. She was just too young to handle the uncut story, and I had too many karmic investments tied up in her. Forget it. She'd get the radio-safe version.

"There's this woman . . ." I sighed. "Look, when a celebrity's on the hot seat like Hunta is, it's inevitable that a bunch of no-name 'victims' will pop up and cry foul. Usually you can swat them away because their connection to the accused is tenuous and their stories are weak to begin with. But now . . . let's say there's a big one coming down the pike. She won't be so easy to dismiss."

"Oh my God. Are we talking about rape? Is she going to say she was raped by Hunta?"

"Pretty much."

"Jesus. Who is this woman? What's her name?"

I couldn't say. At the time there was still a sizable chance her name would be Lisa Glassman.

"You'll find out very soon. Everyone will."

"Wow. God. So it's like your job to stop her?"

I laughed. "I can't stop her. Nobody can. I just need to chart her damage, look for weak spots, and make recommendations accordingly."

"Wow," she echoed. "I'm sorry to be so . . . That's just so cool. I mean it's so cool to be a part of this. I was never a fan of Hunta's—"

"Neither was I."

"—but I am so psyched to help. Just tell me what to do."

I told her. Five hours later, I told her mother. If I didn't, who would?

```
>What's your job? What's HER job?

My job is somewhat complex. I'll try that one later. Madison's
job, however, is very easy to explain. Using my PC, she's going
to keep tabs on about 40 mainstream media websites (the New
York Times, Washington Post, MSNBC.com, etc.). That may sound
like a lot but she's only tracking one developing story. Her goal
```

```
isn't to rehash what people are saying but to read between the
lines and sniff out the bias. That I'm teaching her how to do.
So far she loves it. It actually works out great for both of us.
I need to know which way the wind is blowing and your daughter's
going to be the one with her finger in the air (no, not THAT
finger).

You've got a great kid, Jean. I really enjoy working with her. If
you have any more offspring to lend me, please do. I could always
use a collator.

Off to the races,
Scott

PS—Thanks for the great gift. IT'S WAY TOO MUCH! But thank you.
```

With all my Harmony- and Madison-related business, I had completely forgotten about Jean. I wanted to e-mail her and hose her down before she hit me with some immoderate present. Too late. It wasn't until she pulled up in front of my building at six o'clock that the present hit me from behind.

"Oh shit!" said Madison, poring through her book bag. "I was supposed to give you something."

Sandwiched between two textbooks was a pristine *Uncanny X-Men* comic, complete with Mylar sleeve and cardboard backing. From Madison's disparaging look, she might as well have been holding the latest issue of *Hustler*.

"Scott, please tell me my mother's wrong and you're not into this stuff."

I chuckled a little too defensively. "I wouldn't say I'm *into* it. I mean it's not like I dress up and go to . . . uh . . ." I got lost in the issue's cover. "That's not what I think it is, is it?"

"How the hell should I know?"

"It can't be." I took the comic out of her hands. "Holy goddamn crap. This is X-Men 137."

Madison groaned. "Oh no. You're just like her."

"You don't understand. This issue's a milestone. This is the one where Phoenix dies."

"No, *you* don't understand. You guys are adults."

"Yeah, but I was your age when this came out. Jesus. This must be worth several hundred dollars. Is it a gift or a loaner?"

"She said it's a gift."

"That's insane. I can't take this. It's too much."

"Her collection's worth a gazillion dollars," she replied, unfazed. "She lives for it. And she loves discussing it. Just wait. She's going to spam you with geek talk until you hang yourself."

Damn, this issue brought me back, all the way to the house I grew up in. My parents never understood what I saw in these "funny books," either. Now, in this one, I saw them.

I walked Madison to the door. "I should really thank your mother."

"No, Scott. Don't. Please. You're just going to trigger a long, boring conversation about comics and I'm going to have to translate. Don't put me through that. Can't you just e-mail her? Please?"

I eyed her briefly. "All right. Fine. But you know, these aren't so bad."

"They're stories for kids."

"Whatever. Just tell her I'm very appreciative."

"I will. I will."

Madison threw her book bag over her shoulder. She stopped at the door and, after a moment's debate, rushed back toward me. She stood on her tiptoes and put her mouth near my ear.

"You may be a nerd," she whispered, with a kiss on the cheek, "but you're the best thing that ever happened to me."

Before I could even fathom her words, she was back at the door. She turned around and threw me a grin that was alarmingly mature.

"Don't worry. That's the last time I'll ever get sappy with you. From now on I'm all business."

And with that, she dashed off, in the extra-springy way that only a kid could run.

I studied the comic book again. The issue was a real heartbreaker. I actually cried when Phoenix first sacrificed her life on the blue area of the moon. I could feel the pain of Cyclops as the love of his life died screaming his name (and mine). This was how I got my drama fix, back when I was Madison's age. I don't know if it was a simpler time but Jesus Christ, I was a simpler kid.

As far as puzzling figures went, Madison was a one-piece jigsaw compared to her mother. At 9:30, I received this square oddity:

>PS—Thanks for the great gift. IT'S WAY TOO MUCH! But thank you.

Judging from the response, I can tell you're a reader, not a collector. Allow me to shed some light. Per the latest Overstreet Comic Book Price Guide, that issue, despite its great significance, is worth roughly $40 (mint condition). So I wouldn't call it "way too much." And considering that I gave you my spare copy, I wouldn't call it a GREAT gift, either.

Actually I wouldn't even call it a gift. The more I think about it, the more I see it as a subconsciously jealous ploy to bring you down a step or two in Madison's high esteem. Normally my subconscious isn't so vain and petty, but let's face facts. The cooler you is, the cooler I ain't. Okay, so I was never exactly a rock star in her world, but damn it all, there was actually a time when she and I would talk for hours. I'd make her laugh. She'd ask me questions about everything. We actually gelled. Now all I am to her is an endless source of anguish and transportation.

So if that is indeed what my nutty subconscious is up to, all I can say is oops, and I'm very sorry. But then again, who knows? Maybe the cigar is just a cigar. In that case, ignore my silly ranting. Sometimes I get all a'Freud for no reason. And yet this note seems strangely justified.

Enjoy the comic,
Jean

...who has plenty more issues where that came from.

Normally, I'd say this was a woman with way too much free time, but it had taken her just seven minutes to read and respond to my message. Seven minutes to express a few crazy thoughts, drop a few clever puns, and—most amazing—frame it all at exactly seventy-one characters per line. Her perfect right margin was completely manual. How the hell did she do that in seven minutes? Why the hell did she do it at all? This was how they got their kicks at Mensa. What made her think I'd be impressed?

Seven minutes. Okay, I was impressed. By the time I'd finished admiring her handiwork, I noted the time. 9:43. All right, lady. Not only will I step up to the box, I'll even give it a little twist.

```
                          O
                         Jean,
                       don't let
                     Madison's new
                    esteem for me get
                   you down. By no means
                  does it indicate that you
                 somehow pale in comparison. I
                have several unfair advantages in
               that I'm not the one who tells her to
              brush her teeth, finish all her broccoli,
            write that thank-you note to Grandma for that
             horrible green sweater, and so on, and so
              forth. It's all just part of the pain
                of raising a teenager (not that I
                   would personally know). Look,
                    you did one hell of a job
                     with her. The kid is
                      a real diamond in
                       the rough. Oy!
                        Squarely,
                         Scott
                           S
```

```
...who has a number of classic issues himself.
```

I sent it off at 9:55. Twelve minutes. Damn. And I'd only worked in half the amount of text that she did. There was no denying it. Jean had kicked my ASCII.

And yet instead of being squarely smug, she simply shined on my crazy diamond. By her account, she had been composing a normal e-mail (well, as normal as she would get) when she noticed that the first four lines happened to be even. From there, she merely made a game out of it. She was only challenging herself. She never expected me to join in with my own text sculpture. Jean confessed that as far as speed went, she had the unfair advantage of being prelingually deaf. She thought in letters. I thought in sounds. But given my natural limitations, I had done arousingly well (her words).

Of course she framed her entire response in the shape of a large "Z." And she did it in five minutes.

But I didn't have time to respond to her letter. Hunta's interview was about to hit the nation, which meant Harmony would be calling, which meant it was time to get back to doing what I did best.

"That's so messed up!" cried Harmony from the foot of her bed. "They making it look like that reporter guy was in the room asking all those questions. But he wasn't even there!"

I grinned into the red phone. "Welcome to the backstage, hon."

Those tuning in to watch an all-new *Judging Amy* were in for a disappointment, as CBS ran a special edition of *48 Hours* in its place. The network had won the Maxina Howard sweepstakes, but victory came with a price. In order to keep her carefully crafted interview from devolving into one big episode of *Judging Jeremy,* Maxina had worn the producers down into a state of childlike submission. Yes ma'am, we will limit our footage of Mr. Sharpe to what you've provided on the videotape. Yes ma'am, we understand that means no raunchy bits from any of his videos, none of his randy appearances on MTV, and no out-of-context sound bites from any of his previous interviews. And yes ma'am, we promise to air each and every quote that you have earmarked as mandatory, including the part where your client stresses twice that he has no criminal record.

Most important, Maxina forced them to stick to the script. In other words, no rephrasing questions. No mixing and matching answers ("Have you ever assaulted a woman?"—*rewind, rewind, snip-snip*—"Sure"). Hey, never underestimate the power of creative editing. And never overestimate the scruples of a producer during sweeps month.

Nevertheless, they behaved. Harmony and I watched the whole show together, in the only way we could. She was curled up in front of her ancient thirteen-inch bedroom TV. I was in my living room, rolled out on my extra-long couch. Every time the reporter asked Hunta a question, or nodded to one of his longer answers, Harmony freaked out. She just couldn't get over the deception.

"Here's a helpful hint for the future," I offered. "Any time you see a one-on-one interview and they never show you both people in the same frame, chances are it's a cut-and-paste job like this one. They probably never even met."

"But how did they get the room to look the same and all that?"

"I don't know. Either they set up a background facade at the studio, or they just filmed that reporter in another room at the same hotel."

"That's so dirty!"

"Well, in this case Maxina didn't give them a choice. But just wait. In a year or two I'm sure they'll be faking the side-by-side shot, too. You know, like when an actor plays twins."

"Goddamn, Scott. You scare me sometimes."

"I didn't say I'd be doing that stuff."

"You know, Alonso's kind of scared of you too," she teased. "He said he likes you a lot but you make him glad he's getting out of the game."

"Oh, and why is that?"

"He told me you were like . . . damn, how did he put it? Oh yeah, you were an 'East Coast shark in a West Coast fishbowl.' He said that with a brain like yours, you should be making and breaking presidents instead of dealing in celebrity shit."

"That's nice," I replied, only mildly flattered. "Did you tell him I got out of politics years ago?"

"Yeah. I told him you left Washington behind and all that. He said no you didn't. You just brought it with you."

"Ooh. He's *so* profound."

She giggled along. "I know. He talks like Jesse Jackson. But he's nice, though. You know, he wants to put me up in a hotel for the next week or so."

"I know," I said. "It was my idea."

"Yeah, but who's paying for all that?"

"It won't be you. That's for damn sure."

"Wow. So are we talking a big-money Hunta-style hotel or, like, Motel 6?"

I smiled. "Somewhere in between, closer to Hunta style."

Speaking of Hunta style, he continued to defend himself with intelligence and poise. Maxina had done a great job coaching him. Too bad he had to ride the interview couch alone. In the end, Maxina relegated both Simba and Latisha to the B-roll. From what Doug had told me, Simba remained in highly uncooperative spirits, enough to trigger some closed-door emergency sessions between the Judge and Maxina. I assumed it was simply a matter of time before she'd become my problem too.

"Speaking of big money," I added, giving Harmony her cue to thank me.

"What about money?"

"Uh, did you happen to check the rest of the package I gave you?"

"What? You mean the box with the phone in it?"

"Yes. That box."

"Wait. You saying there was money in it?!"

I paused. "Yes. Fifteen hundred dollars. Do you still have it?"

"No, Scott! I threw it out! Why the hell didn't you tell me?!"

I kept silent as I analyzed the data. Just from the slight bump in her voice, I wagered a good 80 percent chance that she was just messing with me.

Soon enough, she cracked up. "No, I'm just messing with you. I got the money. Thank you."

I played the dupe anyway. "Man. Don't do that to me."

She laughed triumphantly. "I got him! I tricked the tricksta! I slicked the slicksta!"

"You know, I'm starting to think I'm a bad influence on you."

"You a *terrible* influence on me."

Hunta slowly grew within the confines of the TV screen. The close-up meant he was about to say something important.

"Whoa. Quick. Turn up your TV," I told her. "This is a good part."

"How do you know?"

"Trust me."

"I know I got a responsibility," he declared with dyed-in-the-wool candor. "I mean as an artist. And I take it very seriously, you know what I'm saying? I never hurt a woman in my life. I never forced a woman into sex. And I never, ever told anyone they should do that stuff. Never said it. Never wrote it. Never rapped it."

"There it is," I said.

"There what is?"

"The dinner bell," I replied, shamefully excited. "He just put himself on a plate and rang the dinner bell."

When Hunta assured the nation that he had never forced a woman into sex, the publicists of America collectively winced. Goddamn, you just don't say that, even if it's true. And to understand why, one would only have to look to the journalists of America, who collectively drooled. See, if you're a reporter and you're looking to bite into a piping-hot celebrity, it's a far better thing to yell *"au contraire"* than *"j'accuse."* In the media world, catching someone in a seeming contradiction is just as good as catching them in the act.

So on Wednesday, February 7, the gold rush truly began. The news brigades stepped all over each other, swinging their pickaxes high and low in the search for even the tiniest nugget of evidence that Hunta had indeed protested too much. I, of course, knew the location of two rich deposits. My urgent goal was to steer the press toward one and away from the other. I knew that today would be the last leg of the race between Harmony and Lisa Glassman. By midnight at the very latest, one of them would be discovered.

I woke up at nine to the ringing of the red phone. At first I wasn't sure if I was dreaming. In my dreams, apparently, I was still a guy with a cell phone.

"Hello?"

"Scott! I got a reporter woman on the phone! What do I tell her?"

"Harmony?"

"She's waiting on the other phone! She wants to talk to me! What do I say?"

"Get her number," I said. "Call her back."

"Okay . . ."

Finally, I came back to reality. What the hell was I talking about?

"Wait. Harmony? Is that Gail Steiner from the L.A. *Times*?"

"Yeah. She's waiting!"

I sat up. "Okay. Tell her you're not supposed to talk to anyone. If she has any questions, she can call your lawyer."

"That's all I'm supposed to say?"

"Just that," I urged. "She'll try to ask you questions anyway. Don't answer a single one. Don't give her anything even close to an answer. Just keep telling her to call Alonso Lever. Repeat it like a mantra if you have to. And if she asks for the number, tell her to look it up."

"But . . . I'm confused. I thought you wanted—"

"Trust me. Send her off and call me back."

"Okay."

I had only gotten six hours of sleep. It wasn't fair. I needed at least seven hours to be functional. Eight to be clever. Of course it was being clever that got me into this jam in the first place. Jean made cleverness a contact sport. I wound up playing until 3:00 A.M. That wasn't very clever at all.

Gail Steiner was lagging way too much for my comfort. I had expected her to call Harmony sometime last night, soon after talking to Big Bank. Didn't happen. Maybe it was the demands of motherhood, or maybe she had simply lost her edge after eight months away from the beat. Whatever it was, I may have backed the wrong horse.

After a shower and coffee, I initiated Plan B. Cradling the phone on my shoulder, I logged on to the Hotmail website and created a pseudonymous account.

"All right," I told Harmony. "Let me explain where you're coming from. Officially, you don't like or trust the media."

"I don't?"

"No. You believe this is between you and Hunta. It's nobody else's business. All you want, besides some compensation, is for Hunta to acknowledge what he did to you and to apologize for it. Not to the world. Just you. In fact, and I want you to say this often, you wish your lawyer had settled the case back in January, before the whole Bitch Fiend mess. Oh, by the way, you don't think Hunta's responsible for that."

"I don't?"

"Do you?"

"Wouldn't I?"

I flipped through a thin stack of Alonso's legal papers until I found a copy of the CH-100 judicial form. This was the prenotarized version, but I had scribbled down the official court docket number in the upper right-hand corner.

"A lesser person would," I explained, while composing a message through Hotmail. "But you are going to ride the moral high ground all the way to the twist ending. That's why you're never going to look like you enjoy the publicity. That's why you're never going to take pleasure in Hunta's public crucifixion. And most important, that's why you're never going to take a dime from anybody but Alonso."

Oof. That didn't come out right at all. Her silence was piercing.

"I mean just until you recant," I stressed.

"You said I'd be getting all sorts of money."

"And you will. Once you clear Hunta's name, you can go crazy. Sell your autobiography. Endorse Revlon. Pose nude for *Penthouse.* Believe me, they'll offer. It's all up to you. But until that happens, you can't do anything that's even remotely self-serving. The name of the game . . ."

I clicked and sent the e-mail.

". . . is credibility."

Harmony was still frosty. Shit. Things were so much easier when I was handling her from the driver's seat of my car.

"I'll be honest, Scott. I'm lost again. You just lost me."

With Plan B now in motion, I pushed away the laptop and stretched out on the couch.

"Well, then let's go over it again," I said. "We've got nothing but time."

I didn't want the story to begin on the Internet. Planting a seed on the World Wide Web was like conceiving a child on Three Mile Island. Who knew what kind of mutated freak I'd end up with?

But at least the Net worked fast, and on Wednesday I needed speed. My backup leak was The Smoking Gun, an online rag that regularly served up telling documents and court records, all legally obtained through freedom-of-information statutes. The site was a celebrity publicist's nightmare, filled to the brim with big-name divorce petitions, arrest reports, civil claims, and ludicrous contract riders. One such proviso revealed that Britney Spears, a well-paid Pepsi endorser, secretly demanded a six-pack of Coke in her dressing room at every stop on her 2000 world tour. Oh, the scandal!

So, in electronic disguise, I pointed the way to the L.A. County superior court clerk's office, where a nice fat CH-100 was waiting to be discovered. Obviously, the good folks at The Smoking Gun were just as hot to nab Hunta as everyone else. So you could imagine their delight in learning that Mr. Never-Hurt-a-Woman had come *this* close to getting slapped with a temporary restraining order. And just last month, too.

Over the next six hours, the seed became a sprout, the sprout became a plant, the plant bore fruit, and the fruit tasted funny. That's what I got for using the Internet.

"Goddamn it!"

Madison looked up from her work. "What?"

It was four o'clock. While I surfed the Web from the couch, Madison sat lotus-style on the living room floor, surrounded by a sea of online printouts. To my relief, she had finally deep-sixed the junior-executive wear and simply came to work as a junior.

"The Smoking Gun," I told her. "They just posted a restraining-order request that some woman filed against Hunta."

"Oh shit. Who is she?"

"I don't know. They grayed out her goddamn name. Everywhere it's mentioned." I scrolled through the digital pages. "They even grayed out her lawyer's name. I don't get it! They almost never gray out names! Why this one? Why now?"

Madison cocked her head. "Well . . . isn't that sort of good?"

"No. I need to know who we're up against. I need to hear her *name*."

Thanks to The Smoking Gun, the world just learned that somebody was allegedly abused by Hunta at the Mean World Christmas party, and somebody was allegedly mad about it. That did me absolutely no good, considering that "somebody" could still be Lisa Glassman.

"Goddamn it." I leaned back and eyed Madison. "This is all your fault."

"Me? Why me?"

"Because you work with the Internet and the Internet sucks."

"Oh, act your age."

I managed to simultaneously laugh and yawn, which triggered a successive laugh and yawn from Madison. For the fourth time since she arrived, I went upstairs to my bedroom, closed the door, and made a private call from my spy phone.

"Did you talk to her?" I asked.

"I talked to Ms. Steiner," replied Alonso. "I gave her all the information and confirmation she could have ever possibly hoped for. She was very pleased, to say the least."

"And you gave her permission to use Harmony's name?"

"I assured her that neither Harmony nor I would make a fuss if she revealed the victim by name. Will you be making a liar out of me?"

"Pretty much."

He chuckled. "Oh well. One less person to buy my novel."

"What time did you finish the call?"

"About fifteen minutes ago."

I checked my alarm clock. "She's never going to make her deadline."

"She'll make it."

She better. Ten minutes later, I went back downstairs. On the way, I got the bird's eye view of Madison's work. She was adrift in a sea of highlighted articles.

"Jesus," I said. "They really don't like him, do they?"

With a tired sigh, she capped her marker. "No. No, they don't."

The minute she arrived at my place, I had put her to work. I'd printed the natterings of thirty different columnists, each one offering their own postmortem analysis of Hunta's appearance on *48 Hours*. Madison's task was to go through them with a pair of colored highlighters. Every word that benefited Hunta—positive modifiers, supportive quotes, mentions of his wife and child, and so on—was to be marked in green. By contrast, every word used to cast Hunta in a less flattering light was to be marked in orange. By four o'clock, her work looked like a pumpkin patch.

"God, Scott, you were right about the adjectives. Most of the articles refer to him as the 'lascivious' rapper, with his 'libidinous' style of rap music. They also use 'lecherous,' 'licentious,' 'lewd,' and 'libertine.' 'Libertine' is bad, right?"

"In this case, it is."

"Shit, they call him everything short of a horn dog. And the only three songs of his that they keep mentioning by name are 'Chocolate Ho-Ho,' 'Keep Ya Head Down,' and of course 'Bitch Fiend.' But I looked up the album on Amazon. He has at least six other tracks with perfectly respectable titles, including a sweet one called 'Dear Papa.' Funny how no one listed that."

I smiled. "Are we learning?"

"We are freaking."

"I do notice a couple of green words in the mix."

"Oh yes," she replied with perfect wit. "Apparently he's quite buff."

I searched my junk drawer. "Okay. You're doing a great job. So now I'll throw in one more color."

With that, I tossed her a pink highlighter. She caught it. "What's this one for?"

"All the mentions of Annabelle Shane."

"I see. And what will I learn from this?"

"That pink is worse than orange."

She yawned again. "All right."

With an old man's moan, I hunkered down on the sofa. The very moment I got comfortable, the red phone rang. Crap. I didn't want to take it all the way back upstairs. Screw it. I'd just talk around Madison. It'd be fine as long as I didn't call Harmony by name.

"Scott Singer."

Harmony spoke in a panicked whisper. "Scott. It's me. I think I'm in a lot of trouble."

"What's the problem?"

"Some reporter guy just called for me . . ."

"Andy Cronin?"

"Yeah. But I was out at the store when he called. One of my room-mates took the message. Now they asking me all kinds of questions. What should I say?"

"What *did* you say?"

"I said I couldn't tell them nothing."

"That's fine. Just keep saying that. But listen, the more nervous you act around them, the more nervous they'll get. So the next time they corner you with questions, deal with them confidently. Say, 'Look, I love you guys but I'm not ready to talk about it. At some point soon I will be, but in the meantime, if you love me, you're just going to have to trust me.' "

I could just see Madison's mind working to process the conversation. Who does he keep talking to? Is it business? Pleasure? Both?

"But what happens when the story breaks? What do I say then?"

"You say good-bye," I informed her. "I just talked to our mutual friend. He's going to get you out of there tomorrow. You'll be set up somewhere nice."

She squeaked something inaudible.

"I'm sorry. I can't hear you."

"I said I don't want to lose my roommates. They the only family I got."

I casually eyed Madison as she worked. "You won't lose them. They may freak out a little, but they'll get over it. When this is all over, they'll understand. Trust me. These are the kinds of things that only make a friendship stronger."

God, that was trite, not to mention bullshit. I knew that as soon as the tabloids started waving around the cheddar, all bets were off. All loy-alties were subject to immediate reevaluation. I really should have pre-pared her for the possibility that one or more of her friends would sell her out. I really should have taken the phone upstairs.

"You mean that?" asked Harmony.

"It'll be fine. But if you still feel guilty when everything's said and done, screw it. Use your money and fly them all to Cancún."

I felt terrible. I'd never been this deceitful with her before. Each fraudulent comment, each creative omission, was a crack in the ice. A few more of those, Mr. Singer, and you're in for a really cold swim.

But at least she felt better. "Damn, Scott. You always know what to say."

"Hey, it's my job. I'm your lifeline."

She laughed. "I'm gonna keep this phone with me forever. So, like, twenty years from now, when I'm in a jam, I'm still gonna call you up and go 'Scott! What do I do?' "

It was a cute thought, but I knew Harmony wouldn't be under my wing forever. In the media world, you tend to grow up fast. I figured in a week she'd be a black belt at this. By Presidents' Day, she'd be permanently speaking in eight-second sound bites.

Meanwhile, under my other wing, Madison was still busy highlighting all the mentions of Annabelle Shane. Once I closed the phone, she threw me a teasing grin.

"Girlfriend?"

"No thanks."

"Come on. Who was that?"

I folded my hands over my chest and closed my eyes. "My mother."

"You told me your mother was dead. You just said it like an hour ago."

"Okay, then it was your mother."

"Somehow I don't think so."

"Well, she sounded like your mother."

"Fine," she replied, sufficiently irked. "Sorry I asked."

I suddenly remembered something Jean told me. "Hey, your dad's a college professor, right? I mean your real dad."

Madison eyed me warily. "I know who you're talking about. And yes. He is."

"Forgive my ignorance, but how does he teach classes? I mean being deaf and all. Does he use special technology, an interpreter, or what?"

She smiled coyly. *Oh, look who wants information now?* "You ever been to D.C.?"

"I used to live there."

"Me too. There's a school there called Gallaudet. It's a famous deaf university. They pretty much do everything in sign language."

"Ah. I get it now."

"My dad's been teaching there for over twenty-five years. Why did you want to know about that?"

"No big reason. Your mom mentioned it in one of her e-mails and it made me curious."

"I see," she replied frostily. "So you guys aren't just talking X-Men. You're talking X-spouses."

Clever girl. It was definitely genetic.

Last night, at the stroke of midnight, I had replied to Jean's Z-shaped note with a Y-shaped apology for not getting back to her sooner. Unable to resist the thematic convergence, she quickly countered with an X-shaped tribute to her favorite team of comic-book mutants. Very cute, but the text-sculpting thing was getting old. So instead of burying my next message under a great big "W," I discussed my favorite X-Men (Beast, Rogue, Storm) in words of five letters or less.

Never one to be outdone, she described all the things she loved about her namesake heroine, Jean Grey, in words of four letters or less. That may seem like an easy task, but try to keep it up for more than a line or two. It's very, very hard to pull off. And yet she had sent me a flat-out full-page mash note, just ripe with hep puns, fun gags, and sly bon mots. And she did it all in no time.

The challenges only got harder from there. Anagrams. Palindromes. Cryptoquotes. Syllacrostics. As long as the game didn't involve phonetics, she was indomitable. The English language was her bitch, and so was I. I did everything I could to keep up but she threw me around the virtual room, breaking every lamp and mirror. By the end of the lightning pun round, I was begging for mercy. Please. No more. Need rest . . .

And yet Jean had barely broken a sweat.

```
Wow, Scott! That was an AMAZING run! As you've noticed, I love
these kinds of word games. Sadly, few ever want to play with me
and the ones who do, sadly, suck at it.

So thank you! It's been ages since I've had a good mental
challenge. It makes a nice break from all the emotional ones. :)
```

In response, I admitted I was feeling somewhat mentally-challenged myself. But in her own gracious style, she waved me off.

```
Oh, stop. I told you I had the natural advantage. And I learned
from the master. Not only was my first husband twice my age and
IQ, but he was also an English professor. He wiped the floor
with me (literately, not literally). He found my tenacity to be
"cute," but all I wanted to do was wipe the smug off his mug.
So I kept taking him on, losing and learning, losing and learning,
```

until that ONE FATEFUL DAY...ha ha ha. He divorced me. Typical
man.

(Shit. I'm never going to hear from you again, am I?)

Don't worry, I wrote back. I'm not the typical man.

I didn't think so, but I had to be sure. You see in my book, a
typical man is someone who'd rather surround himself with fawning,
admiring young women (*cough cough* Madison) than take on someone
his own age and cranial capacity.

Her teasing insinuation torqued me; only because it made me wonder. Clearly I did enjoy Madison's fawning admiration. And not just hers (*cough cough* Harmony). So what did that make me? Insecure? Lecherous? Lewd? Libertine? I remembered the way Miranda had teased me when she detected my May–September crush on the voluptuous Deb Isham.

So what was it you liked about her? Besides her knockers. Is it that she's young and naïve? That she could gaze upon you with a sense of awe and wonder?

No. Sorry. In hindsight, it was her knockers. And you, Miranda, were simply projecting your husband's flaws onto me. *Et tu,* Jean? Are you doing the same thing with your own professor ex? Are you merely handing me one of your old issues? Because if so:

You should know that the two major relationships I've had thus far
were both with strong-willed, freethinking, devastatingly
brilliant women. One was my age, the other was a good deal older.
Not only did they teach and challenge me in every conceivable
fashion, but they also made gobs more money than I did. Amazingly,
none of this intimidated me.

Neither do you. I'll be more than happy to continue playing these
little word games, losing and learning, losing and learning. I just
hope that when that ONE FATEFUL DAY comes, you won't pout too much,
like a typical woman (see how sexist it sounds when _I_ say it?).

Toodles for now,
Scott Singer

```
PS—Since I know you'll ask: I was dumped both times. Surely by now
you can see why.
```

Once I sent the message, I reread it and winced. Damn. That was persnickety, Singer. Defensively so. You might as well have typed TOUCHED A NERVE seventy times and then sent it off. I never would have said it if I hadn't been so obscenely tired.

And yet instead of going to bed, I waited for her response:

```
>PS—Since I know you'll ask: I was dumped both times. Surely by
>now you can see why.

Surely I can't.
```

That was it. No comeback jab. No witty puns. No clever little postscript. The note was suspiciously terse for a woman with her mastery of the written language. Three simple words. Stranger still, it took her eight minutes to write them.

By Wednesday night I was ready to scream. I had been cooped up in my apartment all day, percolating with a nervous energy that I didn't know how to vent or defuse. I felt like one of those old-fashioned dads-to-be, pacing back and forth outside the maternity ward. Believe me, I would have rather been there in the delivery room, telling Gail Steiner to push! Push, damn it! But obviously, I didn't want to open myself up to any paternity claims. I just had to wait for the miracle to happen.

It happened at eight o'clock. At long last, my baby got to see the light of day. After five days of labor, Harmony Prince was finally born.

Maxina was the one to call with the good news. "Scott, I just got word from my sources at the L.A. *Times.* They just burned the plate for tomorrow's front page. Gail Steiner's piece is all over it."

"Does she mention Harmony by name?"

"Many times."

I deflated into my easy chair. "Oh, thank God . . ."

"You did it, Scott."

I did it. The copyright to the Christmas-party rape claim was now officially ours. In a matter of hours, the *Times* would trumpet their coup all over the newswires, making Harmony the truest of overnight sensations.

"Thank God," I breathed again. "Thank God."

"I don't know," Maxina teased. "I have to say I'm a little disappointed. I hired you to get ruthless and mean with Lisa Glassman, and here you managed to stop her without touching a hair on her head."

I loved her all over again. "Sorry. Next time I'll do better."

"This *is* next time," she replied. "You got this plane off the ground. Now you've got to land it."

I managed to suppress a hysterical laugh. "I will. I will."

"Not that I want to get into this tonight, but what's your estimated flight time?"

"One week," I told her.

"One whole week?"

"Look, I'm not just giving you the cure for Lisa Glassman here. I'm giving you the cure for Annabelle Shane."

"In one week we'll be needing the cure for Harmony Prince."

"She comes with her own cure. That's the great thing about this. Trust me. I know this can work."

Maxina took a good long breath. "I'm too tired to discuss it right now. Let's see how the press reacts tomorrow and we'll go from there."

"Fair enough."

"I'll let you call the starlet yourself."

"Oh, you bet I will."

"Tell her to rest up," she added. "She's in for a quite a day."

Maxina wasn't as joyous as I was. It was easy to see why. To think of the power being put in Harmony's hands. To think of the power I wielded with Harmony in *my* hands. My God. I'd be writing both sides of America's latest and greatest drama. Forget "he said/she said." Now it was all about what *I* said. No wonder I couldn't fake an air of professional detachment. I was about to score with an entire nation.

I sat alone in my apartment, in absolute silence, gazing out at absolutely nothing. I didn't move but I was very, very conscious of the phone in my lap. If I told Harmony she was about to wake up famous, would she even sleep? Would I? And if I assured her that from this point on, her fate was safe and snug in my loving hands, could she believe it? Could I?

Screw it. I'd just hand her the facts and let her sort them out. No more creative omissions. No more giving her the kid's version of things. She was in for the crash course now. The Bitch was about take her places even I never went.

14

SANCTIFIED LADY

Her name came up with the sunrise. East to west, all across the nation, wherever there was sound or light, there was—

"—Harmony Prince," said the talk-radio people in Tampa.

"—Harmony Prince," said the morning TV anchors in St. Paul.

"—Harmony Prince," said the newspapers in Reno.

"—Harmony Prince," said the websites all over.

"—according to a story from this morning's L.A. *Times*—"

"—*Los Angeles Times,* a woman by the name of Harmony Prince—"

"—Harmony Prince—"

"—nineteen-year-old Harmony Prince is filing a civil claim—"

"—civil suit against rapper Jeremy Sharpe—"

"—rapper Jeremy Sharpe—"

"—aka Hunta—"

"—the controversial rapper Hunta—"

" 'I never hurt a woman in my life. I never forced a woman into sex.' "

"—Hunta, for purported sexual abuse—"

"—sexual abuse from an alleged—"

"—alleged rape incident stemming from a—"

"—claimed he never forced a woman into sex."

"—incident at a record-label Christmas party."

"—was a dancer at the Christmas party of—"

"—forced the woman into sex."

"—forced her—"

"—raped her—"

"—*raped* the woman, for God's sake—"

"—raped the dancer—"

"—the nineteen-year-old dancer—"

"—the nineteen-year-old woman—"

"—the nineteen-year-old victim named—"

"—victim by the name of—"

"—name of—"

"—Harmony Prince."

"—Harmony Prince."

"—the victim, Harmony Prince."

"Holy shit!" yelled Harmony from her bathroom. "Scott! What do I do?"

I ran downstairs. "Okay. Step one: move away from the window."

"There's gotta be a hundred people outside!"

"Move away from the window," I said, turning on the TV. Lo and behold, there it was. Her apartment complex. On almost every channel, a roving newshound reported live from right outside her building. I could see at least six satellite news vans in the background. Four police cars. Two ambulances. A fire truck. It was like Melrose all over again. And Harmony didn't even have to kill anyone.

"Holy shit, Scott . . ."

"Take a deep breath, sweetheart. Alonso's coming. He'll be there as fast as he can."

We could have gotten her out of there yesterday, of course. Easily. Quietly. But where was the fun in that? The media needed pictures. Quality pictures. All they had so far were two JPEG images of Harmony and Hunta (courtesy of the L.A. *Times* (courtesy of Alonso (courtesy of me))). Later, I'd scan that wonderful Polaroid and anonymously send it off to UPI. Later, though. It was only 7:30 in the morning. I had to keep her sane until Alonso got there. I had to hold her together. I had no clothes on.

"Did you pack your essentials?"

"What? Yeah. Yeah. I did it last night like you told me."

Someone kept pounding at her door.

"My roommates! What do I tell my roommates?"

"Tell them to use the other bathroom."

"They wanna know what the hell's going on!"

"Tell them to leave you alone."

"LEAVE ME ALONE!"

"You should probably say 'please.' "

"PLEASE!"

I rubbed my eyes. "Harmony, please don't cry. Everything that's happening right now is good. This is good."

"It don't feel good."

"It will. It will. It'll feel great."

"Scott, I am so scared . . ."

"I know you're scared. Alonso's coming."

"I wish you were coming."

"I'm already here. You already have me."

Her roommates kept pounding. "I DON'T KNOW, OKAY? PLEASE LEAVE ME ALONE!"

My other cellular rang. "Harmony, just breathe."

"They'll never forgive me."

"They'll forgive you. They'll understand."

"I'm so scared."

"I'm here for you. Just keep talking to me."

"Is that your other phone?"

"I'm not answering it."

"What if it's Hunta?"

"It's not."

On TV, the chaos boiled over. The newshounds swarmed around a new figure. He looked crisp and fresh in his three-piece suit.

"He's there!" I yelled. "Alonso's there!"

"Thank God!"

"You're all dressed?"

"I'm all dressed. And I got my essentials."

"Then you're all set."

"What do I tell my roommates?"

"Tell them you love them," I said. "Then tell them good-bye."

Alonso made his way into the building. Harmony stepped out from the bathroom. The reporters got in pounce position. The phone kept ringing. This was better than sex.

———

Harmony shared a three-bedroom apartment with four men and one other woman. The men—McB, B-Nasté, Vertikal, and Whitey—formed the core of an aspiring rap group called The Jury. The woman, Tracy Wood, was a receptionist at Aftermath Records. Tracy and Harmony had been good friends in high school, up until the accident. When Harmony was released from the convalescent hospital thirteen months later, they reconnected. Tracy had taken care of her ever since. They all did. Harmony seemed to bring out the protective sibling in everybody.

As such, they'd all been concerned about her these past couple of days. Harmony's behavior was strange and erratic, but she wouldn't tell them anything. The going theory was that she had found herself a sugar daddy. It was a common thing for hostesses to be lured into an outside arrangement, but *Harmony*? For her to take a gentleman client, he'd have to be a *real* gentleman. One who'd pay for the sizzle without demanding the steak. One who had uses for her beyond the most obvious one.

They were so close to the truth, but they could never have imagined this.

At 7:40, on the morning of Thursday, February 8, Harmony Prince made her live television debut. Alonso led her down the walkway like Allan Quartermain, fighting off the savages with one arm while securing the damsel with the other. He was wonderfully telegenic. The cameras added a healthy fifteen pounds and all but erased his goofy, showboating nature. You could almost believe he wasn't enjoying the attention. He even got in a few quality bites. *Stop it! Act like adults, for God's sake! This is not news!*

But the real star of the show, of course, was Harmony. She was beautifully helpless as she clung to her lawyer. No Oscar-winning actress, no precious child, nobody could broadcast their state of being like Harmony did. Her face was a vortex. You couldn't see her without getting sucked into her. You couldn't help but share her righteous horror as the reporters pawed at her, pelting her with unbelievably rude questions. *How much are you asking for? Have you ever been raped before? Why didn't you go to the police? Did Hunta videotape your sexual assault? What would you say to him right now? Would you shoot him if you could? Would you shoot yourself?*

I couldn't have prayed for a more powerful premiere. She couldn't have made a stronger impression if I had tried. Just think of all the morning viewers, staring slightly agape while the cereal dripped from their raised spoons. Think of her poor roommates, who watched their sweet little sister step out into the media storm only to be digitized, miniaturized, fictionalized. She walked out the door and came back five seconds later through the TV screen, a character no more real to them than Frasier or Buffy.

How strange it must have seemed. How odd it must have been for

Lisa Glassman to wake up and find her leverage missing, to learn that she was the secret butt of a nationwide joke. It could have been worse, sweetheart. I could have dropped the mountain on top of you instead of in front of you. I would have found a way. I always find a way. I'm very, very good at what I do.

———

The police followed along, if only to prevent the world from losing Harmony the way it lost Princess Di. But here in America, we chase our cars from above. The local news choppers trailed Alonso's black Audi with military precision. This wasn't just a provincial affair. CNN, MSNBC, Fox News, the sister affiliates in all other markets, everybody picked up on the feed. Only ABC abstained, refusing to interrupt the live opening ceremony of Disney's new California Adventure theme park. There were over twenty news crews down in Anaheim that morning, and with the exception of the Disney/ABC synergy squad, they were all preempted by Harmony. Her first step into the limelight and already she had the world's biggest mouse on the bottom of her shoe. Holy shit. Sorry, Mickey.

It was a short trip north from Harmony's apartment to the Fairmont Miramar on Wilshire Boulevard in Santa Monica. Greta Garbo used to stay there when she wanted to be alone. John F. Kennedy stayed there when he *didn't* want to be alone. And Marilyn Monroe fled there when the media pressure was getting too intense. Now it was Harmony's turn. Her tower suite was a bright and airy wonderland complete with bathroom Jacuzzi and balcony overlooking the Pacific. Ordinarily it would cost $645 a night, but by the end of the day, Alonso would finagle a free tab in exchange for hosting at least one press conference from the hotel's new garden room. That, too, would happen by the end of the day.

At a quarter after eight, Harmony dropped onto the king-size bed. I could hear her popping open the aspirin bottle. Emotionally, she was a twirling, flying coin. I wasn't sure if she was going to land on numbness or hysteria.

I, on the other hand, crackled with wild, euphoric energy. My thoughts, my senses, were amplified to a mad degree. This was what my wedding day would have felt like, if Gracie and I hadn't gone out of our way to sterilize it. We had removed every trace of pomp and circumstance, every emotional and legal facet. In the end it was little more than a neoteric theme party. We thought we were being cool in our postmodern detachment but we had gypped ourselves. I never realized how much until this morning.

"That was the craziest shit I ever saw," said Harmony, swallowing her tablets. "They was standing everywhere. In the mud. In the flowers. On each other. I mean the way they pushed all over each other to get to me . . ."

"Yeah," I replied, smiling. "They live for this kind of stuff."

"And the wires. I never seen so many wires in my life. Everyone had at least six wires coming out of them." She let out a precarious laugh. "I was like 'Shit, where do they all go?' For a second I thought maybe all the people was all hooked up to each other. Like they was all just part of one big machine."

"You're not entirely wrong."

"Yeah, but who decided I'd be the big story? Who decided that I'd be what people wanted to see?"

I turned off the TV. I could feel Harmony, inching her way to tears. She needed my full focus.

"It's all a business decision," I explained. "The income's based on ad rates, the ad rates are based on audience numbers and so far this Melrose thing has drawn in huge numbers. People who don't normally watch the news are now watching the news."

"So what am I, the next Annabelle Shane?"

"Yes, but to them you make a much better lead character."

"Why's that?"

"Because unlike her, you're still walking and talking. Unlike her, you don't have a killing spree on your record. And unlike her, your beef is with the original Bitch Fiend himself. He's the one they're after. He's the reason you're hot property right now."

"Shit. If that's how they treat me, I don't even want to think about how they gonna treat Hunta."

"They've been setting him up as the bad guy all week. With or without you—"

"It's with me," she argued. "If I'm the better story, then he's in a lot more trouble with me."

"Yeah, but you're forgetting the twist. This is a rescue operation. You're saving him. You know it. I know it. He knows it."

"My roommates don't know it."

"Honey, you're going out of your way to upset yourself."

"They know I'm lying," she said, teetering. "They saw me right after the Christmas party. I was fine. I was—"

"Harmony—"

"I kept saying it was the easiest money I ever made . . ."

There she went. Whether she was covering her mouth or the receiver, I didn't know. But I could read the silence.

"Harmony? Harmony, listen to me. Are you there?"

"I'm here." She sniffed.

"You just went through one of the most intense experiences a human being can go through. Your mind is moving a million miles an hour right now, and it's taking you to dark places. Just slow it all down, okay? Step back into the light."

"What are people gonna think about me?"

"Only good things," I assured her. "This is my story now. And I'm not going to stop until the world sees you the way I do."

"As a victim," she groused.

"That's not the way I see you and you know it."

After a few more sniffs and gasps, Harmony settled down. I desperately wanted to put her at ease and then get started on my task list. All I'd managed to do so far was throw on a robe and make myself a Venti-sized cup of coffee.

"You got any family, Scott?"

"Not anymore. Both my parents are dead."

"Did they know what you do? I mean, for work?"

I smiled wanly. "They knew I was a publicist, if that's what you mean."

"But how did they feel about you doing, you know, this kind of stuff?"

I'd never done *this* kind of stuff before, but that wasn't the thing to tell her.

"They knew I loved my job. They knew I was good at it. They were just happy with that, I guess." I switched beats. "Although they had a good friend. A rabbi. He gave me a hard time. I remember once he pulled me aside and said, 'Scott, what you do is not a good living. It may be a job. It may be a well-paying job. But you're playing tricks on people, and that's not a good living.' "

"Damn. What'd you say to him?"

"I simply looked him right in the eye and said, 'Silly rabbi! Tricks are for kids!' "

Harmony screamed with laughter. "You didn't really say that!"

"No. But I would have."

"If?"

"If any of that stuff actually happened."

She screamed again. "You set me up?"

"And you walked right in," I crowed. "I'm still the tricksta. Still the slicksta."

"You're terrible!"

"Anything to get a smile out of you, my dear."

"You're too much."

I checked the clock. "Listen, sweetheart, you're done for the day. I want you to rest and enjoy your new digs, okay? Take a nice long bath. Order a huge meal. Watch some movies. Spoil yourself. You're a celebrity now. Besides, you need to recharge your phone. I don't want to lose you to a low battery."

She took a deep breath, then let out a stretching moan. "Maybe I'll take a nap. If I can."

"Good. Recharge your own battery."

"Thank you, Scott."

"For what?"

"For making me feel better, like always."

I looked out the window, beaming. "Harmony, I'd move heaven and earth for you. You know that."

"I know," she said softly. "You the only one I trust."

That lit me up in dangerous ways. As my feelings and senses were heightened, so were my urges. I wanted to devour a huge rack of lamb, even though it was only breakfast-time. I wanted to sprint down the street, even though I was barefoot. Now I wanted to hug Harmony, hard. I wanted to envelop her, to wrap myself around her so tight that I wouldn't be able to tell her heartbeat from mine. Although the feeling was hot, my reasons were shamefully cold. This was a woman who, just by leaving the apartment, had managed to upstage the forty-million-dollar opening to a hundred-million-dollar theme park. This was a woman who, in just forty minutes, had scored at least thirty million dollars' worth of comparative ad exposure. Oh, sweetheart. I liked you from the moment I met you, but now—God help me—you turn me on.

Once Harmony had disappeared inside the Miramar, the major networks reluctantly went back to their regularly scheduled programming.

The news channels, however, continued to squeeze every last drop out of Gail Steiner's peach. They paraded an endless list of experts, authors, lawyers, pollsters, professors, prognosticators, the whole Goya beanery.

And yet as cerebral as these people were meant to seem, their conclusions were jam-packed with masturbatory drama. This new development has HUGE implications! For Hunta. For the entertainment industry. For the victims of Melrose, their families, their families' lawyers. For all of us! God, yes! This affects all of us!

Surprisingly, very few of the strokes were devoted to Harmony herself. To the media, she was still just a stamp-sized pinup, a thumbnail tease. You could practically hear the news editors howling for more as they launched their flying monkeys out the window. *Go, my pretties! Find me everything you can on this girl! Go! Go!*

Fortunately, one of the minions had been given a secret head start. Hell, I had slipped Andy Cronin the key to Harmony's whole life story. By now, of course, he knew exactly where it fit in. By now, he was typing as fast as he could.

Scott. It's Maxina. We need to convene. Come to my hotel at 10:00 A.M. Eighth floor. L'Escoffier Room.

I was just stepping out of the shower when she left the message. I knew I was freshening up for some kind of emergency meeting, but I figured Maxina would summon me to Hunta's room, as usual. Why the change of venue? Why the fancy meeting room? Who else was coming?

At a quarter to ten, I arrived at the Beverly Hilton. Maxina had been staying there for the past week, courtesy of the Recording Industry Association of America. She wasn't taking a dime from Mean World's coffers. They couldn't afford her. But Maxina wasn't in this for the money. Like the RIAA, she remained focused on the larger battle. Why else would she leave her beautiful home in Atlanta? Her husband and sons. Her orthopedic chairs. To save one measly rapper? No way. In her mind, in her heart, she was fighting to save *music*.

Simba, on the other hand, had no love for the business. Many were starting to wonder if she had any love left for her husband. But when Maxina summoned her to the Hilton, she arrived just as promptly as I did. She was standing in the elevator bank when I caught her dark and lovely scorn.

"Is it me," she asked facetiously, "or have you gotten even taller?"

She was dressed in a loose black blouse and tight gray jeans. Her long hair was clipped back. She hid herself under a hat and dark glasses, but nobody seemed to recognize her. A hefty bodyguard flanked her left side, just in case someone did.

"Simba. Hey. I wasn't expecting to see you here."

"Oh, and why not?"

"You want the real answer or the polite one?"

An elevator opened. The bodyguard escorted us in, gently pushing back a plump tourist who tried to embark with us.

She removed her glasses. "Let me guess. You heard I was being a real pain in the ass."

"Something like that."

"That's okay," she replied as the doors slid closed. "I heard you were fucking Harmony."

Shit. I knew there would be a downside to chewing out the Judge, aside from his lifelong enmity. Shit, shit, shit. That was not a constructive rumor. And worse, it was the kind that denials only strengthened. I merely grinned with mock amusement, but I knew I'd have to say or do something clever to counter the buzz. Whatever it was, I'd save it for the meeting.

"I *was* being a pain in the ass," she offered, three floors up. "I was sick of that hotel. Sick of Maxina telling me what to do. And I was definitely sick of Jeremy acting like he was the only one being put out."

"But then?"

Through the mirrored doors, she bounced a glare. "Let's just say I got a wake-up call this morning."

"How's he holding up?"

"How do you think?"

"It's just medicine," I assured her reflection. "This is all just medicine. It may taste like crap but it's going to make everything better again."

"So you say."

"So I mean. Just stand by your husband. You can't go wrong."

The elevator stopped at the top floor. After sniffing for reporters, Simba's bodyguard led us down the hall to our meeting place. A pair of hotel security guards blocked the entrance. They checked our IDs against their lists, then opened the double doors to a massive, sun-drenched room.

"For the record," Simba added, "I don't think you're fucking Harmony."

"Good to hear."

She put her shades back on. "I'd like to think you have better taste than that."

We stepped into the light.

———

In its heyday, L'Escoffier was the swankiest of swank places to dine, a place where you could rub shoulders with the Hollywood elite over a rich crème brûlée. Eventually Merv Griffin's people shut the restaurant down and left a chamber in its memory. The place could comfortably seat three hundred people, but there were only twelve of us here. We formed a tiny cluster in the center of the room. None of us looked very comfortable.

"See, to me this personifies Los Angeles," Maxina joked to her squinting guests. "Too much sun and too much space."

And yet the loop was looking awfully crowded as of late. Lord only knew how many folks were in on the gag now. The white people at the table were all strangers to me. Four of them were from the RIAA. Two were from Interscope. The final two were from Universal, Interscope's corporate parent. They weren't mere envoys. They were all high priests of the music industry.

The Judge sat with the Interscope reps. He threw me a cordial nod. I assumed it meant détente, but it was hard to tell. The sun gleamed so strongly off his bald head, I could barely see him.

For the first time this week, Maxina wasn't dressed like she was going to Denny's. Decked out in a stylish gray power suit, she walked around the table introducing everybody. Despite their importance, I didn't bother remembering their names. I hoped to God they would extend me the same courtesy. This was stupid. It was unnecessary. It was dangerous. Nothing good ever came out of a committee, especially one filled with such nervous and powerful people.

At 10:00 A.M. Maxina sat down and began the meeting.

"All right, gang. Let's talk about Harmony Prince."

It wasn't long before the shouting began.

———

"They have every reason to be scared," the Judge explained, while cutting into a veal medallion. We were dining at Trader Vic's, an aggressively chic eatery next to the hotel. Our tête-à-tête lunch was his idea, but I gladly accepted. The Judge was the one paying my invoice. That made him my client more than Maxina, Harmony, even Hunta. But for me this wasn't just about customer service. I needed a new friend on the inside, especially since I had left the Beverly Hilton with a brand-new enemy.

"You know how we got the Parental Advisory sticker in the first place, right?"

"Yeah. Tipper Gore had a thing against Prince."

"She got the ball rolling," said the Judge, "but it was her husband who did the real damage. See back in '85, when they were having those rock-and-roll obscenity hearings, the music labels didn't give a shit. Controversy only led to higher sales. What did hurt was the increasing number of kids who recorded songs off the radio instead of buying the albums in stores. So at the time there just happened to be a bill on the Senate floor that would tax all blank audiotapes and give the revenue back to the record industry. We're talking a handout worth hundreds of millions of dollars. Who fostered that bill? Al Gore. Who sat on the panel at the obscenity hearings? Al Gore."

"So the labels took the sticker."

"Right. The RIAA gave in. Not for principle. For profit. And what really sucks, Scott, is that we're in the same jam again."

"How so?"

He eyed me. "Think about it."

I did. "Napster."

"Napster's dying, but the problem's still there. The labels despise the Internet. It terrifies them. What they want more than anything is for Congress to make life hard for all the song-swappers and webcasters. What Congress wants, as always, is to suck up to their soccer-mom constituents. And what do *they* want?"

"To protect their kids from the evils of rap."

"As long as it keeps making the goddamn headlines," he added. "You saw those guys at the meeting. They're pissing their pants. Once the heat turns up, the first thing they'll do is turn on Mean World. They'll cut us out like a tumor. I don't know how familiar you are with the music business but without one of the Big Five behind me, I won't get any albums into stores. I won't get any pay-for-play with the radio stations. Without Interscope, Universal, Vivendi, whatever, I might as well board up the windows. Can you see now why I'm a little stressed?"

He threw his napkin down, then finished his second beer. The Judge had skimped down on the bling-bling today. That was fortunate. In that sunny room, he would have blinged us blind.

"You sure you don't want a drink, Scott?"

"You know, maybe I will have one."

The bar was only twenty feet away. The Judge and I both had a nice clear view of the hanging television, currently on CNN (your source for nonstop Hunta speculation). Once again, they showed that lightning-fast clip from "Chocolate Ho-Ho," in which a skin-baring Harmony pressed and shimmied against a shirtless Hunta. She was completely in-distinguishable from the woman on Hunta's other side. For clarity's sake, the network had dimmed the picture, and then highlighted her head with a light bubble. It made her look angelic, tragic.

The Judge scoffed at the TV. "That song is crap. Half the album is crap. It's not Jeremy's fault. It's mine. His material was all so heavy at first. It was full of all this street angst and family drama. So I made him balance it out with some fun tracks. 'Sex it up,' I said. 'Once you carve a name for yourself, *then* you can start doing the soulful-artist thing. But in the meantime, you've got to think about the market. You've got to play it safe.' "

He jingled his empty beer glass at the waitress. "I'm just a business-man, Scott. I never claimed to be smart."

"You couldn't have known."

"Well, I was certainly worried about 'Bitch Fiend,' " he admitted. "But only because I thought they wouldn't play it on the radio. I spent a lot of money getting those sample rights. You know how goddamn ex-pensive the Rolling Stones are?"

"He samples the Rolling Stones?"

The Judge eyed me like I just fell from space. "Yeah. 'Shattered.' You never heard the song?"

"I've heard 'Shattered.' "

"But you've never actually heard 'Bitch Fiend.' "

I smiled. "I've heard *of* it."

"Damn, Scott. Do yourself a favor. Do me a favor. Buy the CD."

Actually, now I planned to download the song off the Internet, but that wasn't the thing to tell him.

"I kept my word," he said somberly. "I let him do his second album his way."

"So is it good?"

"It's exceptional. It's revolutionary. Too bad it's not what he'll be re-membered for. Too bad it'll probably never even hit the shelves."

I finished my chicken and sat back. Although I was enjoying the lunch and the company, I was still only half there. The other half was thinking about Maxina. I had really pissed her off. It felt shamefully good at the time, but now I was worried. And more than half-worried. I may have just made a fatal mistake.

It was one of those meetings where I would have loved to have been a fly on the wall, instead of actually there. It was all bosh and bunkum, a bunch of skittish suits trying to enforce their own changes to the script so they felt like they had some control over this big-budget gamble. Most of their suggestions were laughably clueless. *Can you get Harmony to mention that she doesn't blame Universal? Can it be a popular song that inspires her to confess? Can't we end this today?*

I didn't have to be there. Neither did Simba. We were both empty garnishing. I was the token white man to appease the other white men. Simba was merely a visual representation of Hunta's faith in Maxina. This was news to Simba. She didn't enjoy being clip art either.

But we both looked pretty and kept our mouths shut. I only joined the din on three occasions; once to assert Alonso's loyalty and twice to challenge proposals that weren't in Hunta's best interests. I had at least a dozen opportunities to stand up for Harmony, but I dodged each and every one. I didn't want to add fuel to the gossip, especially in front of the Judge. If he didn't start the talk about me and Harmony, he certainly encouraged it.

I'll give the man credit, though. He did just as well as Maxina in defending my scheme, assuring his patrons that all the necessary precautions had been taken. Bottom line: we controlled Harmony. This story would end exactly the way we wanted it to.

"Yes, but *when?*" asked an Interscope man. "The longer this goes on—"

"I know. I know," Maxina replied with a heavy breath. "We're not talking weeks. We're not even talking *a* week. The plan is for her to confess on Monday."

She checked my reaction, which I buried a mile deep within me. Nothing would be gained by arguing with her. Not here. I smiled my way through the rest of the meeting. I listened. I waited. At 11:30, we finally dispersed. Simba practically left skid marks. The Judge walked his associates out. Maxina stayed to console the RIAA people. For me that meant more waiting and smiling. By a quarter to twelve, it was only the two of us in the cavernous room.

"I'm really sorry, Scott. If it were up to me, I would have kept them in the dark. But the last thing we want is for them to overreact and make premature concessions."

"That's fine."

"You don't look fine."

"That all depends," I said.

"On?"

"On whether or not you're serious about Monday."

With a pained groan, she sat back down in her seat. "I am."

"That's way too soon. I told you I needed a week."

"And I told you we'd wait to see how the press reacted before making any decisions. Sit down. You're giving me neck cramps."

I took a chair. "They reacted. They ate her up with a spoon. What did you expect?"

"I expected her to be news. I didn't expect her to be breaking news. There's a big difference. It makes the story much harder for us to control."

"I can't believe you're even surprised."

"Of course I'm surprised. In case you haven't noticed, Harmony is a black woman. A lower-class black woman. From the way they've already canonized her, she might as well be rich, blond, and dead."

"I told you this wasn't about race."

She chortled. "I'm sorry. I didn't take you as an authority on the matter."

"What exactly are you afraid of?"

"I'm afraid she'll get too strong for us to handle. I'm afraid that if she chooses not to confess—"

"She will."

"If she *doesn't,* a scratchy audio recording might not be enough to bring her down."

"And if she confesses on Monday," I countered, "it won't be enough to bring her back up. The public won't know her well enough to forgive her."

Maxina finally understood my concern. "Can't we speed up the process?"

"How? If we rush her, she'll look like a media whore. Nobody likes a media whore."

"They might not like her, but they'll forgive her."

"Are you willing to bet on that?" I asked. "Because if you're wrong, they'll ruin her life. She might even get prosecuted."

"Don't you think you're being a little dramatic?"

"Hey, *you* were the one who demanded I look out for her! *You* were the one who said that our plan had to be foolproof! And *you* were the one who threatened to be my—how did you put it?—my bane, my karma, my comeuppance, if I used her and threw her away like Kleenex! And yet that's exactly what you're asking me to do!"

My voice bounced off the walls, hitting her from all sides. She rested her fist against her lips.

"Look, when this is over, I will use every available resource to—"

"That's bullshit."

She paused. "Are you doubting my word?"

"No. I'm doubting your effectiveness. You may have powerful connections but your playbook needs to be euthanized."

Suddenly, the sun didn't feel so hot anymore. "Scott, I'm hoping to keep this civil."

"This is civil. And I'm telling you, in a civil tone, that Harmony will not be confessing on Monday. Or Tuesday. And probably not even Wednesday."

"Scott—"

"She will confess when I feel it's safe for her to confess, and not a minute sooner. I'm the one she trusts. If you go behind my back, she'll just bring it right to me. And if you try to undermine my authority with her, you'll only drive her away from both of us. You'll all but guarantee her defection. I know you're smarter than that."

"I thought you were smarter than this," she said with frozen ire.

"Apparently not, because I'm willing to risk my entire career in order to get this job done right. If I could offer you more collateral, I would. You're just going to have to trust me to do the right thing."

"I don't."

"Well, then you're in for a tough week."

With that, I stood up, turned around, and made the long trip to the door. My heart pounded. My kneecaps twitched. My stomach produced enough acid to melt a horse. But still, it was a moment of dark and primal victory, like beating up a biker gang. It felt great to be alive.

The Judge was waiting for me in the hallway, well out of earshot. He threw me a casual grin. He wasn't as dumb as I thought. Clearly he understood the importance of being my friend.

It was two o'clock, and we were still at Trader Vic's. The Judge had finished his sixth and last beer an hour ago and was waiting for his blood alcohol level to fall back below the DUI line. I was in a similar bind, except I was being held captive by two ten-ounce Zombies. I didn't expect them to be so strong. They were still eating my brains.

"Marvin Gaye," he uttered out of the blue. "Now there was a talented artist. I knew him."

"Really."

"Yup. Brilliant man. Troubled man. Died way before his time, just like Tupac. And just like Tupac, they milked his corpse for all it was worth. I was working at Columbia Records when they released his first posthumous album. This was the same year as the obscenity hearings, so the public was still very wary of the music industry. So what did my bosses do? They changed the name of one of his songs from 'Sanctified Pussy' to 'Sanctified Lady.' Chickenshit bastards."

"I have to be honest with you, Judge. I like the second one better."

"It's just a title, for God's sake. You could call it 'Kumbaya' and it wouldn't change the fact that the song is all about the joys of fucking a religious woman. Changing the name was like calling a gun a flower. Just call it what it is. Let Marvin be Marvin. But no. They had to mess with his art. They had to mess with his memory. And all because they were afraid of the few loud morons who judged a song by its title."

He leaned back and rested his hands on his belly. I wanted to pat his head for luck.

"You married, Scott?"

Humbly, I held up my unadorned left hand.

"So is there anyone special in your life?"

Had I been less sober or more forthcoming, I might have held up my other hand. Instead, I went for the big lie.

"I'm seeing someone."

"What does she think about all this shit going on?"

"Actually, she doesn't keep up with the news at all."

"She doesn't?"

"No. She doesn't even watch TV."

"That's weird. What is she, religious?" He raised his eyebrows. "Is she a sanctified lady?"

"No, no." I laughed. "She's deaf."

Sorry, Jean. This had absolutely nothing to do with you. I was just fighting a nasty rumor and you were the nearest available weapon.

But if Harmony made a good distraction from Annabelle Shane, Jean made a great distraction from Harmony. The Judge was fascinated. He barraged me with questions, some of them stupid enough to make me feel better about my own deaf-related ignorance. For others, I had to improvise my answers. *"Can she drive?"* Yes [but not well]. *"What if there's an ambulance coming?"* Well, um, there's a special device in her car that flashes [was there?]. *"Was she born deaf, or did she lose her hearing?"* She lost her hearing at a very early age [from what I gather]. *"How do you guys talk in bed?"* None of your damn business. [Don't know. Don't plan to find out].

At a quarter to three we finally left the restaurant. The Judge had paid for both of us and left a supremely generous tip. I waited with him at the valet area, even though I'd parked the Saturn myself.

"You know, I spent twelve years building up that label," he told me. "And the real irony is that up until last week, I got crap for *avoiding* controversy. It's true. I steered clear of all the real troublemaker talent. The ones who couldn't keep out of jail. The ones with strong gang affiliations. The ones who always picked beefs with other rappers. My artists are choirboys by comparison. You know how hard it is to market a roster of well-behaved rappers?"

"It's got to be hard," I said.

"It's hard. It's even harder to trust my livelihood to some smooth-talking publicist and his doe-eyed little victim."

"What do you want me to say?"

"I don't want you to say anything. I just want you to remember your loyalties, especially if it comes down to a choice between her well-being and ours."

His black Bentley arrived. He handed the valet a twenty and didn't ask for change.

"Her well-being is directly tied to yours," I said.

The Judge laughed. "Funny. That's just what I told her."

"I didn't like the way you said it."

"Too bad," he replied, grim-faced. "Because your well-being is directly tied to hers."

He got in his car and drove off. Pity our détente didn't outlast his buzz. Pity he'd talk to Maxina before I had a chance to set things right. I must have been doing something wrong, because there were more and more people being added to the conspiracy, but I didn't seem to be making any friends.

At three o'clock Andy Cronin's piece hit the newswire hard. The updates had been coming in fast and light all day, making pebble-sized splashes. But Andy hurled a two-ton boulder with his article: RAPE ACCUSER'S LIFE A STORY OF TURMOIL, ABUSE. In nine hundred words, he covered every nasty beat of Harmony's past, skillfully avoiding the cheap, theatrical embellishments that were all too common in journalism today. He left the emotion to his quoted sources: Harmony's former documentarians, her former social workers, and her current lawyer. They all gushed over her strength in the face of such monstrous adversity. Powerful stuff. I could just hear the collective "Jesus Christ" being uttered in every newsroom across the nation. Story-wise, ratings-wise, and otherwise, this woman was magnificent. She was a franchise unto herself.

Predictably, the media outlets strapped on Andy's piece like a jetpack and took off with it. I was stuck in construction traffic on Santa Monica Boulevard when a succinct but slightly jumbled version of Harmony's background hit me from the radio. I had to laugh, not at the announcer's mistakes (it was her stepfather who impregnated her, not her father) but at the sheer insanity of it all. It shouldn't be this easy. It shouldn't be this easy to manipulate the news.

By the time I got home, it was twenty after three. Once again, Madison was crouched outside my door, waiting.

Upon seeing me, she defensively raised her palms. "I'm fine. Seriously."

"I believe you."

I unlocked my apartment door. She eyed me through a mask of concern.

"How are you doing?"

"You're a sweetheart to ask, but I'm fine, too."

"You look a little stressed."

"Just busy."

She rose up. "Oh my God, Scott. I've been waiting all day to talk to you about Harmony Prince."

"Well, you're in luck," I said. "It's your turn."

I held the door open. She hustled inside. Thank God for Madison.

Her excitement was a perfect antidote to the Judge and Maxina. To the RIAA. Interscope. Universal. Simba. I could understand why they were all so scared. I could even understand why my assurances were always taken with twelve grains of salt. But the cloud of mistrust was starting to choke me. I had to take greater care in the future, or this giant new machine of mine would fall apart from the inside.

15

ARE YOU IMPRESSED YET?

This book is dedicated to Him. And her.

So read the new top sheet of my copy of *Godsend,* Alonso Lever's magniloquent sci-fi opus. I had fed the title page to the shredder, along with my discarded mail. I'd been shredding my mail for many years now, especially my financial statements. In this day and age, when everyone was worried about online security and electronic fraud, few seemed to realize that their trash bin—their physical trash bin—was an information warehouse for wily scavengers.

As for the title page, that was a Madison-related concern. She wasn't a crook, to my knowledge, but she did keep up with the news. I could just imagine her confusion upon finding in my possession an unpublished novel by the now-famous lawyer of our now-famous enemy. It wouldn't be a major crisis, but why face it at all?

Madison stood up and took a stretch break from her highlighting duties. As her arms rose, so did her T-shirt, exposing at least four inches of flat white stomach. I felt like a criminal just for noticing.

She spied the manuscript on top of the TV, studying it.

" 'This book is dedicated to Him. And her.' What the hell is this?"

I continued to navigate the Web from my couch, scanning the knee-jerk reactions to Andy Cronin's piece. "I have a friend who fancies himself a novelist. He gave me a copy to critique."

"Oh, a 'friend,' huh?"

I met her simper with a sneer. "If it was mine, I'd take credit for it."

"So who's 'Him'? God?"

"Most likely."

"And her?"

"No idea."

She skimmed the first few pages. "I have an urge to highlight all the adjectives."

I grinned. "Take a break."

"So is it good?"

"He probably shouldn't quit his day job."

"What's his day job?"

"Lawyer."

"Is he at least a good lawyer?"

"Yes," I said without hesitation. "He's a very good lawyer."

Alonso had only two full days to prepare for the media onslaught. Two days to fill a six-week-old case file with fake notes, fake phone logs, fake letters, what have you. He was playing the game on two levels: as a man who was genuinely representing Harmony Prince, and as a man who was genuinely fooled by Harmony Prince. He had to start building himself up as a dupe now. Once the confession hit, there'd be an immediate investigation, and he didn't have the cozy distance that I had.

Then there was his staff to deal with. They were used to assisting him in legal maneuvers that weren't entirely legal, but never on such a high-profile case. On Tuesday he made them all sign a new series of contracts, guaranteeing them each a five-figure bonus, payable at the end of the year and contingent on absolute media silence. What he didn't tell them was that the money would be part of an extended severance package. He didn't like deceiving his own crew, especially about their impending layoff, but he knew that lame-duck workers weren't the most loyal or efficient people to have around.

If that wasn't tricky enough, he had his personal life to worry about. He feared the press heat would spill over into his private affairs, so he scrambled like mad to tidy up. He didn't detail me on that part of the effort, but he did once mention that he was in a complicated relationship with a complicated woman, the circumstances of which, regrettably, had some story value. I figured she was either criminally young or famously married.

Doug's theory was a little more exotic. "I bet she's a he," he mused with a cackle. "I mean, come on. Look at Alonso. Can't you just picture him as the 'husband' to some high-heeled trannie?"

I wasn't so sure, but the fact that Alonso had split his novel's dedication between God and her suggested that the relationship was as serious as it was mysterious.

Media-wise, he had little to fear. The only woman he'd be associated with, now and forever, was Harmony Prince.

Since this morning, a phalanx of reporters had stationed themselves outside his office building. His firm received an average of seventy-five press calls an hour, not to mention an endless stream of faxes from talk-show producers begging him to book his client on their show. By 10:00 A.M. he had brought in a freelance publicist to establish order. She was a young and perky thing, and she didn't know any more than the public did, but she cracked the whip like a skilled dominatrix. Within the hour, the media folks were kissing her hard leather boot. The journalists were especially docile, only because they knew she was hand-picking the audience for the end-of-day press conference.

It was quite a show. At 5:20 the national news outlets and West Coast affiliates cut away to the Garden Room of the Fairmont Miramar. The place was packed with reporters, photographers, security guards, camera crews, and enough electronic equipment to fill a Best Buy. Every network had a different name for the event. On CNN it was the HUNTA ACCUSER: PRESS CONFERENCE. MSNBC billed it as ALLEGED HUNTA SEX ASSAULT VICTIM, ATTORNEY STATEMENT. KTLA 5, Los Angeles, presumed a little too much in their overlay by declaring that HUNTA'S RAPE ACCUSER SPEAKS. Although technically accurate (Harmony could indeed speak), it was a functional misnomer. She remained safely locked away in her tower suite.

"So where is she?" asked Madison, who had scooted up next to me on the couch.

"I doubt she'll be there."

"Why not?"

"Credibility," I replied. "A good victim wouldn't parade herself in front of the media. At least not right away. If her handlers are smart, we won't hear a peep out of her until next week."

"You sure?"

I shrugged. "That's what I would do."

To the abject disappointment of the press corps, Alonso made a solo entrance. He threw his guests a priggish little grin. *Sorry, people. This is only the first date. And we're not that easy.*

"Thank you for coming," he said into the microphones. "I have a statement from Miss Prince."

As the cameras flashed and popped, he retrieved a folded sheet of paper from his suit pocket. He looked a little too pleased for my comfort, but then again, so did I.

" 'I appreciate the concern and support that people have shown me in this trying time,' " he read. " 'And as much as I understand the public's need to learn more about me and my situation, I consider this a personal matter. I'm sure if you or someone you love was victimized, you wouldn't want it to become national news. So I ask the members of the press and the community at large to please respect my privacy and the privacy of my loved ones. I never asked to be abused. And I certainly never wanted to be famous for being abused. Thank you for your understanding.' "

Madison snorted. "That was so written by committee."

Actually, the committee was sitting right next to her, although Alonso did provide the "I never asked to be abused" part. He was afraid my speech lacked quotability. I regretted listening to him. The words were pure overkill, and worse, they were completely uncharacteristic of Harmony, who didn't have a self-pitying bone in her tight young body.

At the conference, the floor opened itself up to queries. One by one, Alonso took them on. This was always a tricky part of the game, like juggling knives. But the press was on our side. They wanted to believe Harmony. They just had to sell her to their audience, and for that, they needed more to go on.

If she was sexually assaulted, why didn't she go to the police?

"To put it mildly, Miss Prince does not have a lot of faith in the Los Angeles Police Department. Or the criminal justice system."

Would she cooperate if there was a police investigation?

"I won't speculate on that."

What evidence does she have to support her allegation?

"I will not discuss the particulars of the case."

Why did she withdraw her request for a temporary restraining order?

"I will not discuss the particulars of the case."

How much money are you asking for?

"We're still in prenegotiations. We haven't determined an amount yet."

Is Miss Prince upset that the Los Angeles Times *revealed her by name?*

"Absolutely. So am I. When I spoke to Ms. Steiner, I was led to believe that my client would remain anonymous. Obviously I was misinformed."

If you're so protective of your client's privacy, why did you cooperate with the Associated Press when they—

"By then the cat was already out of the bag, and there was no way to get it back in. The least I could do was make sure that Andrew Cronin got all his facts right, which he did."

So then it's true that she had miscarried—

"Look, I'm here on behalf of my client. I'm asking you, as she asked you, to keep a respectful distance. Miss Prince doesn't want to be an enticing headline. She doesn't want to be a ratings grabber. And she certainly doesn't want to be a tool in the public crusade against rap."

Are you saying that she doesn't have an issue with rap?

"I can't say. We never discussed it. I do know that she has an issue with Jeremy Sharpe, and it's not because of his music."

Alonso continued to parry, thrust, and dodge the questions for six more rounds before calling it a day. His responses—our responses—were nothing but sound and light. But they were quick, they were interesting, and they were easily repurposed. The press was satiated for now. As soon as Alonso thanked his audience, the networks kicked back and burped out commercials.

I looked to Madison. "So, what do you think?"

She squeezed her chin, chewing on her answer as if I were grading it. "I don't know. I mean to me the whole thing reeks of bullshit. But I might just be biased, working for Hunta and all."

"Back it up. Which part smells to you?"

"Well, for starters, there's the fact that the lawyer held a big press conference just to ask the press not to make a big deal out of this. I mean, come on."

I laughed. "That's just part of the game. Everyone knows it."

"I figured. But I still get the sense that . . . I don't know. This seems too well organized. The timing seems too perfect. The victim seems too perfect. It's kind of like with Britney Spears. Every time she moves, you can just feel this big corporate force around her, controlling every molecule of her existence."

From the TV, a Claymated chili pepper whistled at us, desperate for our attention. I muted the volume.

"So you feel this whole thing is a professionally engineered event."

"That's just the sense I get," she said unsteadily. "But maybe I'm just being cynical."

I rested against the arm of the couch, grinning like a proud . . . whatever I was to Madison. Boss. Mentor. Friend. None of those terms felt right. At the moment I had the strange but overwhelming desire for a more indelible connection. Cousin. Uncle. Father. I didn't care, as long as we were linked by blood. I wanted to share my DNA with her. I wanted to plunder her lineage, to steal her away like a Viking and make her one of my own. Knowing her, she'd come along willingly. Happily. If only it were possible. If only we could get away with it.

As odd as it was, the impulse didn't seem to have much do with Madison herself, just like this morning's quasi-sexual twinge had little to do with Harmony. I was still hypercharged from the day's events, feeling potent and virile. Why wouldn't I? I had just brought the Bitch to a screaming climax. I'd left her moaning for more. There was no greater thrill, but that didn't stop my id from looking. There must be other worlds to conquer. There must be other precious treasures, forbidden pleasures, to seize with my very own hands.

"So what do you think?" she asked.

"I think you're right. I think this is a supremely organized effort by a bunch of people we're not seeing."

"But why? What would they get out of it?"

"I don't know. There are a lot of powerful conservatives out there who see rap as nothing more than black culture infecting white teenagers. Obviously, they'll do whatever they can to limit its influence, but the only way to break through the First Amendment wall is with continued public outrage."

"God."

"I'm just speculating," I disclaimed. "I truly don't know."

"But don't people find the timing suspicious? I mean this woman is accusing Hunta of rape one week after the whole Melrose thing."

"Actually, that's not true. She filed for a restraining order over a month ago. That's what's killing us here."

"Can't that stuff be faked? You know, backdated or something?"

I smiled at her. "Not without the help of the Mean World lawyers."

"Well, maybe the label's in on it too."

"Why?"

"I don't know. To sell more albums."

"This isn't a marketing stunt. Trust me."

"Well then what the hell is it?"

From my bedroom, my red phone rang. I tousled Madison's soft, light hair, then started up the steps, throwing her a shrug and a lie along the way.

"When I find out, you'll be the first to know."

Some people had a natural charm that exuded from them effortlessly, like a rainbow. Harmony was one of those people. Alonso was not. His charisma was synthetic and boldly conspicuous, like a neon sign. But he had a winking self-awareness about it that made him endearingly campy. And I had to give him points for consistency. He kept his sign lit twenty-four hours a day. Always bright. Always colorful.

Well, not always. Just as my force field occasionally sputtered, so did Alonso's glow. When he called me at a quarter to six, the lights were cold and dark.

"Scott, do you mind telling me what the hell's going on?"

I closed the bedroom door. "What's the matter? I thought it went fine."

"I'm not talking about the press conference. I'm talking about Maxina."

Ah, shit. This couldn't be good. "Where are you?"

"In the stairwell, working my way up to Harmony's room."

"Something wrong with the elevators?"

"I'm venting excess energy."

"So what did she say to you?"

"Maxina? She said—she *decreed* that I was to bring Harmony onto *Larry King Live* tomorrow."

"Tomorrow?!"

"Her orders."

"No. No way. Absolutely not."

He clopped harder. "See? I knew you would say that! Who's running this show, you or her? I mean, how do you people expect me to function under conflicting directives?"

My gut told me it wasn't a directive at all. More like a test. Maxina and I had a big split this morning, and now she wanted to see which way Alonso would jump. She was in for a disappointment.

"It's too soon," I said. "Harmony just got done telling the media to leave her alone. If she shows up on *Larry King* the very next day, she'll have no credibility."

"As it stands, I agree with you. But I'll ask again—"

"I am. I'm in charge of this side of the effort and I'm saying no. It's not happening."

We both paused for a long, deep breath. I spent the time looking out the western window. The sun was almost gone, painting the sky in dazzling purple ribbons. Filmmakers call this the magic hour, for very good reason. Los Angeles had its faults, but it gave great twilight.

As the lampposts flickered on, so did Alonso. I could hear the bright hue come back to his voice.

"Ah, bureaucracy," he said, continuing his climb. "This is why I never liked working at the big firms."

"Same here."

"Still, I can understand why they're all so panicked. Between you, me, and our lovely Miss Prince, we could do quite some damage."

"But we won't."

"I wasn't suggesting we should," he stressed. "Quite the opposite. I think we—'we' meaning you—should throw Maxina some kind of bone. We don't want her making secret moves against us."

I couldn't shake the feeling that she already was, but Alonso had a good point.

"Have your girl call Larry King's people," I said. "Tell them you'll do Monday's show. Assure them it's still an exclusive, but they can't announce it until noon that day."

"Eastern?"

"Pacific. We're only giving them six hours to plug her. Make them understand that if they jump the gun, even by a minute, you're canceling the appearance and freezing out the whole network."

He chuckled amicably.

"What?"

"Nothing," he said. "I'm just not accustomed to having this much leverage."

I smiled. "Same here."

"Will you be calling Maxina?"

I watched the street as a black SUV was approaching my building. I recognized the dented grille.

"No," I replied. "She'll be calling me."

By the time I got off the phone, Alonso had reached the top floor. Jean had reached my front curb. The sun was gone. The moon was hiding. There was nothing left but artificial light.

On my way downstairs, I got another bird's-eye view of Madison's work. Once again, her news clippings were littered with orange words: pinprick stabs at Hunta that were tiny enough to preserve the illusion of objectivity. The supportive green words, by contrast, were as rare as four-leaf clovers. But there was encouragement to be found in the pink. The mentions of Annabelle Shane were a mere fraction of what they were yesterday. There would be even less tomorrow. By next week the Melrose demon would be all but vanquished. I wasn't just a publicist anymore. I was an exorcist. And my elaborate ritual was working. Can't you see it, Maxina? Can't you see it working?

Madison looked up from her notepad. "Oh. I was just leaving you a message."

"I'm here."

"So's my mom."

"I saw."

"Do you need me to stay late tomorrow? I can."

"I don't think there's a need."

She lowered her voice, as if her mother were somehow listening. "Or I could come early. I mean, my afternoon classes are a joke."

I patted her back. "As I much as I appreciate your willingness to sacrifice both school and family . . ."

She sneered at me. "Shut up. Look, I know how big this is. I just want to help."

"You are," I said earnestly. "You're an amazing help."

"But I want to do *more* for you."

"You will. You will. Trust me."

Actually, I had no idea what I was alluding to. Drea had me marking up newspapers for weeks, until I was highlighting by sight and by reflex. I still see colored words every time I read. It's not a bad power to have, but it does keep me from enjoying a good novel. I always end up reading the author instead of the story.

Slinging her book bag over her shoulder, Madison made her way to the door.

"Oh, wait," I said, fumbling over the top of my wall unit. "I want to give you something."

She stopped and turned around. "It's not a comic book, is it?"

"No. It's for you."

I retrieved a small, dusty key ring and tossed it to her. "The smaller one's for the apartment. The other one's for the building, although you always seem to get past that door."

From her face, you'd think I was on my knees, proposing. "Oh, wow. Scott."

"It's no big deal. I just don't want you waiting in the hallway anymore."

"So then if you're not here tomorrow—"

"Knock. If I don't answer, come in. Log on to my laptop. Start printing articles. Easy, right?"

"Wow. I really appreciate this."

"Listen, those keys only exist on weekday afternoons. You understand what I'm saying? I don't want to come home on a Saturday night to find you here, hiding out from your family."

"You won't!"

"This isn't your new airport."

She clenched her hands together, drowning me in the kind of life-or-death intensity that makes adults so scared of teenagers.

"Scott, I swear to God I won't abuse your trust. I would never do anything to jeopardize our relationship. You are—" She cut herself off, waving her open hands. "Whatever. I'll do anything you say."

Outside, Jean remained in her SUV, patient and silent. It really wasn't fair, was it? She had carried Madison for nine months and thirteen years. She made every sacrifice. And yet I was the one with all the power and influence over her precious little girl. I had more power than I knew what to do with. A lesser woman would have hated me for it. A lesser man would have given her a reason.

So I couldn't help but notice, typed Jean, *my daughter's two new keys.*

Yeah, that was me, I typed back, less assuredly. *Why? Did I screw up?*

We were done with e-mail word games. We were even done with e-mail. On Wednesday night Jean had introduced me to EyeTalk, a freeware application that allowed Internet users to communicate one-on-one in real time. Just minutes after registering myself with a user name and password, I had Jean at my virtual doorstep. I'd accepted her chat request, just to try out the software, but I was too jazzed up to be much of a conversationalist. All I could think about was Harmony's impending fame.

Never one to be discouraged, Jean buzzed me again on Thursday, two hours after picking up Madison. This time she only had *Friends* competing for my attention. I turned off the TV and let her into my laptop. It wasn't long before she brought up the key thing.

\<jeanx\>	You didn't screw up at all. I'm just glad to see things going well on both ends.
\<ssinger\>	What do you mean both ends?
\<jeanx\>	I mean I knew _she_ was happy with the arrangement...
\<ssinger\>	So am I. I told you everything was fine.
\<jeanx\>	Well of course you'd say that to me. I'm her mother.
\<ssinger\>	Ah. I get it now.
\<jeanx\>	Right. Keys don't lie. Unless they're somehow misengraved.
\<ssinger\>	She's a great kid.
\<jeanx\>	I always thought so.
\<ssinger\>	She's definitely got your smarts.
\<jeanx\>	No. Her father's the one who passed down the brains. I gave her volatility.
\<ssinger\>	But she's been doing okay recently, right?
\<jeanx\>	Yeah. For the most part.
\<ssinger\>	What do you mean?

Now that we were linked up live, I could see her pause. Her cursor blinked steadily for a few silent moments, then

\<jeanx\>	You know what? This is the exact reason why she doesn't like me talking to you. She has a point too. After all, I'm her mom. You're her boss.
\<ssinger\>	True.
\<jeanx\>	And she takes her job very, VERY seriously.
\<ssinger\>	I noticed.
\<jeanx\>	Nobody wants their mom dishing dirt to their boss.
\<ssinger\>	Forget I asked.
\<jeanx\>	Forget I hinted.
\<ssinger\>	Forgotten.
\<jeanx\>	Shit.
\<ssinger\>	What?
\<jeanx\>	Now I'm afraid that in the absence of information,

you're going to assume the worst about what I was
                            going to say.

<ssinger>   [blinks stupidly]

<jeanx>   She really is a great kid.

<ssinger>   I know!

<jeanx>   A lot less trouble than I was at her age.

<ssinger>   You were a problem child?

<jeanx>   I used to cut my arms and legs with razors.

<ssinger>   Eeuu.

<jeanx>   I was the youngest in a mob of blue-blooded Virginia
                            Catholics. They were all dumb as posts. I was just
                            deaf as one. I might as well have turned Iranian.

<ssinger>   Nobody else in your family was deaf?

<jeanx>   Nobody else in my life was deaf.

<ssinger>   Yeesh.

<jeanx>   Yeah. My folks didn't know what to do with me. I was
                            like the toaster they just couldn't fix. Though they
                            did attempt to make me as passingly functional as
                            possible. They took me to otologists, audiologists,
                            speech pathologists, child psychologists...

<ssinger>   Speech pathologists? As in talking?

<jeanx>   There was indeed a time when I, under strict duress,
                            attempted to squeeze words out through my throat. It
                            was about as easy as farting a sonnet. Gave it up real
                            fast, I did.

<ssinger>   Your family never learned sign language?

<jeanx>   No. Neither did I. Not until I was 16. Not until the
                            Great Professor came along.

<ssinger>   You met your husband when you were 16?

<jeanx>   Yah. One of the frustrated psychologists called him in
                            to help me. He drove from DC every night, ninety
                            minutes each way.

<ssinger>   That was nice of him.

<jeanx>   Sure. He opened my mind. My heart. My legs.

<ssinger>   At 16?!

<jeanx>   Well, I wasn't exactly passive in the process.

<ssinger>   Yeah but you were 16!

<jeanx>   Didn't you say you had shacked up with a much older
                            woman?

```
<ssinger>    Not until I was 21.
<jeanx>      Well, I was a mature 16. And as much as I loathe the
             man now, he was my saving grace at the time. If it
             wasn't for him, I would have killed myself.
             Eventually. Probably.
<ssinger>    Wow.
<jeanx>      But instead I ran off with him to Gallaudet and never
             looked back. Best move of my life. By 21, I was a
             completely different person. I was married. I was
             signing like a pro. I had friends. I had pride. And to
             top it all, I had Madison. My sweet little angel. I
             carried her through the whole Gallaudet revolution.
<ssinger>    The who to the what now?
<jeanx>      The "Deaf President Now!" protest. March 1988. It
             was the biggest Deaf uprising in history. We shut the
             whole campus down. You never heard about it?
             It made world news.
<ssinger>    It's not ringing a bell.
<jeanx>      It was a school for the Deaf but it never had a Deaf
             president. So we fought. We won. It was historic. For
             us, anyway.
<ssinger>    Wow. My ignorance is staggering.
<jeanx>      You're not that bad.
<ssinger>    Really? I feel like ever since I met you, I've made
             every stupid mistake in the book.
<jeanx>      What book?
<ssinger>    I don't know. Is there a book to help me become less
             ignorant about deaf issues?
<jeanx>      Like what? "The Complete Idiot's Guide to Dummies"?
<ssinger>    Oof! Ouch! See, now if _I_ made that joke...
<jeanx>      You'd be in a lot of trouble, mister.
<ssinger>    I've been fighting the urge to ask you stupid
             questions.
<jeanx>      Oh, just ask them. Everyone else does.
<ssinger>    How'd you lose your hearing?
<jeanx>      Explosion at a chemical plant. It left me deaf but it
             heightened my other senses to a superhuman degree.
<ssinger>    I don't think so.
<jeanx>      Fine. Spinal meningitis. I got it when I was two.
```

```
<ssinger>   So you're 100% deaf.
<jeanx>     90% in the left ear. 95% in the right. I still get
            certain frequencies a little. I can always hear when
            the TV is on. It gives off this faint, high-pitched
            squeal.
<ssinger>   That's just the truth being tortured.
<jeanx>     Jesus. Did I just give you my whole life story?
<ssinger>   Only the first few chapters.
<jeanx>     Okay. So what's your origin?
<ssinger>   My origin?
<jeanx>     Yeah. How'd you get to be you?
<ssinger>   I was bitten by a radioactive asshole.
<jeanx>     You're not an asshole.
<ssinger>   No, but I have the proportionate strength and speed of
            one.
<jeanx>     . o O (This man is not very forthcoming.)
<ssinger>   Actually, I have no idea how I got to be me. I've
            lived a life virtually free of
```

Next to the laptop, my red phone rang. I figured it was either Maxina or Harmony. Unfortunately, both of them trumped Jean on my priority scale.

"Hello?"

"Hey, baby."

"Harmony! What's the poop? What's the scoop? What's the rumpus?"

She laughed. "Damn. What's with you?"

"I was just about to call you."

```
<jeanx>     You've lived a life virtually free of...?
<ssinger>   I've got to go.
<jeanx>     Already?!
<ssinger>   Work beckons.
<jeanx>     Oh come on. I'm enjoying this.
<ssinger>   So am I, but work beckons.
```

"Are you typing something?"

"Just finishing up a correspondence," I said. "Talk to me. How you feeling?"

"Full. I ordered up a huge dinner."

"Yeah? What'd you get?"

"Chicken-fried steak. Black-eyed peas. Country green beans."

"Mmm. Southern."

```
<jeanx>      Mr. Singer, you are leaving me unsatisfied.
<ssinger>    You're not the first.
<jeanx>      And you won't even stay to snuggle.
<ssinger>    Bye.
<jeanx>      Wait! What did you live a life virtually free of?!
<ssinger>    Adversity. Bye.
```

I signed off, closed the laptop, and then stretched out on the couch.

"So. Your new boyfriends still in the room?"

Harmony laughed. "Shut up. It ain't like that and you know it."

Before he left the Miramar this morning, Alonso had stationed a private security crew outside her suite. Harmony was quick to establish an open-door policy with her new protectors. The first watch, Anthony and Chuck, spent all day in her room: playing Nintendo, watching movies, and generally talking up a storm. By midafternoon they were unburdening their deepest woes. Anthony was having serious communication problems with his long-term squeeze, and Chuck was so busy working off his debt load that he didn't have the time or energy to meet people.

Harmony, of course, played the veteran hostess—listening, empathizing, doing whatever it took to make them feel good (within reason). In this case, distraction was her reward. It wasn't easy to think about the outside world, especially when the outside world was thinking about her. What better way to escape than into the hearts and minds of others? If only everyone handled their stress as constructively as she did.

"I'm glad they around," she added. "I never had this much space to myself before."

"I'm sure those guys fill up space."

"Actually, none of them are all that big. Not like Hunta's guy."

"Yeah. He's a house."

"How's he doing, anyway?"

"Big Bank?"

"You know who I'm talking about."

My smile tapered off. "Let's just say he's in good spirits. And substances."

"Yeah. I'd probably fry my brains too if I was in his shoes. Poor guy."

"Sweetheart, I guarantee that everyone will be kissing his ass next week."

"Yeah? And what about me?"

"You can kiss his ass if you want."

"You know what I'm talking about!" She laughed. "Man, you are acting strange tonight."

"I know. I'm in a nutty mood."

"It's been a nutty day."

"Have you been watching TV at all?"

"I keep trying," she said, "and I keep turning it off. It's just too much for me. Either they trash Hunta, which makes me feel bad, or they talk about all the shit from my past, which makes me feel worse. And still none of it seem real to me."

"Don't worry. It's all going to slow down to a more comfortable speed."

"That ain't what Maxina told me."

Of course not. I wasn't the least bit surprised that Maxina had called. But it still made me nervous. It shouldn't have. I knew she was only doing with Harmony what she'd done with Alonso. Poking. Prodding. Sniffing for an ulterior agenda. I didn't plant one. I didn't have one. So then why did I feel so edgy? Why did it feel like a Wal-Mart just opened up across the street from my general store?

"When did you talk to her?"

"This afternoon. She said it's only gonna get crazier from here. Today it's just the media reacting. Tomorrow it's both the media and the public."

"That's not exactly—I mean, yes. She's right. But she was talking about the uproar against rap itself. Not the situation with you and Hunta."

"No, she said specifically the situation with me and Hunta."

Goddamn it, Maxina. We're in the same rubber raft and you're throwing darts.

"Listen, Harmony, Maxina is . . . She's an amazing woman. She's a very accomplished woman. But this kind of operation is outside her field of expertise. That's why she called me in."

"I know."

"She's just a little anxious, that's all. Not for you. Not for Hunta. She

knows you'll both be okay. She's just worried about the long-term effects on the music industry."

"She said all that."

"Really?"

"Yeah, like word for word."

"Oh."

She giggled. "That's it. You ain't Scott! Put Scott on!"

"I'm here," I said weakly. "It's me."

"What's going on in that big bad brain of yours?"

In other words, talk to me. Distract me. Let me in. My big bad brain
told me to proceed very carefully. I didn't want to flood her with my
own neuroses. I was her anchor. I had to look sturdy, for her sake and
mine. Yet at the same time, there was Maxina, setting up shop on Harmony Drive. In order to stay competitive, I had to offer up something.

For a moment I considered playing the Jean card, like I did with the
Judge. That would certainly occupy Harmony's mind, but as far as lies
went, that one was a bramble patch. Sooner or later, I'd get tangled up.
For now I'd just have to skate by on controlled honesty.

"If it wasn't such a white question," I quipped, "you'd probably ask
me about *my* big dream."

She chuckled. "Okay. Pretend I'm white. What's your big dream?"

"This."

"You mean me?"

"I mean this. You. Hunta. The whole story."

"Why?"

I stared up at the ceiling. "I don't know. Everyone wants to make
their mark. It's just a matter of how. Hunta has his music. Alonso has his
novel. You have your children's books. I've got this."

"Yeah, but we put our names on our shit. You don't get credit for
yours."

"So?"

"So don't you want people to know it was you?"

"I know it was me."

"And that's enough for you?"

"I don't care about impressing others," I bragged. "Just me."

Her voice took on a teasing lilt. "So are you impressed yet?"

"Yeah," I admitted, a little too readily. "I'm pretty impressed."

"That's dangerous, Scott."

"I didn't say I was cocky."

"I didn't say that, either. I'm just worried about you tempting fate. And I wouldn't worry so much about that except when you tempt fate, you tempt *my* fate."

Harmony had this simple, bungling, but ultimately airtight way of phrasing things. She drove her point right into me. I sat up on the couch and sighed.

"Damn," she said. "I'm sorry. I didn't mean to bring you down."

"No. You didn't. I just wish you were up here with me."

I could almost see the thoughtful look on her face, the pensive way she held herself in that giant bed. She wore her guilt and fear like a heavy cloak, but I could feel her trying to escape.

"You know, I spent over a year in that convalescent hospital," she told me. "After the police car hit me. It was just me and a bunch of old people. Really old. They were all messing themselves, forgetting where they at, dying left and right. It was depressing as hell. What was even worse was that none of them had any family, so as soon as they died, they became city property. They'd go straight to the city morgue, get burned up in the city oven, and then have the ashes hauled off to the city dump. I was thinking about that the night I met you. When I said okay to your crazy plan, I was thinking how I don't want to go like that."

I smiled. "You want to make your mark."

"I want to make my mark."

"You want to make your presence known."

"I definitely want to make my presence known."

"You want to raise the roof."

She laughed. "Yeah."

"Raise the roof!" I yelled.

"Yeah, raise the roof!" she yelled back.

"Well, what do you think we're doing? We're raising the roof!"

"I know!"

"So enjoy it!"

"I will."

"Enjoy it!"

"I will!"

She was more amused than infused, but I had reached her. I'd lifted her up just a little bit.

I, on the other hand, was bursting with wild energy again. And fierce desires. This morning's twinge was back in full force, except now I found myself melding the fantasy to reality. I planned out the logistics of my gratification as if it were a jewel heist. The hotel was crawling with journalists, many of whom knew me, but I could sneak past them. I could work my way into the tower, all the way up to Harmony's suite, all the way to her giant bed. Her abstinence was the final lock but even that could be overcome. Consciously or not, I'd been chipping away at her defenses from the very beginning. A few more taps of the hammer and I'd be in. The seduction would be complete.

It was a dangerous thought, a conceited one at that, but my higher functions chased it away. For the first time I could see the edge of the cliff that so many influential men had driven off. All the evangelists and politicians. Actors and athletes. Singers and rappers. With extraordinary success came a sense of sexual empowerment, entitlement, plus the ability to rationalize even the basest of urges. I could do it. I could have it. I could get away with it. It's not a crime anyway. She wants it. Nobody will tell. Nobody will know. Nobody will care. I've worked hard. I deserve it. I should do it.

So many men have fallen into that trap. So many crises have come out of it. I was smart enough to stop where I was. I'd only tempt fate so much.

"I will," Harmony repeated. "I'm gonna enjoy it from now on."

"Good," I said, back to my old cautious self. "As long as you don't look like you're enjoying it."

———

In his opening monologue, Jay Leno joked that investing in stocks now was about as smart as leaving your daughter alone with Hunta. When guest Cameron Diaz referred to her boyfriend as frisky, David Letterman quickly followed up with "You mean like cat frisky, or Hunta frisky?" On *Politically Incorrect,* Bill Maher and his guest panel spent eight minutes discussing the new allegations. The most generous sentiment came from veteran rapper LL Cool J, who claimed it was ridiculous that the deplorable actions of one man were being held up against the entire music industry.

I guess it wasn't right to celebrate when the man I was hired to save was still drowning in the river. From his point of view, all I'd done was heat up the water. Despite my assurances to Harmony, I had no idea how he was doing. I never once tried to call him. It was callous and cowardly of me, but then what could I say that I hadn't said a thousand times before? What new assurances could I possibly give him? I was all out of words. I felt the urgent need to do something, anything, if only to remind myself that I was still on his side.

At half past midnight I opened up the laptop, created a new account through Yahoo! Mail, and composed a quick note. The message was, like the recipient, short and explosive.

```
Harmony Prince is lying.
```

From the very beginning, I knew I'd be portioning out Harmony to three different journalists. Andy Cronin got her past. Gail Steiner got her present. And now, with a click of the button, Miranda Cameron-Donnell just got her future. Well, a hint of it. This was a gift that came in installments. The final piece would be the big prize: the confession. There was no real strategy in saving the best for Miranda. Truth be told, I simply owed her a climax.

The moment I sent the e-mail, my guilt spun like a compass needle from Hunta to Harmony. That was exactly how the media's rage was going to flip. God, let them forgive her. Let her forgive me. Let the story end right. And since I'm here on my knees, Lord, let the writer get away, alive and uncredited.

16
SLICK'S WOMAN

The Bitch was always talking, but she only spoke in numbers. As the nation went to bed, the data from five thousand Nielsen boxes were parsed and tabulated, translated from raw digits to industry language. On Friday morning the trades spelled it out in common tongue: Harmony Prince was a hit. The people—at least those with Nielsen boxes—had taken her into their homes and kept her there.

That was all the affirmation the networks needed to pick her up for a full order. The morning telecasts changed their over-the-shoulder box graphics to incorporate Harmony's image, usually the one from the Polaroid. Her written statement to the press was chopped up and spit out so often, you'd think "I never asked to be abused" was her personal catchphrase. And in the headlines and readers, the teasers and bumpers, she was no longer introduced as the "Hunta accuser" or the "alleged Hunta victim." She was simply Harmony Prince. Her tale was eponymous now. Her name was laser-burned onto the cultural landscape.

And the story grew. It seemed that everyone wanted to add to the script, just to score some quick prominence. Witnesses at the Christmas party ("I saw them dancing up close. He was all over her. She didn't seem to like it"). Her former cohostesses ("She told me what happened the next day. She was a mess. I said, 'Girl, get a lawyer' "). Even her roommates supported the story. The most genuine and compelling statement came from Tracy Wood. She was a squat and unattractive woman, but her tears fell like bombs. "She never told me," she cried to the camera. "She never said a word. But she wouldn't lie about something like that. Even for money. She's . . . she's the best person I know."

That clip, which played several times on CNN, sent Harmony into her own wailing fit. Still, her guilt was all internal. Nobody else faulted her.

Hunta, by contrast, was an enemy of the people. The unattributed details that had sprung up overnight were pointed and cruel. He threatened to kill Harmony. He tried to kill her. He sodomized her with a beer bottle. He tied her up. He smacked her down. And, of course, he videotaped the whole thing. That was the rumor that just wouldn't die. It was UPI that reported, through anonymous sources, that Hunta liked to plant a Panasonic digital minicam at the scene of his sexual encounters. At the end of the article, a Los Angeles police detective claimed that if Miss Prince had only come to them, they could have seized the damning footage, which by now had surely been erased or destroyed.

The drama was getting bigger, stronger, and meaner by the minute. By next week it would be absolutely feral. I didn't expect the attacks to get so vicious, so soon. I had assumed that in the spirit of political correctness, the media would keep themselves to body blows. Apparently, I miscalculated. Apparently, there were psychological forces at work here beyond the drive for profit.

If there's one thing I learned in my many years in the field, Maxina had said, *it's that the press always finds a way to make the black man the bad guy.*

No. Sorry. I worked in the same field and I still couldn't subscribe to that, not when the airwaves were seeping with hypertolerance to the point of condescension. I wagered this had more to do with our sexual neuroses. We could handle a man who looked like a young god, but not a man who looked like he *fucked* like a young god. That pushed some serious buttons with us, both men and women. It made us uncomfortably jealous, aroused, insecure, or just plain wanting. Watching Hunta squirm, especially at the hands of such a sweet and virginal young beauty, was like aloe for the mind. It was balance. It was justice. I was providing cheap relief to millions of people. That didn't make me feel good, considering how easily I could relate.

Whatever it was, it was moving too far, too fast. From now on I'd be putting all my strength into the hand brake. I'd be working against my very own momentum. Already I could feel the resistance.

"What in God's name are you talking about?" yelled Alonso from his speeding Audi. He had just graced CNN's *Burden of Proof* with his appearance (via satellite) and was feeling mighty smug after getting the last word on Greta Van Susteren.

I cradled the phone as I worked on my laptop. "I just need one of your staff members to talk to Miranda Cameron-Donnell. On the record, but anonymously."

"Why?"

"So they can voice their suspicions that Harmony isn't on the level."

"Meaning I'm not on the level."

"No. Their story is that they initially shared their concerns with you, but you dismissed them."

"Why?!"

"Because you believe in her."

"No, I mean why do this at all?"

I gathered all my personal electronic files into one folder, then set an encryption lock. Madison was a great kid, but a kid nonetheless. I didn't want her snooping in my absence. On a whim, I also deleted the many e-mail messages between me and her mother. God knows why. It was all nerd talk and word games.

"We need to start planting a few seeds of doubt," I told him. "We have to set the stage for Harmony's confession."

"That's your reason for risking my credibility? You want to *fore-shadow*?"

"I just don't want her confession to come completely out of the blue."

"It could come out of the blue, red, or pink!" he snapped. "The media won't care because it'll make good copy, and the viewers won't care because they're idiots. What you're proposing is great risk for no gain. And considering that it's my risk, I won't do it."

I got up from the couch. "You're not seeing the big picture."

"Actually, I am. You're the one who's dabbling at the canvas like you're Renoir. This is not a work of art, Scott. This is not an epic drama. It's a media campaign. Get a grip."

Damn. Alonso sure had his Wheaties this morning. Was he right? Was I being an artistic perfectionist? Or was I merely being thorough? I let the issue drop, but when I asked him to publicly dispel the rumor about Hunta filming the incident in Room 1215, he refused, on the grounds that it would be out of character.

And still the story grew.

At noon the Hunta contingent released their first official response to Harmony. Doug avoided the traditional press conference in the way that most of us would avoid a traditional caning. His faxed missive, though blandly worded, was clear in tone:

Mr. Sharpe, his wife, and his supporters at Mean World Records categorically refute the allegations of Harmony Prince. Her charges are completely without merit, and we intend to fight them to the end. We are confident that the truth will ultimately prevail, and that Mr. Sharpe will be vindicated.

The press delivered the message verbatim, but with a cynical sneer. The headlines on the news sites varied from the insidious (HUNTA DENIES SEX CRIMES) to the insane (BITCH FIEND RAPPER SWEARS VINDICATION). I made a mental note to buy a new orange highlighter.

At one o'clock another woman came forward to claim abuse. Fox News broke the story of Mary Austen, a twenty-five-year-old dancer-cum-flight-attendant who'd dated Hunta back in 1998. In a four-minute segment, she confirmed the public's worst suspicions. He was into the rough stuff. He told her he liked his women to scream. He left her with numerous bruises and contusions. Eventually, it got to be too much for her, so she left. He harassed her so many times following the breakup that she considered getting a restraining order.

Mary was so full of shit, you could see the stink lines. She had the veracity of an infomercial, with her glossy lips, her neon fingernails, and her dark, desperate eyes that begged for acceptance. She was an empty plastic shell. I found her tragic, all right, but not in any interesting or admirable way. Most of the press agreed. Ultimately, she, like the rest of the knockoffs, would orbit Planet Harmony a couple of times before being cast back into the void.

At two o'clock the National Academy of Recording Arts and Sciences officially canceled Hunta's performance at the upcoming Grammy Awards. "We're not making any moral judgments," said NARAS president Michael Greene. "We're not saying he's guilty. We just don't want the Grammys to be overshadowed by this kind of controversy."

Words to live by. What really happened was that a vocal family council pushed the Grammy advertisers to push CBS to push Greene to dump Hunta like a bad enchilada. The process began on Monday, right after the world learned of the "Bitch Fiend" sex tape. To his credit, Greene initially told CBS to tell the advertisers to tell the family council to go fuck themselves, but that was back in the beginning of the week, when Hunta was only the center of a First Amendment debate. That was the good kind of controversy, the kind that brought in young viewers. Once Harmony exploded on the scene, however, toodle-oo. Last night, Greene had warned the Judge of his new resolve in the hope that he could persuade him into persuading Hunta into canceling his own performance. But Hunta, on a strict diet of pot and righteous indignation, told the Judge to tell Greene to go blow a schnauzer.

And still the story grew. At three o'clock the Los Angeles Police Department officially began an investigation into the sexual assault of Harmony Prince. That was when Madison arrived at my home with a smile usually reserved for game-show winners. Her excitement was justified. At that moment she was the only person on earth who had good news for Hunta.

———

"So Slick finally hollas," said the rapper, from his hideout. "Thought maybe you forgot about me."

I paced my bedroom floor. "That would be difficult."

"Really? All my friends did it. All my brothers in the hip-hop community. L-Ron. Hitchy. All the motherfuckers who hung out with me before. They all acting like I don't exist now. My agent ain't even calling me."

"I'm calling you."

"Aw. That's very sweet of you. Taking time away from Harmony to talk to me and shit."

Sigh. "I'm not spending any time with Harmony."

"Well then I guess it's that deaf woman of yours who's been keeping you busy."

Christ. Lies traveled fast. "I see you talked to the Judge."

"I heard it from Doug." He laughed. "When he first told me, I thought he meant 'def,' as in 'D-E-F'. I was like 'Shit, man, only Russell Simmons still uses that word. Just say she's fine.' "

I smiled uncomfortably. "She is pretty fine."

"What the fuck you doing to me, man?"

"I'm saving your ass. You just don't know it yet."

"The cops want to talk to me now."

"It's just for show. They know they can't nail you without Harmony's cooperation, and they know they'll never get it."

"Yeah? What about Mary Austen?"

"She's nothing," I assured him. "She's filler."

"She's lying! I didn't do none of that shit to her! All I did was dump her ass for Simba! Then the bitch got all psycho on me! *I'm* the one who almost got the court order. I ain't lying! Ask Doug!"

"Look, I believe you. And so do—"

"And what's this shit about the Panasonic? I don't even own a camera!"

"It's crap. I know."

"Yeah, but who's planting that, man? How does that shit get started?"

"I'm sorry. What kind of camera was it?"

"Panason—" He caught my drift. "Oh, get the fuck out of here. No way."

"I don't know for sure. But it wouldn't surprise me if one of their marketing people saw the opportunity and took it."

"No way! No fucking way!"

"It's just the business."

"Yeah, well the business is fucked up! I mean I thought the music industry was bad, but that business—*your* business—is straight from hell, man. Fucking flacks."

"Hey, you know 'flack' and 'rap' are just two words for 'blame.' "

The line was silent.

"You know, you *catch* the flack. You *take* the rap . . ."

"What the goddamn hell are you talking about?"

"Look, Hunta, the important thing is that the kids are still behind you. Your fans—"

"Bullshit."

I opened the door. My client didn't seem to have any direct concerns about Harmony, so I figured it was safe to include Madison. As I traipsed down the stairs, she watched me eagerly from the edge of the couch. She knew damn well who I was talking to.

"It's not bullshit. My assistant—"

"You got an assistant?"

Madison beamed at a thousand watts. I sat down next to her, poking her thigh.

"I've got a lovely young assistant," I said. "She's very good. On her own initiative, she went around her school today, polling her classmates. Guess what she found out? They're behind you in overwhelming numbers. They have absolute faith in your innocence."

"You're full of shit, man. You can't even call me by my real name."

"I'm not full of shit, *Jeremy*. She talked to over ninety kids."

"You just saying that. I bet you ain't even got an assistant."

"I do."

"Yeah? She there now?" Crap.

"She's around." Crap.

"Then put her on."

Crap. "You want me to put her on."

Bug-eyed, Madison covered her mouth. I hadn't prepared her for this. I wasn't prepared for it myself. This wasn't good. If I didn't put her on, Hunta would never believe anything I said again. And if I did . . .

"All right. I'll go get her. But just so you know, she believes you too. I mean she just took one look at Harmony Prince and . . ." I snapped my fingers. "Just like that. She could tell the woman was lying."

"Yeah, of course she could. You told her, didn't you?"

"No," I replied, keeping a wary eye on Madison. "She's thirteen."

"So?"

"So be nice to her, okay? She's my most valuable asset."

"Why didn't you give her the whole story, man?"

"Listen, I'm very protective of her and I'm not going to put her on until I know you're going to be nice to her. You understand what I'm saying?"

Madison threw me a mortified glare. *Christ, I'm not a baby, Scott.*

Fortunately, Hunta got it. "Fine. Whatever. I won't tell her. Just put her on."

"All right." I handed the phone to Madison, covering the receiver. "It'll be fine. Just tell him like you told me."

I leaned back and exhaled, right as Madison shot forward. She primped herself, cleared her throat, and then greeted Hunta in an absurdly professional voice.

"This is Madison."

The facade was only verbal. You could see her glowing rapture from a mile away. She wasn't even a fan of his but hey, you put a guy in the news long enough and he takes on a legend of his own. For Madison, this was the ultimate thrill. For me, it was a blowout waiting to happen.

"Hi." Pause. "Madison McKnight. I'm a big—" Pause. "No, I really did. It all started when I asked a couple of friends what they thought about Harmony Prince. They were just as convinced as I was that she was lying through her teeth. So then I started asking other kids, and they felt exactly the same way. I have the responses of over ninety different—"

She opened her notebook to pages of scribbled data. It wasn't the most objective or scientific of surveys, but certainly no worse than the half-baked pie charts they ran in the papers.

"Right. Exactly. We can tell the difference. Teenagers have a special nose for bullshit, because we're exposed to so much marketing."

I told her that, but it was mostly bullshit itself. Marketing didn't make kids wiser, just more cynical. The biggest reason Hunta was so popular right now was because he was a public scourge, the bane of stodgy adults everywhere. In teenage eyes, that made him cooler than Jesus.

Madison, however, was abnormally sharp for her age. Right away she saw the puppet's strings. She just didn't see me pulling them. *Please, Hunta. Jeremy. I know you don't owe me anything right now but please don't ruin the good thing I've got going with this girl. I've got a lot invested in her. Hell, she's half my portfolio.*

Gazing forward, she nodded. "Exactly. We are. But the important thing is that there are still a lot of people behind you, even if the media won't show them. Your fans are totally with you."

She beamed again, squeezing my arm.

"Thank you. That's very sweet. Everything I learned, I learned from Scott." She listened. "I'm sorry?" Pause. "No. I come here after school." Pause. "No, his apartment."

With a giggle and a blush, she glanced at me. "No, no. We're just . . . no."

I rolled my eyes. I thought those jokes would go away when I stopped calling her my intern.

Hunta chatted her up some more. She listened, enrapt, for well over a minute. Suddenly a new oversight caught up with me and hit me like a seizure. Oh my God. I was so worried about him spilling the beans on Harmony that I forgot about the other secret. The other lie.

So what's the deal with Slick's woman? You know, the deaf woman.

There would be a mushroom cloud over Brentwood if Madison ever heard those words. God, what would I say? *No, no. He meant "def," as in "D-E-F."* That would never work. Neither would the truth. How could I explain that I lied about seeing her mother just so people wouldn't think I was seeing Harmony? I'd have to explain Harmony.

"Uh-huh," said Madison, still absorbed.

Expressionless, I sat and waited, silently praying to fate. Of course fate had every reason to laugh at me. I got myself into this hole. I didn't have to use a real woman for my fabrication. I certainly didn't have to use Jean, although she'd probably get a kick out of the ruse. Madison wouldn't. That's what made my stomach acids churn. I should have never given so much weight to this skinny little girl. I should have never gotten hooked on her adulation. It wasn't smart or healthy. Jean definitely wouldn't get a kick out of that.

"Wow," she said. "That's beautiful."

After a little more small talk and a cordial farewell, Madison relinquished the cellular. She was on cloud nine. I was a stupid, lucky man.

"I like that girl," said Hunta.

I threw Madison a shaky smile. "So do I."

"You should tell her the whole story, though."

"I will. Someday. In the meantime, hang in there, okay?"

"Yeah, right. Say hi to your woman for me. I mean the one who ain't deaf."

"You know, believe it or not, she cares about what happens to you."

"I'll believe it when she clears me."

"She will," I promised. "It's happening—"

He hung up before I could even say "soon." With a weary sigh, I dropped the phone.

"Oh my God," said Madison, pressing her chest. "That was so intense. My heart is going like boom boom boom."

So was mine.

"Why did you say that?" she asked.

"Say what?"

"That believe it or not, I cared about what happened to him."

"I wasn't talking about you."

"Oh."

"What was all that stuff he was saying to you?"

She flashed me a coy grin. "It's a secret."

"That's fine," I replied, still waiting for my heart to slow down. "You're entitled."

The news simmered down on Friday evenings. It was officially the weekend, and weekends were all about escape. On weekends, the Bitch usually went to the movies.

This weekend, however, reality caught up with the big screen. In every city, keyed-up parents formed vigils around theater ticket counters. The cause of their wrath was *Hannibal,* which had just opened today. They weren't boycotting. They were simply ensuring that children under seventeen wouldn't be allowed to watch Dr. Lecter sauté a piece of Ray Liotta's brain. Sadly, it was children under seventeen who fueled the box office nowadays, especially for movies in which somebody ate somebody's brain. Poor MGM. They needed a hit so badly. Poor Keith Ullman. As the marketing czar, he took the flack and the rap for all the studio's lemons. How the hell could he have predicted the "Annabelle Shane reaction" (as punned in *Entertainment Weekly*)? Even Annabelle didn't know what she was starting.

Meanwhile, on the other side of Hollywood, the publicity team at Paramount Pictures invited Alonso to Monday's star-studded premiere of *Down to Earth,* the new Chris Rock reincarnation comedy that was opening next week. Alonso was, naturally, encouraged to bring Harmony and all her free media attention. Wisely, he declined. His only mistake was telling Harmony about it.

"But I *love* Chris Rock," she whimpered to me. "I want to meet him."

"I'm sure you will someday."

"So when do I finally get to go out and do the celebrity thing?"

"Monday," I promised. "That's when you mix it up with Larry King."

"I'd rather mix it up with Chris Rock."

Ironically, Chris Rock was originally scheduled to mix it up with Larry King on Monday, until they bumped him for Harmony. Little did she know she was dissing him twice. She certainly wouldn't hear it from me.

"Be patient, honey. If we get you out there too soon—"

"I know. I know. Credibility. You want me to play hard to get."

I grinned. "Just think of it as abstinence on a wider scale."

Harmony wasn't amused. She wasn't in good humor at all.

"All right. Something's up. Talk to me," I said.

"I'm just starting to feel a little cooped up in here," she admitted. "I'm even getting sick of looking at the ocean."

"You want to change hotels?"

"No. The hotel's fine. I guess it's just . . . I don't know. I'm kind of feeling isolated."

"Tell me what I can do to help."

"Well, for starters, you could come visit me."

She knew it was a long shot. That didn't make me feel any better. I would have loved to see her again. My new fantasy, my *chaste* fantasy, was to smuggle her out of the hotel and take her on a nice long drive. Anywhere. It didn't matter. The smell of smoke was gone from my car. My passenger seat was looking awfully empty. It'd be nice to have her back. There were, of course, logistical problems.

"Sweetheart, you know I would, but the press is all around your hotel. It's like the Oscar preshow out there."

"Chuck said he could sneak you in."

"What are you telling those guys about me?"

"Nothing," she said. "I never even gave them your last name. What's the big deal?"

"No. It's fine. Just don't—just be careful what you say around them. About everything."

Christ, that was dumb of me, not to mention cruel. Here she was complaining of isolation, and I'd just put a wall between her and the few people she could see.

"I just thought you might like to see the new drawings I made," she replied dejectedly. "I can't show you over the phone."

Dumb. Dumb. Dumb. "Is this for your book?"

"No. That's still all in my head. I was just doing landscapes and stuff. I'm practicing for the book."

"I still think it's a great idea. I can't wait to see it."

"Yeah."

Our conversation hit a sudden patch of cool, dead air. This new awkwardness was driving me crazy. A few more seconds of silence and I would have grabbed my car keys. I would have told her to order up dinner for two.

"Scott, when this is all over, are you still gonna have to hide from me?"

"I'm not hiding from you. I'm hiding from them."

"Yeah, but how long are you gonna have to hide from 'them'?"

I sighed. "I don't know. It'll be a while before you and I can go out for Chinese food."

"It's not that. I was just hoping you could be my official publicist or something. I mean when this is all over."

As much as I liked the notion, and as much as I loved that she asked, I knew it could never happen. Even if the Judge paid me under the table, there were still several dotted lines connecting me to Mean World. Officially attaching myself to Harmony would only invite suspicion, most likely investigation.

"I'm more of a crisis manager than a celebrity rep. I wouldn't be the best person for you. We'll set you up with someone good."

"Okay."

"But that doesn't mean we can't be friends."

I was hoping she'd be touched by that. Instead, she fell into an odd fit of giggles.

"What?"

"I'm sorry," she said, still snickering. "I want to be friends. I mean we are friends. I just got a picture of you chilling at my place, kicking back with a 40 and listening to Wu-Tang."

I smiled along. "That's more than I can picture."

Of course, I didn't tell her what I *could* see. My newest fantasy was to fly her around the world in a two-seater plane. We'd land at exotic ports, stay at exotic hotels, and at each scenic vista, I'd stimulate her mind with fascinating bits of local history. It wasn't an entirely chaste vision. I couldn't seem to get us out of the exotic hotels.

But my media high was finally beginning to subside. I could feel my galvanized id slowly settling back to normal. What a relief. It was getting a little too raucous here in my psyche. All in all, I preferred the quiet.

```
<ssinger>   Yo.
<jeanx>     Yo yo.
<ssinger>   I tried buzzing you for a chat this morning.
<jeanx>     Sorry. I only come out at night. During the day I
            pretend to be a web designer.
<ssinger>   How's that going?
<jeanx>     The pretending? Quite well. What are you doing home?
<ssinger>   What do you mean?
<jeanx>     I mean it's a Friday night. Shouldn't you be out on
            the town?
<ssinger>   What makes you think I'm an "out on the town" kind of
            guy?
<jeanx>     Because when I first met you, you were just some dude
            cruising around Westwood at 3AM. At least that's how I
            struck you. :}
```

```
<ssinger>    I was coming back from the airport.
<jeanx>      Really? So were we.
<ssinger>    Another 'find & retrieve' for Madison, huh?
<jeanx>      No comment.
<ssinger>    Right. I forgot.
<jeanx>      But I did notice that you weren't alone in your car.
<ssinger>    That was just a friend from New York.
<jeanx>      [scans for subtext]
<ssinger>    A _married_ friend from New York.
<jeanx>      Okay, but someone in this household thinks you have a
             special woman in your life.
<ssinger>    That seems to be the rumor.
<jeanx>      Do you?
<ssinger>    Nope.
<jeanx>      Special man?
<ssinger>    Nope.
<jeanx>      But you _are_ hetero.
<ssinger>    Yes. Non-practicing.
<jeanx>      You and me both, pal.
<ssinger>    But you're married.
<jeanx>      Scott, if you think marriage implies constant,
             frequent, or even occasional sex, then you're
             stunningly naÅ¨ve.
<ssinger>    I think you meant "naive."
<jeanx>      I did. This program seems to barf its umlauts.
<ssinger>    You mention your ex-husband all the time but you never
             talk about the current one.
<jeanx>      What would you like to know?
<ssinger>    What's his name? What does he do? How long have you
             been married? How does he put up with you?
<jeanx>      Neil. Captions. Four years. Shut up.
<ssinger>    Captions, as in "closed captions."
<jeanx>      For the hearing-impaired. Yes. He's one of the guys
             who types them up, usually for live broadcasts. He
             does a lot of sports events. I believe he's doing the
             Grammys in two weeks.
<ssinger>    He must haul ass on the keyboard.
<jeanx>      220 words a minute.
<ssinger>    220?!!
```

<jeanx>   I know. That used to really turn me on.

<ssinger>   How is that even possible?!

<jeanx>   It's not a keyboard. It's a 10-key touchpad, like
                the stenographers use. He just plugs it into the
                network console, and it all gets encoded into the
                broadcast.

<ssinger>   I think I read something about this.

<jeanx>   Television runs on 20 visible lines of data. The 21st
                line is hidden, right out of view, until you press the
                Captions button. Then it gets pushed up to where
                everyone can see it.

<ssinger>   I did read something about this.

<jeanx>   Damn. I thought I was impressing you.

<ssinger>   You are. You know a hell of a lot about TV for a woman
                who doesn't watch any.

<jeanx>   I just know a lot about Neil's job. YOURS, however,
                remains a mystery to me.

<ssinger>   You might say I also work with hidden messages.

<jeanx>   You mean like "VOTE FOR FRED" or just "BUY THIS
                PRODUCT"?

<ssinger>   Buy this product. Buy this person. Buy this story.

<jeanx>   So what are you peddling now? Product, person, or
                story?

<ssinger>   Actually I seem to be making a product out of a
                person's story.

<jeanx>   Wow. That's vaguely ominous.

<ssinger>   Hey, I'm a candy striper compared to the "VOTE FOR
                FRED" people.

<jeanx>   See, this is why I keep my nose buried in comic books
                and fantasy novels. Every time I look up at reality, I
                get depressed. Or repulsed. Or just plain pissed. I
                don't even like fiction that takes place on Earth.
                Earth sucks.

<ssinger>   How do you know?

<jeanx>   Because I've lived here all my life.

<ssinger>   It's just that the people who complain about the state
                of the world today usually base their opinion on what
                they see in the news. That's a big mistake.

<jeanx>   I'm not one of those people, but I'll bite. Why is it
                a mistake?

<ssinger>   Because the news is all emotion-based propaganda. It's
                ·all about showing you the worst of humanity. Not the
                common worst, the SHOCKING worst. And then they spin
                the shocking worst to make it look like it's common.
                School shootings! Rapper assaults! It could happen to
                YOUR child! It could happen to YOU!

<jeanx>   You're talking about the tabloids.

<ssinger>   I'm talking about all the news.

<jeanx>   They can't ALL do that.

<ssinger>   Now who's being naÅ¨ve?

<jeanx>   God, I am so far removed from this. For good reason,
                it seems.

<ssinger>   It's all just part of the business.

<jeanx>   Yes, and apparently so are you.

<ssinger>   I never denied it. And I never claimed to be above it.

<jeanx>   So you like what you do.

<ssinger>   I love it.

<jeanx>   You love planting hidden inflammatory messages in the
                news.

<ssinger>   Yup. I think I'm good at it, too.

<jeanx>   And _I_ think you're trying to get an inflammatory
                reaction out of me. That's what I think.

<ssinger>   Yeah, I probably am. And I should probably stop. I
                don't want you pulling my assistant out of her job.

<jeanx>   No. God, no. That'd be like pulling her heart out of
                her chest.

<ssinger>   Good, because I've come to rely on her. The girl's got
                talent.

<jeanx>   For planting subtext?

<ssinger>   For digging it up.

<jeanx>   Think she has potential to plant it?

<ssinger>   Like a mad farmer.

<jeanx>   See, that's the part that makes me cringe a little.

<ssinger>   Don't worry. You're particularly safe from our evil
                mojo.

<jeanx>   Me? Why me?

```
<ssinger>   Because we mostly work with noise, and you're immune
            to noise.
```

On-screen, the cursor blinked twelve times before she responded.

```
<jeanx>     You're very interesting.
<ssinger>   Ha ha ha.
<jeanx>     What?
<ssinger>   You did this once before. You took a really long time
            to give me just a little bit of text. I sit here
            expecting twelve paragraphs and then I get three or
            four measly words.
<jeanx>     I was censoring myself.
<ssinger>   Don't worry. I can take an insult.
<jeanx>     Actually, it was a compliment.
<ssinger>   You censor your compliments?
<jeanx>     I censored this one. It was pretty harsh.
<ssinger>   I have absolutely no idea what to make of that.
<jeanx>     Look, it was a good decision. I don't make good
            decisions very often. Let's just skip it and
            move on.
```

We moved on. When I finally finished my chat with her at 4:30 A.M. (if seven straight hours of dialogue could be considered a "chat"), her censored compliment lingered in the back of my tired mind. As much as I hated to be teased, something told me that a compliment from Jean, even a harsh one, would be a uniquely gratifying experience.

Before I fell asleep, I spent another half hour playing back our exchange. In my thoughts, she spoke with the sharp, quirky panache of an actress in a 1940s comedy. Maybe the lead from a Preston Sturges film. Veronica Lake in *Sullivan's Travels*. Or better yet, Barbara Stanwyck in *The Lady Eve*. Her character was also named Jean. She was a card sharp: a sexy, quick-witted flimflam girl who ran circles around poor, hapless Henry Fonda.

Jean, *my* Jean, seemed too much of a pleasant wreck to be a hustler. And we seemed to be circling each other at equal speed. Increasing speed. That made me a little nervous. As much as I wanted to diversify my emotional holdings, I was wary about putting too much stock in Ms. Spelling. She could be dangerous to let inside, much more dangerous than Madison or Harmony. And yet part of her was already here. I could hear that damn Stanwyck voice, teasing me about being a typical man, pegging me as a guy who'd rather surround himself with fawning, admiring young women than take on someone his own age and cranial capacity.

All right, Jean. Maybe I'll take you on, just to spite you. Maybe I'll let you in, despite my own better judgment. Over the moat, through the gate, and past the sentries. Welcome to my neurotic high esteem. I may be sorry, but at least I won't be typical.

17

HIGH TECHNOLOGY

On Saturday morning Maxina drew Harmony a nice poster-sized illustration of my shortcomings.

Their rap session began at 9:00 A.M., while I was still in deep, recuperative slumber. Once again Harmony bemoaned her increasing feelings of isolation, but this time she complained to the right person. Maxina immediately advised—she *demanded,* in that definitive but tender way of hers—that Harmony call her long-lost roommates and invite them up for a visit.

Naturally, Harmony was stunned. To her it was like learning the shortcut out of Oz. *Wait, you mean all I had to do was tap my damn slippers three times? I can* do *that?*

It wasn't hard to imagine her real questions. "Why didn't Scott tell me? Why did he make me think it was so dangerous to talk to them?"

No doubt Maxina, artful as she was, merely shrugged and kept her mouth shut, but she knew the answer as well as I did: it *was* dangerous. I didn't trust Harmony to keep her friends out of the loop and I didn't trust them in the loop, especially when the news rags were offering cash for dirt to anyone even remotely connected to the story. Hell, by Friday no fewer than six of Hunta's former contemporaries had sold him out for a four-figure payoff. It'd be careless to assume that Harmony's friends would be any different.

Yet apparently, they were. As of Saturday not a single one of them had grabbed the tabloid carrot, even the *Enquirer*'s twenty-thousand-dollar carrot. That was pretty damn impressive considering the amount of conflicting testimony they could have already offered, and especially considering the relative value of twenty large in that household.

Okay, so I had underestimated their integrity, not to mention their love for Harmony. My real mistake was not realizing how little it mattered. By Friday, she was already bulletproof. Even if one of her roommates did run to the scandal sheets with tales of false claims and shady dealings, it would have barely put a dent in her credibility. If anything, it would have given me the foreshadowing that Alonso was all too unwilling to provide.

By the time I woke up, at a quarter after eleven, the reunion was well under way. I could hear them all partying in the background, blasting rap music. Harmony and I had to shout to be heard.

"What?"

"I said I'm sorry for not suggesting it myself!"

"That's okay!" she yelled back. "Even you can't think of everything!"

"So you're not mad?"

"I ain't mad at all! I'm too glad to be mad!"

Everyone in the background cheered. That was a lot of noise for five people. Where the hell were the bodyguards? Probably partying with them. Jesus. That was stupid. It was reckless. There were still a number of journalists skulking around, posing as guests. If even one of them got wind, or worse, got footage of this shindig, it would come back to hurt Harmony. She wouldn't be bulletproof after her guilty confession. A shot like that could kill her.

My first instinct was to warn her, to tell her to at least turn down the music, but the last thing I wanted to do was rain on her parade. I was on thin enough ice, despite her assurances.

"Was there anything else, Scott?"

"What? No. I'll let you go. Have a good time."

"Don't worry," she replied with a touch of frost, "I won't say nothing about you."

Five minutes later, I was cursing in the shower. Goddamn it, I was losing her. I was losing her, all because I *could* think of everything. I'm sorry, sweetheart. It's just the way I am. I don't know how to err except deep on the side of caution. I don't know how to exist besides very, very carefully.

On Saturday afternoon I channeled all my energy into a personal productivity blitz. I drove off in a dented black Saturn and came back five hours later in a rented white Buick, filled to the top with overdue purchases. By six o'clock, my chore list was a thing of the past, a period piece. For the first time in what felt like ages, I got a taste of my old, comfortable existence before Hunta and Harmony, Jean and Madison, Annabelle, Maxina, Miranda (the adulterous version), Keoki Atoll, all the crazy things that February had thrown my way. It was as if my life had been plotted out for sweeps. Everything was louder, more pronounced. More intense. There was even more nudity.

That was why I appreciated Ira.

If ever there was a stable presence in my world, it was him. I hadn't heard a peep out of him since last Sunday, but even his absence was stable. It was just the way he operated. Sometimes he'd disappear from my life for weeks on end. Other times he'd bug me so often I considered cutting my phone line. It all depended on whether or not he had an interesting project to work on.

He must have had something good, because he never called to give me grief about Harmony. That surprised me. I figured Ira would be the first one to tell me how screwed my client was. Even Keith Ullman, the man who had set me up with Hunta before washing his hands of the matter, had called to offer his condolences. Yet not a word from Ira. Something was up. I decided to pay him a visit before I did something crazy, like miss him.

At 7:30, I boarded the *Ishtar* and was immediately hit by an eerie sense of sameness. All of Ira's clutter, his clothes, his empty take-out boxes, seemed molecularly unchanged from my last visit. Even Ira was the same. He was still wrapped up in his ratty blue robe, still curled up in his computer command chair, still conjuring up some sort of virtual house on his PC. This was more than stability. This was a six-day time warp.

"Hey," he said, affording me only a moment's glance. "I thought I heard footsteps."

I kept looking around. "Jesus, Ira."

"What?"

"This is exactly how I left you last week."

"What'd you expect me to become? A butterfly?"

"No, but I expected you to move a little bit. You're even working on the same 3-D house thing."

He glanced at his monitor, then laughed. "Oh, that. Yeah. You seem to have caught me in construction mode again. It's just one small part of the program."

"What, you're developing something else now?"

"This isn't mine. It's from a bunch of guys in San Francisco. I'm just beta-testing it."

"Yeah, but what is it? Some kind of game?"

He finally spun toward me, his wide face filled with rapturous awe. "Holy crap, Scott. This is more than a game. This is the future. And I don't just mean the future of gaming. I mean this is the future of *being.*"

Despite my soft protests, Ira spent the next twenty minutes guiding me through his new passion. The yet to be titled program was just one entry in an emerging form of nerd entertainment known as the Massively Multiplayer Online Role-Playing Game (MMORPG). In short, it was a new type of diversion: a 3D networked environment in which users from all over the world could interact with one another as anything or anyone they wanted to be. Tall or short. Young or old. Human or otherwise. They could reinvent themselves in ways that reality had proved most inflexible. Ira showed me his own rendered incarnation: a trim and WASPy fellow who was nice-looking in every sense of the term. He reminded me of *ER*'s Noah Wyle. He certainly didn't remind me of Ira.

Whereas most of these games were mired deep in the fantasy and sci-fi realms, this one was based in the here and now. It was designed to be a spin-off nation, a utopian refuge for today's jaded pilgrims. By signing on as a tester, Ira was living and toiling among the country's first settlers. By Monday, he had his own business selling custom texture maps for walls and floors. By Wednesday, he had enough virtual money to start his own township. By Thursday, he had thirty loyal Netizens, and by Friday he was married to two of them. And I thought I had a busy week.

He had been dedicating an average of sixteen hours a day to his digital life. He swore that was the norm among his many friends and spouses.

"It's definitely a commitment," he said. "I mean this isn't just a glorified chat room. We're building a whole new society here. You can't do it halfway."

"That's pretty cool," I affirmed.

"Yeah, right."

"What?"

"I can already feel the intervention coming."

"I'm not intervening. I'm just quietly hoping that this won't impact our progress with Move My Cheese."

"It won't. Jesus. When did you get so maternal?"

"I'm not being maternal," I said. "I didn't come over here to nag you. This was a purely social visit. In fact, I was hoping I could pull you off this boat for an evening. I say we do something fun in the real world. After you shower."

He kept working on the PC. "Can't."

"Can't shower?"

"Can't go out. I've got a meeting in fifteen minutes."

"What? Here?"

He pointed to the house he was renovating. "There."

"You're talking about the game. You've got a meeting in the game."

"Yes, but I'm meeting with real people. It's very important. I'd like to finish the roof before they get here."

Now I could feel an intervention coming, but I wasn't in the mood for heavy discussion. I wasn't in the state of mind to convince anyone of anything. The engine was off today. I was coasting on sail power.

I stood up. "Okay. Fine. It's your choice. I guess next time I'll call ahead."

"Yeah. Definitely. I'll clear a night."

"Hope things continue to prosper in Iraville."

He emitted a patient smile. "It's not called Iraville. I'm not even called Ira."

"Well, whatever your name is. Stay healthy, all right?"

He didn't acknowledge me until I was halfway out the door.

"Oh, wait. Scott."

I turned around at the door as he swiveled his chair.

"If someone e-mails you a JPEG of Anna Kournikova, don't open it. It's a virus."

I didn't know whether to laugh or scream. Ira and I were never two peas in a pod, but now we weren't even sharing the same planet. No wonder he never called to bug me about Harmony. He probably hadn't even heard of her yet. The news had yet to reach the shores of Alt-America. It seemed a little bizarre and pathetic to me, but then who was I to judge? Ira had a whole new nation to explore on his Saturday nights. My social options were down to virtually one person.

```
<jeanx>     You think we have a problem?
<ssinger>   What, you mean like a 12-step problem?
<jeanx>     I don't know.
```

I didn't know either. I had returned home at a quarter to nine with the express intention of not opening my laptop. Not opening up Eye-Talk. Not checking to see if Jean was online and, if she was, not ringing her up for another marathon chat. It did seem a tad unsound, especially after coming from Ira's. But I took some comfort in the fact that she and I came as we were. At least we were playing ourselves.

```
<ssinger>   If you weren't talking to me right now, what would you
            be doing?
<jeanx>     Probably re-reading one of my Terry Pratchett books.
<ssinger>   I'd just be watching cable.
<jeanx>     Yeah. The girl watches a lot of tube. It drives me
            nuts.
<ssinger>   Is that what the girl is doing right now?
<jeanx>     No. The girl is out with the man. They're seeing
            "Hannibal."
<ssinger>   WHAT?!
<jeanx>     WHAT?!
<ssinger>   You let your husband take an impressionable 13-year-
            old to see that corrosive R-rated filth?!
<jeanx>     I sense and hope you're kidding.
<ssinger>   I am. But if your daughter eats my brains on Monday,
            I'll have a legitimate grievance.
<jeanx>     Don't bother suing us. We're broke.
<ssinger>   You are?
<jeanx>     Not really.
<ssinger>   In other words, yes, but you regret telling me.
<jeanx>     In other words, yes, but you damn well better take my
            check for that auto damage.
<ssinger>   Hey, not a problem.
<jeanx>     AND you better cash it.
<ssinger>   . o O (Damn!)
<jeanx>     Seriously.
<ssinger>   Seriously. I'll take it. I'll cash it. I promise.
```

```
<jeanx>     Good. It's been hanging over me for nine days
            now.
<ssinger>   Are you okay?
```

The question earned me a few moments of radio silence.

```
<jeanx>     What makes you ask? You can't even see me.
<ssinger>   Subtext, baby. Subtext.
<jeanx>     Oh, you're good.
<ssinger>   I'm good.
<jeanx>     DAMN good.
<ssinger>   Damn right. So what's the problem? Can you talk about
            it? Or is it part of the Subject We Dare Not Speak?
<jeanx>     No. It's not maternal. It's marital.
<ssinger>   Oh.
<jeanx>     But I won't get into that either.
<ssinger>   Right. Fair enough. You want me to piss off, then?
<jeanx>     No. I want you to stay and talk to me. All night.
            Again.
```

This time I was the one who paused, apparently long enough to
cause concern.

```
<jeanx>     Look, in case you're worried, I don't see this as an
            escalating thing. Our relationship is purely textual.
<ssinger>   I know. We just seem to be having an awful lot of
            text.
<jeanx>     Okay. You tell me your problem with that and I'll tell
            you mine.
<ssinger>   I just don't want to become an issue in your family.
<jeanx>     You mean marital or maternal?
<ssinger>   I don't know. You tell me.
<jeanx>     Well, I can rule out the former. In order for you to
            become a marital issue, we'd have to screw. Outdoors.
            In his garden. Right on top of his azaleas. And his
            cat.
<ssinger>   Wow. It sure takes a lot to upset Neil.
<jeanx>     No it doesn't. Now should we talk about the maternal
            issue?
```

```
<ssinger>    Yes, because I'm not quite sure what it is.
<jeanx>      I don't know. I just feel like we're cheating on
             _her_.
<ssinger>    Actually, I've felt that a little too. It's silly,
             though.
<jeanx>      Not in her head.
<ssinger>    Why? What do you think is going on in her head?
<jeanx>      I'm guessing pictures of you.
<ssinger>    Oh come on.
<jeanx>      It's true.
<ssinger>    How do you know?
<jeanx>      Because I can read minds. Didn't I tell you?
<ssinger>    I think you're misreading this one.
<jeanx>      I think you're just being humble.
<ssinger>    No. I'm serious. If she's in love with anything, it's
             the work.
<jeanx>      How do YOU know?
<ssinger>    Because I can read subtext. Didn't you notice?
```

I didn't like the direction this was heading. I didn't think it was fair of Jean to push her daughter out on a limb like this. More important, I didn't think she was right.

```
<ssinger>    I'm serious. I would know.
<jeanx>      Yeah. I think you would too.
<ssinger>    So then what's the issue?
<jeanx>      I guess the issue is what you would do with that
             knowledge.
<ssinger>    Ahhhh. I was wondering when we'd finally get to this.
<jeanx>      It's my biggest fear.
<ssinger>    Hey, I don't blame you for having it. I just wish
             there was something I can say or do to ease your mind.
<jeanx>      It's not that I think you're evil or twisted or
             anything...
<ssinger>    Praise indeed.
<jeanx>      It's just that you're human. She's pretty. And she
             would do anything you wanted. Anything. You'd just
             have to ask.
<ssinger>    Uh...
```

```
<jeanx>      And the worst part is, I'd never know. She'd never
             tell. You two would totally get away with it.
<ssinger>    You enjoy torturing yourself like this?
<jeanx>      A little. But only when I'm in a pissy mood.
<ssinger>    Yeah, well stop it. You're weirding me out.
<jeanx>      Fine. What's YOUR biggest fear?
<ssinger>    You mean about you?
<jeanx>      No. In general.
<ssinger>    Mediocrity.
<jeanx>      Wait. Back up. You have a fear about me?
<ssinger>    Currently, yes. But it's a nutty one.
<jeanx>      What, that I'm a psycho-killer?
<ssinger>    No.
<jeanx>      A vampire? An alien? A Lutheran?
<ssinger>    No, that you're Madison.
```

The cursor blinked for a good twenty seconds. Poor thing. If she could see my face, my own sardonic smirk, she'd know I wasn't very committed to this particular nightmare. It was just one of a million bleak angles that crossed my field of vision, one of many droll predictions being whispered among the viewers in my own private cineplex. There was always a twist. There was always a wild third-act surprise, especially when a promising thing looked a little too promising. It was just Hollywood dharma.

Admittedly, I had gotten an early start on my suspicion. Last Sunday, in Jean's first e-mail to me, I had noticed a nonmotherly use of the word "cool." That was enough to trigger an opening round of What If . . . ? What if Madison was posing as Jean? What if she had co-opted her mother's account? What if she had set up a server function to redirect all incoming messages from me before Jean could ever read them? It's much easier than it sounds, especially for someone as sharp as Madison. Ultimately the real Jean would try to contact me, but what if her daughter was sly enough to set up a two-way deception? What if Jean was hearing from "me" all along, and hearing that everything was fine?

It was exactly the kind of stunt I could see a bright but unstable teenage girl devising, until she was inevitably caught. As the week progressed, small observations kept fueling the uncertainty. The fact that I only heard from Jean at night, when Madison was home. The fact that

Madison kept yawning after Jean and I had our first late-night exchange. The fact that she delivered the classic "Death of Phoenix" comic herself, then demanded I thank her mother by e-mail. That was certainly a chin-scratcher. What if Madison was a closet X-Men fan herself? Or what if she'd done some quick Web research, enough to make her fluent in X-talk, and then swiped a pivotal issue from her mother's collection?

Like Jean, I often tortured myself with dark, exotic notions, but this one never kept me up at night. It certainly didn't stop my relationships from evolving. And the more I got to know them both, the quieter my theories became.

But then Jean had to shake the whole damn tree, just moments ago, with her bizarrely suggestive rant about what her little girl would do if only I asked. Her grim supposition instantly resurrected mine, only now that I knew those two, now that I cherished my rapport with both mother and daughter, the thought was downright terrifying. It was enough to make me queasy.

\<jeanx\>	Wow. I'm not sure how to take that.
\<ssinger\>	Try it with a grain of salt.
\<jeanx\>	No. Still doesn't wash. Either you think she's amazingly mature for her age, or I'm amazingly immature for mine.
\<ssinger\>	I didn't say I believed it. I just said it was a fear.
\<jeanx\>	So then for the record, you do not believe, assume, or hope that you are electronically flirting with a 13-year-old girl.
\<ssinger\>	I thought we weren't flirting.
\<jeanx\>	Oh wake up. We're flirting like mad. We're just not escalating.
\<ssinger\>	Maybe I should read more carefully.
\<jeanx\>	Maybe you should answer me.
\<ssinger\>	NO. I DO NOT BELIEVE, ASSUME, OR HOPE THAT I AM ELECTRONICALLY FLIRTING WITH A 13-YEAR-OLD GIRL.
\<jeanx\>	And if it turns out you are?
\<ssinger\>	Is that a confession?
\<jeanx\>	It's a query.
\<ssinger\>	Okay. To answer your query: I'd be upset. I'd be angry.

<jeanx>   How upset and how angry?
<ssinger>   Upset enough to kick you out of my life and angry
            enough not to miss you. Is that a satisfactory answer?

She took a few long beats to process my words.

<jeanx>   You know what? It is. Wow.
<ssinger>   Good.
<jeanx>   I really, really believe you, Scott.
<ssinger>   Glad to hear it.
<jeanx>   Yeah. Wow. You just killed my biggest fear. You don't
            know how happy that makes me. I mean it. I'm even
            crying a little.
<ssinger>   I swear, woman, you get weirder by the minute.
<jeanx>   Would you like me to kill YOUR biggest fear? Or are
            you willing to take on faith that I am not my own
            teenage daughter?
<ssinger>   I don't think you're Madison!!
<jeanx>   Yes, but there's still that tiny seed of doubt in your
            mind. I can see it. I can kill it.
<ssinger>   You can prove you're not Madison.
<jeanx>   I can prove it in four words. No, make it five.
<ssinger>   Five words, huh?
<jeanx>   I'm giving you a choice: proof or faith. What will it
            be?
<ssinger>   I don't know. I'm tempted to say "proof," but it feels
            like the wrong answer.
<jeanx>   This isn't a quiz show, Scott. I'm only asking for
            your benefit.
<ssinger>   Yeah but I can't imagine anyone choosing faith over
            proof.
<jeanx>   Neither could I. But I just mustered up some faith
            right now, specifically in you, and it feels REALLY
            good. Care to try some?
<ssinger>   No. I'll take the proof.
<jeanx>   You sure now?
<ssinger>   I'm sure.
<jeanx>   You want the proof then.
<ssinger>   If it's not too much trouble.

```
<jeanx>      It's not. But I'd be remiss in not giving you one last
             chance to back out.
<ssinger>    I'm not backing out! Will you give me the damn proof
             already?!
<jeanx>      Okay! I'll be right over!
```

She disconnected. The lower half of my screen went blank. For a minute I sat there, staring at my laptop like an idiot, wondering why she couldn't just deliver her proof through the computer. Then I reread her last five words. Damn. I guess she did. Whatever made me think I was dealing with an adolescent? This woman was far too smart to be a child in disguise. This woman was smarter than me.

For the eighth time in seven days, MRVL GRL pulled up in front of my building. She left the lights on and the motor running. She didn't get out. I watched her through the window, even though I couldn't see the driver. I knew who it was, of course—and who it wasn't—but why was she just sitting there?

Suddenly, my old but trusty gray cell phone emitted a short series of beeps. I pulled it off the kitchen counter. I had a new text message.

YOU COMING OR WHAT?

I had no idea what she had in store for me, but I liked the way she spared me the thorny issue of inviting her in. By no means did I want her in my duplex. I didn't want her by my stairs. I didn't want her anywhere near the concept of escalation. Apparently the feeling was mutual. That was all I needed to know before putting my night in her hands.

After clutching my wallet and keys, I took a somber look at my other cellular. The Bat-Phone. That red, clunky, overembellished rigamajig that had come to symbolize my secret relationship with Harmony. I'd been carrying it around all week like a ten-pound sack of flour. For God's sake, it was Saturday night. The news flow was just a trickle, and Harmony was rich in friends. Wouldn't it be nice to leave the phone behind for once? To leave *her* behind?

Ultimately, it was fear of irony that set me straight. The minute I left home, of course, something would happen. The moment I became inaccessible, Harmony would need me. I was already two steps in the doghouse with her. I couldn't afford any more mistakes. Once again, I took her with me.

As I approached the SUV, I could see the inscrutable Mrs. Spelling, smiling at me through her window. I hadn't laid eyes on her since last Saturday, back when she was little more than a bad driver, a worried mother and, naturally, a Deaf Woman. Now that we'd exchanged thousands of words, now that I had at least eighty more colorful terms to describe her, she looked completely different to me. She was still forcibly cute in that Katie Couric/chipmunk sort of way, but there was a deep intricacy to her face that I had definitely missed before. It made her almost impenetrable. She was what Katie Couric might look like in a weird and cathartic mood. She was the world's most complicated chipmunk.

At the moment, her face was dedicated to making fun of me. Feigning confusion, she lowered her window and flashed me her handheld.

MADISON SAID I HAD TO RUSH OVER HERE. ANY IDEA WHAT THIS IS ABOUT?

"Read my lips: you're not funny."

Grinning, she jerked her thumb at the passenger seat. *Get in.*

"And where are you taking me, exactly?"

She didn't catch that. Another thing I'd learned from her this past week: lipreading was hard. The human mouth was nowhere near as versatile as the human throat. Many word sounds were doubled, tripled, quadrupled in a single phoneme. Even veteran readers like Jean still routinely missed or misread at least 25 percent of everything said. Try ....sing or mass-reeding......twenty-five ....cent of everything ridden. Not fun, is it?

So when she motioned again, I shut up and followed. I got into the very car that had crinkled mine. As I closed the door, Jean turned on the interior light. She was wearing a sleeveless white blouse, turquoise capri pants, and old white sneakers. Her short black hair was held back by a plastic green hairband. She was dressed more for a day of spring cleaning than a night on the town. Okay, so she wasn't exactly a fashion template, but there was something wonderful about the way she existed in her own continuum, far beyond the reach of *Marie Claire* and Laura Ashley. None of her insecurities, none of her neuroses were media-fueled. She was her very own mess.

And she was still one fine-looking mess. Nature may have stolen one of her senses but it left her a number of gifts: perfect skin, a seductive jawline, and what I could only assume was a divine metabolism. She had an incredibly trim body for a woman who sat at her computer all day.

She studied me for a moment, then scribbled into her handheld.

IT'S NICE TO SEE YOU.

"Thank you. You, too."

YOU READY?

"Where are we going?"

JUST TRUST ME. YOU'RE IN FOR A REAL EXPERIENCE.

She locked the doors and turned off the light. Before pulling away, she closed her eyes and genuflected. Whether she was really praying or just messing with my head, I didn't know. She didn't clue me in. But as always, I had my suspicions.

There is an electronic device known as an Emergency Response Indicator that picks up the noise from police, fire, and ambulance sirens and signals it to deaf drivers through a series of blinking red lights. It even indicates the proximity of the emergency vehicle. I got to see it in action on the way to our mystery destination. I thought it was incredibly cool. This was a magnificent age we lived in. There was clearly no better time to be deaf.

At half past ten we arrived at the Third Street Promenade in Santa Monica, only two blocks south of Harmony's hotel. Jean expressed some guilt at using her handicap placard to get a good spot, but it was either that or drive around for ages.

With covert glee, she held my arm and led me through the bustling crowd of pedestrians and street performers. She took me down an alley, between two restaurants, then up an unobtrusive stairwell. There, on the second floor, across from a Greek optometrist's office, was the entrance to Club Silence.

At the door, she adjusted my collar, then retrieved her handheld from her purse.

YOU ARE NOW LEAVING EARTH, she wrote, AND ENTERING MY WORLD.

She wasn't kidding. Never in my life had I been to a place where everybody was talking but nobody was saying a word. All throughout the posh little establishment, patrons cut their hands through the air in quick, elegant motions. There didn't seem to be a single verbal conversation transpiring, yet there was more than enough noise to keep the scene from becoming eerie. The shuffling of clothes. The clapping of hands. The clumps and clods of footsteps. And the normal human interjections: moans, sighs, laughs, cries. There were just no words and no music. It was enough to make a wonderful difference. I'd never seen anything like it before in my life. I didn't even have a film or television reference to compare it to. I was completely off-script.

Jean paid my cover charge (she insisted, although I suspected my expression alone was worth the price of admission), then pulled me to a row of small tables on the east side of the room. Fastened onto each surface were numerous clamshell iBooks, linked together by LocalTalk cables.

It cost another ten dollars to score us an hour of table time. We sat across from each other. The setup was very similar to EyeTalk, with one major difference. From behind her own screen, Jean threw me a small and mysterious grin. I had no idea what was fueling it. Reading her face was like reading the NASDAQ page. There were too many details. Too much going on.

<So,> she entered, <is your mind sufficiently blown?>

Unlike her, I wasn't a touch typist. I had to look down at my fingers.

<Yeah. Wow. I didn't know places like this even existed.>

<Yup. They're all over. At least they used to be. The Deaf Club is dying out.>

<Why?>

She shrugged. <High technology, I guess. We've got the Internet now. TTY. DVD. Closed-captioned TV. Basically, like the rest of you, we have a lot more excuses to stay home. I haven't been here in at least two years. Thanks for giving me an excuse.>

<Thanks for bringing me. This is pretty amazing.>

Jean leaned against her fist, studying me through a squint. <Tell me. Why do people find deafness so fascinating? Are they the same way about blindness?>

<No. Blindness is boring as a dog's ass.>

<I don't get it. Why?>

<Because Hollywood's already given us a million blind people. We know they're all kind-hearted, plucky, super-capable individuals, and we don't give a shit.>

<But why aren't there a million deaf people? And when they DO show deaf people, how come they're always oralists? The oral deaf are an extreme minority.>

<My guess is that nonverbal deaf people, like yourself, are much harder to adapt for the screen.>

Jean raised a skeptical eyebrow at me.

<Look at this,> I wrote, then motioned between us. <Look at us.

Come on. We're both very pretty, but who wants to watch us typing for twenty minutes?>

She made a vast sweep with her hand. <Look around! Look at THEM! ASL is a visual language! It's beautiful to look at. It's even beautiful on ugly people! Look!>

<I'm looking. I'm agreeing. It's gorgeous. But even if you show two people signing, even if you show subtitles, there still won't be any sound.>

<So?>

<So viewers don't like long periods of silence, especially in the theater. It weirds them out. It causes them to think.>

Jean rolled her eyes. <Remind me not to ask you any more questions.>

<You should be glad they're leaving you alone. They'd only get you wrong.>

<Me personally?>

I grinned. <Yes. You're completely unadaptable.>

The overhead lights flashed on and off, until everyone stopped to look at the middle-aged man at the switch. He stepped onto a small wooden stage and cheerfully signed to the room for a few moments.

<Well,> I quipped, <I guess we know where he stands on the economy.>

<He's the club owner. He was basically telling everyone not to go away. There's a live comedy act starting in a few minutes.>

<I assume that'll be in sign language too.>

<What can I say, my dear? You're a stranger in a strange land.>

<That's okay. I'm loving it.>

She lost a good chunk of her merriment. <It'll wear thin. Trust me. This was Neil's life. He was a hearing boy raised in an all-Deaf family. Exact opposite of my upbringing. If I was a fish out of water, he was a bird in the sea.>

<Yeah, but he grew up speaking the language, didn't he?>

<It's not the same,> she wrote. <When you can hear, signing just doesn't take on the same import. There's only so far a coda can go into the Deaf World. For Neil, it was like growing up inside a diving bell. It gave him issues, to say the least.>

<Coda. I remember Madison using that word. What does it mean again?>

<Child of Deaf Adults.>

<Right. I guess she's one too.>

<That's a big reason my first marriage ended. I didn't want to raise her at Gallaudet. I didn't want her to grow up alienated. Like I did.>

Sarcastically, she shook her fist. <And a BANG-UP job I did, too!>

<I think you're underestimating her,> I stated.

<Um, wasn't it just an hour ago that you thought/feared/suspected she was secretly playing me?>

<Yes. I underestimated her. Now that I've been proven wrong, I'm preaching the gospel of Madison. I think she's a wonderful, amazing girl.>

<You're only getting a fraction of her,> she typed with a heavy sigh. <With you, she puts her best feet forward.>

Before I could type a word of protest, she cut me off. <Not because she's in love with you! I think you're right. I missed the boat on that one, okay? My bad. But you are still the light in her otherwise dreary existence. She idolizes you. Of course she's going to want to impress you.>

<She does impress me. A lot.>

<And that makes me happy. It makes me jealous. I would love to see the Madison that you see. I only hope you never get the Madison that I get.>

I didn't hide my frustration. <You make her sound like the Antichrist.>

<Oh, don't give me that. You know I would die for her. You know I would die without her. What I'm trying to say is that beneath her Greatest Kid in the World exterior is some really dark stuff. She has no friends at school. She's been suspended a number of times for cheating, cutting, fighting. She gets into trouble with boys. She doesn't eat. She barely sleeps. She LIES a hell of a lot. And she gets depressed. She gets so goddamn depressed that I get scared for her. I haven't been sleeping too well either.>

I thought about Madison's school survey, the one she'd shared with me and Hunta. I could picture her sitting alone in the lunchroom, carefully fabricating the input of classmates who wouldn't give her the time of day, much less participate in her straw poll. I could see the faculty isolating her, fearing her like she was the sequel to Annabelle Shane in development. I didn't want these images. Madison certainly wouldn't want me to have them.

<Why are you telling me this?>

<Because that's the stuff she hides from you. She seems to be doing a good job, but it can't last forever. I just don't want you bailing at the first sign of trouble.>

<What makes you think I would?>

<Because I have this fatal tendency to assume the worst in others. Sorry, Scott. We can't all be Pollyannas.>

I matched her snide leer. <I thought you mustered up some faith in me.>

<It wore off.>

<Well, stow it. I'm not going anywhere.>

<Good. It would be a damn shame because beneath all that dark stuff, she truly is the Greatest Kid in the World. So while you're loving her platonically, you might as well love her unconditionally.>

I stared at her, flabbergasted. <Jean, you wear me out.>

<I know. I've got my own problems. I've got a failing business, a shattered marriage, a horrible self-image, and a daughter who can't stand me.>

<Yes, but on the plus side, you've got a neat device in your car that blinks every time it hears a siren.>

She grinned. <True. I've also got you.>

That didn't hit me very well. Sensing my discomfort, she frowned at me. <I'm not talking seduction. I'm just talking human connection.>

It still felt like seduction, and I didn't like it. If she had a problem with her husband, she should work it out with him instead of seeking outside affirmation. Miranda had done the same damn thing, only she happened to catch me tired and jet-lagged on my thirty-fifth birthday. My defenses were down that night. Now they were on full shield alert.

<You still don't know me that well,> I wrote.

<I know. That's why I like this. Your real face says a lot more than your typeface.>

<And what is my real face telling you right now?>

She threw me a dashed pout. <That I'm freaking you out a little.>

<Close enough.>

<Scott, look at MY face. Read my subtext.>

With some trepidation, I closed in to read the fine print. I could see she was disappointed and a little annoyed that I was missing her point.

And yet I couldn't see her point. All I could do was acknowledge the possibility that maybe, just maybe, she wasn't playing me against her own frustrations.

Giving up, she spelled it out for me. <I find you a very attractive man, Mr. Singer, but sex is not what I'm about. I was never a big fan of it and frankly, I was never very good at it. Call me a nerd, but I'd rather spend my nights swapping bad puns and double entendres than bodily fluids. I'd rather explore your mind than your body. And you give good mind, my dear. I can fly around in that big, mysterious head of yours for a thousand years and still not hit the edges.>

I kept my eyes on the screen and my reactions deep inside me.

<What frustrates me, Scott, is that I can tell you feel the same way. You don't want to screw me, you want to know me. I think it's beautiful the way you want to know me. And what a convenience that there's no law in church or state that prevents you from knowing me. But there's something about that. There's something about the way we're connect-ing that obviously scares the hell out of you.>

I looked up at her. <Where are you GETTING all this from?>

<What do you mean?>

<I mean you're putting all this stuff on me, like we have some pro-found thing between us. And not just between us, but between me and Madison. You're telling to me love her unconditionally and to not break her heart. That's fine but Jesus Christ, I'm her BOSS! She works for me fifteen hours a week. She's worked for me fifteen hours TOTAL. Where is all this coming from?>

<Hey. If you want to fry me with your eyebeams, fine. But don't take this out on her.>

I laughed. "Oh, you don't want me bringing her into this? You're the one who—"

It wasn't until she glanced at me askew that I realized I was speaking out loud. I took a deep breath and channeled my thoughts back into my hands.

<Jean, you're driving me nuts. I mean I like you. I like you both a hell of a lot, but I don't want to get sucked into your lives.>

<That's the thing. I think you do.>

<You're wrong. You are very, very wrong.>

<Scott, I'm looking at your face. And I can see you're very lonely. That's—>

I slammed my iBook shut, with the same satisfaction I'd get from

slamming her mouth shut. Muted, frustrated, she leaned all the way
back in her chair and blew cool air at the ceiling.

How strange that I would take that moment to admire her body
again. I drank it in. Her wonderfully toned arms. Her sturdy shoulders.
Her terrifically humble breasts. She might have given me too much
credit. Despite my rage, I couldn't stop thinking about screwing her.
There was something very comfortable about that. There was something very safe and appealing about sex with an unhappily married
woman. Not just any sex but bad sex. Unfulfilling sex. I wanted to make
love to her badly. For the life of me, I couldn't figure out why.

Taking a break from each other, we watched the strangers in the
room as they all spoke in hands. I wished I knew a little of the language,
at least enough to eavesdrop. Jean was right. This was wearing thin.

Soon enough, a rotund little man flipped the light switch several
times, until he had our attention. He climbed the wooden stage and addressed the room with meaningful gestures. Within seconds, he had
everyone laughing except me and Jean. She was, however, idly amused.

I cocked my head at her. In response, she slipped me a futile smirk. *I
can't help you, buddy. You sealed my lips.* I reopened the laptop.

<"What do a duck and a dog have in common?"> she typed.

I shrugged at her. She shrugged back.

<"They both fly, except for the dog.">

Wincing, I shook my head.

<It works better in signs,> she conceded.

I emitted a soft grin.

<It's more than a different way of talking,> she explained. <It's a
different way of thinking. ASL is the cleanest, leanest language ever invented. There's no rhetoric. No hairsplitting. No mincing or prancing
or beating around the bush. To speak it is to cut right to the heart of the
matter, all the time. It's wonderful for us, but for people who can hear
and talk, even codas . . .>

Saddened, she tossed up her hands. <I know I'm hard to take. Believe me. I try to censor myself as often as I can. But somehow I always
end up snapping back to me. It's just the way I am.>

<Believe it or not, I like the way you are.>

<I know,> she wrote with a half-smile. <I know it. In fact, I
brought you out tonight because I was in a fairly desperate need to be
around someone who appreciated me.>

<I'm in short supply of those myself.>

<See, I don't understand that either. It truly baffles me.>

<You're only getting a fraction of me.>

She wasn't buying it. <Right. This is the part where you once again allude to the fact that you're secretly an asshole.>

<It's not a secret.>

<You're not an asshole,> she wrote back. <You're just feeling-impaired.>

She stood up and leaned over her keyboard. <I'm going to "freshen up." Then we'll skedaddle. They should be back soon anyway.>

I watched her walk away. She looked good from behind, too. She looked good from every angle. I couldn't seem to escape my lower functions, but the more I stayed down here, the more I realized that I was simply hiding out. I was afraid to go back upstairs. I was afraid to look into my very own mind and see how much of it she'd already conquered. She was taking me over, bit by bit. That was scary enough, but what really made me cringe was the thought, the fear, the suspicion that she knew exactly what she was doing.

Serves me right for letting her in. Serves me right for pulling her out of my laptop. I should have kept her in there, just like I kept Harmony trapped inside my big red cellular. Complicated gadgetry standing in for people. Are we embracing the future, Ira? Or are we both in need of a serious intervention?

As I sat there alone, as the comedian's silent jokes flew miles above my head, I thought about everything Jean had said. Then I realized I didn't have to think about it. I had an electronic transcript right here in front of me. Technology at work again.

I scrolled through our conversation. I got to the part where I cut her off. I noticed she had typed a few more words, even after I slammed my laptop shut. I was curious—deeply afraid but curious—to see how she finished the sentence.

Scott, I'm looking at your face. And I can see you're very lonely. That's okay. We're lonely, too. And we're inviting you in.

18

"HARMONY THIS/HARMONY THAT"

There was no escaping irony. I returned home from my excursion at half past eleven, only to remove the phone from my pocket and discover that it had been accidentally switched off. It must have happened somewhere along the way to Club Silence because I had a message waiting for me that was over an hour old. It wasn't from Harmony, but it was about her. Apparently there were big, bad things happening at the Fairmont Miramar.

"Finally!" yelled Alonso. "Where were you?"

"I'm sorry. My phone was off. I didn't realize."

"Well, we've got a pressing matter."

"You said that. Now can you please elaborate?"

In his message, Alonso had only stated that Harmony had . . . a visitor. He had said it with such delicate discretion that for a moment I thought he was referring to her period. If only. Harmony was indeed dealing with her very own blood, but it was all in the form of a fifty-eight-year-old man whose arrival I probably should have anticipated.

At ten o'clock he approached the main entrance to the hotel, only to be stopped by doormen. From his stained army jacket, his torn jeans, his duct-taped shoes, it was obvious he wasn't a distinguished guest of the Miramar. And yet despite his pauperlike appearance, the man insisted he was a Prince.

"You show her this photo," he demanded. "You show her my ID. She'll know me."

Sadly, he wasn't the first one to try to ride his way in on the long-lost-relative ticket. He wasn't even the first one who proclaimed himself

Harmony's father. But he was the first to offer evidence. In addition to a long-expired driver's license, he bore a photograph from 1981, the only known picture of Harmony's two natural parents.

The proof was sent upward, from hotel management to Harmony's bodyguards to Harmony herself. She hadn't seen hide nor hair of Franklin Prince since she was an infant. She wouldn't know him from Adam. But even with her fractured memories, she could recognize her own mother. She could see Franklin's strong resemblance to his other progeny, Kenneth Prince, a man Harmony knew and cherished. Kenneth was long dead, but the elder man had somehow made it through the years. Now he was back, presumably to make amends with his long-lost, famous child.

Nobody could blame her for wanting to meet him, if even just to confront him. Nobody could blame me for assuming the worst in him. At thirty-eight, he had knocked up his adolescent foster daughter and then abandoned his family to live with her in Modesto. Shortly after Harmony was born, he discarded both lover and child for a new teenage squeeze. He wasn't the villain of Harmony's life (that would be her stepfather), but he wasn't a beacon of virtue, either.

I was dying to know how she was doing. The phone rang six times before she answered. She sounded tranquilized.

"Hello."

"Harmony. It's me. I heard. Jesus. How are you?"

"I can't talk now."

"Is he still there?"

Pause. "Yeah."

"Listen, I want you to call me the minute he leaves, okay? Don't worry about the time. I'll be up."

"Okay."

"You promise to call me?"

"Yeah," she said after another discomforting silence. "I gotta go."

I put the phone down, then stretched out on the couch. It was hard to think, especially with Jean still running loose in my head. To distract myself I watched *Saturday Night Live* until I closed my eyes. When I opened them again, it was two-thirty in the morning, and my red phone was ringing.

"Harmony?"

She didn't respond, but I could hear her soft sniffles. I sat up.

"Okay, are those good tears or bad tears?"

She sniffed again. "I don't know."

"Well, how did he seem?"

"Terrible," she said. "He was missing teeth. He had these sores on his hands. And he smelled awful. I felt so bad for him."

He must have been a pathetic sight indeed. I couldn't imagine anyone, even Harmony, being anything less than furious.

"So was he all apologies?"

"Yeah. He said he's a different man now. He's been living in shame over what he did. He said he's been trying to find me for a while. Then he saw me on the news."

I resolved not to say anything. No misgivings. No warnings. No theories. I was just going to follow Maxina's cue and be supportive.

"Okay, what?"

"Nothing," I urged. "I'm just listening."

"No, you ain't. You thinking shit."

"I'm always thinking shit. But right now I'm just here to listen and be your friend."

"Yeah, right."

"I'm serious."

"Scott, just say what you wanna say!"

"Look, I don't know this man. I can't judge his motives." Wincing, I rubbed my temple. "All I'll say is that it took me one afternoon to find you."

"Well, maybe he ain't as smart as you."

"You didn't change your name. You didn't even leave the area."

"So maybe he just ain't smart, okay? He's still my father!"

"I know that. I know. I can't even pretend to relate to what you're going through right now. But in case you haven't noticed, I'm very protective of you. I don't want to see you get hurt."

She unleashed a jaded laugh that was unique for her. And worrisome to me.

"It's not that I think he's out to hurt you. I just think he's . . ." Damn it. Shut up. Shut up. "Can I ask you a very important question?"

She let out an acrid sigh. "What?"

"Did he ask you for money?"

Her lack of answer was answer enough. I threw my head back, mouthing a curse.

"Did you *give* him money?"

Still nothing.

"You gave him all the money I gave you."

After another lull, her crying gasps started up again. Son of a bitch. He was better off staying out of her life. Franklin Prince was not a nice man, nor was he a subtle man. And Harmony wasn't stupid. She could tell from the start that her father was looking at her through dollar-sign eyes. All I was doing was confronting her with her own worst suspicions. I didn't expect any medals for my effort. I could hear Jean's gloating whisper in the back of my mind. *Hypocrite.*

"Look, sweetheart, I'm sorry I—"

"Stop calling me that."

"What?"

Her voice was low and guttural now, full of teary rasp. "Stop calling me 'sweetheart.' Stop calling me 'honey.' Stop talking down to me like I'm your goddamn bitch."

I leaned forward, stunned. "I'm sorry. Harmony. God, I didn't even know it bothered you. If I knew—"

"Just stop talking! I am so sick of you talking! I'm sick of you talking, and playing me, and acting like you care about me and shit!"

"I do care about you."

"You never cared about me! You only care about getting what you want!"

I stood up. "Harmony, I'm not the one you're mad at right now."

"Yes you are! I'm mad at *you,* Scott! I'm mad at you for always talking down to me! I'm mad at you for always telling me how I feel! I'm mad at you for trying to keep me away from my friends! For not telling me about Lisa Glassman!"

"Wait. What?"

"For promising me all this money and then not letting me take a dime!"

"Hold it!"

"And I'm mad at you for kissing me and promising me the world and then locking me up in this MOTHERFUCKING ROOM THE REST OF MY LIFE!"

"Wait!"

"FUCK YOU!"

The line went dead. The phone fell out of my hand. I put it back on the coffee table, then lay down on the couch again. My eyes were wide open. I spent the next few hours staring up at the ceiling, connecting the stucco dots into images that were both grand and intricate.

Although she didn't tell me, Harmony had another visitor on Saturday. At three o'clock a lovely young woman of Korean descent approached the bodyguards outside Harmony's suite. From her small white bikini, she seemed to be a guest who'd stumbled off (*way* off) from the pool area. She wasn't. After greeting the men, she removed the towel from her waist and slowly spun around for them. Her goal, aside from causing erections, was to prove that she wasn't hiding any recording equipment. She wasn't with the press. She was simply a businesswoman who required a few moments of Harmony's time.

Like most women who caused erections, and like most erections, she was indulged. The bodyguards let her deliver her pitch through a two-inch crack in the door.

Harmony, my name is Kathy Oh. I'm a publicist. A very good one. Now you can listen to me or not, but I'm telling you right now that whoever's handling you is wasting you. You've got a kind of spotlight on you that few people ever get, even celebrities. You shouldn't be hiding from it. You should be using it before it goes away. Make a difference. Make some money. Whatever you want, I can help you get it. I can get you enough offers in the next seven days to set you up for the rest of your life.

To give Harmony a taste of her own potential, Kathy brought a ready-made deal. On behalf of the Coca-Cola Company, she was authorized to offer Harmony fifty thousand dollars, all up front, in exchange for being seen with a can of Coke in her hand. Left or right. Diet or regular. The variables didn't matter as long as the can was caught on the news. The arrangement was completely confidential, and it was valid whether or not Harmony signed with Kathy. She would return, with cash and paperwork, at 6:00 P.M. Think it over. Have a nice afternoon.

Naturally, the offer provoked much discussion among Harmony, her bodyguards, and her visiting roommates. Even her friends, who had each turned down tabloid money on principle, couldn't find a problem with the Coke proposal. Neither could Harmony. The one thing standing between her and free money was the stern specter of me.

Circumventing me altogether, she called Alonso, the lenient parent, hoping he could bless the deal. No such luck. He simply told her everything I would have. Despite Kathy's grand fancy, word of the arrangement would inevitably reach the press, and the press took a harsh eye to secret shills. Harmony was better off sticking to open endorsements, and not until after the twist.

But, sensing Harmony's resentment, Alonso adjusted his spiel. *Look, that's just how Scott explained it. If it were up to me, I'd be having a Coke and a smile right alongside you. But this is his show. And we both know his take on this.*

I didn't learn about this until Sunday morning, when Maxina gave me the secondhand story. I had to laugh, not just at Alonso's cheap evasion but at Kathy Oh's resourcefulness. Like me, she was a freelance operative. Unlike me, she was renowned for her effective lack of subtlety.

Yet we were both minnows compared to Maxina. She was never one for the bikini trick, thank God, but she had her own way of getting things done. By the time she showed up at my doorstep, bearing news and gifts, she knew who was in the superior position. I couldn't blame her for being smug. I couldn't even blame her for being superior. I lost Harmony on my own, with only a little help from others.

———

"She'll come around," Maxina assured me from the bottom of my front steps. "That thing with her father really threw her for a loop. You just got caught in it."

She stood. I sat. She was clean and well rested. I still wore my clothes from last night, plus a new dark circle under each eye. I was miserable. She was not. But her joy had little to do with me. On Friday night, while in the lowest of low moods, she had returned to her hotel room only to find her husband and sons waiting there, fresh from Atlanta. They had conspired with her staff to surprise her. It was the best kind of deception, and it worked. Maxina told me she screamed so loud, she probably set off every car alarm in the area.

Currently, her three men—all big and burly fellows—waited patiently outside her rented Lexus. They were all about to take a nice, relaxing jaunt up the Pacific Coast Highway. Maxina only stopped by to deliver her latest coup, which I now held in my hands. It was a cardboard box the size of a toaster oven. There wasn't a news director alive who wouldn't club me for its contents.

"Well," I admitted, "you certainly put me in my place."

"I didn't do anything."

"You told her about Lisa Glassman, I assume."

Less than contrite, she unwrapped a peppermint candy. "Yes. That I did."

"Kind of like the scorpion stinging the frog, don't you think?"

"It was a calculated risk."

"It was your first bad move."

She popped the candy in her mouth, then slipped the wrapper into her shirt pocket. "You had way too much power over her. Every time I talked to her, every other sentence out of her mouth was 'Scott says this' or 'Scott says that,' 'Scott thinks this' or 'Scott thinks that.' " She laughed. "I mean you really won her over. I was trying to ride my way in on the surrogate-mother train, but *you,* you seduced her."

Maxina brushed a ladybug off her shoulder. "Not literally, of course."

I had the urge to become loud and nasty, but her family was just ten yards away.

"Ordinarily, that wouldn't concern me too much," she added. "Except that you yourself were getting a little too 'Harmony this, Harmony that' for my comfort."

I lowered my head and laughed. Maxina didn't share the humor.

"I've been in this game a long, long time, Scott. One of the reasons I've endured, I think, is because I've always kept an inch of space between me and my causes. It doesn't stop me from fighting passionately. It doesn't stop me from working eighty-hour weeks. It just stops me from losing myself in the mission. I've seen some bright and talented people burn up that way."

She tossed me a meaningful glance. "So have you."

I twirled the box in my hands. It didn't make a sound. Whoever packed the tapes sure packed them tight.

Maxina sighed. "Okay, I have better things to do than stand here and annoy you. I just wanted to drop off the present. To be honest, I was hoping I could convince you to convince Harmony to end this sham tomorrow, but obviously—"

"She's not even talking to me."

"She *will*. For God's sake, it's just a snit. If you weren't so wrapped up in her, you'd see that."

Try as I might, I couldn't disagree. With Harmony, I didn't have a shred of detachment left. Funny how just twelve hours before, another highly perceptive woman had called me feeling-impaired. It was doubly ironic, considering that I was using my odd feelings for Jean to distract myself from Harmony, and vice versa. I was standing them against each other, holding Madison for ballast.

"I am not here to meddle in your life," declared Maxina. "Frankly, I could care less about whatever personal issues you're dealing with. All I know is that this whole giant mess revolves around Harmony, and she, for reasons I can't even begin to fathom, still revolves around you. That makes you crucial to me, to Jeremy, to Mean World, and to the entire music industry. I don't like it. Believe me, if I thought I could persuade her on my own to do what she has to do, I'd write you out of the story in a heartbeat."

She glanced back at her family, waving for more patience. "I need you for this. You're the one who started it. You're the one who has to end it. And if you just took a step back, if you just got some *distance,* you'd see that the Larry King show is a perfect place to end it."

"It's too soon."

Maxina pointed to the box. "We've got the documentary now. We've got hours of sympathetic footage to help break her fall."

"It's still too soon."

"You saying that out of spite?"

"I'm saying it out of reason. I'm talking about a few more days. Jeremy, Mean World, and the entire music industry can survive a few more days of Harmony, much more than Harmony can survive a confession tomorrow. She's barely said a word to the public yet."

"And whose fault is that?"

"Mine. Obviously. If I was overcautious, I was overcautious. But I'm not going to be reckless to compensate." I flashed her a facetious grin. "Not with my dear, beloved Harmony at stake."

That was said out of spite. Maintaining her perpetual evenness, Maxina pressed her hands together, resting the tips of her fingers against her lips.

"I'm going up the coast," she proclaimed in a demonstrably chirpy tone. "I'm going to spend the day with the men I love. At the moment, you are not a man I love."

"That's okay. I wouldn't have fit in the car anyway."

She dissected me one last time.

"Scott, do me a favor. Don't watch those tapes right away. Take a day for yourself. Run some errands. Spend some time with your lady friend. Just take a break from the mission. Please."

I tried that yesterday. It didn't quite work. There was no escaping Harmony. But I appreciated the concern.

When the nation's hottest new victim asked the nation to leave her alone, the cynics didn't buy it. This was the age of Jerry Springer. And

Harmony Prince, like it or not, was firmly entrenched in a demographic that lined up to exploit itself on trashy vessels like his. She was a hostess dancer. A hip-hop hoochie. A low-rent ass-shaker who'd presumably bite the head off a chicken if it gave her the chance to get bleeped on somebody's talk show.

And yet the media—the legitimate media—had been standing outside her hotel for three days, waiting for her to spill her guts. Even Jesus popped up after three days. Who the hell was this woman?

She certainly wasn't Jesus, but through her silence, her restraint, she was rising above the pathetically low expectations of her demographic. She was rising above the caricature of the lower-class black woman. How very strange that this was all engineered by the whitest of white men, an apolitical flack who gagged at every form of mass-market idealism. I wasn't doing this for black women. I was doing it for Harmony. I wanted the world to appreciate her for more than her entertainment value. I wanted them to get her right. How very sad that she, of all people, resented my efforts.

I wasn't the first high-minded artist to get caught up in his subject. I wasn't even the first one to get caught up in Harmony. Four years ago, a progressive filmmaking duo followed her around with a camera, studying her in her natural habitat like she was an exquisite gazelle. They amassed 102 hours of raw video, all of which fell into a deep legal crack once the couple split hard.

By Thursday every network was pounding at their respective doors, looking for some way, *any* way, to untie the Gordian knot that was keeping all that beautiful footage from being released. Then Maxina cut right through it, not only freeing the product but getting an exclusive hold on it. When I asked her how, she said, "Who cares?" I could only assume she brought both Jay McMahon and Sheila Yorn into the ever expanding fold, describing the gag, explaining how crucial their aborted documentary would be in saving Harmony's attritional ass.

As soon as I reentered my apartment, I opened the box, closed the shades, and popped in the first of the eighteen videotapes. In my state, I must have looked like a moping ex-boyfriend, losing himself in old, happy images of the woman who dumped him. There was a little of that, but mostly I was working. I held a notepad in my lap, marking the most poignant segments. I wanted to explain to the masses, in an airable nutshell, why Harmony lied. Why she stopped lying. Why everyone should forgive her and ultimately admire her for the person she is. I had my work cut out for me, especially since I was building my case off the person she was.

Outwardly, Harmony at fifteen was little different from Harmony at nineteen. Her hair was longer. Her teeth were crooked. She had some mild acne. All to be expected. What jarred me was the vastly different way she carried herself. There was a sharp edge to her that didn't exist anymore. This Harmony was still two years away from being mowed down in a crosswalk by a wayward police cruiser. This one had an undamaged brain. She talked quicker. She moved quicker. I could even see her think quicker.

She also had clearer access to some very bad memories, and it showed. The more I watched her interact with people, the more I noticed a *jagged* edge. She was polite to her teachers, funny to her friends, even a little sexy to the boys who paid her attention (and there were more than a few), but a lot of it seemed artificially generated for the cameras. Behind the act was a thin layer of contempt that never seemed to reach the surface. I could see it best when she turned to face the lens. She seemed to have a special disdain for her chroniclers. Or maybe it was for her eventual audience.

Either way, Jay and Sheila adored her. Since this was all rough copy, I could hear their off-screen chatter. They had fallen for Harmony just as hard as I did, although I wouldn't have been as easily roped in by this version. This one was a little less than genuine. This one put her best feet forward.

Twenty hours into the footage (and eight hours into my viewing), Harmony dropped the mask. She was sitting on a couch in her shabby group home, drawing into a sketchpad. It was yet another maddeningly dull segment to fast-forward through, but there was something about her increasing discomfort that made me slow down and watch. She kept peeking at the camera through the corner of her eye, increasingly vexed.

"*I don't know what y'all find so interesting about this.*"

"*We think it says a lot about you,*" replied Sheila, invisible as always.

"*Yeah, well, I don't know what you find so interesting about me.*"

Now Jay voiced in. "*Don't sell yourself short. You're pretty remarkable.*"

I rolled my eyes. So did Harmony. "*Why? Because I'm less fucked up than I should be?*"

"*You're a girl who grew up in a culture of violence and abuse—*"

"I'm a black girl who grew up in Inglewood," she countered. *"And you only calling me 'remarkable' because I don't got a pimp, two kids and a crack habit."*

I laughed. The filmmakers didn't.

"Harmony, we admire you for the things you do have. You're intelligent. You're talented. You're affable."

"We look up to you."

"Yeah, but you looking down to look up," said Harmony. *"You admiring me like I'm the nicest dog in the pound."*

The next few seconds were pure nerve-racking silence. I sat forward, mesmerized.

Vindicated by the filmmakers' silence, Harmony got back to her drawing. *"Don't worry. I'll play along. I'll give you your show. I'll even roll over and beg, if it'll get me out of this place."*

The mask went back on. The film kept rolling. The scene would never have made it into Jay and Sheila's final cut, had there been one. I couldn't even work it into my own product. For the media, it would only be a tool to simplify her. They'd only use it to squeeze her into one of their preexisting molds. The world would never get her right. But I was finally starting to.

On Monday, February 12, the word got out fast: Harmony was breaking her silence. CNN lifted their own gag at 8:00 A.M., four hours earlier than promised. In a business where each rating point was worth millions of dollars, and in a month when the broadcast nets took great pains to trounce their cable competitors, the network couldn't hold it in anymore. *We've got Harmony Prince, and we've got her tonight! Exclusively on CNN! Kiss our cheeks, Fox News! Oh, happy day! Happy day!*

It certainly wasn't a happy day for MGM. The final first-weekend box-office tally for *Hannibal* came in at $22.4 million, way lower than even the most skeptical forecasts. Move My Cheese had predicted a $58.1 million opening, a miss so wild that it shaved at least three points off the program's overall accuracy rating. Ira briefly returned to the corporeal world to check the numbers and mutter a few expletives before vanishing back into his monitor.

Also cursing: Alonso. The *New York Post* ran a malevolent piece on his spotty reputation as a lawyer and citizen. The story included damning quotes from disgruntled ex-clients, ex-employees, ex-girlfriends, and a leery investigator from the California Bar Association who'd been sniffing after Alonso since the mid-1990s. If that wasn't bad enough, the article contained two cleverly veiled references to transvestism, ambiguous enough to avoid a libel suit but clear enough to get the insinuation across.

When Alonso called me at 10:00 A.M., he was sputtering with rage. He was convinced that the story had been planted by none other than Doug Modine.

"So, that's the way we're playing it now?" he bellowed. "We're using *live* ammo on each other?"

I only had to scan the byline to know the true culprit. The author, Jenny Alvarado, was the maid of honor at Gail Steiner's wedding. Gail Steiner had harbored a mad-on for Alonso ever since he publicly blasted her for revealing Harmony's name (after privately giving her permission). She should have seen it coming, but alas, journalists were a sensitive bunch. And they stuck together. This, I explained, was simply revenge by proxy.

"Double proxy," he snapped. "I'm being punished for *your* maneuver."

"Hey, you made me the heavy with Harmony for that Coca-Cola thing."

"I'm entitled to a little latitude! I'm out here on the front lines, while you're safe and snug in your hidden bunker!"

Okay, okay. Whatever. I promised I'd help him with the counterspin. Anything to get him out of his own problems. His first and foremost task was to prep Harmony for her *Larry King* appearance, since I obviously couldn't. She had yet to lift her grudge, and it was driving me insane.

"Harmony, Harmony, Harmony," griped Madison at the start of her second work week. "You know, there are other things going on in the world besides Harmony."

She was talking to me but she was scolding the media. I couldn't blame her. She must have highlighted Harmony's name at least five hundred times since Thursday. It didn't help that I was watching yet another tape from the Jay and Sheila archives when Madison arrived. When she asked me how I obtained the footage, I gave her the loaded truth. "Never underestimate the great Maxina Howard," I told her. When she asked me what I hoped to gain by watching it, I gave her a loaded lie. "Know your enemy," I said. "Know your enemy."

Madison was more interested in getting my take on the Kournikova

virus, which had also scored considerable attention today. All throughout the weekend, all over the world, tens of thousands of computers
were infected by a tainted JPEG of eminently screwable tennis star Anna
Kournikova. Not being a tennis fan, I only learned of her existence and
screwability recently, thanks to the virus.

"That's my point," said Madison. "I bet her publicist was behind it."

I gave it some thought. "I don't know. That seems a little risky. I
mean they almost always catch the guys who start those things."

"So what? You just talk some teenage hacker into planting the bug
and then deny the hell out of it when he points the finger at you."

"That's a horrible thing to do."

"What? He's a kid. He'll just get probation."

"Yeah, well, how would you like it if I hung you out to dry like that?"

"I wouldn't like it at all," she replied. "But then I'd be smart enough
to record our conversations as insurance."

Goddamn, she had a future. "Get back to work."

At four o'clock Eddie Sangiacomo called me back with his investigative summary of Franklin Prince. Nothing surprising. A few statutory-
rape charges in the eighties. A number of drunk-and-disorderly arrests
in the early nineties. After that, he went liquid. On paper, he ceased to
exist. No reported income. No recorded addresses. No legal or medical
problems. Too bad. I was hoping there'd be something I could use to get
him out of Harmony's life forever. Whether she loved me or hated me,
I was still her guardian angel and would keep looking out for her best interests until one of us died.

At a quarter to five she stepped out of the Miramar and back into the
media swarm. Only the news channels broke in with live coverage of
her reemergence, but every network this side of Telemundo would be
rolling the tape tonight.

We watched her on CNN. Madison booed. Ever since she rapped
with Hunta, her fealty to him was unshakable. He could do no wrong
with her. Even when I told her he was a habitual philanderer, she denied
it. "If he never admitted it himself, then you have no proof. All you have
is hearsay." Well, I did hear it from numerous sources, including his
wife, but I let Madison have the point. I even joined in on the booing,
despite the fact that Harmony never looked better to me. She wore a
form-fitting white blouse with slit sleeves over wide-legged trousers.
Her hair was done up, salon-style, and her jewelry adornments were
formally chic.

Once again Alonso held her in defensive position, but now they had a throng of bodyguards to keep the press at bay. Harmony looked a lot calmer now than she did during her last walk of fame. She made eye contact with the cameras. She was wise enough not to smile.

With a derisive cluck of the tongue, Madison resumed her highlighting. "She's loving this. You can tell."

"I don't know. I heard a major soft-drink company offered her a lot of money to be seen with one of their products, and she turned them down."

"Does that stuff really work? I mean are people gonna go out and buy Pepsi just because they saw some rape accuser holding a can?"

I shot her a crafty smile. "I only said 'soft drink.' What made you think of Pepsi?"

"Thinking is not the same as buying."

"It's all cumulative. Wallets are opened by hands, hands are controlled by brains, and brains are full of other people's ideas. Nobody's immune to it. Not even your mother."

She threw me a teasing grin. "What made you think of my mother?"

"Get back to work."

Ducking questions, Alonso and Harmony scuttled into a big white limousine, courtesy of CNN. As soon as it drove off, the network went back to relevant polls and pundits.

"Man, those guys sure love Harmony Prince."

"I know you're talking to her," said Madison, still highlighting.

"You know I'm talking to Harmony Prince."

She fought a smirk. "I know you're talking to my mother. A lot."

I kept my gaze on her until she looked up again.

"It's okay," she assured me. "I'm not accusing you of anything. I mean I think you're secretly seeing someone, but considering that you're always talking to her on that weird red phone of yours, I know it's not Mom."

"Madison . . ."

"I'm sorry. It's not my business. I just wanted—"

"I'm not seeing anyone, secretly or openly."

"It's not my business. I just wanted to say I'm okay with you and my mom talking. That is my business. And I'm telling you, in case you wanted to know, that I don't have a problem with it. Not anymore."

She had her mother's ability to exasperate me. "What *was* your problem?"

Sighing, she resumed her work. "It's just that she always freaks out about me. I didn't want her freaking you out, too."

"I can form my own opinions."

"I know," she said warmly. "I can tell. It's appreciated."

Ever since she cried at my tardiness last Tuesday, Madison had declared a ban on all unprofessional emotions and expressions. I wasn't sure if she was trying to impress me or imitate me. Either way, she succeeded far too well. I could have used some mushy sentiment at the moment. I could have handled hearing what a wonderful guy I was.

Still, her genial praise was enough to get me out of the grim mood I'd been hiding. And what excellent timing, too. At five o'clock my "weird" red phone rang. As I carried it upstairs, Madison held up her hands. *Not my business.*

Although my face was cool and bemused, the inner me was howling with relief. Thank God. Thank God. Thank God. With just one hour to go before speaking to Larry King and the world, Harmony was finally speaking to me.

"Hey."

"Hey yourself," I replied, closing the bedroom door. "You look wonderful."

"Oh, you saw me?"

"I never miss you."

She was quiet. I threw myself down on the bed. I could hear the hum of the limo's engine. I could hear Alonso chattering away in the background.

"Who's he talking to?" I asked.

"I don't know. He's always talking to someone on the phone."

"He's always talking."

She chuckled. "Yeah."

"Well, for tonight he's been given firm instructions to shut up and let you speak for yourself."

"I know. That scares me."

"You'll be terrific," I promised. "This is the part we've all been waiting for. This is the part where you really get to shine."

She let out a long, tired breath. "You make me crazy, Scott."

"I know."

"I mean you really drive me nuts."

I closed my eyes. "I know. I'm sorry."

Now I could even hear the bumps in the road. I could hear Alonso bitching about the *New York Post*. Jesus. Get over it, already.

"I decided what to do about my father," she offered. "If he wants to be a part of my life, I'm going to let him in. To see if he's worth getting to know. But if he asks me for money again, even once, I'll know he's not for real. I'll know he's just playing me."

"I think that's very smart."

"Not that I've been doing much thinking about him today," she added with a nervous titter. "Ever since I woke up, I've been all about Larry. Larry, Larry, Larry."

I smiled. "I'm sure Larry's been thinking about you, too."

"Yeah, but he's not scared of me like I'm scared of him. And these guys haven't helped. Maxina and Alonso have been telling me things all day. They're like 'Okay, if Larry asks you this, don't say this. But if he asks you that, definitely say that.' And they keep reminding me how he's been doing this stuff for a million years. I get the point already."

We sighed in tandem, then Harmony groaned.

"Scott, what do I do?"

That was all I needed to hear to come alive. I sat up. "I'm glad you asked me that."

She chortled. "Come on. You think I'd go on live national TV without talking to you first? You're the only one who makes sense of this shit for me."

Life was good again. I hopped out of the bed, pacing. "Okay. First I want you to forget everything that Maxina and Alonso told you. Can you do that?"

"Oh, that's not a problem."

"Good. Now forget that proper diction you seem to be using. Just talk the way you normally talk."

"Oh no, Scott. I've been practicing all day."

"I don't want you wasting precious energy on grammar. It's unnecessary."

"Yeah, but I don't want to sound stupid."

"You never sounded stupid to me. And I'm pretty smart."

"It used to be easy for me," she said with lament. "Before the accident. I used to be able to turn it on and off like a light switch."

I knew that. By now I was very familiar with the "before" model. She was a good kid but she never could have smiled from a Polaroid the way this Harmony did. This was the Harmony I wanted.

"Just turn it off and leave it off. Will you do that?"

She loosened up already. "Yeah. Okay. Shit, so far this is easy. You only telling me to forget things."

"Yes, but here comes the hard part. This next and last one is very important. You want everyone to like you, don't you?"

"Of course."

"Okay. I want you to forget that too."

She paused. "Forget I want everyone to like me?"

"Absolutely. Anyone who presumes to judge you from the other side of a TV screen and a big bag of Ruffles is not worth impressing."

She laughed loud enough to quiet Alonso. "But what about Larry?"

"Larry's just a big old softie. And he already loves you for the numbers you're bringing him."

"Yeah, but—"

"Harmony, take a step back and look at yourself. Look at what you've got."

"What do I got?"

"You've got five roommates who turned down large amounts of money to protect you. You've got at least six bodyguards who'd probably guard you for free if it came down to it. You've . . ."

I stopped at the window, momentarily stuck for words. "You've got a talent for affecting people," I said. "Even the ones who aren't so easily affected. It's what you do. You do it without even trying. All I'm saying is don't start now."

She was dead quiet, but it was all warm silence.

"Harmony, when that camera light comes on, you're going to snap into place. You're going to become more yourself than you've ever been before in your life. Mark my words. You were born for television. I saw it before I even knew you and you knew it before you even met me. Don't shit a shitter."

She let out a soft, cracked laugh. "What you doing to me, Slick? You trying to make me cry before I even get there?"

"No. I'm just trying to hold your hand."

"I wish you were."

"I wish I were too."

"I don't know why you mess me up so much, Scott."

"I don't know," I said, resting my head against the glass. "I don't know. Somehow you and I just got tangled up, I guess."

"Yeah, but I don't see us ever getting married."

"No. Doesn't look likely."

"I mean I knew from the beginning that you too old, too white, and way too smart for me."

Grinning, I paced again. "Yeah. And I knew you were too young, too short, and far too nice for me. But I probably could have overlooked those things."

"If?"

"If you weren't so goddamn famous."

She didn't laugh. I was almost hurt until I heard the faint sounds of cheering from the other end of the line.

"Harmony? You there?"

"Yeah. I'm here. Holy shit."

"No, I mean are you there at the studio?"

"Yeah. I guess so. Oh my God. Holy shit! Are you watching this?"

"No," I said, fighting the urge to run downstairs. "Tell me what's going on."

"There are people," she began, then stopped to listen to Alonso. Come on. Shut up and let her talk to me.

"Scott, there are people all over the street. Outside the CNN building. They got signs. They all got signs with my name on them!"

"Don't keep me in suspense! What do they say?"

"Oh my God . . ."

"All right. I'm going to let you go deal with this."

"No! Don't go! Stay with me!"

"What do the signs say?"

"There's, uh . . . 'Harmony rules.' 'Go Harmony.' Uh . . . 'Stand strong, Harmony.'" She laughed, incredulous. "'Give them hell, Harmony.' 'Harmony Prince forever!' 'Inglewood High School loves Harmony Prince!' That's my school! And there's, uh . . ."

"What?"

She lost some steam. "'We believe you, Harmony.'"

I stayed with her, hiding out inside her big red cellular. When she stepped out of the limo onto Sunset Boulevard, she took me with her. She carried me through the gauntlet of cameras, cops, and spectators. As she proceeded, she described everything she saw, everything she felt. When she felt fear, I told her to stow it. I'd gotten her this far. I'd bring her the rest of the way. When she felt guilt, I told her to save it. She'd need it soon, but not tonight. Tonight was her night to bask in the world's unadulterated affection. It was such a rare thing nowadays to see a blameless celebrity. The Bitch had a tendency to bite and scratch the people she took into bed with her. Just ask Hunta.

But Harmony was in for nothing but warm, sweet love, and lots of it. If anyone deserved it more than she did, they should have come to me. I would have helped them too. Once again I felt divinely empowered, but this time my strength was matched by an otherworldly kindness. I was a benevolent force of nature. I was the Great Karmic Equalizer.

I was Superman.

And once I carried Harmony into the CNN building, I let her go, told her to be careful now, and flew back to my own office before anyone even knew I was gone. I came back downstairs as Clark Kent, wearing only the tiniest hint of satisfaction on my innocent face.

"Did I miss anything?"

Of course, Clark Kent had the luxury of being surrounded by extremely dense people who couldn't see through a pair of glasses. I had Madison. She turned away from CNN and looked at me strangely, as if I'd just changed into a cocktail dress.

"What?"

"She has the same phone," she uttered, still working it all out. "Harmony Prince has the exact same phone as you."

Oh. "So?"

"I just saw it. She was just talking on it while you were upstairs. Talking on yours."

"Madison, what would you like to know?"

"I'd like to know what would happen if I took your phone, did a star-sixty-nine, and asked for Harmony Prince. That's what I'd like to know."

Expressionless, I sat down on the easy chair, near her workspace. I thought about it for a moment, but what else could I do? I handed her the phone.

19

"NO."

"Well?"

My trusting assistant listened into the receiver, then handed the cellular back to me.

"Nothing," she said. "It's not working."

Of course not. Our phones may have been big and weird but they were loaded with enough advanced technology to thwart the FBI. What chance did ★69 have?

"Now do you want to ask me directly?"

She tried to maintain solid eye contact, but she didn't have the confidence to pull it off. "I'm sorry, Scott."

"Don't be sorry. Your suspicion isn't so crazy. This can be a very dirty business. People screw each other over all the time."

"But you're not."

"Not what?"

"Screwing over Jeremy."

Smiling softly, I shook my head. I fought the urge to call her "sweetheart." Harmony had made me all too aware of my tendency to patronize.

"I've made mistakes, Madison, but I've never betrayed a client. And I have absolutely no intention of leaving this one in the mess he's in. In fact, you could say I'm quite obsessed with getting him out. Do you believe me?"

"Of course I do," she said, flustered. "I'm just . . . It's stupid. I did the same thing last week, when you were late. I just jumped to the craziest, darkest explanation and assumed that was it."

Who was I to fault her? I used to wonder if she was secretly winning me over as a thirty-four-year-old deaf woman. Her miss was a lot closer than mine.

"I just get the feeling there's a lot you're not telling me," she said.

"There's a lot I'm not telling you," I admitted.

"Why?"

"Because as incredible as I think you are, you're only thirteen. And you're still new at this. I have other responsibilities that I can't share with you. I can't even share the reasons I can't share them with you. All I can say is have patience, have faith, and stick with me. Someday I'll tell you everything. I promise."

Madison curled her arms around her bunched knees, staring forward. "I know," she sighed. "I just—"

"—wish you could do more. Yes. You and me both. At least we can be frustrated together."

She looked up at the TV. CNN reminded us for the hundredth time that the hour of Harmony was nigh upon us.

"There's got to be some way to stop her," she insisted.

"How do you prove that someone wasn't raped? Either we'd have to find hard evidence that she lied or she'd have to confess it herself, on record."

"That'll never happen."

"Probably not," I sighed, fighting to stay in character. "But it'd be a hell of a nice surprise."

At 5:55, MRVL GRL returned to its now familiar spot at my front curb, near the hydrant. Madison shot to her feet the moment she heard the horn. This was not a nice surprise.

"Oh no! What the hell is she doing? She's early!"

Normally, Jean would be right on time, but today there was a schedule change. At the beginning of her shift, Madison asked if she could stay to watch *Larry King Live* with me. I told her it was fine as long as her mother approved. Using her two-way pager, Madison buzzed Jean. Jean buzzed back. Everything was spiffy. Except . . .

"Shit! She always does this! She always flakes out on me!"

"Hey, it's okay."

"It's not okay! I wanted to stay! Now I can't!"

"Sure you can."

"She's not going to want to drive away and come back in an hour!"

"Of course not."

"So what are we going to do? Make her wait out there?"

"No," I replied in a calming tone. "We're going to invite her in."

From her reaction, I might as well have suggested we all take a shower together.

"Oh my God. You can't be serious."

"I thought you didn't have a problem with us talking."

"Scott, you only deal with her electronically. You have no idea what she's like in person."

I had some. "Listen, you don't have to convince me she's nuts. I know it. She knows it. But she also knows that this is your workplace, and she respects that."

"She doesn't respect anything I do! All she does is ruin things!"

"Look at me."

Madison wasn't in good shape, but I had never felt better. I was still crackling and glowing with superhumanity. In my elevated consciousness, my floating-lotus position, I was sure I could heal at least some of the damage between mother and child.

"I know she embarrasses you, but there's nothing she can say or do to make me think any less of you. What *you* do, however, is very important. Now you can freak out, and freak me out, or you can invite her in and impress the hell out of both of us. "

She glared at me defiantly. "I'm not freaking out."

"Prove it."

"Fine. Whatever. I'll invite her in."

Instead of moving toward the door, she stood at the window and signed. They had a natural wireless connection. How cool.

She spoke along with her hands. "I said seven. Seven!" She sneered. "Yeah. 'Whoops.' Just park the car and come in." She shrugged brusquely. "It wasn't my idea. It was Scott's. Just come in."

Madison turned around and plopped down in the easy chair, shooting me a scowl. "She won't want to watch TV."

"Then I'll give her something to read. Go let her in."

She got up and shuffled toward the door. "You know, you might find this hard to believe, but I don't live to impress you."

I smiled. "And that's just one of the many reasons you do."

She left. I really couldn't blame her for being upset. She'd built a nice haven for herself here. The last thing she wanted was her mother storming in, bringing all the family baggage. Mom herself didn't seem too keen on the idea. *I would love to see the Madison that you see,* she had typed two days ago. *I only hope you never get the Madison that I get.*

Well, one of us was in for an education. And that was just the sideshow to what was happening on TV. I put a blank tape in the VCR and began recording. It was six o'clock. Zero hour. For 150 million television sets around the world, Harmony was just a click away.

Lawrence Zeiger and I had a few things in common. We both grew up in New York. We both hailed from German Jewish ancestry. We both changed our names at age twenty-four, mostly for aesthetics but a little bit to hide our German Jewish ancestry. I became Scott Singer. He became Larry King. And he did it ten years before I even became at all.

Larry King Live had been a staple of CNN since 1985. During that time, Larry had interviewed pretty much every name you've ever heard of, plus a few thousand you haven't. He'd even chatted up people who technically didn't exist. Aside from Jay Leno, no media figure had crossed the fourth wall more times than Larry, appearing as himself in over two dozen Hollywood properties, from *Ghostbusters* to *Murphy Brown* to *The Exorcist III*. Not being a CNN viewer, Harmony didn't learn of Larry's actuality until she was booked onto his show. She always assumed the guy with the suspenders was just another fictional character.

But Larry certainly believed in her. On Thursday and Friday he had devoted the entire hour to Harmony, bringing in his usual panel of experts to squabble over the merits of her case (and the demerits of Hunta's). He closed the show by promising a "very, very special guest" on Monday whom he couldn't announce until that morning.

And now here she was, sitting across the desk from him, in front of his signature light map. All throughout his intro, she smiled and fidgeted with palpable anxiety. I felt for her, even though I knew she'd loosen up quickly. She was in good hands. Larry King was not a gorgeous man, but he had a heart of gold and a steadfast neutrality. He wasn't emotionally manipulative, like Barbara Walters, or completely insane, like Connie Chung. He was a throwback to gentler times, when objectivity ruled the news.

On Harmony's left was Alonso, the sharpest-looking one of the bunch. Despite his commendable appearance, the poor man had been reminded by everyone, from me to Maxina to Larry's producers, to keep his big trap shut. This was Harmony's vehicle. He was just the airbag.

Okay, before we even start, do you want to explain that button you're wearing? What does that mean, "The Jury"?

With a pleasant laugh, Harmony raised the round button clipped above her right breast. The camera briefly zoomed in on it.

"This has nothing to do with the case. The Jury's just the rap group my roommates are in. They're gonna be real big, real soon. But I thought since I'm here, I might as well do a shameless plug. Hey guys! Hi Tracy!"

Madison shot back into the apartment and practically vaulted onto the couch. "What did I miss?"

"Nothing. It just started."

So you're a big fan of rap.

"I love rap. I always have. East Coast. West Coast. It don't matter to me, as long as it's good."

"Well, if it don't matter to her," teased Madison, "it don't matter to me."

I looked to the open door. "Where's your mother?"

"She's coming. She's just paging Neil."

"Oh. Is he expecting you guys at home?"

She shot me a dark look. "Was that a joke?"

"No. Why would that be a joke?"

"Scott, I'm trying to hear this."

A lot of people expected you to have a problem with rap, given the circumstances.

"I never had a problem with rap, Larry. Rap never hurt me. It was just a man who happened to be a rapper. I mean, if he was a milkman, nobody would be blaming milk."

Madison gaped in affront. "Oh my God. Is she for real?"

Yes, but that line couldn't have been more forced. Come on, Harmony. Stop trying to be cute. Stop trying to be anything.

Okay. I know this isn't easy, but let's talk about Hunta for a second.

Alonso was about to speak, but Harmony cut him off. "Actually, I'm trying not to talk about him. I don't want to talk about him. Anything I got to say about him, I'm saving for the trial."

Harmony patted Alonso's shoulder. "See? I listen to you."

Better. Much better. It took all my energy not to smile. Damn it. I shouldn't have let Madison stay. I should have watched this alone, without anyone watching me.

So you expect it to go all the way to trial. No settlement.

"I don't know what to expect anymore. I'd just love for this whole thing to be over right now. Actually, I wish it had ended back in January, before the whole Melrose thing."

Finally, Jean entered my apartment. For once she was actually stylish: professional gray blazer, short skirt, high heels, expensive earrings. She looked pretty damn formal for a self-employed graphic designer. She looked pretty damn good.

She closed the door, then flashed me an edgy grin. *Hi. Thanks for having me. You must be insane.*

I returned an acknowledging shrug. *Sorry. I meant well. I'm scared, too.*

"Have a seat," I said, motioning around. "Anywhere."

She took off her blazer, revealing the sleeveless white blouse she'd worn to Club Silence. If she was embarrassed to be seen in the same shirt twice, she didn't show it and I didn't care. With arms as perfect as hers, she could wear that top for the rest of her life and I wouldn't mind. God help me. I had yet to recover from Saturday night's tumult. All I did was put my attraction on layaway while I dealt with Harmony. Terrific. Now I had to process both women at the same time, while masking it all from Madison. I was just full of bad ideas tonight.

Jean sat down on the couch, on the other side of her daughter. From the way she held herself, you'd think there was a spitting cobra between us.

I leaned back to get a clear view. "Do you want anything to drink? Or eat?"

"Scott, you're missing this."

Jean shook her head. I sat forward again, muttering to Madison, "Should I turn on the captions?"

She was still fixed on CNN. "Don't bother. She's going to get up in a minute and start thumbing through your magazines."

Now, on Thursday, you told the press to leave you alone. You wanted them to respect your privacy. Why are you speaking out now?

"Because I'm already all over the place," Harmony replied evenly. "I mean, I know they're just doing their job, but . . . I don't know. Ever since Thursday, I been reading all this stuff about me, and it's all been . . ."

You feel you've been misrepresented.

"I feel like I've been simplified."

I had to laugh at how right she was. As Harmony spoke, the network ran alternating text bites on the bottom third of the screen, under her

name. WAS RAPED AND IMPREGNATED BY HER STEPFATHER AT AGE 11 /
DISCOVERED MURDERED BODIES OF MOTHER, HALF BROTHER IN 1994 /
SPENT 13 MONTHS IN HOSPITAL AFTER BEING HIT BY POLICE CAR.

"I mean, I see these experts and psychologists talking about me like
they know me. Complete strangers are talking about these things from
my life like I was a TV movie or something."

Well, you've been through an awful lot for someone so young.

"Yeah, but I don't want to be defined by the bad things that happened
to me. I mean, everyone has had something bad happen to them at some
point. It affects the person they are but, I mean, it doesn't necessarily de-
fine them."

Madison mocked her again. "I mean . . . I mean . . . I mean . . ."

"Oh, like you're so eloquent."

"Shut up."

So what do you think defines you?

After a few seconds of stumped silence, Harmony laughed. "Wow. I
guess I brought that on myself. Uh, let me think about that."

Larry took the opportunity to cut to the first commercial.

"She's good," I said with false frustration.

Madison tied her hair back. "I don't know. She seems awfully perky
for an alleged rape victim."

"That's the thing. She's downplaying it beautifully. If she went on
TV going 'Woe is me, woe is me,' there'd finally be some backlash
against her. Everyone likes a victim, but nobody likes a whiner."

"I didn't know she had braces. I bet they're fake."

"Why would she wear fake braces?"

"So she doesn't look too perfect."

I tugged her ponytail. "Not everything is a calculated move."

Meanwhile, Jean continued her efforts to exist inoffensively. I smiled
at her. "You must be bored out of your mind. I'm sorry."

She gently waved a hand. *I'm fine. I'm fine.*

Madison signed to her, smirking. "Relax, Mom. You're not embar-
rassing me."

Jean quickly signed back. Madison laughed, then squeezed her
mother's arm.

"What did she say?" I asked.

" 'Give it time.' "

Kicking off her shoes, Jean approached my wall unit and began
thumbing through my old issues of *Brandweek*.

"She just can't sit still in front of the TV."

"That's amazing," I said.

"Yeah, but it's made her all weird. I mean we barely have any culture in common. She doesn't even know who Jerry Seinfeld is."

Finding no interest in *Brandweek,* Jean keep browsing until she discovered my untitled copy of *Godsend* on top of the TV. She skimmed a few pages, then held the stack up to me, intrigued.

Madison signed to her. "It's just some novel his friend wrote."

She tilted her head, mouthing her query. *Ira?*

"No," I replied. "A different friend."

Ironic that Alonso, the friend and author in question, just materialized behind her pelvis.

"Mom, move. We can't see."

Jean sat down with the manuscript. As the show continued, I found myself frequently checking in on her. She seemed at turns both enthralled and bewildered by Alonso's prose. At one point she caught my glance and threw back a look that was way too complex to decipher. There was definitely some sadness there. I couldn't tell what it was related to. Madison? Neil? Me? None of the above? I motioned for her handheld, fumbling with the stylus.

YOU JUST COME FROM A JOB INTERVIEW?

With a scowl, she wrote into the device, then handed it back. YES. IT SUCKED. I HATE THE WORLD.

Smiling, I scribbled back. BUT YOU LOOK NICE DOING IT.

She studied me, deadpan, before passing her reply.

THANKS. YOU WANT TO FUCK HERE, OR SHOULD WE GO UPSTAIRS?

I bit my lip to keep from laughing, but it was a losing battle. Jean was a cruel woman, the kind who'd fart at a funeral just to watch the faces around her quiver and crack with painful suppression. But she fell into her own trap. She found my tortuous struggle so amusing that soon enough we were both red-faced and rumbling, shooting quick breaths through our noses.

It was hopeless. We were caught.

"Scott, you're supposed to be watching this!"

I let out a sobering cough. "It's okay. I'm taping it."

"Maybe I wanted to analyze it with you! You ever think of that?"

"You will," I promised. "We'll do it tomorrow. We'll go through it piece by piece. I swear."

Madison stood up, muted the TV, then aimed her hot glare at her mother: the human virus. Twelve minutes and already she'd contaminated the apartment, the work effort, me. No wonder Madison fought to keep me away from her. If I had known she was such an infectious presence, I would have kept away myself.

Jean grimaced, expecting the worst, but her daughter remained spitefully mature. With a stern glower, she addressed us in two different languages.

"Okay, fine. But instead of passing notes behind my back like a couple of third-graders, how about including me in the conversation?"

I shut off the handheld and tossed it back to Jean. "Sure. We'll talk. You can translate. Just turn up the sound a little. I want to keep an ear open."

Madison adjusted the volume, then faced us from the easy chair. "All right. Let's talk."

For a few awkward moments, none of us could come up with a topic. Then Jean pointed at the TV, signing.

"She wants to know what we're watching and why. Can we tell her?"

"Of course. It's hardly a secret."

"This won't be easy. Trust me."

She wasn't kidding. Jean was so far removed from the cultural spectrum, she didn't even know what rap was. It took several minutes for us to explain the background, the main cast of characters, and our role in the drama. She wasn't entirely pleased.

"It's not so simple, Mom."

"What did she say?"

"She said we've got it ass-backwards. We're saving the villain from the damsel in distress."

I shook my head. "It's a lie. He never even touched her."

" 'How do you know?' "

Because it was my lie. "Because his wife knows him better than anyone else. She has no illusions about him. And she believes he's innocent with every fiber of her being."

Madison translated my defense with gusto. Her mother backed down.

" 'If you're right,' " she offered, " 'then this Harmony woman is either malicious or deranged.' "

I scoffed at Jean. "It's not so simple, *Mom*."

" 'Why do you say that?' "

The question came from both of them. I leaned back and shrugged. "I just think people are complex. That's all."

Jean signed with sarcastic wonder. Madison giggled. " 'Ooh. You're *so* deep.' "

With a tight smirk, I flipped Jean the one piece of sign language I knew. She punched my arm, then gestured to Madison, who was still laughing.

"She wants to know what other crazy projects you've worked on."

Delving into the crisis-management archives, I told them about the time I fought to save a Stanford professor whose correct but unfortunate use of the word "niggardly" had raised quite the brouhaha. Ironically, it took four months and ten angry phone calls to get him to pay my invoice. I also shared the tale of my one political client: a California congressman whose sanity was called into question when he held a public moment of silence for Detective Bobby Simone (Jimmy Smits), who had passed away the night before on a very special *NYPD Blue*. The congressman was simply injecting some droll levity into a long and dull assembly meeting, but newspapers all over the country painted him as a schizoid "Nurse Betty" figure who couldn't tell fiction from reality. With my help, he got better.

And, of course, I filled them in on the recent fun and games at Keoki Atoll. Madison was impressed with my ability to talk 128 respectable young women into stripping naked for me. Jean wasn't, but she withheld her objections. Even when I told her about Deb Isham's hateful reaction, she hid her thoughts behind a mask of lead. That frustrated me. I was challenging her, testing the walls of her moral outrage. At first I thought she wasn't playing along, but as soon as Madison wasn't looking, she threw me a quick, hardy squint. *If you want to scare me, buddy, you'll have to do better than that.* I could, but it didn't look promising. She seemed strong enough to love me unconditionally, which made her strong enough to like me platonically, which apparently made her stronger than me.

Through Madison, she segued to a crazy project from her own career. Three years before, she was hired to come up with a nifty box design for Morning Faith, the world's first and only Christian-themed breakfast cereal. Oddly enough, her client was an Israeli investor who thought he could make a quick buck in the States. After all, America had millions of Christians. It had millions of cereal eaters. There had to be some overlap.

There was, but not enough to pull the flock away from the graven images of Cap'n Crunch and Count Chocula. Jean blamed the product's failure on her own generic "heaven sky" design. Madison and I faulted the lame title. Putting on our thinking caps, we came up with our own. Madison suggested "Angel Bran." I liked "Genu-Flakes." Jean took the prize with "Honey Frosted Monogamous Heter-O's." She also offered "Left Behind: The Cereal (Now with 25% Less)," but that one left us scratching our heads. Rolling her eyes, she told us to forget about it and move on.

The conversation devolved from there. It got so silly that Madison couldn't even translate anymore. Unlike EyeTalk, the poor girl wasn't built to handle the relentless back-and-forth between me and her mother. Soon she was laughing so hard, she had to escape to the bathroom to recuperate.

Jean and I were left alone, smiling but not laughing. Reclining against the wing of the couch, she kicked up her bare feet, leaned her head against her fist, and stared at me with that maddeningly unsolvable face of hers. I studied it. I set every neuron to work translating her complicated message. She didn't make it easy. There were so many missing pieces, and yet I could recognize her lingering issue from our Saturday-night tryst. *This is lovely, Scott, but I can see you still have problems.* Of course I had problems. What the hell did she expect? She claimed we had some profound cerebral rapport, but what if I wanted to explore her mind *and* her body? She claimed she was inviting me in, but what if the seat I wanted was already taken? What if I didn't want to spend the rest of my days coveting another man's wife and stepdaughter?

I matched her pose, nearly overtaking her small feet with my 11Es. I matched her stare, but her frustration couldn't hold up to mine. It wasn't fair what she was doing to me. It wasn't fair to tease me with her perfect wit, her perfect warmth, her perfect arms, her perfect *child,* this perfectly wonderful domestic scene, and then pack it all up at the end of the day. It wasn't healthy to invest more of myself in what was ultimately a time-share arrangement. I was loving them on the clock, renting them out like a pair of hostesses. If that was all I got out of them, this was all they got out of me. I may have been lonely, but I still had pride. Worse for Jean, I still had Harmony.

Raising the volume of the television, I sat forward and lost myself in the show. It was 6:45. The fourth commercial break had just come to an end. This was the part where Larry took calls from the audience. This was the part I worried about the most. I trusted Larry. He only threw softballs. Who knew what his viewers were waiting to hurl?

He introduced the first caller: a fast-talking man from Nyack, New York.

Hi. Harmony, first I want to say how sorry I am for all the terrible things you've been through.

Over the course of the hour, out of the corner of my eye, I watched Harmony grow more and more comfortable in front of the cameras. But now she seemed a little off balance. Furrowing her brow, she cocked her head. She was hearing the caller through a tiny earpiece. It took some getting used to.

"Uh, thank you."

My question is, uh, don't you think you're sending out a bad message to other rape victims by not cooperating with the police? I mean you're asking for money, but don't you want justice?

I could see Alonso's jaw tighten. He desperately wanted to jump in and tear this guy a new one. So did I. Harmony remained perfectly level. At some point her "smart" grammar had reemerged, but she wasn't trying. She didn't even seem to notice.

"I understand where you're coming from, sir, but I'll say it again: I don't need to see him go to jail. Jail's not going to make him a better person. Jail only makes people worse. And his going to jail isn't going to make *me* a better person. It's not going to help me sleep better or live better. Look, money *is* justice. Anyone who tells you otherwise probably has more money than he needs. And if you think that's a bad message . . ." She shrugged. "I'm sorry. I never asked to be a messenger. I gotta do what I think is best for me. But you're entitled to your opinion."

I leaned my head back and yelled. I could hear the spirit of Ayn Rand yelling back: *She's magnificent, Scott! How did you find her?* Just got lucky, ma'am. Just got lucky.

Madison rushed back downstairs. "What happened?"

"This woman is unstoppable!" I bellowed through a screen of artificial rancor.

She giggled. "Who, Mom or Harmony?"

"Harmony," I replied, taking a quick peek at Jean. Having given up on me, she had once again lost herself in Alonso's novel. But she did witness my odd cry to the heavens. I met her quizzical look with a childish raspberry. She shook her head, then signed to Madison.

"Mom says you're a troubled individual."

"Sit down. We're watching again."

This time Madison sat down on the floor, in front of her mother. Clapping with glee, Jean undid Madison's ponytail and began running her fingers through her daughter's long mane.

"She loves untangling my hair," she said. "She's a real freak about it."

"Your mom's just a freak."

"What did Harmony say to make you yell like that?"

"I'll explain later. Just watch."

I'd already missed the second call, but considering that Harmony had deferred to Alonso, it must have been a legal question. The third caller was a woman from Ottawa, Ontario. She had a soft, unsteady voice. Larry had to tell her twice to go ahead.

Hi. Uh, Harmony. My name is Jenna. I just wanted to start by saying that . . . I think you're very brave to come forward like this.

She chuckled. "I never planned on coming this far forward."

I know you didn't expect this much attention. But still, you took on a famous person with a lot of money and a lot of resources. That's not an easy thing to do. I . . .

Larry edged the woman on. *What's the question?*

I was in the same position as you. I was . . . I was raped by a man who . . . He hurt me pretty bad. And I was too afraid to come forward. This man was very well respected in the community and . . . I just couldn't find the courage to do it. I couldn't do what you did. And I'm a lot older than you.

The caller was crying now. Harmony bit her lip and gazed down at her ceramic mug.

I guess my question is how? I mean, this only happened to you eight weeks ago. It's been almost a year for me, and I still can't . . . I still don't even know how to handle it. Harmony, you're an inspiration to me. How did you get so strong?

Although the average viewer couldn't tell, the woman was disconnected. It was something producers did when a caller rambled on too long. In this remote-control world, when Nielsen boxes measured ratings in ten-second intervals, uncomfortable beats were a business hazard. As dramatic as the whole scene was, Harmony had only five seconds to reply before Larry gently pushed things forward. She almost missed her window.

"It's an act," she replied with a trembling smile. "This whole being-strong thing is just an act for the cameras. But I'm glad you fell for it, ma'am. I'm hoping someday I'll fall for it too. Maybe someday we'll both trick ourselves into being strong."

Magnificent. She was more profound than I could have possibly imagined. She was a young prodigy. She was wunderkind.

Madison was less impressed. "You think that call was for real?"

"I have very little doubt."

"I don't know. It sounded like a plant to me."

She was getting under my skin, but it was my own fault. I was the one who brought her backstage. I was the one who pointed out all the grease and grime, all the ropes and pulleys. I'd hoped that Madison's new enlightenment would make her less cynical, not more so. Either I was failing her as a mentor or she was just too damn young to cross the curtain. This was a problem I'd have to address soon.

At 6:53 something happened. Larry paused, expressionless, as he listened to his producers through his own earpiece. You'd never tell from his level face that he had a heavy decision to make and a split second in which to make it. But he was a seasoned veteran of the business. In retrospect, he did what any broadcaster would have done. And there were consequences for others—lots of consequences for lots of others—that he couldn't have possibly known about.

He simply and innocently introduced the final caller as "Los Angeles, California."

Harmony, hello. Before you react, I just want you to know that this isn't an ambush, okay? I'm not calling to attack you. It's just that you and I both have a lot invested in this, and I wanted to talk to you, straight up, woman to woman.

Harmony didn't recognize the voice. She had heard it only once before. Alonso had never heard it at all. I, however, pegged it immediately. That put my surprise about nine seconds ahead of everyone else's.

"What the hell is this?"

Madison looked to me. "What? Who is it?"

Larry asked the caller to identify herself. Who is this?

"It's his wife," I said.

"Whose wife?"

I'm the wife of the man you're accusing of rape. My name is Simba Shange.

A thousand alarms went off in my mind. A thousand dark angles were analyzed and explored. Behind each and every one of them, unfortunately, was Maxina.

"You didn't know about this?"

Wide-eyed, I sat down on the floor, next to Madison. "No. Not at all."

Neither had Alonso. He had done a marvelous job keeping quiet, but now it was time for the airbag to go off. He became quite vocal with his objections, drowning both Simba and Larry in chaotic crosstalk. Harmony merely gazed out at the cameras, at me, with a helpless expression. *Scott, what do I do?*

Listen, Harmony, you don't have to say or do anything. I just need to you to hear me out, okay? This isn't part of the game. I'm talking to you straight now.

Alonso continued to bury her in his own stir. Absolutely not! This is not appropriate! This is tantamount to harassment! I will not have my client harassed!

Madison shot forward. "God, shut the lawyer up!"

Harmony, you better tell your lawyer to shut up, or I won't just talk, I'll sing.

That shut him up. Her veiled threat made us both go slack. This couldn't have been Maxina's work. Maxina would have kept her a mile away from a very dangerous comment like that.

Look, I know all the things you know. I know what you're doing. I know why you're doing it. And I don't blame you one bit. You had all these smart, slick people telling you that everything's good. Everything's fine. Everything's gonna work out great for everyone, especially you. But they're misleading you, Harmony. They're using you for their own agendas, and none of them give a damn about you or my husband.

Madison held my arm. "What is she talking about?"

Larry asked the same question, but they were both ignored. The camera was fixed on a tight shot of Harmony. It was just her face reacting to Simba's voice. Both were starting to crack.

It only took you a few days to become famous. It took Jeremy years. He had to work through years of setbacks and disappointments and bad contracts and greedy executives, but he did it. He made it past all of them. Then came Melrose and then came you, neither of which he's responsible for. He never did anything to hurt you. But now everything he's ever worked for is being undone because everyone thinks he hurt you.

With a trembling hand, Harmony covered her mouth. Now both women were crying.

You're killing him, Harmony. Nobody told you, but I'm telling you now. You're killing him. You're killing our whole family and I'm asking you to stop.

Harmony's wet face was being beamed out through 21 satellites, to 212 countries, into Lord only knew how many television sets. There was no true way to measure the number of people watching her from their homes and dorms, from the bars and hotels, the hospitals, the airports. There was no way to measure how people watched her, whether their jaws hung slack or their hands touched their mouths. And there would never be a way to know what people were thinking as they saw Harmony's quiet tears fall live on global TV. I could only guess. I could only assume they were all watching, thinking, and talking just like Madison.

"Oh my God. She's gonna confess . . ."

The people in the loop—and there was no way of counting them anymore—were all dealing with heavier thoughts. What if she confesses everything? What if she sinks the whole ship? What if she tells the world that she was really working for Hunta/Mean World/Interscope/Universal/Vivendi/the RIAA/Maxina Howard/Scott Singer? Oh please, God. Please, Harmony. Don't take us down with you.

That thought was running strong in my head, but I was also on the other side of the issue, with Harmony's roommates and bodyguards, her admirers and well-wishers, rape victims and rap bashers alike. I was praying right along with them. Oh please, God. Please, Harmony. Don't do it. Don't go down at all. You keep going. You keep going.

I'm begging you to stop, Harmony.

At long last, Harmony uttered something, but it came out as wet air. She bowed her head, still choking back sobs. Whatever she said was so low that even her collar mike didn't pick it up.

"What did she say?" asked Madison.

What'd you say?

"She said something. I couldn't hear it."

Larry leaned in closer. Harmony, what did you just say?

She lifted her head again, showing her tear-streaked face. Despite her red and puffy eyes, there was a sharpness to her expression, a hard contempt I hadn't seen since the ghost of her old self glared at me from a four-year-old documentary.

"I said no."

The studio was silent. The camera remained fixed on Harmony. She wiped her cheeks and saw the world dead on.

"I said no, and he didn't listen . . ."

Madison and I both leaned back against the couch. In the reflection of the TV screen, I could see Jean behind us, still running her nimble fingers through Madison's hair. She was watching with us, but she didn't seem to be watching Harmony. Through the television, through the reflection in Harmony's face, she was watching me.

On TV, the tears kept coming, stronger and stronger, as Harmony sealed tomorrow's headline.

"I said no. And he didn't listen."

That pretty much finished the show. Larry segued to a commercial. By the time he came back on, it was 6:59 and he was alone. He told us, in sympathetic fashion, that Harmony Prince and her attorney have left the studio. She's okay. Boy, it's never easy though, is it? She's a brave woman. A brave woman. He then plugged tomorrow's guests, a standby panel of experts who'll talk and argue about—who else?—Harmony Prince. Hope you'll join us.

By the end of the hour, I was already in my bedroom, Bat-Phone in hand. As I had made my way upstairs, Madison threw me a simple but poignant question: "Scott, what does this mean?" The subtext of her concern was obvious: *Scott, what if she's telling the truth?*

She wasn't, but the fact that Madison began to wonder meant big trouble for everyone. If Harmony could put doubt in the mind of Hunta's most zealous defender . . .

Sorry, *second*-most zealous. Congratulations, Simba. You just made the biggest public fuck-up since DEWEY DEFEATS TRUMAN. You just scored a place in the High Hall of Well-Intentioned Bunglers, right next to Ralph Nader. You just became our iceberg.

From her own lovely face, Jean had a different inquiry. *What are you not telling us?* She had seen me in the reflection of the TV screen. Surely she suspected by now that my attitude toward Harmony was somewhat less than adversarial. *But what does that mean, Scott?*

She'd just have to wonder for now. I had higher priorities. This was the part where the ship began to sink. This was the part where everybody got loud.

"How is she?"

"What the hell is going on?"

"Alonso, how is she?"

"She's not talking to me! She's not talking to anyone! She's in the bathroom right now, crying, screaming and calling everybody a mother-fucker!"

I tried to call her, but she didn't answer her phone. I was hoping she'd at least be fuming from the inside of a limousine.

"Get her out of there," I demanded. "I don't care how. Get her out of there and get her back to the hotel."

"Scott, she's not listening to me! She thinks I was part of the ambush! She thinks we all set her up!"

"Keep your voice down! Be careful!"

"I'm in the senior producer's office. Don't worry. I'm alone."

"You're still in the CNN building, for Christ's sake! Use your head!"

He snorted scornfully. "Ah yes. Ever the vigilant one. No wonder things are going so smoothly."

I clenched my teeth. "You know I had nothing to do with that."

He lowered his voice to a hiss. "We wouldn't be in this mess if you hadn't started that pissing contest with Maxina."

"*She* had nothing to do with that. It was all Simba."

"How do you know?"

"Because Maxina wouldn't be so stupid. Trust me."

Alonso exhaled. "This is bad, Scott."

Stop. Using. My. Goddamn. Name. "We can still salvage this."

He spoke in a harsh whisper. "How? If she confesses now, after that emotional scene, everyone will think she's demented. She'll freak people out. To be honest, she freaked *me* out a little."

"Alonso, were you ever raped?"

"Of course not."

"Me neither. But Harmony was, many times, by her stepfather. We have no idea how that . . . Look, we'll get some experts to explain that she was channeling an earlier trauma. She never mentioned Hunta by name."

He thought about it. "I don't know. That might satisfy some people—"

"We'll make it satisfy everyone. The bigger issue right now is that the anti-Hunta sentiment is going to reach critical mass."

"So what are we supposed to do about it?"

I rested my back against the wall, running my hand through my hair. Damn it.

"We've got to end it," I said. "We've got to end this thing fast."

Alonso wasn't happy about it either. "She doesn't seem ready to come clean now, does she?"

"We'll get her ready."

"Frankly, I don't think it's in her best interests anymore."

"There's nothing else to do," I replied. "There's no alternative."

"Actually, that depends."

"On what?"

"On whatever measures you and Maxina have established to prevent there from *being* an alternative," he said pointedly.

I fell quiet, quiet enough for me to hear the footsteps coming up my stairs. That wasn't my pressing concern. Madison was too deferential to step within earshot of a private conversation and Jean didn't have an earshot at all.

"In other words, you'd like to know what's stopping the three of us, or maybe even the two of you, from going all the way. Past the second star on the right and straight on till morning."

"I'm talking about the death of quid pro quo," he replied. "Deny it if you like but we are rapidly approaching a situation where somebody is going to win and somebody is going to lose."

"I don't want to hear this shit."

"I'm just giving you the reality of the situation. If you truly cared about Harmony—"

"Hold on a second."

I opened the door, startling Jean. She'd been writing me a sticky note, but now she simply held up her hands. *I come in peace!* Nodding, I held up a finger, then turned away from her. I didn't want her reading my face or lips for this one.

"Sorry. You there?"

"Yes. I'm here," he said. "All I'm asking—"

"I know exactly what you're asking. And here's my answer. You want to know what's stopping us? *I* am. You want to know how averse I am to the idea of screwing over Jeremy? *Very* averse. So averse, in fact, that if I catch you planting alternative ideas in Harmony's head, I will dedicate my life to killing your novel. And by 'life,' I mean 'afternoon.' You'd be amazed how easy it is to keep a bad book down."

Say what you will about Alonso, the man had skin of iron. From the way he laughed, I might as well have thumped him with a wiffle bat.

"Self-righteousness does not become a man of your résumé, my friend. And save your threats. There's nothing you or Maxina can do to me now that Harmony can't do with a single well-placed quote. She's the one with the power, and she's the one I'm loyal to. So while I won't actively steer her toward one outcome or another, I'm informing you right now that I will go where she goes. Take that as you will. And call me when you're feeling more constructive."

He hung up. I lowered the phone, counted to five, and then turned around with a chirpy grin. "Hi there."

With a cautious wince, Jean flashed me a pair of neatly scribbled stickies, one in each palm.

I was just going to tell you we're leaving / May I borrow your friend's weird book?

He wasn't a friend anymore. "That's fine."

She wrote a new note. *Are you OK?*

"I'm okay. Better than my client, anyway."

Do you need Madison to stay?

"No. I'll be all right. Thank you, though."

Not buying the brave act, she amended her message. *Do you WANT Madison to stay?*

"I want you both to stay."

The words didn't hit her well, but her bad reaction was like sunlight to me. She rolled her neck, she grimaced, she chafed and whined through a *What are you doing to me?* look, as if she were on a diet and I just offered her a big block of chocolate.

And what a dense block I was. This whole time I was analyzing her like an alien dispatch. She was so damn strong to me, so damn clever, that I just assumed she was pulling me along some Byzantine path toward . . . something. Not sex, but something. It was driving me crazy that I couldn't figure it out, but at long last it occurred to me that she had absolutely no idea what she was doing. Worse, she might have thought she was following me. No wonder she was so frustrated. *Where are we going? I thought you knew! Great! How do we get out of here? I have no idea.*

But at least now we stopped wandering. Now we knew we were both lost. I didn't think I was hiding it, but then she probably thought she was screaming her dither at me. How very strange for a woman who could read minds and a man who could read subtext.

With a lovely sigh, she thumped her forehead against my chest. Once, twice, three times. I gently rubbed her back. Yeah. I know, Jean. You never set out to infect me, but you did. I never set out to escalate, but here we are on the second floor. I would have loved to address this, but given events, I didn't even have time to ask "What now?"

She pulled away. After fixing her hair, she wrote a quick blurb on another sticky note, then pressed it on my upper back. I was about to reach behind and grab it, but she stopped me, shaking her head. *Not yet,* she told me. *Wait.*

It would have to wait anyway. The phone in my hand rang. Groaning, I flipped it on.

"This is Scott."

"Scott, you know I had nothing to do with that."

I'd never heard Maxina this stressed before. From her quick and heavy footsteps, I knew she was going somewhere fast.

"I know," I assured her. "It's not me you need to worry about."

Jean backed away, throwing me a heavy look and a wave before disappearing down the stairs. God only knew what Madison was thinking.

"This is a nightmare," said Maxina through short breaths. "All we need is one smart journalist to really analyze Simba's comments."

"We might get some crackpot conspiracies, but nothing in the mainstream. They wouldn't dare accuse Harmony of anything. Especially not now."

"I hope you're right. How is she?"

I found myself pacing to her rhythm. "Not good. Apparently she's mad at all of us. How's Simba?"

"She's a mess. She just left the hotel. We think she just left Jeremy."

"That's crazy."

"No it's not. I just got off the phone with Doug. She took Latisha and a suitcase."

"Jesus Christ! She ended the call fifteen minutes ago!"

"Things are falling apart fast, Scott. Now, I don't have time for bullshit. I need to know if you're going to be a help to me or a hindrance."

"What do you want?"

"I want this over! I want Harmony to recant no later than tomorrow morning!"

"You got it."

Her shuffling came to a sudden stop. "You're serious now."

"Dead serious. This show isn't good for anyone anymore. I figure if you and I present a united front, we can talk her into cooperating."

Maxina let out a shaky laugh. "Wow. I'm afraid to ask what your catch is."

"My catch is that you stick to your word. Once I help you save Jeremy, you do everything in your power to help me save Harmony. That's all I ever wanted."

She started up again. "You got it. You got it. Oh, bless your heart, Scott. I knew you'd come around."

"No you didn't."

"No. I didn't. But you are now officially a man I love."

From the window, I watched Madison and Jean cross the street. Without looking back at me, or even at each other, they both entered the SUV. I pulled the small yellow slip off my back.

We moved out.

"Scott? Are you there?"

"Yeah," I said, meeting Jean's glance through two windows and fifty feet of dark air. "Yeah. I'm here. What now?"

By eight o'clock I was in Beverly Hills. I parked my rented Buick on Doheny Drive, in front of a small Spanish-style house. I had dropped Simba off at this very place a little over a week ago, on that fateful day we (I) selected Harmony to be our media snare. Before leaving my car, Simba had reached over, squeezed my leg, and asked me to promise her, *promise* her, that I'd do what's right for her and Jeremy. I promised. Obviously she stopped believing me.

The door was answered by a striking woman in her late twenties. She was dark-skinned, and almost six feet tall. She was surprised to be looking up at me.

"Can I help you?"

"Yes. I'm Scott. I'm one of the smart, slick people your cousin's been complaining about."

She leered with grim humor. "She mentioned there was a white one in the bunch."

"Can I please see her?"

"What makes you think she's here?"

Hunta had an inkling, which was passed from Doug to Maxina to me. Also passed along was Hunta's strong desire to see Harmony go under the wheels of a cargo truck. He reportedly had similar sentiments for me.

"I'm only working a few hours ahead of the reporters," I stressed. "It's in her best interests that I get to her before they do. Please."

I didn't ask to be here. I really wanted to minister to Harmony, but

Maxina opted to handle that herself. *She's too close to you, Scott. You're only going to set her off more.* I didn't necessarily agree, but I liked the idea of Maxina taking the brunt of Harmony's ill will for a change. It would make things easier for me when I called her later.

In the meantime, Maxina had another way for me to be useful.

Warily, the cousin let me into her living room and left me waiting there for ten minutes. I spent most of the time studying the black-and-white photos on the walls, all artistic nudes of the cousin herself. I was impressed, not just with her lithe form but with the healthy amount of nerve it took to decorate her home with naked pictures of herself. In every shot, she sported a white plaster cast on her left forearm. There was a statement in there somewhere, but damned if I knew what it was.

Soon enough, she came back, cradling a sleepy Latisha. "She's ready to see you. She's on the back porch."

"Thanks." I gestured to a photo. "Was your arm really broken?"

She leveled a cool stare. "No."

As I passed her by, she kept a strong eye on me. "You enjoy playing with other people's lives the way you do?"

I stopped and made a half-turn, not entirely facing her. "Usually."

There were only two chairs on the porch, each in the shape of a giant cupped hand. I sat down in one, leaning back against four tight fingers. I didn't like the idea of a big palm holding up my ass, nor did I like the assemblage of vertical penis sculptures that adorned the patio like a cactus patch. All in all, I preferred the nude-cousin motif of the living room.

On the other hand, there was Simba. She was a vision, as always, even with strained red eyes. She had just showered. Her hair was slicked back. She wore an Asian silk robe, short enough that she had to cross her legs to keep our talk from becoming more awkward. At her feet were a pack of cigarettes and a box of tissues. Currently, she was working her way through the cigarettes.

"You here to tell me I fucked up?"

"Only if you think it went well," I said.

She let out a smoky chuckle. "No. I'm pretty unhappy with how it turned out."

I kept quiet as she tapped her ashes into a tray on the thumb of her chair.

"He told me I fucked up. Those were the first words that came out of his mouth the minute I walked back into the room. 'You fucked up.' "

"Did he know what you were doing?"

"It was his idea. He wanted to call in himself but I said 'No. Let me do it. It'll sound better coming from me.' "

She shook her head at me, incredulous. "I mean, shit. You guys did such a good job with her. She was so damn good, the way she claimed how rap didn't do this to her. Rap never hurt her. Don't blame rap. Blame the rapper. That was some quality stuff. I'm sure it was a big relief for the Judge, for Maxina, for everyone at that whole meeting. It must have been a huge goddamn relief for all of them."

Right. Now get to the part where you chide me.

"See, you were different to us. You were our one ray of hope. Everyone else was focused on saving the label or saving the music business, but *you,* you were all about Jeremy. Until suddenly you became all about Harmony. Harmony, Harmony, Harmony. Even Maxina was worried about you."

"It was gossip," I insisted, as calmly as possible. "Childish, cynical, paranoid gossip. If you chose to believe it, fine. But what you did—"

"I did what I thought was necessary!"

"I told you both to have patience and to have faith in me, and you didn't. Now you made it ten times worse for everyone."

She closed her eyes, choking back tears. "You've never been through something like this. You've never been on our side of the crisis. We can't turn on the TV, we can't open a newspaper without seeing some former friend telling lies about us. We can't check our own answering machine without getting death threats. Death threats, Scott! I'm twenty-two years old! I have a baby! How do you expect us to be patient? How do you expect us to have faith in you when *you're* the one who made it ten times worse?"

For a taut minute, we sat in silence, facing each other from opposite hands.

"Do you know how much the *Enquirer* offered me to speak out against my own husband? Two hundred and fifty thousand dollars. A quarter of a million dollars. Nobody's offering me money to defend him. Just to attack him. Can you believe that?"

"Yes," I said meaningfully.

She scrutinized me. "Ah. So that's why you're here. You heard I left Jer, and you're wondering if I'm going to become an even bigger problem."

I matched her harsh expression. She extinguished one cigarette and immediately lit up another.

"You know, when he was eighteen, he won this freestyling competition at a local club. He just blew everyone away with his rhymes. That was when he met Yak Fula, a guy his age. He's dead now, but at the time he was part of Tupac's backup group, the Immortal Outlaws. He and Jer got to talking, and they became friends. Soon enough Yak introduced Jeremy to Tupac, and then they became friends. He was a good role model for Jeremy. Artistically, that is. Personally . . . Well, this was his Death Row phase. He was really getting into the whole gang shit. When you're with Suge Knight, you're with the Bloods. You are red from head to toe.

"As much as Jeremy loved being 'Pac's protégé, the whole scene kind of scared him. He was the Reverend's last remaining son. He promised his dad he'd stay squeaky clean for the rest of his life. His *long* life. That was the idea. That meant no gang affiliations. No thug tattoos. He also promised no drugs, but . . ." She laughed. "Well, that was the only one he broke. You just couldn't hang out with 'Pac and his crew without getting high. Not unless you stopped breathing. Besides, Jeremy had his big dream. He was going to live a long, *rich* life. And 'Pac was going to show him the way.

"So soon enough, one of the Outlaws got kicked out of the group because he smashed up 'Pac's new car. Suddenly Yak was saying things to Jeremy like 'Hey man. We're gonna make you one of us. You're gonna be an Outlaw.' Jeremy was like 'Holy shit,' but he knew what that meant, too. When you're officially part of 'Pac's group, you were branded with a big tattoo that said THUG LIFE, right here." She motioned across her abdomen. "Right across the stomach. That was a problem. I mean, would he disappoint his father by getting a big THUG LIFE tattoo? Or would he risk falling out with 'Pac?"

She looked out at the night sky, shooting smoke up at the stars. "Turns out it didn't matter. In September they all went up to Vegas to see Mike Tyson fight. Everyone from Death Row was there. All sorts of celebrities. This was Jeremy's first real taste of the big life. Everyone was drunk and high and throwing money around like crazy. People were out of control. Right after the fight, right in the lobby of the MGM Grand,

'Pac started whaling on this guy who had supposedly stolen something from somebody. It was a gang thing. I don't know. But before long, everybody in the group was kicking this guy on the floor. Even Suge Knight was getting in on it. Jeremy didn't know what to do. Yak's like 'Come on, man. You down with us or ain't you?'

"What else could he do? He started kicking this guy too. It was the only time he ever did anything like that. And he still feels bad about it. See, that's the thing about Jeremy. He's always looking at himself through his father's eyes. He's always making up for the mistakes of his brothers. And he still feels bad about this thing he did four and a half years ago. For kicking a man he didn't even know. Can you imagine what he'd be like if he ever hurt a woman he did know?"

She didn't have to tell me who she was really talking about.

"Anyway, it only got worse that night. The whole gang was running around town in a caravan. They went from the MGM Grand to Suge's house off the Strip, and then from Suge's house, they were all fixing to go to some club. Nobody stopped for a minute and Jeremy was caught up in the wave. It wasn't so fun anymore. He said it felt a lot like drowning."

She took another deep hit off her cigarette.

"And then it happened. Right at a stoplight, a white Cadillac pulls up next to the car Tupac was in. Four guys with guns get out and BAM! BAM! BAM! BAM! Jeremy was only one car behind, right next to Yak. They saw the whole thing go down."

"Jesus . . ."

"Yeah. It was a mess. Everything got crazy. Everyone's trying to chase each other. The cops are all around and Death Row people are telling Jeremy 'Don't say nothing to the police! Don't say nothing to the police!' Meanwhile, Tupac's all shot up. He couldn't even breathe. They got him to the hospital, but he was already gone. It took six more days for his body to die, but he was already gone."

Her eyes welled up. Her mouth began to quiver. "That's not the part that messes me up. I mean, I never knew Tupac. I wasn't even a fan of his. I just knew Jeremy. He told me the story not long after I met him. And he . . . and he told me how he had finally gotten in to see 'Pac at the hospital, the day after the shooting. The doctors had already done a million things to him by then. They had to take out half his guts just to keep him alive. But what Jeremy remembered the most was the THUG LIFE tattoo on 'Pac's stomach. There was a huge incision cutting right through it. It was like a big slash between the THUG and the LIFE, and . . ."

She finally wept. "When he first told me the story, he was crying worse than I am. He told me how that was it for him. That was when he knew he wouldn't go down the way Tupac did. He looked to me, he was crying, and he said 'Baby, I chose life.' "

One by one, she furiously pulled tissues out of the box on the floor. She used the whole wad to wipe her eyes. "When he told me that story, I fell in love with him. Right on the spot. He had me. Not just for the night. He had me for the long haul."

She closed up her robe, gazing ahead in anger. "But when he told me I fucked up, that was it. That was the official limit of shit I would take. I have loved him, even though he's betrayed me dozens of times. I've supported his career, even when mine died an early death. And I have stood by his side throughout this whole goddamn nightmare. I never asked him to thank me because I was his wife. It was my job to support him. But when he told me I fucked up . . . no. That was it. I took my suitcase and my daughter. I said good-bye and I meant it."

She crushed her cigarette into a nub, then turned her gaze back on me. "Tomorrow morning I'm going back to Virginia. To my parents' house. I'm going to unplug all the TVs and radios, I'm going to curl up with my baby girl, and we are both going to sleep for a month. That's my only plan. Tell the press whatever you want about me. Whatever you think will help Jeremy the most. I don't care anymore. I just want out."

Simba crumpled her tissues and dropped them into her lap.

"I've seen an ugly side of the world these past two weeks," she said. "It's an ugly world you live in. And it's going to take a long, long time to put it behind me."

After a few long moments, I stood up from the hard chair. Wincing, I arched my spine.

"Death threats," I informed her. "You went away with Latisha because of all the death threats. It was Jeremy's idea. He just wants to see the two of you safe."

She glanced up at me, sniffing. "That's good. That's really good. You just think of that?"

I shrugged. "It's my job."

"Well, then you keep doing your job, Scott Singer. You get him out of this shit. He never raped a woman in his life. You don't stop until the whole world knows that. You hear me?"

I heard her, but I was looking at the patch of clay erections behind her. I couldn't help but relate. Again I found myself fleeing to lower functions to avoid the complexity of my thoughts. It would be so nice to fly away to Virginia and curl up in bed with Simba for a month, or two, or six. It would be a grand relief to escape all the budding developments in my life, even the ones that looked promising (*too* promising). I was a weak man. I was a coward. And the women around me just kept getting stronger.

At nine o'clock CNN America aired its regularly scheduled encore of *Larry King Live*. All over the nation, all the people who had missed Harmony the first time around were settling onto their sofas, eagerly anticipating the explosive finale that everyone was shouting about. No doubt many of them shunned the spoilers: *Don't tell me what happens! Let me see it for myself!* The ratings would spike significantly toward the end of the hour, especially on the West Coast. Everybody who missed the fourth-quarter drama of Monday-night football, everybody who didn't give a crap how *Third Watch* ended, everybody who loved Raymond but hated *Becker*, they would all have an interesting place to go at 9:53.

As the show began again, I made a sudden left turn off Wilshire Boulevard, just to get away from the silver Acura behind me. When I had left Simba's hideaway, I noticed the car resting behind mine. The moment I started off, it came to life and followed. All along Wilshire, it trailed me, just as Jean once did. The driver even had a small silhouette like Jean's. It was déjà vu all over again.

Only this time there was no incident. I turned. The driver kept going. There was no reason on earth to think she was Jean. There wasn't even much reason to think she was following me. I was simply occupying my mind with cinematic scenarios. I could have used a good car chase at the moment. I needed something familiar, even cliché, to hold on to. With each Hollywood device came the promise of a Hollywood ending, where every good person gets everything they want: love, justice, success, or just plain closure.

For the moment, all I wanted was air. I pulled up to a not-so-legal spot of curb (permit parking only, fuck it), shut off the car, and began a late-evening walk through residential Westwood. It was just me and my thoughts, but they weren't good thoughts. Two hours ago, Alonso had pronounced the death of quid pro quo. That didn't faze me until Maxina confirmed his diagnosis. Once she had smuggled herself out of the

Miramar, she called me for an update. I told her Simba wasn't going to be a problem anymore. She told me Harmony was just getting started.

"Scott, I think it's time we began discussing Plan B."

"Not yet. Let me talk to her."

"Don't call her tonight," she warned. "Give her time to wind down. Trust me."

Sound advice, but what kind of friend would I be if I didn't at least call to check on her? How could I pass up the chance to play good cop? After three blocks, I took the cellular brick out of my pocket and dialed Harmony for the hundredth time tonight.

At long last, she answered. I could hear her own voice blaring in the background. Even she was watching CNN.

"Hey baby!"

Her odd pep threw me. "Harmony."

"Took you long enough."

"Your phone was off."

"I know. I thought that would get you to come over here. Instead I got Maxina."

"Sorry. She told me to stay behind."

"Why?"

"I don't know," I replied with dark levity. "Maybe she was afraid we'd run off together."

"You know, she said that whole thing with Simba was your idea."

That smacked the grin right off my face. I froze in my tracks. It didn't even occur to me that Harmony was joking until she broke out in harsh giggles.

"I'm just messing with you, Slick! Come on! Lighten up!"

"That's not very funny."

"Listen to you, all freaked out and shit. How the hell do you expect me to trust you guys when you don't even trust each other?"

"Harmony, look—"

"Ooh! Wait! This is the part where I talk about abstinence. Hold on."

I had missed that segment. I tried to listen in but I couldn't make out the words. Instead I resumed walking, waiting for her to come back to me. My stomach hurt.

"Damn," she said with a laugh. "My motherfucking grammar was all over the place. I didn't even notice. I wish Alonso had told me. Or you could have called me during the commercial."

"Look, you know I had nothing to do with that. I mean what Simba did."

"Yeah, that's what everyone's saying to me. You, Maxina, Alonso, Larry."

"Right now I'm just talking about me. I want you to believe me."

"Oh, I believe you," she responded sharply. "But that just means you didn't see it coming. So every time you tell me now that things are under control, that things are gonna be okay, I'm less inclined to believe that. The name of the game is credibility, Scott. And you just lost some."

I slowed down my pace, sighing. "You are indeed in a foul mood."

"Actually, I'm not. That's the weird thing. This was still the best night of my life. You were right. When those camera lights came on, something snapped into place inside me. It was like, I don't know, getting superpowers or something. I felt like I was moving faster than everyone else. Nothing could hit me. Nothing could hurt me."

"I thought you were absolutely—"

"Except the phone calls," she interjected deliberately. "That little thing they put in my ear really messed me up. I could only hear half the words the callers were saying, and the other half gave me a mean headache."

"That's normal. I had—"

"I guess it worked out okay, though. If I had heard everything that motherfucking bitch was telling me, I probably would have given it all up."

I closed my eyes. "Harmony . . ."

"I would have given *you* up, too."

Shit. Shit. Shit. I spun around and started back for the car. "Okay. That's it. If you're not dressed, get dressed."

"Why?"

"Because I'm picking you up," I said. "You and I are going out for a drive."

She thought about it. "No."

"I thought you wanted me to come over."

"Not anymore," she said. "You're just gonna tell me the same shit Maxina told me. Except I know you. Once you get me alone, you gonna lay all your words on me. You're gonna talk me into doing something I don't want to do. And I don't want you doing that."

"Harmony, you knew this part was coming—"

"You never said it'd be so hard! You never told me it'd be so hard! You tease me with all this fame, all this respect, all these money offers, and then you just pull it all away from me right when I'm starting to like it! Like it was all some goddamn joke! That shit ain't funny, Scott! I don't find that shit funny at all!"

"None of that stuff has to end."

"Oh, no, I'll still be famous," she fired back. "I'll be famous for being the bitch who let everybody down. The bitch who lied!"

"You'll win them back."

She laughed. "Yeah. In other words, things are gonna be okay. Sure, Scott. Sounds good to me."

I walked faster. "Look, let me come pick you up. We'll go for a drive, and we'll—"

"No!"

"I won't even talk! I won't even open my mouth! You can sit there and yell at me the whole time! You can yell at me all night! I don't care! I just want to be with you, okay?"

"Why?"

"Because tonight you were the most magnificent goddamn thing I have ever seen in my entire goddamn life! And I only caught half the show!"

That stumped her. "You didn't watch the whole thing?"

"No. I had people over."

She paused in amazement. "You're shitting me."

"It's all right. I taped it."

"Is this another one of your tricks?"

Grimacing, I swung a tight fist through the air. "Goddamn it! This is not a trick! I am not lying! This is not part of my master plan, okay? Tomorrow morning you and I are going to have that conversation. *That* conversation. But tonight I just want to see you. I don't want to talk. I just want to see you, live and in person. Can I? Please?!"

I was so flustered, I forgot where I parked my car. I couldn't even remember what kind of car I'd rented. I twirled around, scanning the street. Shit. Now what the hell do I do? What do I do if she says yes and I can't find my car?

"No."

"Harmony—"

"No, Scott. You go home. You watch the rest of that show. And you save your strength for tomorrow. I already know what you're gonna ask. And you already know how I'm gonna answer."

"Harmony, wait!"

With a click, the line went dead. I stopped looking for the car. It was a lost cause. And to think that three and a half hours ago, I was Superman. Now I was just helpless, hopeless. Three and a half hours ago, I was the benevolent author of other people's fates. Now I was just another hopeless, hapless character, getting swept along with the plot.

All I could do was pray for a decent ending, but it wasn't so easy to stay sunny when I could hear those dark whispers out there in the cineplex. This is the part they've all been waiting for. This is the part where things get ugly.

FOUR

BLAME

20
DISHARMONY

The strife got off to an early start on Tuesday. As dawn crawled over the west, a sheet of paper dribbled out of the fax machine in the management office of the Raffles L'Ermitage hotel. The text was hand-drawn and sloppy, but it didn't take a scholar to interpret the message. *BITCH FIEND: KA-BOOM!*

Within minutes everyone inside the hotel was evacuated onto the street, including poor Hunta. Given the hour, there were only two bodyguards on hand to protect him from the camping flock of reporters, photographers, and protesters. Hunta had to be held back when one of the journalists asked him if he had ever raped his own daughter. It was simply a setup for the cameras (as was the bomb threat, one might argue), and it worked beautifully. Shots of the rapper in all his savage fury would be online and on-air in a matter of minutes.

At 6:45, Big Bank and the rest of the reinforcements arrived, but by then the scare was already over. The police questioned Hunta in his suite. *Do you recognize this handwriting?* "No." *Has anyone threatened you recently?* "Yeah, man, everyone's threatened me recently!" *Where are your wife and daughter?* "Fuck you."

Ten minutes later, Doug was on the scene, ripping into both the police and hotel management. The police suggested that Mr. Sharpe leave the premises immediately. Management insisted on it. By 8:00 A.M. the crew had checked out and was en route to the rapper's next roost. Only a handful of people were trusted with the secret of Hunta's new location. I wasn't one of them. I didn't even know how to reach him anymore.

It was just as well, I suppose. All I would have done was offer more assurances and more help. He'd already had enough of my assurances. By Tuesday morning, he'd suffered quite enough of my help.

I woke up at 7:56, four minutes ahead of my alarm radio. I took that as an encouraging sign. Beating the clock, keeping a quick step ahead of the world's noise, was a good note to start the day on. I hopped out of bed. I stretched. I pulled Jean's momentous sticky (WE MOVED OUT) off the floor, crumpled it, and threw it in the wastebasket. All the loose files in my head were organized into neat little folders, and the folders were put away. I would not be encumbered by personal issues this morning. I was a lean, sleek vessel, optimized for maximum performance.

I brushed my teeth. I showered. I threw on my best casual work ensemble, then drank my morning coffee. The TV and the laptop remained off. I didn't need to know how much worse things had gotten since last night's blowout. Screw Larry King. Screw the news. Screw all the people who let their lives become affected by this colossal nonstory. None of them were welcome in my apartment. As far as I was concerned, the universe consisted of just me and Harmony Prince. Pity. With all that space to ourselves, surely there were better things to do than battle.

At 8:35 I took a deep breath and then rang her up. She sounded awake and alert. She was ready for me.

"So did you watch the rest of the show?"

"I did."

"Wasn't I good?"

"You were better than good," I told her. "You were absolutely entrancing."

"Always the sweet-talker."

"You asked me a question. I gave you an honest answer."

"Scott, are you in love with me?"

Jesus. She was jumping right in, wasn't she? I refused to be thrown.

"I don't know," I said. "I know I'm infatuated with you."

"Yeah? You ever have fantasies about me?"

"Yes."

She laughed. "Damn. You're surprisingly direct this morning."

Glad she noticed. For this conversation, I was determined to stick to raw sincerity. No rhetoric. No mincing. No witty evasions. Harmony, by contrast, seemed more polished than ever. Every word out of her mouth sounded like a sixth draft.

"I had a dirty dream about you last night," she told me. "We were sitting in someone's living room, probably yours. We were on the couch watching TV. Except it was me on TV. And you were talking all through it. You were telling me how I was so good about saying this, and why the press would love me for saying that. And as you were talking, you started touching me. It was all casual at first but then before I knew it, you had my shirt undone. You're even sneaky in my dreams."

"Harmony—"

"There's more. Don't you want to hear it?"

"No. Not really."

"Why not?"

"Because this smells a lot like strategy to me."

"Yeah," she replied in a hard tone. "Now you know how *I* feel."

I stood up from the couch and wandered. I wasn't quite comfortable, in places.

"Harmony, I've done a lot of things. I've patronized you. I've underestimated you. But at no time did I ever manipulate you through some emotional charade."

"You kissed me."

"We kissed each other. If you think that was strategy on my part, then you're overestimating me."

She didn't believe I was genuinely affected by her, and yet here I was, walking off the proof. It would have been funny if it wasn't so tragic.

"This is my idea of the future," I announced while opening my balcony doors. "I want you to hear me out, because it's very important, okay? At one o'clock there'll be a press conference in the garden room of your hotel, just like Thursday. Just like Thursday, you won't be there. Only Alonso. Once again he'll read a written statement, which you and I will compose together."

"No."

"Later this afternoon, I'll come by your hotel with a small production crew. We'll shoot a forty-six-minute interview that will then be peddled to the networks, just like Maxina did with Jeremy last week. We'll hire Kathy Oh to be your new official representative, replacing Alonso. She'll make sure that whoever gets the interview airs it in its proper context."

"It won't do any—"

"It'll just be you, on tape, explaining the circumstances. You made a bad pact with some bad people. You regret it. You just couldn't live with the lie any longer."

"After the way I cried—"

"You *could not* bear the fact that you were ruining the life of an innocent man."

"How do you know he's innocent?" she asked.

"Of raping you?"

"Of raping Lisa Glassman!"

"He didn't rape her."

"How do you know?"

I sighed. "Because his wife knows."

"Oh, *that* bitch? You believe anything that bitch says?"

"She has no reason to lie."

"Of course she does! Hunta's got another album coming out. That album means money. She only puts up with his shit for the money. Everyone knows that."

I shook my head. "There are so many things wrong with that, I don't even know where to begin."

"Yeah, well, you don't know what he was like at the Christmas party," she countered. "I was there. He was out of control. I saw him grabbing women by the ass, calling them bitches. I saw him on the couch with his hands all over that woman. I saw them leave together. And I saw her come back crying."

"Well, then I guess she was raped. Did you report it?"

"Don't put this shit on me like I'm acting all crazy. They called you in just to stop her. Why else would they do that? Why would they pay you a hundred and sixty thousand dollars to stop this woman if there was nothing to her story?"

"The story was enough," I said. "In case you haven't noticed, a little nothing can go a long way."

"Yeah? Well, if it was no big deal, then how come you kept it from me?"

"Because of this! Because I didn't want you to justify screwing over an innocent man!"

"You took that woman's story! You took her story and you put it on me!"

"I took her lie and I made it yours! And I only did that so you could kill it once and for all! That's the point! That's the key to this whole operation!"

"The key is saving him by making everyone mad at me!"

I took a deep, calming breath, then pressed my hands together.

"Look, I've told you time and time again that you will not be the villain. The only villains will be the invisible white conspirators you turned against."

"You keep *saying* I'll be okay—"

"I *know* you'll be okay. I know that nobody would ever dare attack a contrite and telegenic young black woman. That's just suicide. These venues are all ad-supported, and advertisers always—"

"I'm not talking about the goddamn media, Scott. I'm talking about people. I'm talking about the people out there. If I do what you want me to do, I'm gonna be a bad memory forever. Every time a woman's raped now, people will say 'Oh, that bitch is probably lying. Remember Harmony Prince?' Every time a black woman accuses anyone of anything, people will say 'Oh, that bitch is probably lying. Remember Harmony Prince?' Wherever I go the rest of my life, I'm gonna be the bitch who lied! Who's gonna trust anything I say? Who's gonna wanna read my books to their kids?"

Some neighbors began squabbling on the street. I closed the balcony doors.

"Harmony, I know it's hard to get perspective when you're inside the fishbowl, but take my word for it. You are just a tiny blip on the world's radar. Out of the six billion people out there, there are only a few thousand who actively give a shit about the things you say or do, and most of them are in the media. To them, you're revenue. To everyone else, you're entertainment. You're a fun distraction. A cheap way to avoid thinking. That's why stories like this are so popular: because they require no thought. People aren't thinking about you, they're reacting to you. And they're reacting the way the television tells them to react."

"And what if the television tells them to hate me?"

"It won't. The television loves you. It will continue to love you. You're still sympathetic. You're still great to look at. And you still keep getting more and more interesting. That's what I've been trying to tell you. This isn't an ending. It's a beginning. Once you clear Jeremy's name, we're going to rebuild. You and I together. We're going to rebuild you, and we're going to paint you right this time. Not as a victim. Not as a liar. We're going to start over, and we're going to do you right."

She was silent, but I could feel her distance. I was holding out my hand, and she clearly wasn't taking it.

"They're just words, Scott. You're just giving me words."

"Yes, but if you could see me saying them—"

"I'm glad I don't! It was seeing you that got me into this shit in the first place!"

I sat down on the stairwell, lowering my head. That was it. We were officially jammed. She didn't want to see me. She didn't want to hear me. She didn't even want to smell me. To her I reeked of strategy. She could feel me coming from every direction, even though I was simply standing right in front of her, naked and stuck.

From the wind static, I figured Harmony stepped onto her seafront balcony. She had been a clenched fist from the moment she picked up the phone, but I could feel her opening up.

"I didn't really have that dream about you," she admitted.

"I figured."

"I was just making a point."

"Yeah," I replied with a grim chuckle. "I figured. But it was a good point."

"I do have fantasies, though."

"Really."

"Yeah. Ever since you kissed me and promised me the world, I've had this fantasy where you and I are married. You're my husband and my publicist. I'm like the world's most famous woman, and I travel all around with you, talking to kids, signing my books, handing out words of wisdom. And folks in the media give us shit because we're so different, you and me, but every time we leave a place, people always say 'Damn. Now those two make a good couple. Those two made it work.' "

I kept my head down and my eyes shut.

"You believe me, Scott? Or do you think I'm still just making a point?"

"I believe you," I said.

"You like that fantasy?"

"I think it's beautiful."

"Yeah? You don't sound very touched."

"I don't sound very anything," I sighed. "I don't look very anything. I've got a poker face. A poker voice. A poker everything. It's just the way I am. But I do have feelings, even if I don't show them. And I do care for you, even though you think I'm lying."

I heard the flick of a cigarette lighter. She spoke through one side of her mouth. "You want to convince me you're for real, you find a clever way to get me out of this shit. One that saves your client without sinking me."

"There's no other way."

"Or even one that doesn't save your client. I don't care. Quit the job. Tell them to keep their goddamn money. Just stay with me. Keep going with me."

"Harmony, that's not—"

"If you do that, Scott, I'll finally know you're for real. I'll know you weren't just playing me. And then I swear to God I will fall into you completely. I'll marry you. I'll travel the world with you. I'll make love to you every day and every night. I'll give you lots of kids. I'll die old and happy, right by your side. Do you believe me?"

"It doesn't matter what I—"

"It's a simple question! Do you believe me? Yes or no?"

"I don't think you're lying, if that's—"

"That ain't the same as believing me and you know it!"

"What do you want me to say? This isn't one of your fairy tales! This is real life! You're talking about the rest of our lives!"

"And you're talking about the rest of *my* life!"

"Fine! You made your point! I get it!"

She thrust a sharp and jagged laugh into my ear.

"You're a goddamn hypocrite, Scott."

"Yes! I'm a hypocrite! Congratulations! You got me! That doesn't change the fact that I'm doing what's best for you."

"We got nothing left to talk about."

"Yes we do! Harmony—"

She hung up on me yet again. With a muttered curse, I closed the phone and dropped it.

The worst part was that I believed her. I believed she would love me as promised, but I could see the string attached. She'd be mine as long as I kept her pretty. It was frightening to realize how little that bothered me. I probably could have done it—spent the rest of my days keeping her pretty and the rest of my nights basking in her fame, her love, her secondhand smoke. I could have even drowned an innocent man, just for a taste of the life she promised.

Ultimately, it wasn't my conscience that saved me from treachery. It was a little crumpled sticky note in my bedroom wastebasket, a more tenuous hint of a less conditional union. In the end, it was Jean who saved me from Harmony. I didn't take that as an encouraging sign, especially since I knew what was coming. I knew that by the end of our next conversation, I'd no longer have Harmony to save me from Jean.

Before I left for Century City, I'd finally caught up with the news. The dark upshot of the L'Ermitage bomb threat was that it punctuated our cover story for Simba's departure. At nine Doug faxed the official word to the media. *For their own safety, Ms. Shange and child have left for an undisclosed location, while Mr. Sharpe remains in Los Angeles to fight these false allegations. Ms. Shange continues to support her husband wholeheartedly and hopes the family can be reunited soon under better circumstances.*

Simba naturally earned a lot of coverage for her televised ambush but it was hard to vilify her, particularly since the attack was so remarkably civil. At best, it was a desperate plea from a loyal wife in denial. At worst it was a cheap PR stunt that backfired horribly. Fortunately for us, her vague insinuations of a conspiracy were either ignored or written off as paranoid rambling. But that was only a temporary relief. I knew her cryptic words would be revisited once Harmony confessed.

"*If* she confesses," said Doug in the elevator.

"She'll confess," I assured him. "I'm not worried about that."

With a nervous snort, he adjusted his bow tie. "You're a step ahead of us, then."

This was not a fun time to be working at Mean World Records. Ever since Melrose, the hate mail had been piling up to the roof. The harassing phone calls had been coming in so fast and so furious that the Judge was forced to abandon the landlines and assign brand-new cell phones to all his staff. On Thursday someone messengered a box with a dead rat in it, causing one poor assistant to pass out. On Friday a man charged in with a bucket of red paint and proceeded to splash it all over the reception area, plus the receptionist. The vandal was promptly arrested, but his belligerence cost the label twenty-four hundred dollars, plus the receptionist.

By Tuesday morning security was airtight. I practically had to give a

DNA sample before building security notified Doug that I was there. He came down to the lobby to retrieve me himself. As soon as I stepped onto the twentieth floor, I was security-wanded. Once I arrived at the outer doors of the Mean World office, another guard asked me to raise my arms.

"This is insane," I griped as large hands patted me down.

"It's necessary," said Doug.

"It's insane that it's necessary."

He shrugged. "We're the richest nation in the world. We've got to blame someone for something."

Once I was officially pronounced clean, Doug pushed open the heavy cedar doors. "Just be prepared, Scott."

"For what? A cavity search?"

He didn't smile. "For blame."

For the record, I never assaulted Annabelle Shane. I wasn't the one who riled her into a shooting frenzy. Nor did I trigger Lisa Glassman, whose face would be on the front page of everything right now if Harmony hadn't come along. Six of one, half a dozen of the other. Unfortunately, no one here seemed to care about the alternate reality. The Mean World office was a parallel universe in itself, a strange Bizarro realm where Hunta was the victim, Harmony was the villain, and rap was not a fan of me.

As Doug led me past the sea of cubicles, young heads sprouted up to observe me: the tall and wicked white man who played with other people's lives like they were pieces on a chessboard. I met their hot glares with an insurgent sneer. On a good day, I wouldn't even bother myself with the thoughts of strangers, but this was not a good day. My early talk with Harmony had left me wounded and hobbling. I needed to rest up for our next encounter.

Unfortunately, I'd been summoned to face the Judge.

"In case you didn't pick up the vibe," he said, "nobody here likes you. In fact, we all pretty much think you're an asshole."

We eyed each other from opposite ends of a giant conference table, while five of his most scornful lieutenants flanked the long edges. Behind every angry black man was a poster of another angry black man. The glass walls were covered in promotional reproductions of Mean World album covers. L-Ron. X/S. Hitchy. Hunta. For the cover of *Hunt-away,* Jeremy stood arms akimbo in front of a pure white backdrop. He was naked except for six figures worth of jewelry and a large parental-advisory placard obscuring his naughty part. His seditious snarl sealed the message. *Y'all better be advised of* this *now, 'cause your daughters want it, and I'm ready to give it.*

On some unspoken level, he must have gotten a thrill from watching us uptight prigs cringe at his raw sexuality. His mighty manhood was a threat to the whole nation, a juggernaut erection tearing across the countryside, shattering dams, destroying cities. Even his fellow braggadocio rappers were diving out of its way. That had to be worth a few cackles. As the current fiend in the office, I felt like cackling myself.

"Well," I said in perfectly glib spirit, "I guess I won't be invited to your next Christmas party."

An executive shot to his feet. "You think this is fucking funny?"

"No, I think this is unproductive. Where's Maxina?"

"She's not coming," said Doug, the only nonhostile force at the table. "She threw her back out this morning. She's practically immobile."

"Can we at least get her on speakerphone?"

"Why don't you deal with us yourself," huffed the Judge, "instead of hiding behind Mommy?"

With a laugh, I held up my palms. "Fine, Judge. If it'll make you feel better to chew me out in front of your people, go ahead. If you want to blame me for what Simba did—"

"It's not what Jeremy's woman did! It's what *your* woman did!"

Standing up, he slid today's *Los Angeles Times* all the way down the table. Above Harmony's crying face was the headline she wrote herself: I SAID NO AND HE DIDN'T LISTEN!

"You see that shit? You see that?"

"I see it."

"She's fucking us over! She's killing us! And all because she believes her own goddamn story!"

"What'd you do?" asked a subordinate. "Hypnotize her?"

"Or is she just a psycho?" asked another.

"She panicked," I replied in a nice, tranquil tone. "She was put in a tight squeeze and she panicked."

"Funny how well her panicking served her," a third executive remarked.

I stood up and wandered the room. Business psychology 101: the person closest to the ceiling always takes the floor. Anything to silence the rabble.

"Look, Harmony is scared to death right now. She doesn't want to go against us but she's afraid to go along with us. She's stuck on a high ledge with everyone watching, and she doesn't trust us to catch her if she jumps."

"That was your job," said Doug. "You were supposed to have her complete trust."

"There's no such thing as complete trust, especially in a situation like this. Now, I am doing everything in my power—"

"Are you?"

I gave the Judge a winsome smile. "Let's skip over the insinuations and get right to the suggestions. What would you have me do?"

"Use the goddamn audiotape!"

"She has to understand that she can't win," added Doug. "If she doesn't confess, we'll have to do it for her."

"That is an absolute last resort," I said.

The Judge slapped his hand down. "What the hell are you waiting for? We are out of time! We are all out of time! If you don't clear Jeremy's ass, we're going to have to drop him from the label! You think we want to do that?"

"He's a good artist," said one lieutenant.

"Our best artist," said another.

"And even if we drop him," the Judge continued, "the political fallout is going to kill us in a matter of weeks. We have to fix this now!"

"We're not saying leak the tape," Doug assured me, as if I were simply worried for myself. "We're just suggesting you use it as a bargaining tool."

"It's not a bargaining tool. It's a threat."

The Judge laughed in bleak wonder. "He's afraid to threaten her. Our whole goddamn world is crumbling, and he's afraid of upsetting his new fuck buddy."

I knelt beside him, speaking in a sardonic stage whisper. "Did it ever occur to you that if we threaten her, my new 'fuck buddy' might confess a hell of a lot more than we bargained for?"

He grabbed my shirt collar. "I told you, goddamn it! I told you from the start it was a mistake to tell her who she was working for!"

"Get your hands off me."

"You put my whole life's work at the mercy of this stupid little bitch!"

"Get your hands off me."

"You get her to end this thing now or I will end your fucking life!"

Doug stood up. "Judge . . ."

"It's okay," I said, keeping my cold gaze on the Judge. "If your boss wants to take a swing at me, he can go right ahead. I won't swing back. I won't bitch or sue. I won't even go home and take it out on my loved ones. I'm a grown man. And no matter what he does, I'll continue to act like one."

That was just white-pacifist bravado. I truly didn't want to take a punch today, or any day, but a sock to the jaw was nothing compared to the prospect of blackmailing Harmony. All I could do was stall for time until I came up with a better solution.

Still burning hot, the Judge let go of me. He held his finger in my face.

"A grown man takes responsibility for his actions. And your actions, your whole scheme, has gotten us into a world of shit! So what are you going to do about it, 'Slick'? What are you going to do to fix the mess you made?"

With that, all eyes were upon me again. Glancing at the poster image of Hunta, I idly wondered how much this whole crisis mattered to him now. How much did Harmony Prince matter to him now that his wife and daughter were gone? Did he blame me for that, too? Sorry, man. In the end, that was all your fault, just as Harmony was all mine. So what are we going to do about the problems we've caused, Jeremy? What are we prepared to sacrifice in order to make things right?

In the heated silence, I made my way back to my seat, exhaling toward Doug. "You're going to want to get Maxina on the phone," I told him. "She's going to want to hear this."

———

At half past eleven, I returned to the parking garage. Thankfully, it only took a few minutes to locate my rented Buick. Last night I'd spent nearly an hour wandering the residential streets of Westwood, trying to re-member what I drove and where I'd parked it. By the time I found the damn thing, there was a fresh new forty-dollar parking ticket pressed against the windshield.

Today there was only a sticky note.

I didn't notice it until I got in the car. The message was scribbled on the glue side. I could read it through the glass.

YOU'VE BEEN A BAD, BAD BOY.

In a wild heartbeat, I scrolled through several theories. Jean came first, just by association, but she was quickly disqualified. Her handwriting was clean and curvy. This was sharper and more erratic. Best case scenario: mistaken vehicular identity. Worst case: Jean had a creepy Jekyll/Hyde thing going on. Most likely: I had a journalist on my tail, and he or she was getting smarmy.

This was cause to be extra careful but not extra worried. Being connected to Mean World was manageable. Being connected to Harmony was not. Thank God I didn't pick her up last night. Thank God for the red phones. And what a lucky convenience that my freshly mended Saturn was ready and waiting for me as of nine this morning. This was a perfect time to switch cars.

From Mean World, I sped to West L.A. and returned the Buick to the good people at Avis. From there, I hoofed five blocks to the auto-body shop. Nobody seemed to cruise behind me. If I truly had a shadow, it probably quit at Century City, signing off on a smug note. It wasn't worth worrying about at the moment.

Once I was reunited with my Saturn, I drove west, all the way to the Santa Monica beach. The parking lot was shooting distance from the Fairmont Miramar, a fact that wasn't lost on others. Three spots over, an intrepid young photographer—a real Peter Parker type—waited patiently from the bed of his pickup truck. His telephoto lens was fixed squarely east and upward, presumably on Harmony's balcony. It was smart business. A nice, clean shot of her would pay his rent for three to six months, depending on neighborhood.

Crossing the strand of bladers and joggers, I stuffed my shoes with my socks, then made my way across the sand. At the water's edge, I rolled up my pant cuffs and dipped my feet. Only in California could you do this in February. Only in L.A. would you see a man in Fendi shades and Banana Republic attire stepping through the ocean with a pair of leather shoes in one hand and a cell phone in the other. For me, there was no better place to work. The sea washed away all my extraneous issues. I was ready for Harmony.

It was 12:30 when I made the call. Her mouth was full of something crunchy.

"I told you we got nothing more to talk about."

"Yeah. Turns out you were wrong."

She paused. "I hear waves. You near the ocean?"

"I'm in the ocean."

"Really? You near me?"

"You can probably see me."

"Bullshit . . ."

I could hear her open her balcony doors. I couldn't spot her myself, but I certainly just made the photographer's day. Smiling, I cradled the phone and waved.

"Where are you?" she asked.

"Keep looking straight ahead. I've got at least fifty yards to myself."

"Is that you waving your hand?"

"Hi there."

She screamed with laughter. "Oh my God! I can barely see you! You're like a dot!"

"I'm still bigger than you."

"What the hell you doing out there? You trying to charm your way up to my room or something?"

I scanned the other incognitos on the beach. "No. That's not part of the plan."

"Good. Because I told my boys not to let you in for any reason. I told them to get rough if they had to."

"Now why would you go and do a thing like that?"

"Because I don't want you pulling your tricks on me."

"Why would I do a thing like that?"

"Because all you care about is saving your client. You made that clear enough."

"Harmony, be honest with me. Who do you think I like better? You or Hunta?"

"It ain't about like. It's about money."

"Shows how much you know," I taunted. "I just forfeited my entire fee."

"Yeah, right."

With a laugh, I began walking through the Pacific, soaking my shins in ice-cold seawater. "I know. The guys at Mean World thought it was a trick too. Fortunately, Maxina knew better. She knew exactly what I was doing."

"What *are* you doing?"

"Giving away my money."

"To who?"

"To you."

For once, her disbelief was enjoyable. "You're such a liar."

"As we speak, Doug Modine is cracking open the piggy bank he set aside for me. We're going to get you eighty thousand in cash today and then deliver the other half tomorrow. We'll get a courier to rendezvous with one of your roommates. I assume you can trust them to deliver the money."

"You can't be serious."

"I'm dead serious."

"What is this? A setup?"

"It's a not a setup."

"So you're bribing me then."

"It's not a bribe. It's proof."

"Proof of what?"

"Proof of me."

Sadly, my scheme hadn't done much to stop the "Scott loves Harmony" rumors. Even Maxina saw fluttering hearts around my head. When I first presented my idea, she immediately asked to speak to me alone. She was strung up in her hotel bed, zonked out on painkillers, but she was lucid enough to explore the angles. *Scott, are you sure you know what you're doing?*

"I don't get it. Why you doing this?" Harmony asked.

"Why do you think I'm doing it?"

"I don't know," she retorted. "I just smell strategy."

I kicked up water as I walked. "It's funny. You seem to think I'm all brain and no heart. They seem to think I'm all heart and no brain. And you all seem to think I'm double-crossing one for the other. Harmony, Jeremy. Jeremy, Harmony. So allow me to tell you what I told them: screw you. Maybe I want to do what's right for both of you. Maybe that's more important to me than a silly paycheck. Maybe, just maybe, I'm a *warm* conniving bastard. You ever think of that?"

"No."

"I know." I sighed. "That's why you and I would never work. Fortunately, my plan will. And if I can't earn your trust, I can at least buy your lack of distrust."

"What makes you think a bribe will change my mind?"

"I told you. This isn't a bribe. It's a token of faith. I'm giving up the one reason I'd ever have to screw you over. I don't care who gets the money. I'd tell them to keep the money, but then you wouldn't believe me."

"Scott, why do you even think this is about you? Maybe I'm doing this for me!"

"So am I!"

"Bullshit!"

"Why would I lie to you now? What would I have to gain from it now? Prestige?"

"I don't know. Maybe they threatened your career. Maybe they threatened your life. Maybe they threatened your *girlfriend's* life. I don't know what's really going on. All I know is that you want me to throw myself at the mercy of the media, and all I see is they don't got any."

"I told you—"

"I know what you told me, goddamn it. I heard you. And I don't agree. If you ain't lying, then you're just wrong."

My left shoe fell out of my grip, into the ocean. Cursing, I rolled up my sleeve and retrieved it. I hadn't left my shoes on the beach because I thought someone would steal them. Another bad idea. Son of a bitch. I just gave up my entire paycheck. I just sacrificed $160,000 and one shoe in order to clear this fatal blockage, but it didn't do a damn thing.

"You think I'm stupid, Scott."

I closed my eyes. "I don't think you're stupid."

"Well, you think you know more about the world than I do."

"No. I just think I know more about the media."

"You probably do. But maybe someday you'll go on this ride yourself instead of pushing someone else through it. Maybe then you'll understand why it's so hard to do what you're asking me to do."

My pant cuffs were soaked. I started to get a chill from the water, but I kept splashing through.

"Harmony, victims come and go. They're a dime a dozen. If you keep going this way, people will run out of ways to praise you. They'll get tired of feeling for you. Worse, they'll resent you—not the media, but you—for filling one too many headlines. And once they turn away, that's it. You're off the menu. You're a blip. You're pop trivia. You think I'm lying? I can give you a list of twenty names that'll sound vaguely familiar to you. Twenty names of people who rode and fell off the victim track, just like you're doing."

"Well then I'll just have to jump to a better track," she challenged.

"I'll just have to use this time to make something better of myself. I was hoping you'd help me, but I guess that ain't happening."

"No," I replied with a heavy breath. "I guess it ain't."

"You just love talking down to me, don't you?"

"No. I hate it. But you're giving me no other choice."

"So what happens now? You guys come after me with all you got?"

"Of *course* we do. What do you think I've been trying to prevent? Why do you think I just gave up my whole damn fee?"

"And are you gonna help them, Scott? You gonna help them take me down?"

A midsize wave broke a few yards ahead of me, drenching me up to my thighs. By now my legs were completely numb.

"If it comes down to that," I mused, "I'll be blamed, which means I'll be fired."

"Which means you wouldn't get your money anyway."

"You know, you really are stupid."

"Fuck you."

I chuckled. "Fuck me. Right. I'll tell you what. Why don't you hang up on me a twelfth time? Why don't you kick me out of your life for good? Then you'll find out which one of us is more fucked."

She paused but she didn't hang up. Shit. Don't make me do this.

"What are you talking about?"

"I'm talking about consistency. Since I truly am the smart and evil bastard you pegged me for—good catch, by the way—don't you think I would have established a solid Plan B? Do you really think I could have sold my crazy idea to Hunta, Maxina, and all the others if I didn't offer some kind of insurance policy?"

She paused to mull it over. "Alonso said you'd have something up your sleeve."

"Alonso is a flaming jackass who just shot himself in both feet. But in this case, he's right. I guess you decided not to trust him either."

"What's your insurance policy?"

"We have you on tape," I informed her. "When I first drove you, when I *liberated* you from the Flower Club, I recorded our conversation."

"You taped me? You *taped* me?"

"Of course I taped you. I can't believe you're even surprised."

"But it don't make sense! It's all you! That ride was just you talking!"

"Not just me. I did a lovely job describing the plan but you contributed some nice tidbits yourself. 'Wait. You want me to tell people he raped me? But it's a lie. He never raped me. Hunta never even touched me.' "

"You're crazy! That gives up the whole game!"

"No, no, no. Selective editing, my dear. I picked a nice two-minute chunk that covers only the plot to frame Hunta, not the plot to save him. See how smart and evil I am?"

"Bullshit! If you play that tape, you go down with me!"

"Wrong. In order to prove it was me, you'd need voice experts to match it to a second recording of me. Legally, there are only two ways for the authorities to ever obtain such a thing: A) if I cooperate, or B) if they pull it from the public domain. I have no intention of cooperating. And I don't have my voice in the public domain."

"Then I'll just say it wasn't me on that tape either!"

"Uh, maybe I should clarify the term 'public domain,' honey. It includes CNN. It includes *Larry King.*"

"You motherfucker! You motherfucker! You gave me all this shit about having an invisible rope around you! That if I go down, you go down too!"

"Yeah, well, turns out I had a safety line."

"You motherfucker! You goddamn motherfucker!"

My lips began to quiver. My teeth chattered. The ocean was freezing me. I didn't care.

"Sweetheart, you should be less concerned about me and more concerned about yourself. See, once that tape is released, it'll go to at least three independent audio experts who'll compare the pitch, the tone, and the frequency of your voice on *Larry King* to your voice on the recording. Within hours, they can prove beyond a shadow of a doubt that it was you, and then you're in for a bad time. You won't even have remorse to hide behind, because hey, you never bothered to confess. You were caught. You were exposed."

"I'll tell them everything! I'll give them the whole story!"

"Go ahead. Sing like a bird. It doesn't matter. You're stuck on the wrong side of Occam's Razor. Nobody sane is going to believe that you were trying to help Hunta all along, especially after the way you cried last night. And nobody credible would support your story anyway. Your roommates. Lisa Glassman. All people with dubious motives and zero evidence. The truth is just too improbable. It's too complex for the audience to handle. Hell, they couldn't even handle Whitewater, and that was just a land deal."

Sometime during my spiel, I crossed into the realm of fiction and just kept going. In truth, the recording would put me at huge risk with both the media and the authorities. If it was ever released, Harmony would have everything she needed to drag me straight down to hell. It would be a living nightmare. As if this wasn't. As if her hot tears weren't enough to damn me forever.

"I'll give you up! I'll give them your name!"

"Knock yourself out. But consider this: if I'm such a smart and evil bastard, what makes you think I'd even give you my real name?"

"You showed me your license!"

I laughed. "Oh, well then I *must* be Scott Singer."

By now I was soaked to the waist and shivering all over.

Harmony screamed her sobs. "You motherfucker! I hate you so much! I hate you SO MUCH!"

"I never wanted it to come to this! I did everything possible to keep it from coming to this but you just wouldn't listen to me! You wouldn't trust me!"

"I HATE YOU!"

"I did everything for you! I risked my career for you! I gave up my money for you! I put my heart and soul into you and you threw them right back in my face!"

"You ain't got a heart! You ain't got a soul!"

"I've got them. You just refused to see them."

"You motherfucker! You are a sick motherfucker! You're a sick child!"

A large wave crashed down, knocking both shoes out of my hand. I didn't chase after them. I was so cold, I could barely stand.

"Harmony, shut up, stop crying, and listen to me very carefully. You have exactly one hour to call Maxina and tell her that you're willing to cooperate. If she doesn't hear from you in one hour, the tape goes out to the press. If you value your own well-being, you'll use your head for once and do the smart thing."

She kept crying. "You are the saddest, most pathetic man I ever met in my whole life."

I couldn't stop shaking. "Whatever."

"I don't care what your real name is. I don't care what you think you're accomplishing. I don't care what happened in your life to make you this way. There's no excuse. There's no excuse for a man like you."

"You don't even know me, bitch."

I hung up, then closed the phone. By now my shoes had made it safely to shore. For a moment I considering following them. For another moment I considered going the other way, walking deeper into the water until I disappeared entirely. After a few more seconds of quivering indecision, I met my footwear on dry land.

I picked them up. I studied them. I launched them back into the sea. They were both ruined forever. Not just my shoes, the ocean. I ruined the whole ocean. Every time I'd look at the sea now, I'd think of the time I forced Harmony Prince into doing something she didn't want to do, of the time I pinned her down, had my way, and ruined her forever.

Slowly, vacantly, I trudged back to my car and started it up. I didn't like the way my bare foot felt against the brake pedal, or the way my wet pant legs felt against my thighs. And still I couldn't stop trembling. Inside, I was caught between the urge to flee the scene of the crime and the realization that I was in no condition to drive anywhere. I was an accident waiting to happen. I had just gotten my car back. I couldn't take any more accidents.

Giving in to common sense, I turned on the heat and stared ahead at the flying seagulls. I became lost in their looping patterns. Forty-five minutes later, I finally stopped shivering. My slacks were merely damp. My body and mind were nearly thawed.

I'd never called a woman a bitch before.

"It's done," said Maxina from her hotel bed. "I just spoke with Harmony. She's agreed to cooperate. She's going to record a videotaped confession for us tomorrow morning."

"Tomorrow morning?"

"Her condition. She wants to write the speech herself and she wants a whole night to prepare it. I tried to bargain with her but she was pretty inflexible. It's all right. I'd still rather play her videotape tomorrow than our audiotape today."

I rested my head against the window. I wasn't entirely lucid yet.

"It'll be okay," she added. "We still have final cut. There won't be any bombshells. There won't be any names named. I supported your pseudonym story, by the way. Very clever thinking."

My stomach churned. "Any other conditions?"

"She wants your money. All of it. I stuck to my guns on that one. Half now. Half on delivery."

"Any other conditions?"

"Scott . . ."

"Just say it."

Maxina sighed. "She doesn't want to hear from you ever again. You knew that. You knew what you had to do, you knew the consequences, and you did it. You fell on your sword."

I watched another photographer set up by the curb, waiting for that precious glimpse of Harmony.

"Scott, I know it hurt like hell, but you did the right thing. You saved Jeremy."

"Who's going to save Harmony?"

"I will. I'm keeping my promise. I'll hire a publicist tonight to be her new official handler. I'll coordinate everyone on this side of the effort. We won't level a single bad word against her. Even Jeremy will forgive her. All of his rage, all of *our* rage, will be channeled at the conspiracy. Trust me. Your plan will work. Your plan is going to work out beautifully for all of us."

Funny how ridiculous it sounded when coming from someone else.

"For the record," she conceded, "I'm sorry I told her about Lisa Glassman. You were right. That was a big mistake."

"That's not what screwed things up and you know it."

"I know."

I was starting to become hot and bothered. I turned off the air, but it didn't help. I was percolating, pulsating with pent-up energy that I couldn't quite release. I didn't even know what form it would take. Screams. Tears. Maniacal laughter. Who could say? But I refused to let Maxina become the lucky earwitness to such a rare emotional event. I wanted to reserve it for Harmony. I wanted her to hear me crack into tiny pieces.

"I didn't mean for it happen like this," I offered, weakly. "I didn't mean for us to get so . . ."

"Listen, do you know how many singers and actresses get married to their agents? Their managers? Their *publicists*? Too many to count. That little dance between star and starmaker is as old as fame itself. You were just the latest pair to get caught in it. I knew there'd be trouble from the moment I saw you two together."

"But I never meant for it to happen. It was an accident."

"I know."

"*She* doesn't."

"Of course not," Maxina replied with a motherly chuckle. "You've never seen yourself through a young girl's eyes. You're a dashing tomcat, all suave and confident. In your world, there are no accidents."

"Apparently there are."

"I know. I'm not a young girl. I see them. You screwed up. But you know what, Scott? They were honest mistakes. And in the end, you got the job done."

She was certainly in a magnanimous mood. Who could blame her? Twenty minutes ago, she was looking at World War III. Now she had the pleasure of calling all her cronies in the music business and telling them they can finally breathe again.

"Go home," she said. "Get some sleep. The best thing you can do now is distance yourself. I assume you've been careful in covering your tracks."

YOU'VE BEEN A BAD, BAD BOY. "I have. At least with Harmony. I mean, no one knows about my connection to her except the twelve thousand of you."

"Well, the twelve thousand of us have a very strong interest in keeping it quiet. You'll be fine."

I'd never called a woman a bitch before.

"Go home."

That part would follow me forever. I could have said so many other things. I could have even just said "You don't even know me" and ended the call with a modicum of virtue (at least in my book). The fact that I'd garnished my last words to her, littered my very own message, only justified everything she said and felt about me. It was all the proof she needed.

After five more minutes of self-flagellation, I put the car into gear and left the beach behind. I escaped through the 10 East, but despite my right foot's discomfort, I passed my exit and just kept going. I wondered how far I could get from the ocean. What if I went all the way? What if I drove all the way to the other coast?

The thought was so appealing, I actually smiled. I would make a cross-country pilgrimage, stopping only for gas and rest. I'd sleep in the car. I wouldn't eat at all. I'd fast for absolution. I'd fast and speed my way to the opposite shore. The moment I dipped my soiled feet into the crisp Atlantic, I'd be clean again. I'd be absolved. Then I'd call a local journalist with the story. It'd make a nice human-interest piece. BASTARD PUBLICIST DRIVES ACROSS NATION, BEGS FORGIVENESS FOR BASTARD WAYS. Once it was published in the *Wilmington Post-Gazette,* or whatever they call their paper, I'd clip it out and send it anonymously to Harmony. Maybe then she'd get it. Maybe then she'd get me right.

No. She wouldn't believe it. She'd probably think it was just more words. Just more strategy.

"Fuck her," I said, fifty miles from the coast. By that point, I was completely dry and sound again. I ran the numbers in my head. I'd paid a thousand dollars for the phones, twelve hundred for Eddie Sangiacomo's PI services, and another three thousand in cash disbursements to Harmony, most of which she squandered on her father. I also had at least twenty-two thousand in taxes due, thanks to a fairly lucrative year. On the plus side, that same good year had left me with sixty thousand in savings and assets, and I had another eighteen thousand in fees and reimbursements coming from Mertens & Fay for the Keoki Atoll job. This wasn't the end of the world. There was no reason to get dramatic. I'd survive this.

I took the nearest turnaround exit, then began the long trek home. Fuck her.

I didn't return to Brentwood until shortly after four. The whole way back, I had Madison on my mind. I suffered flashbacks to last Tuesday, when she had waited outside my apartment door, thinking black thoughts. I must have abandoned her. I must have hated her. I must have hated her so goddamn much that I actually avoided my own home in hopes that the little bitch would go away forever. It was inconceivable to her that a man like me could simply be running behind schedule.

Everyone else is scrambling around like they don't have a clue, she'd said to me after her crying jag. *But you're totally above all that. You seem to have a handle on everything.*

Yes, I did seem that way, didn't I? It's all smoke and mirrors, my dear. A grand illusion. I've been doing it all my life. I've gotten pretty good at it, too. Too good, for some people.

As I stood outside my apartment door, I fixed my hair, adjusted my shirt and then summoned up a fresh batch of composure. I was myself again, the shoeless version. I even had a good cover story for that. I had just come back from a meeting with Maxina Howard. Like a typical tourist, she insisted on walking the beach. Like a typical idiot, I kept my shoes on. Along came a tenacious wave, and SKLORP! A hundred and fifty dollars' worth of footwear down the drain. I donated them to the first homeless man I saw. Maxina said it was good karma. I said it was going on my invoice.

Madison sat cross-legged on the couch, shooting Internet articles from my laptop to my BubbleJet. She seemed a little anxious.

"Hi."

"Hey. Sorry I'm late."

"I knocked several times like you told me. Then I used the key."

"That's fine," I told her. "That's why I gave it to you."

I dropped my wallet on the kitchen counter, then peeked at my answering machine. Exhaling, I collapsed to the easy chair. "I did the dumbest thing today—"

"Scott, you had a visitor."

"What?"

"A woman stopped by twenty minutes ago. She was looking for you."

"Can you be more specific?"

Madison squinted, scouring her memory banks. "Shit. She told me her name. I just forgot it."

"You didn't write it down?"

"No. I remembered it. But then you sort of came in, barefoot and smelling like salt."

"I'll explain that," I promised. "Once you remember this woman's name."

"Marina . . . Malina . . ."

"Maxina?"

She snapped her fingers at me. "Yeah. Maxina."

"That doesn't make sense. I just spoke with her less than two hours ago. What did she say?"

Madison winced, hesitant. "She said she knows you're up to something with Harmony Prince."

I took a fierce breath through my nose, then lowered my head. I will not explode. I will not implode. I will not crack into tiny pieces. Not in front of Madison.

"Are you okay?"

No. "Yeah. I just haven't eaten all day. My blood sugar is down."

"You want me to get you something?"

"Sure. A glass of apple juice would be great."

"Okay."

Goddamn it. What kind of game was Maxina playing? What kind of game did she think I was playing? Did she think this whole thing was an act? That Harmony and I were pulling off a complicated con job? Wow. Wouldn't that be a clever twist? I'd almost prefer it.

Madison brought me a full glass of juice. I took a deep sip. "Thank you."

She faced me from the couch again. "I've never seen you this stressed."

"I'm not stressed. Just hypoglycemic."

"You can't tell me what's going on, can you?"

"I don't even know anymore. I just know there's some serious discord among my associates. Things aren't going well and everyone seems to think I'm the reason."

"Why you?"

"I don't know. I guess someone has to take the blame."

"But do they really think you're working for Harmony Prince?"

"I don't know," I said, throwing up a hand. "I don't know what they're thinking. I just know that I've busted my ass to make things right and nobody believes me."

"I believe you."

"Do you?"

"Of course," she replied without a beat. "We had this talk. I was stupid to ever doubt you. And so are they."

It took all my energy not to run over to the couch and squeeze her like a little boy would squeeze his mother. I wanted to hold her, to have her rub my back and tell me that everything would be all right again. Sadly, that would violate the unspoken covenant that she and I had established last Tuesday. In this office, we were absolute professionals. In this apartment, we were perfect adults.

She curled herself up against the wing of my couch, watching me from the same place, wielding the exact face her mother had used on me last night. They were so eerily alike sometimes, in such beautifully subtle ways.

I leaned back with a wobbly grin. "This was not the best project to start you on."

"Yeah. Sounds that way."

"It's almost over. Very soon I'll be a free man again. And then you and I are going to spend some serious time together. I have been woefully remiss in my mentoring duties."

"Shut up. You have not."

"Trust me. I have. And trust me when I say I look forward to it. I swear to God, Madison, you are . . ." I waved my hand. "Whatever. Things are going to get better from here. I promise."

She smiled, and I found myself moderately functional again, functional enough to remember that Maxina threw her back out this morning. She was in no shape to leave her bed, much less drive all the way over here to deliver vague messages.

"Madison, this Maxina woman who stopped by. Did she happen to be middle-aged, black, and somewhat . . . expansive?"

She cocked her head, confused. "No. She was your age, white, and somewhat condensed."

Of course.

"And her name just happened to be Miranda."

Madison slapped her head. "Miranda! That's right! Shit!"

Of course. "It's all right."

"I'm sorry, Scott."

I could barely hear her. All the blood in my body seemed to rush to my head. I gazed down at my feet. They were naked, white, and pale, like the feet of a dead man. All they needed was a tag hanging off the toe and the picture would be complete. Of course.

"Are you sure you're okay?"

"I'm fine," I said, staring past my feet and all the way down to my future. "Everything's fine."

21

GODSEND

The traffic was heavy at Ralph's. The five o'clock rush made it nearly impossible for Miranda to squeeze her cart down the produce aisle. She didn't mind the congestion. To a native New Yorker like her, it was like sailing the wide Sargasso Sea.

"Now *this* is a supermarket," she declared majestically. "I'm so used to shopping at some tiny, overpriced D'Agostino's. This is heaven to me. Look at all these choices!"

Much had changed since our last encounter, twelve days ago. Miranda had flown home, filed for marital separation, got it, filed for a work transfer, got that, flew back here, leased an apartment, leased an Acura, and then began a passionate rebound affair with Ned Caruso, a fellow beat reporter at AP Los Angeles. Amazing how she managed to do all that and still find time to stalk me.

"What's great is that Ned and I eat the same things," she bragged. "No red meat. Lots of chicken and fish. We both love fresh steamed vegetables, Basmati rice, and a nice dark merlot with dinner. The man's definitely got style. And unlike some people, he knows how to fuck a woman."

Judging from the expressions of all those within earshot, it would take some time for L.A. to get used to its newest resident. Miranda, on the other hand, was well on her way to becoming a full-fledged Angelino. She wore a form-fitting white tank top and khaki shorts. Her natural brown hair was now a synthetic auburn. She had tanned considerably. Her breasts even looked bigger, but that was either a trick of the light or just some clever padding. To the casual male eye, she was a little bit of honey. To me, she was simply a woman trying to outrun herself. I figured she was on the fast track to some kind of meltdown. Then again, who wasn't?

"Now, before I actually grill you," she said, to an artichoke, "what's the deal with the underage blonde in your apartment?"

I took another bite of my energy bar. Things were not going well inside my body. I was hungry. I was fatigued. I was seeing red bouncing dots in front of my eyes. I would have much rather battled Miranda from the other side of a cozy restaurant booth, but she already had an evening of dinner, wine, and sex on the docket. I was forced to tag along for the preparations.

"You remember that fender-bender we got into on the way back from the airport?"

"As a matter of fact, I do."

"That's the daughter of the woman who hit us."

"The deaf woman," she said.

"Right."

"What, she couldn't settle by check?"

I shrugged in good humor. "It's just collateral. I have to give the kid back once I get paid."

She gave me a jaded grin as she spun a bag of tomatoes shut. "Her name is Madison, and she told me she's your assistant."

"So why'd you ask, then?"

"I'm simply curious to know why you'd take on a kid helper. You hate kids."

"Says who?"

"Says Gracie. She used to complain all the time that you never understood her work."

"Funny how Gracie never complained to me."

"Well, you know how she is," said Miranda. "She could have an arrow sticking out of her chest, and she'd still swear everything's fine. You just have to needle her, that's all."

I could have cracked a watermelon over her skull. I had the motive and the opportunity. If only there weren't so many witnesses.

"I think it's amazing how much Madison looks like Gracie," she added. "When she first answered the door, I freaked out. I thought maybe you cloned her from old hairs."

"Another winning theory," I sniped.

Miranda eyed me coyly. "Look at you, all tense and persnickety. You really have been up to no good, haven't you?"

"You tell me."

"Ah, I knew you'd make me play my cards first. Fine." She paused to examine a honeydew. "I just hope you haven't gotten too close to that deaf woman, because she's the one who ratted you out to me."

"What the hell are you talking about?"

Miranda pushed the cart forward. "As you've no doubt figured out, I've been digging into this whole rap/rape story. I've been skeptical of Harmony Prince from the very beginning, even though it was 'politically insensitive' of me to question her veracity. My editors gave me so much shit. I said, 'Guys, can we at least consider the possibility that she's not entirely on the level?' They said, 'How can it be? She filed for a restraining order four weeks before Melrose even happened.' And I said, 'Well, what if she wasn't on the level four weeks ago?' I mean, shit, I'm not a fan of rap at all, but I know that suing rappers is like a cottage industry to some women, and some lawyers. Especially Alonso Lever." She checked my reaction. "Am I wrong here?"

"Not at all."

"Who knows? Maybe she was genuinely pissed. I hear Hunta's a real sweet-talker with the ladies. Maybe he charmed the pants off her. Maybe he tricked her into thinking this was the start of a beautiful romance, got her to give up her abstinence, and then chucked her aside once he got his jollies. That would certainly piss me off, especially if I had her history of abuse and abandonment. I mean, God, how could she *not* have issues with men?"

I stared ahead listlessly. "Makes sense."

"Or maybe it's something even more sinister," she said with a mischievous glance.

She threw two bags of salad mix into her cart, then moved us along. "See, there's so much reasonable doubt in this thing, but nobody wants to touch it. Nobody wants to rock the boat. Everyone's just printing what they're told, because the story's interesting enough the way it is. It's bullshit. My editors wouldn't listen to me even after I showed them an anonymous e-mail I got, telling me flat out that Harmony Prince was lying. Thanks for that, by the way."

"Whatever."

She examined her yogurt options. "So I said fuck it. I started digging on my own time. On Sunday night I went to this horrid little place called the Flower Club. You ever been there?"

"No," I said, coyly. "What is it? An arboretum?"

Miranda laughed. "You're such an ass. You know damn well that Harmony used to work there as a hostess dancer. Only she went by the name Danesha. Can't say I blame her. I was so embarrassed to be there, I felt like giving a fake name myself."

I greatly enjoyed the thought of Miranda gagging her way through that sleaze pit.

"But I asked around," she continued. "Apparently, Harmony's last day was the previous Sunday. She didn't quit. She just stopped coming to work. Nobody knew why until her face started popping up everywhere. It came as quite a shock to the gals at the club. From the way Harmony talked, she had a pretty good time at that Christmas party."

She liberated a few banana Yoplaits, then shot me a sly sideways glance. "But a few of the girls had some interesting things to say about Harmony's very last customer."

"Such as?"

"That he was really tall. White. Good-looking in a nondescript sort of way. He definitely seemed out of place there. He sat at the bar talking to some guy, but then as soon as Harmony came out of the bathroom, he flew right toward her as if he'd been waiting for her all along."

Oh shit. I could already see the punch line.

"They ended up playing pool for a little bit. Then he gave her five hundred dollars and promised another thousand just to let him drive her home. No sex. Just talking. But once he left, Harmony kind of freaked out. See, unlike her more experienced associates, she wasn't one for the, shall we say, extracurricular activities of her profession. So while she was changing, she told some of the other girls about it. 'What do I do? He says he works for Mean World, but he's white. It doesn't make sense. What if he's a rapist? What if he's a serial killer?' And her friends said, 'Girl, relax. If he's got that much money to blow, he's just an eccentric. He probably just wants someone to cry to.' "

Shit. The car . . .

"So, with much trepidation, she went down to meet him at his car. And the girls, ever so curious, watched from the bathroom window. Given the amount of money this guy was throwing around, they expected to see a limo waiting. Or at least a Bentley. But instead they watched her cross the street and step into—are you ready for this?—a black Saturn sedan."

"With a dented trunk," I added.

"With a dented trunk," she repeated, laughing. "I mean, wow! Can you imagine my surprise that I just happen to know this guy? Can you imagine my crazy luck that I just happened to be there when his trunk got dented?"

In top form, I could have laughed away her implications. But all I could muster up at the moment was some defensive surprise. "You can't be serious. That can't be all you have."

"Well, no. Of course not. But it was enough to get me on your tail, just to see what you've been up to. And wonder of wonders, last night I tailed you to the home of Denise Corwin, who just happens to be the cousin of Kelly Corwin, who just happens to be Simba Shange, who just happened to say some *very* interesting things on *Larry King Live*."

Miranda casually pressed up against me, sinking her fingers down the front pockets of my slacks. Our boundaries were forever muddled by our onetime fling, but there was nothing sexy about this.

"See, I watched that show, just like everyone else. I saw Harmony's eyes well up, and just like everyone else, I thought, Holy shit. She's going to confess. She's going to admit to lying."

"But she didn't."

"She didn't, but I couldn't help but think how very, very clever it would be if she did. What a great distraction from Melrose and Annabelle Shane. What a terrific way to turn all this angry momentum around. I know it sounds far-fetched, Hunta and Harmony secretly working together in an elaborate media hoax, but I couldn't help but think how very, very Scott it would be."

The red spots in front of my eyes got bigger. They danced faster. My head began to throb. "But she didn't confess."

Smiling, she whispered up to me. She practically breathed her words. "I think she will. I think that was the plan all along. I think I'm about to be proven right, and then I think you're in a lot of trouble."

I pulled away from her. "You've lost your mind."

"Then correct me. Enlighten me. If I'm wrong, what you were doing at the Flower Club?"

"That wasn't me."

"What were you doing with Simba Shange last night?"

"Never met her in my life."

"What were you were doing at Mean World this morning?"

"There are over sixty other companies in that building."

"Then what are you doing *here*?"

I rested my hands on the end of her cart. I only had a few more ounces of bullshit left in me. I had to use them well.

"Look, I know how the game is played. If you want to keep hounding me, go ahead. If you want to keep following me and leaving juvenile sticky notes on my windshield, knock yourself out. I don't care." I pointed a harsh finger at her. "But don't you ever hit me through my assistant again. That was low. It was despicable. For God's sake, the girl is thirteen. Your little slanderous message made her cry. Is this part of your new act? Is this what you've been reduced to? Making little girls cry?"

Miranda shook her head at me in wonder. "Scott, look at you. Listen to yourself. You're a mess."

"You're one to talk. What *haven't* you changed about yourself in the past two weeks?"

"I'll be the first one to admit I have problems," she said evenly, "but at least I'm trying to do something about them."

"By what? Harassing me? Harassing my assistant?"

"By being a real journalist for once."

"Bullshit. If you were a real journalist, you'd cover real news. Why don't you try debunking this fictional energy crisis? Why don't you cover the millions of small investors who are being fucked over by the hundreds of large investors? Or here's a crazy thought: why don't you write a story about how real journalism was choked to death by bottom-line economics and replaced by a histrionic tabloid celebrity attack machine? You won't even have to do any research. It's all around us."

Miranda crossed her arms, studying me with clinical detachment. "Right now I'm more interested in the story of the publicist who's starting to drown in his own lies."

I thought about it, then shook my head. "I don't see the audience for it."

With that, I took the last bite of my energy bar, crumpled the wrapper, then dropped it in Miranda's cart. I tossed her a cool wave and turned around.

"Scott, wait."

I turned back. Miranda leaned on the cart. There was definitely an enhancer bra at work. She never used to have cleavage.

"If I made your assistant cry, then I'm sorry. I didn't realize she was that young."

"Well, she is."

"But you've got one hell of a nerve calling my actions low and despicable when you and I both know what you've been up to."

"You don't know anything."

"What did you tell this one, Scott? What bag of goods did you sell this one to get her to humiliate herself in front of the cameras?"

"Maybe you should get therapy."

"Maybe you should get ready," she replied. "Because I'm coming into this story. And I'm coming in through you."

With a hot glare, I walked off. It was a winning act, but the inner me was tearing his hair out. Miranda had a strong rope to hang me with. All she had to do was bring it to Harmony. The minute those two women connected, the moment Miranda spoke my name, the floor would drop out from under me. Miranda would get her story, and Harmony would get her revenge.

And what a grand revenge it would be. What better way to make me sorry, what sweeter way to make me suffer, than to make me famous?

On my way out of Ralph's, I bought a box of cold/flu capsules, some vitamin C, and several cans of gourmet chicken soup. My idiotic stint in the ocean was pulling me under the weather. Hopefully, with a little rest and a lot of self-maintenance, I could nip the illness in the bud.

Still, I didn't feel like going home just yet. I knew Madison was still there, and I couldn't stand her seeing me all cracked and vulnerable like this. Might as well do the cheap thing and wait her out. And since I was already here in Marina del Rey, I knew just the right person to help me kill the time.

Despite the traffic, it took me only five minutes to get to the marina. Once again it was the magic hour. Twilight painted the western sky in vibrant pink hues. Passing cars turned their headlights on. The lampposts buzzed to life.

It was a beautiful sight, to be sure, but as I walked the docks, I kept my hands in my pockets and my eyes on the wooden boards beneath me. So much for my lifelong resolve to never see the Pacific again. I was back already. Worse, the sound of sea waves slapping against pillars was enough to slap me back into very recent history. The awful things I'd said to Harmony. The bile from my mouth that coated and stained what used to be a sterling-silver tongue.

On the plus side, I now had more in common with Ira. The man was a verbal lumberjack whose nasty wit could fell the sturdiest of souls. Next to him, I was still about as caustic as skim milk. In fact, if I told him I had called a woman a bitch today, he'd probably only chastise me for being uncreative. Now there was a perspective I could deal with. There was a set of eyes I wouldn't mind seeing myself through.

I was so busy aiming my gaze at the pier that it wasn't until I reached the edge that I caught the change in scenery. Had I been even less attentive, I might have boarded the sleek new yacht that bobbed in the *Ishtar*'s place.

This was a stranger's ship. Ira didn't have the capital to upgrade his vessel. And if he had merely taken his old boat out for a jaunt, then he wouldn't have relinquished his permanent parking spot. I scanned the other yachts within eyeshot, on the off chance that Ira had traded moors with a fellow seaman. There was no *Ishtar* in sight.

Wearily, I assembled the options. Maybe he moved to a cheaper dock to help support his online role-playing habit. Maybe he sold the boat entirely. Or maybe he discovered a big enough hole between this crappy analog world and his perfect digital one and then sailed right through it, never to return.

Whatever it was that triggered the sudden change of address, Ira never saw fit to tell me. I knew I could still send him a token greeting through voice mail or e-mail, or both, if I was feeling particularly desperate. But in my dark and honest frame of mind, I could only place even odds that he'd ever reply. Not that I blamed him. All in all, we were never really the best of friends. *I* was never really the best of friends.

Whether we reconnected or not, I wished him well in his new life and his new skin. Same went for Miranda. On a better day, in a stronger state, I'd only shake my head at their mad tandem dash to reinvent themselves. But as my body, my soul, and my best-laid plans continued to crumble, I couldn't help but wonder if they were on to something.

My efforts to wait out Madison were thwarted by her mother's slight tardiness. I approached my own building at a quarter after six, only to find MRVL GRL pulling into its usual spot by the hydrant. Instead of ducking into my garage, I parked along the curb, four cars behind Jean. I turned off the ignition and the lights, blending into the scenery.

Within moments Madison popped out of the building and sauntered down my front steps. From a distance, she seemed okay, even though I'd all but abandoned her today. I wasn't so egocentric to think that her sun rose and set on my actions, but the more I thought about Jean's sticky note, the stranger Madison's stability seemed. They had just moved out on Neil. That was a huge thing for an eighth-grader to deal with, but you'd never tell from Madison's calm young face that she was dealing with it at all.

Damn. Maybe she was a clone of Gracie. I didn't see the physical re-semblance as much as Miranda did, but they were definitely built from the same emotional template. My ex-lover was a brilliant, quirky, and benevolent woman. Sadly, she was also closed to the point of being air-tight. At some point she began to suffocate inside herself. Fortunately, she found a man with the right tools to extricate her. Somehow, God knows how, he helped her free.

But what if Madison isn't so lucky? What if she becomes another Gracie and then doesn't get rescued? What would that make her, besides a clone of me?

My hands were shaking again. It was a good idea to hide. I didn't want them to see me like this, all stressed out and full of self-pity. I would have rather suffered another confrontation, another complication, than deal with their compassion for me.

Madison got in the SUV, and Jean drove them away. Finally, I breathed again. I just needed soup. I just needed a little soup and a lot of sleep, and then I'd be myself again, or at least a reasonable facsimile.

———

In my dream, I flew east, into the sunrise. It welcomed me.

———

I sat up on the couch. The living room was pitch black. Everything was off, and yet something had beeped me back into the waking world. I turned on the lamp, but nothing happened. If I was indeed awake, I was in the midst of another rolling blackout. I opened up the laptop and made my way in the light of the start-up screen. From the kitchen counter, my gray cell phone projected a faint green square onto the ceil-ing. I had a new text message.

WE NEED TO TALK, ASAP. WILL YOU MEET ME AT CLUB SILENCE, PLEASE?
IT'S VERY IMPORTANT.

It was ten-thirty at night, my head was aching worse than ever, and
I'd well exceeded my recommended daily allowance for drama. I was in
no shape to take on the indomitable Mrs. Spelling. Still—

OK.

—it was better than sitting here in the dark, thinking about my
nascent cold and my bleak future. If anyone could get me out of the
shadow of Harmony Prince, even briefly, it was Jean.

I gathered myself. After retrieving my flashlight from the junk drawer,
I went upstairs to my bedroom, changed into clean clothes, and dug out
my old eyeglasses. Technically, I was supposed to wear them whenever I
drove at night, but they never seemed to make it into my A-squad of accessories. Tonight I definitely needed them. My naked eyes wouldn't get
me to Santa Monica alive.

The Third Street Promenade was dim and virtually deserted. All the
stores were closed. Only a handful of souls wandered in and out of the
restaurant/bars. At first I went down the wrong alley and up the wrong
stairwell, but eventually I traced my way back to Club Silence.

On a late Tuesday night, the lack of noise was downright eerie. There
were only six other people scattered throughout the establishment: an
elderly couple by the boom box (gesturing), a young couple at the bar
(kissing), a middle-aged bartender (signing something incomprehensi-
ble to me), and Jean.

She watched me from the far end of a laptop table. She wore a long
black T-shirt over jeans. Silver hairband. No makeup or jewelry. The
most striking difference, one that almost kept me from recognizing her,
was her cat's-eye glasses. They redefined her entire face. She could have
passed for a college student, a wry and eclectic theater major who was
into Brecht, Björk, herbal ecstasy, and Vertigo comics. I never wanted to
get under her shirt more.

Clearly, the feelings weren't reciprocated. The look she flashed me
was cold and austere. I didn't get it. Last night she was thumping her
head against my chest, wondering what to do about her attraction to me.
Now she glared at me like she'd just found child porn on my hard drive.

She tossed me a curt nod. <Thanks for coming.>

<What? Why are you mad at me? What did I do?>

She winced at herself. <I must look pretty grim, don't I?>

<Maybe. I don't know. I'm very off tonight.>

<So am I. I was already in bed when I decided to call you. The lights were out. My contacts were out. I was trying to sleep. But then I realized that if I didn't talk to you right now, I wouldn't sleep at all.>

<I didn't know you wore contacts,> I wrote.

<Yeah. The perils of computer work. What's your excuse?>

I tapped my glasses. <I don't wear contacts. I barely even use these things.>

<Take them off.>

With an "as you please" shrug, I took them off, folded them, and dropped them in my shirt pocket.

She tilted her head, studying me. <You look better without them.>

<You look wonderful with yours.>

Expressionless, she retrieved a money order from her purse and slid it across the table. It was $975.50, exactly a hundred dollars more than I'd paid for the Saturn repairs. I had e-mailed her the final cost this afternoon, shortly before leaving for Ralph's.

<Why the extra hundred?>

<For the inconvenience.>

Miranda would have laughed her ass off. <Why a money order?>

<Because if I gave you a check, you might be tempted to rip it up into little pieces.>

That was mildly encouraging. In her mind, I was still the kind of man who was susceptible to random acts of charity. I was about to respond, but then she pulled an item from the floor: a fat stack of papers. I recognized it immediately as Alonso's novel.

<Jesus. Don't tell me you finished that thing already.>

She plunked it down on the table, between our laptops. On the top page, covering the book's dedication, was a single yellow sticky note, filled with Jean's curvy handwriting.

GODSEND

a novel

by Harmony Prince's lawyer

With a droll stare, she raised her eyebrows at me. *See the problem now?* Of course. Of course it had to do with Harmony. Everything in the world, every problem in my life, came back to Harmony.

<You were smart to get rid of the title page,> Jean typed, without

taking her gaze off me. <But if you had actually read the book, like I did, you would have discovered the 12-page afterword at the end. He refers to his novel by name. He also signs it.>

Of course Alonso would be self-indulgent enough to finish his work with a lengthy explanation of what it meant to him. Loquacious prick.

<He's very talented,> she added. <Very strange. Very kinky. But very talented.>

By sheer reflex, my addled mind processed a weak dodge: I was simply studying the enemy. That's the only reason I had the book. I was studying the mind of the enemy.

Shit. I was too sick to lie.

<How did you find out he was Harmony's lawyer?>

<I saw his name on-screen last night. On that CNN show. I remembered it because it looked nice. The letters in "Alonso" kind of look like a little truck, with the O's as wheels.>

Damn it, Jean. Don't do this to me. Don't be all smart and sexy and weird tonight. I'm not strong enough to handle you. I'm definitely not strong enough to handle your scorn.

Reading my discomfort, she vented herself through a long, pensive breath. <Honestly, you gave yourself away.>

<I know.>

<Last night. The way you looked at Harmony when she cried.>

<I know.>

<It made me nervous. I know it's not my business, but you're obviously involved in something murky here.>

"Jean . . ."

<And I wouldn't care about that, except you've got my DAUGHTER involved.>

"Hold it!"

The remaining patrons watched me as I stood up and dragged my wooden chair around the table. I sat so close to Jean, my knees touched her thigh.

"I'm sorry," I said with slow articulation. "I can't type and look at you at the same time, and I need you to see me for this. I'm going to tell you two things that are absolutely, one hundred percent true. I want you to read me very carefully as I say them, all right? Read my lips. Read my face."

Thrown by my intensity, Jean nodded.

I took in a deep swath of air, then held up a finger. "One: yes. You're right. There's more to this job than meets the eye. I'd explain the whole thing to you right now, but it would take an hour, and honestly, the details don't matter. All you need to know . . ."

For a brief and disturbing moment, my inner teleprompter went dark. My words, my thoughts, became scrambled beyond recognition. I suddenly wished I were fluent in Sign, so I could chop through this goddamn jungle of rhetoric and cut right to the heart of the matter.

"I had a plan, Jean. I had a plan that would have channeled a nation's idle rage off a man who didn't deserve it and onto a bunch of people who didn't exist. It was a crazy and ambitious plan, but it wasn't a cruel one. I never set out to hurt anyone. I never set out to betray anyone. I truly and honestly believed that this would benefit everybody. It just got . . . Things took a bad turn. I know that's small comfort to the people involved, but since you're not involved, all you need to know is that I meant well. I screwed up, but I meant well. Did you get that?"

With wide and alert eyes, she nodded. Somewhere on the outskirts of my consciousness was the impulse to run my hands up her arms, up her sleeves, all the way to the peaks of her shoulders, which I'd madly caress with my thumbs for as long as she'd let me. Instead, I merely held up a second finger.

"Two: I have bent over backwards to protect Madison from the more complex aspects of this operation. That is the one thing I've truly done right. Your daughter . . . she is such a marvel to me. She's such a treasure. I would never do anything to jeopardize her well-being. I only want to be a positive force in her life. I want to help her process all the deceptive crap that's floating around out there, but I want to do it in a way that doesn't make her more cynical. There are media literacy books that can help me. There are websites. I'm going to check them out. I'll do whatever it takes. I just . . ."

I turned my head away. "Shit . . ."

Jean put her hand on my cheek, trying to turn it back, but I resisted her. This wasn't what it looked like. I wasn't about to cry. I was about to sneeze.

Finally, it came out. It was one of those full-body sneezes that shorts out the mind, forcing you to reboot. By the time I looked back at Jean, I was covering my lower face with both hands. She had a tissue waiting for me.

"Thank you."

It was just as well. I was getting a little too muddled and desperate for my own comfort. If I hadn't sneezed, I probably would have gotten even scarier. I would have fallen to my knees, begging Jean to accept me, love me, hold me, mother me. And if she couldn't do that, then I would have implored her to at least leave me the healing presence of her daughter. Don't cut me off from Madison. I need her. I need one of you. Both of you. More of you. Just don't cut me off. Please.

I took her tissue and whatever dignity I had left and wandered off to the men's room to clean myself up. I made the mistake of looking at myself in the mirror. I was a mess. The strain on my face was visible for everyone to see. The illusion of me was a mere flicker.

As I returned to the table, I dragged the chair back to its original spot, then sat down. Jean continued to watch me, expressionless.

<You okay?>

<I'll live,> I typed, while trying to keep eye contact.

<Scott Singer, you are an absolute mystery to me.>

<You're not exactly an open book yourself.>

<Tell me what you're thinking right now.>

<I'm thinking how awful I look,> I replied with a sniff. <I'm thinking how great you look. And I'm trying to come up with some clever excuse to work my way back to your side of the table.>

On reading my words, Jean closed her eyes and let out a surrendering moan. She rose to her feet and made her way to me. I was about to stand up, but she pressed my shoulders down and slipped past me. From behind, she embraced me, wrapping herself around my neck like a mink stole.

I closed my eyes and rolled my head back, holding her forearm with both hands. I could feel her breath against my skin. She planted a quick, innocent kiss on my jaw, then rested her lips on my cheek. She kissed the same spot several times, rapidly, as if she were drilling her way into me. It was sweet and strange and almost painful in its potency. Wincing, I squeezed her wrists.

"God, I need this . . ."

Abruptly, the drilling kisses stopped. With her cheek against mine, she pulled her right arm free of my grip. I could hear the sound of slow keystrokes.

Finally, I opened my eyes and looked at the screen.

<i get scared.>

I pecked the keys with my right index finger. <so do i.>

<i'm a coward. i'm a cynic. and i'm a complete wreck right now.>

She held me tighter, kissing the side of my face. She smelled like lime. She must have worn a facial cream to bed and then washed it off. It smelled wonderful.

Jean signed her affections with a quick kiss and then pulled away from me. Straightening herself out, she returned to her seat.

<Sorry,> she wrote. <I would have loved to stay where I was but this place closes in fifteen minutes and I have a lot of my own explaining to do.>

<You moved out.>

She sighed. <We moved out.>

<Just tell me I wasn't a factor in that decision.>

<That's what I need to explain.>

<So I was.>

<You weren't. You couldn't have been.>

<Why not?>

She grimaced sheepishly. <Because we moved out three months ago.>

All I could do was stare at her vacantly as I put the pieces together.

She shrugged. <I told you you weren't a marital issue.>

<You wanted me to believe you were still married.>

<I AM still married. But it's over. I want out, and so does Neil. Since November, we've been trying to negotiate our own divorce, without lawyers. It's been a living hell. We meet at least three times a week in a vain attempt to separate his debts from mine. We always end up crying, cursing, and saying horrible things to each other. Well, mostly I say the horrible things. I know just how to cut him down into little cubes. I'm not proud of it.>

God. With that razor-sharp mind of hers, she could shred a man to pieces. And at the rate we were going, it would only be a matter of months, weeks, days, before she'd crack the last of my access codes, the flaws in my defenses. Soon enough, she'd have the power to break me with just one tap of the chisel. The thought was downright terrifying.

<But then he knows my weakness,> she continued. <He takes her out every Saturday night, and there's not a damn thing I can do to stop it. He poisons her against me. He strikes at me through my very own child. Even her FATHER wasn't low enough to do that.>

The rage on her face made her an entirely different woman to me. Selfishly, I was relieved to be an innocent bystander, but the dark voice inside wondered how long it would take for me to earn my own share. Nine days was all it took to bring the hatred out of Harmony, and she wasn't one who hated easily.

On reading my expression, Jean breathed out a quiet groan. <This is why I didn't tell you. It's an ugly part of my life. I didn't need someone new to complain to. I needed someone new to distract me. I needed someone to laugh with, joke with, flirt with. And on that front, my dear, you have been a godsend to me. The last thing I wanted to do was bring my problems into our nice little sphere. The second to last thing I wanted to do was create new ones.>

She briefly held up her left hand, flashing me her white-gold wedding band.

<So I used the marriage as a preemptive defense. I do it all the time. I chat online with a lot of people. It's my television. I love it, but the downside is that half the time, the other person wants to escalate. Men and women both. Personally, I don't get it. I don't know what they all see in me.>

<I'm afraid I do.>

She rolled her eyes. <Yes. I know that NOW. But you did a damn good job convincing me otherwise. You were sitting right here telling me how we didn't have anything profound . . .>

<It was bullshit,> I confessed. <I just didn't want to fall into a married woman.>

<And I didn't want to fall into another man. Not now. Not when I'm still trying to get rid of the last one. But damn it . . .>

She shook her head at me, drowning me in a face filled with warm chagrin. <I'm not sure I ever had a platonic thought about you.>

I matched her look. <You did a damn good job convincing me otherwise.>

<I know.>

<YOU were sitting right here telling me how great it was that we only wanted to get to know each other's minds.>

<Utter bullshit,> she replied with a tight smirk. <I was picturing you naked the whole time.>

I let out a cracked laugh. <What's wrong with us?>

<We're both scared,> she wrote. <We're both scarred. We're both jaded. And to make matters worse, we're both currently embroiled in our own separate nightmares.>

My head started throbbing again. I looked down at the keyboard.

<I hate to say this but you and that kid of yours are holding me together.>

<You're holding us together,> she wrote back. <Do you know how long it's been since she's let me run my fingers through her hair?>

I glanced up again. <She never told me about Neil either.>

<Of course not. I'd be amazed if she did.>

<I don't get it. Why?>

<Because you're an escape for her too. She was too young to remember the first divorce, but this one's hitting her hard. She's going through hell and she blames me for it. She thinks I'm some kind of gorgon who eats the hearts of men. Why do you think she's been trying to keep me twelve miles away from you? Why do you think I had to sneak out of the apartment tonight like I was the teenager?>

<That's silly that she would think that about you.>

<She's thirteen. It's her prerogative to think silly things.>

<I guess you and I should know better.>

Jean shrugged hopelessly. <Yeah. We should. But that doesn't change the fact that I'm scared of you. I'm scared of you breaking my heart, or cutting me down into little cubes, or taking my daughter as an emotional hostage if things ever got really bad between us. That's why I had to bring you out here tonight. I had to find out once and for all if you were secretly an asshole.>

<I'm not.>

<You're not,> she replied wearily. < I'm running out of ways to distrust you.>

Now I looked at the manuscript, the provocative sticky note on top. I didn't like the way Harmony's name looked in Jean's handwriting. The lettering was elegant and artful, everything that Jean was and everything that Harmony wasn't.

She followed my gaze. <You really care about her, don't you?>

<Yes. But I'm done with her.>

<No you're not.>

<No,> I admitted. <I'm not.>

She reached an arm across the table. <Then let me be your distraction.>

I took her hand. For once I was way ahead of her.

She didn't care that I was coming down with something. I didn't care that her car was a mess. If we wanted this to be a proper love scene, we would have gone to an upscale hotel suite with a roaring fireplace, a bottle of Chablis in a tin ice bucket, and Annie Lennox's "Why?" playing in the background as we tumbled stylishly on the thousand-dollar carpet.

Jean and I were too clever to pursue the cinematic cliché. We were too clever to be good at sex anyway. We were both lousy lovers, by our own admission, and we were too clever to see intercourse as the salve to our current ills.

So we regressed. We stole away to the back of her SUV like a pair of fumbling virgins. In the light of the lamppost, in a handicapped spot near the sea end of Wilshire, we embraced, we kissed, we ran our hands all over each other with nervous excitement. We explored each other carefully. She wasn't wearing a bra, so when my left hand moved up her shirt, all the way to the swell of her nipple, she let out a soft gasp, as if no one had ever touched her there before. When she gently nibbled my ear, I almost cried, as if I'd been waiting for years to have a girl do that to me.

We were so awkward and juvenile in our affections that for a wonderful time, I was simple again. My mind was filled with dumb and pleasant thoughts. As she kissed my fingers, I made a strong commitment to enroll in sign-language classes. I couldn't wait for the day when we would stop relying on technology and Madison to talk to each other. As I moved my hands over her firm stomach, I made the decision to start exercising again. I wanted a body that would drive her crazy. I wanted to be her own private amusement park. And as she rested on top of me, as she pressed her hips against mine, I realized that despite our limitations, we could screw each other senseless someday. When circumstances were better, when we knew each other better, we'd be so comfortable that we could shut off all the noise in our heads and become two bodies working together in perfect passion, perfect instinct, perfect rhythm. God, how I wanted to make her scream with pleasure. God, what a thing to look forward to.

But for now, we were both in shambles. Once we stopped fooling around, the myriad complexities of our adult existence came back into focus. Dozens of unwelcome details flooded back into our field of vision.

Leaning against the passenger door, I held her from behind. I could almost feel her powerful mind start up again, processing multiple streams of thought, observation, analysis, concern. I noticed the laptop on the floor, complete with LocalTalk cable. That was her backup plan. If I had refused to come out tonight, she would have charged straight to my front door, equipment in hand. She would have linked our two portables and set us up. She could have saved me a whole trip to begin with but then she knew that if things went well in my apartment (too well), there would be a whole second floor for us to deal with. A whole bedroom. The opportunity (the temptation) to have sex (bad sex) would probably be too much to resist, and (God help us) not only would we be going too far (too fast) but we'd be making love right above Madison's office (her haven), and that would just be starting our (reckless/dangerous/wonderful) relationship off on two bad feet.

I rested my chin on her head. "God, you're just like me," I said. "You think of everything."

My words, of course, fell outside her notice. I was talking to an audience of me. Sensing the disconnect, Jean retrieved her laptop and booted it up in front of us. She channeled her own pressing thoughts through SimpleText, in eighteen-point Helvetica.

<We are acting out my daughter's nightmare.>

I reached my arms under hers, tapping the keyboard. <Then we're going to have to start a very slow, very subtle campaign to sell her on the idea of us.>

<That won't be an easy project.>

<I've had worse.>

She squeezed my hands, then leaned her head back into me. <You're so much stronger than me.>

<I'm nowhere near as strong as you. I'm just better at pretending.>

<I don't care,> she typed. <I just want to crawl inside you and never come out.>

I held her tight, planting slow and soft kisses on her neck. I kissed her faster and more intensely until she closed her eyes and moaned. Moving upward, I pressed my lips to the side of her face, cleaning away every last trace of lime. I wanted to devour her. I wanted to swallow her whole, like a snake. Then I'd have her all to myself. She wouldn't have to worry about Neil, or Madison, or money anymore. She'd be hiding out inside of me. She'd be hiding out with me.

The laptop chimed at midnight. Jean didn't notice it until I stopped my affections. She glanced at the clock on the menu bar.

<It's Wednesday,> she wrote.

<Happy Wednesday.>

<Happy Valentine's Day,> she replied. <You better leave before I fuck you.>

In the future, at least Alonso's version, there will be two ways to exist: physically and virtually. The physical world will be a giant urban ghetto for the working class, society gone to shit. But the virtual world will be a full-time paradise for all who can afford it. Not only can you customize your appearance, you can customize your senses. If you only wanted to see the world in springtime, you'd only see springtime. If you only wanted to see Baptists, you'd only see the fellow users who were registered as Baptists. Or leftists. Or jazz enthusiasts. There were a million flags you could attach to yourself, and a million types of people you could exclude from your own perceptions. God no longer had to grant you the serenity to accept the things you could not change. With the right software, you could change anything.

Such is the premise of *Godsend,* at least the way Jean described it. At midnight she and I let go of each other. By a quarter to one, we were back in our respective homes, back on our respective computers, back on EyeTalk, where it was safe. By then my electricity had returned, but I kept the lights off anyway. I stretched out on the couch and rested the laptop on my chest as if it were Jean herself.

At first we shared some of the wonderful things we'd like to do to each other, someday, when circumstances were better. We romanced each other speculatively, virtually, and in full lowercase. We finished ourselves. Then we curled up together as best we could, spooning on a bed of ones and zeroes.

The narrator of *Godsend* had no determinate identity, not any that he or she was willing to share with the reader. In the virtual world, s/he was a perpetual metamorph, a disenchanted cipher who changed everything about him/herself on an hourly basis. Name. Shape. Sex. Perceptions. The trouble begins when s/he meets and falls in love with a fellow shifter. All they have in common are their capricious ways and a taste for pansexual debauchery. According to Jean, the two main characters spend half the book screwing in every form imaginable, even as lobsters. Unfortunately, after each blissful encounter, they spend days obsessively seeking each other out again, trying to reconnect through whatever new disguises they've adopted.

<Does it have a happy ending?> I asked.

<Sort of. It turns out the mystery date is Jesus.>

I blinked, stupefied. <The whole time the narrator's having sex with Jesus?>

<Yeah. It's kind of like a weird, soft-porn version of the Footprints parable.>

I laughed. <Wow. That's so stupid, I'm actually offended.>

<I kind of felt the same way,> she replied. <And yet I couldn't put it down. To be honest, the whole time I was reading it, I was thinking about you.>

<I'm not Jesus.>

<Neither am I. But the book made me wonder why I was having such a hard time believing in you.>

<It's not your fault,> I sent her, with encoded gloom. <There's something about me. I give off this oily vibe.>

<No, Scott. I'm just someone who's been hurt badly.>

I grabbed a tissue from the coffee table and wiped my nose. <I wish I could promise I'll never hurt you.>

<I wish I could promise I won't drive you insane someday.>

<So what happens next?>

The cursor blinked steadily for a few silent seconds.

<I'm going to get this ring off my finger,> she typed. <Once and for all, I'm going to close the book on Neil. I'm going to become financially solvent again. And while doing all that, I'm going to wade into you, slowly, and in such a way that doesn't cause me or my daughter great emotional distress. How does that sound?>

<Sounds like a solid plan,> I offered.

<Yeah. You and I are just full of grand designs, aren't we?>

<Not me,> I declared. <I'm all schemed out.>

<So if you don't my asking, what happens next with you?>

I didn't mind her asking. I just didn't know how to answer. In a few hours, the sun would come up. A few hours after that, either Harmony would confess or she wouldn't. If she confessed, Miranda would sink me. If she didn't, the audiotape would be released and would open up a world of shit for me, Harmony, and a whole lot of people.

All told, I was in for another bad day.

The more I thought about it, the more I wished I'd stayed in the car with Jean, instead of fleeing at midnight like Cinderella. I wished I had taken her Hollywood-style, with blazing flames and wild passion. I should have screwed her into a new state of being. Instead I nibbled. I pecked. I brought her into me piece by piece when, goddamn it, I should have begged her to let me out.

22

THE TWIST

I'd left Harmony on the floor of my car. As I'd fled the Santa Monica beach yesterday, the red phone tumbled off the passenger seat and onto the dirty rubber mat. I had yet to pick it up. Harmony had said there was no excuse for a man like me. I told her she didn't even know me, then called her a bitch. There wasn't much to say after that.

Even Maxina, the last person I'd spoken to on that infernal device, had signed off on a note of finality. You're done. It's over. Bye-bye. She was right. For me, the job was finished. I didn't even have a bill to hand them. The only thing left to do, for my sake and theirs, was erase myself from the picture.

Not a single one of my accomplices had the need or the desire to ever speak to me again, and yet from the floor of the Saturn, the red phone rang once more.

I didn't hear it. I was two stories up and fast asleep in my bed. Instead of leaving a message, the caller shook me awake through my landline. It took me three and a half rings to fumble my way to the cordless receiver on the night table. It let out a loud beep, whining to me about its low battery.

"Hello?"

"Uh . . . Scott?"

Despite my languor, I had an easier time recognizing his voice than he did mine. "Hey. Doug."

"Jesus. I thought I got the wrong number. You sound awful."

I felt awful. My head pounded. My throat throbbed with hot pain.

My sinuses might as well have been filled with cement. I was officially ailing.

My alarm clock blinked its digits at me, still confused from last night's blackout.

"What time is it?" I asked.

"Seven. Listen, you need to wake up, because we've got . . . Something very strange has happened."

"What happened?"

"Somebody leaked the tape to the media."

My receiver beeped again.

"What is that?" he asked.

"It's my phone. What are you talking about?"

"The audiotape. Fox News somehow got their hands on a copy."

"How did that happen?"

"That's what I'm trying to find out. It wasn't us."

It began to dawn on me that this was actually happening. I sat up. "Wait a second. Wait a second! Someone leaked the audiotape to Fox News?"

"Yes. Good morning."

"That's crazy! Why would anyone do that? We had her!"

"I know."

"She agreed to confess on videotape!"

"I know!"

"So who leaked the goddamn recording?"

"That I don't know. I was hoping you'd have some clues."

Beep. "I have no idea what the hell's going on, Doug."

"I was afraid of that."

"I gave a copy to you and Maxina," I said. "That's it."

"Hey, mine's been locked in my office safe since last Monday. Nobody's touched it."

"What about the Judge?"

"He may hate you, Scott, but he's not stupid. He knows a video confession is a hundred times better than an audio implication."

"Yeah, but does he have the combination to your safe?"

Beep! "It's not him!"

"Well, somebody leaked the tape!"

"Look, just get dressed and come to my house as soon as you can. We're going to sort this thing—"

The cordless died. I chucked it at the hamper, then hunched forward, groaning. I had gotten only two hours of sleep, and I was sick all over, but my mind was running on emergency power. That recording was 90 percent me. If Fox News had it, it would be playing nationwide in a matter of minutes. By noon my voice would be on every channel. By midafternoon Miranda would expose me as the mystery villain, and by tonight, Harmony would confirm it. Happy Valentine's Day, Scott. You're done. It's over. Bye-bye.

The morning belonged to News Corp. Since 5:00 A.M., the minions of Murdoch heralded their coup all over the airwaves. *Holy crap! We've got a MAJOR twist in the Harmony Prince saga, and we've got it exclusively on Fox News! Bow to your masters, CNN! Bow to us!*

The recording would premiere at noon Eastern, nine Pacific, but the network spilled enough details to get the nation's juices flowing. CNN and MSNBC followed suit with their own prereactive chatter. *Professor, do you think this alleged tape could be for real? Could Harmony Prince be lying? Could this whole thing be a sinister hoax? And if it is* [slobber slobber], *who does the other voice belong to? Who is he working for? What would he have to gain from this?*

I spent a good thirty minutes under the showerhead, pressing my palms against the tile wall, staring down at my feet as hot steam cleared my nasal passages. My thoughts were liquid. I couldn't seem to hold on to anything for more than a second. Mostly, I suffered flashes of droll curiosity. I wondered which picture of me Miranda would use for her story. Ha. Maybe the one from her 1996 Halloween party, when I came dressed as a devil. I wondered what vengeful ornaments Harmony would add to the image. *Oh, he berated me all the time. He touched me inappropriately. He threatened to have me killed. Once he even called me a . . . Can I say the "N"-word on TV?*

Once I shut off the water, my thoughts turned to Madison. There was no way to prepare her for this, no way to make her understand. She was in for a horrible day and a long, sleepless night. And once the pain of my betrayal went away, once her hot tears dried up, she'd close herself forever. The walls would rise up, ninety feet high and twenty feet thick, and there'd be no getting past her formidable defenses.

It was enough to make a grown man weep, but I couldn't even seem to do that. Everything else was failing on me—my clock, my phone, my body, my schemes—but the practical engine inside of me just kept chugging along. It pushed me through the rest of my morning routine: into my clothes, out of the apartment, into the car, onto the road. Always thinking, never reacting. Never, ever reacting.

As I left the garage, I was hit by the strong and sudden urge to drive to Madison's school. I knew where it was. I could be there in ten minutes. I could scour the halls, peeking into every classroom until I found her. Then I'd kneel on the floor, gazing up at her as I squeezed her shoulders. *Look, there are going to be some things on the news today. Things about me. Don't believe them, okay? It's not the way it looks. I can't explain it just yet, but . . . God, just hold on, Madison. Don't give up on me.*

No, that would only freak her out, and it would yank her into the crisis sooner than necessary. The problem wasn't the recording itself, it was me being identified as the second voice. There were only two women with the power and the incentive to rat me out: Miranda and Harmony. If I cut them both off at the pass somehow, I could survive this. There was just one woman with the power and the incentive to help me: Maxina. She would be at Doug's house. Okay. Stick to the original plan then. Go to Doug's house and talk to Maxina. She'll help you out of your jam.

Your jam?

Three lights later, it finally occurred to me what I was doing. I was trying to cut the rope that Harmony had around me. She was falling hard, and I was desperately trying to cut the line around my ankle before it pulled me down with her. I was fighting to make sure she fell alone.

"Jesus Christ."

Abruptly, I pulled into a loading zone. Without shutting off the car or even switching gears, I kept my tense fingers gripped around the steering wheel. My eyes were wide and my breaths were quick and labored. Otherwise, I didn't move an inch.

"Okay," I said. "Okay. Okay . . ."

It took a dozen more of those to defuse me. I'd never been this close to a meltdown before. I was a man of few griefs but the few I had, I muddled through. When my father died. When my mother died. When Drea fell. When Gracie left. I always held myself together. Now I was just a stiff breeze away from structural collapse.

There's no excuse. There's no excuse for a man like you.

Except Harmony didn't know what kind of man I was. She didn't know that I tried. I tried to make everything work for everybody, even her. Especially her. I was a man who tried. I was a man who failed. At the very least, I was a man who meant well.

"I meant well . . ."

Yes, and what a fine comfort that was. Maybe I could yell that to her as she plummeted into darkness. Maybe she'd forgive me on the long way down.

Nobody seemed to follow me, but I parked a block away from Doug's house anyway. As I walked down the quiet street, I focused on my physical ills. The drums in my head pounded at full force. Every breath of cool air scraped its way down my throat. I pictured myself wrapped up in a thick, warm comforter on top of my couch, watching hours of old movies without a care in the world except recovery. If Harmony entered the vision, she'd nurture me with hot tea, a lot of aspirin, a few silly giggles, and a wet kiss on the forehead. If it was Jean, she'd turn off the TV, take off most of her clothes, and then slip under the covers with me, contagion be damned. I loved each remedy. I suppose a less creative person would imagine the simultaneous affections of both women, but Harmony and Jean were so different from each other, they were so much larger than life to me, that they couldn't even fit in the same fantasy. They were matter and anti-matter. My head could barely contain the two of them.

Doug's Land Rover was parked in his driveway, right next to the Judge's black Bentley. I figured it'd be just the three of us until Maxina arrived. As usual, I figured wrong. The door was answered by Big Bank. He wore his typical black ensemble, from boots to blazer.

"Hey. What are you doing here?"

He looked around. "Just get in."

Quickly, I entered the house. He closed the door.

"It was stupid of you to come here."

"I was asked to come here."

"It was stupid for them to ask."

"Don't worry," I said. "I'm not radioactive yet."

"Yeah? What happens when the TV starts throwing your name around?"

"Then I start glowing."

"And then what?"

"I don't know," I admitted. "That's why I came here."

He studied me, expressionless. "You have a hickey on your neck."

Surprised, I examined myself in the foyer mirror. There was a blemish the size of a quarter at the base of my throat, a silly mishap from last night's affections. It pulled me out of the future so fast, I laughed with inertial energy.

"The deaf woman?" he asked cynically, as if Jean were just an urban legend.

"Yeah. You want to hear all about it?"

"No."

"Good," I said, adjusting my shirt collar. "So is Jeremy here? Or did they just bring you over to kill me?"

I knew Hunta had a new secret hideout. I just didn't expect it to be Doug's place. It was a move of pure fiscal pessimism on the Judge's part. He figured this was a lost battle, which meant he'd have to drop Jeremy from the roster, which meant Hunta's second album would never come out, which meant there was no future revenue to deduct all those hotel expenses from. It was record-label dharma: if you can't bill the artist, it's probably not worth paying for.

Since I last saw him nine days before, Hunta had lost a little weight, a lot of sleep, his wife, his daughter, his faith in humanity, and any fondness he may have had for me. I could see it all on his face as I entered the living room. Wearing nothing but an open robe and a pair of red silk boxer shorts, he stretched himself out on the long couch. For once his poisons were legal. He tapped a cigarette into an ashtray on the floor, right next to a half-empty bottle of sloe gin.

"Slick," he muttered lazily. "Get the fuck over here."

I sat down on the wooden coffee table, right between him and the big-screen TV. The bold text overlay stretched all the way across the Fox News banner: HARMONY PRINCE A HOAX?

Before I could say anything, Hunta grabbed my sleeve. His eyes were cracked with red veins.

"Just tell me it's over, man. Tell me this fucking nightmare is over and I'll forgive you for everything."

Through the rippled glass, I could see the wide forms of Doug and the Judge on the porch: pacing, flailing, fretting. Like me, they were waiting for more data. They were waiting for Maxina.

"It looks like the nightmare is over," I said. "At least for you."

"I didn't ask what it looks like! I asked what it is!"

"I don't know what else to tell you. We're just going to have to wait and see."

He sat up, pressing his fingers over his cornrows. The cigarette in his hand looked like a small chimney coming out of his skull.

"They all saying she *may* be lying. She *may* be full of shit. But no one's saying I may be innocent."

"That's not how they work," I told him. "They only have two modes: attack and ignore. If you want vindication, you're going to have to fight for it. You're going to have to get in everyone's faces, with middle fingers blazing, and say, 'Fuck you. You got me all wrong.' "

I thought that might pick him up some, but he continued to brood. I plopped down next to him, slouching into the cushions.

"Or you can just attack the evil white men who framed you," I added accordingly.

"Yeah? Can I mention you by name?"

"I don't think you'll have to."

Sinking with me, Hunta matched my languid pose. We looked like a couple of wasted stoners, spacing out in front of the TV.

"Forget it," he said. "What I been through, I wouldn't wish on anybody. And it don't matter anyway. Even if I got the whole world kissing my ass, it won't mean a damn thing. Not anymore."

"I'm sorry about Simba."

"Yeah. So am I."

He took a long swig of gin, then offered me the bottle. I waved it away. I didn't need his depressant, and he certainly didn't need my flu germs.

"I never been alone for Valentine's Day," he told me. "Ever since I was a kid, I always had someone to be with. I never had trouble finding a woman to wrap myself around." He laughed. "And it was always the same. They'd always end up mothering me. It didn't matter if they was older or younger. They could all see I grew up without a mother. They could all see that hole in me, and they all tried to fill it. And Simba . . ."

Staring ahead, he took a long, shaky hit of nicotine. "I been blamed for every bad thing in the world, man, but that shit's all on me. I fucked up. And you know what the sad part is? Even if she came back right now, even if I apologized to her all day and all night, I'd still fuck up all over again. I'd fuck up in all the same ways."

"Maybe you wouldn't."

"Yeah, soon enough I would," he said before imbibing again. "Soon enough I'd have to."

I studied the bottle in his hand. It idly occurred to me that the words "gin" and "Jean" would look very much the same to a deaf lipreader. So would "medicine" and "Madison." The bizarre revelations nearly triggered an ill-timed chortle. All I needed was gin and medicine. I could survive all this with just a little gin and medicine.

"See, we ain't like them, Slick. There's a kind of love in women, most women, that we ain't got in us. It's a kind of love that we don't know how to handle. That's why so many marriages end up falling apart. That's why there's so much pain in the world."

"That simple, huh?"

"Some things are just that simple, man. It's people like you who make shit more complex."

"Well, you ever rap about it?"

He gave me a jaded look. "Fuck you. I bet you think I haven't."

"Have you?"

"Second album, motherfucker. First track. 'Love Is Real.' "

"Tell me about it."

"Why?"

"Why not?"

Extinguishing his cigarette, he stared at its last wisps of smoke.

"It's a sequel," he told me. "It's all about that guy from 'Bitch Fiend,' 'cept here he finally deals with his problem. Here he finally sees that if he keeps spreading himself out over all these different women, there'll be nothing left of him to spread. And he finally finds a woman he can put all of himself into, not just that one part of him, you know what I'm saying?"

"I know what you're saying."

"So he puts everything into this one woman. And he finally learns how to stop being all scared and shit. You know, scared of someone knowing him. Scared of someone loving him."

"Sounds really good," I said.

"It's better than good, man. It's the best song I ever wrote."

"Simba must have loved it."

With his eyes leveled downward, he emitted a wistful sneer. "Nah. I mean I wrote it for her. I wrote it about her. But I didn't write it *with* her. And that was the problem. I had help on that one. And then I fucked the help."

Ah, yes. Lisa Glassman. How quickly she'd dropped off my radar screen. It felt like months since I'd even thought about her. Months since I'd even wondered what the truth was.

"Jeremy, can I please ask you something?"

He snorted a laugh. "You asking *now*?"

"I might as well ask now."

"What the fuck does it matter now?"

"Because I'd just like to know what really happened that night."

"What really happened," he echoed while lighting another cigarette. "It's funny. She called me last Thursday. Right as that bitch of yours was getting her face put everywhere. I never expected to hear from her again, but there she was on the phone, wondering what the hell happened. How this one lie started this other lie and everything got so out of hand."

"So she admitted she was lying."

He waved me off. "Hell, yeah. She knew it wasn't even a question of that. I mean, we were both there that night, and we were both listening. She only said yes. And she said it like a thousand times."

He dropped his head back, venting smoke at the ceiling fan. "I never raped a woman, Slick. But if lying was a crime, then I'd be a master criminal, you understand what I'm saying? If using women was a capital offense, they'd have given me the chair a long time ago."

Just from her impressive background, Lisa Glassman had struck me as a woman of skill and resolve. A true creative professional. I could only imagine that despite her attraction to Hunta, however deep it ran, she had initially put up quite a roadblock when he starting making advances. Oh, the wonderful things he must have said to her that night. The powerful lines he must have used to bind her better judgment. If that was indeed a crime, and if the system wasn't nicer to white men, I'd surely be on death row myself.

"You know what the saddest part is? She never asked for any money. She never even asked for an apology. All she ever wanted, all she fought to get, was that damn song she helped me write."

I rubbed my nose. "That's all she wanted? The rights to that song?"

"No, man. Not even the rights. She didn't care if I gave it away to L-Ron or whoever. She just wanted a written promise that I'd take the song off the new album and then never sing it again. She said I didn't deserve to sing it. It was too good for me. She felt so strong about it that she was willing to lie to get what she wanted."

There was definitely a poetry at work there, considering that *he* had lied to get what *he* wanted. It all made perfect sense. But there was still one nagging question.

"So why didn't you just give it to her?"

Hunta let out a hearty belly laugh, loud enough to stop the pacing shapes on the patio.

"That's what Lisa asked when she called me up last week. And I'll tell you the truth, man, just like I told her. I didn't want to give up that song. It's just that simple. It was the title track of the album. The best track of the album. If she wanted to quit her job, call me names, call my wife, that was her business. But she didn't deserve to take that song from me. Not because she let me fuck her."

Somber again, he let out a tired sigh. "Once that Melrose shit happened, though, I changed my mind real fast. I was ready to give her anything. But then Maxina came along and said it would look bad to be making that kind of deal. And then *you* came along and . . . Shit, you were the man."

"I was the man," I said weakly.

"You were the man with the plan that was gonna fix everything. And you wanna know what the real sad part is? She told me she would've never come forward." He laughed again. "She was only fronting like she was gonna hit the media. Just to sweat us out. This whole time we're all racing to stop her, and it turns out she would've never come forward. She said she could never do that to another person, even a person like me."

On TV, Fox showed a clip of Harmony and Alonso exiting the CNN building, right after their tumultuous appearance on *Larry King Live*. Although Harmony tried to shield herself from the unrelenting cameras, it was easy to see the pitch-black look on her face. She was vengeful, hateful, out for blood.

Hunta watched along. "All these lies. All this crazy drama. All for what?"

"I don't know."

From the corner of my eye, I could feel him turn to look at me.

"We should've never listened to you, Slick."

"No," I responded. "I guess you shouldn't have."

By eight-thirty, we had all gathered in the living room, spreading ourselves out among the three leather sofas. Hunta sat between Big Bank and Doug, while the Judge and I faced each other from the adjacent love seats. It would take ten Harmonys to match our combined weight, but the one on TV loomed large enough to balance out the room.

The Judge and I were held in our own strange counterpoise. He swore to me that he wasn't the one who leaked the audiotape. I assured him that even if he was, I had no intention of making anyone's life any worse. We didn't believe each other, but who cared? We were too nervous, too clobbered, too battle-weary to start another fight now. All we could do was wallow in the din and blather of Fox News until something pulled us out of our stasis.

As expected, that something was Maxina. At a quarter to nine she joined our little powwow, shattering the casual equilibrium we had established. The moment she walked in, we all seemed to tilt her way.

With a wince, she sat down next to the Judge. Her hair was unwashed, her eyes were dark with pain and fatigue, and her untucked blouse was misbuttoned by one. Like the rest of us, she was clearly at the end of her tether. She kicked off her shoes, then muted the TV.

"My copy of the audiotape," she began, "has been locked inside my suitcase ever since I got it last Monday. Nobody else knew where it was. Not even my staff. Doug?"

"Like I told Scott, our copy was locked in the office safe. Only the Judge and I have the combination."

The Judge sighed with forced patience. "I swear on the life of my children that I did not leak that tape."

"It's ridiculous," Doug declared. "As soon as Maxina told us that Harmony was confessing, we practically threw a party. Why would we screw that up?"

"My guess?" I said. "You got antsy. You didn't think Harmony would actually go through with it, and you didn't want to waste another moment."

Doug waved me off. The Judge simply glared. "Yeah? And what about your original? How secure was that?"

"Locked in my safe," I said.

"You said you have an intern."

"She's thirteen, she doesn't have the combination—"

"And she don't know the whole story anyway," griped Hunta.

That was pretty much what I was going to say. But I was idly flattered, on Madison's behalf, that Hunta not only remembered her from their brief conversation but continued to give a crap about her opinion of him. In that respect, he had little to worry about. By the time Madison checked the news, she'd know for sure that he was innocent. She'd know for sure that I wasn't.

"I am completely stumped, then," said Maxina. "But it doesn't matter who leaked it. We've got to deal with the fallout."

Hunta was puzzled. "What's the problem? Why is this so bad for us?"

"It's bad for Harmony," Doug replied. "And she can make it bad for us."

Maxina cleaned her glasses with her shirt flap. "She was up all night working on her speech. I read the final draft. It was wonderful. Too bad we didn't get a single word of it on camera. Once she found out about the Fox News story, she wasn't in a mood to cooperate."

She threw me a quick, poignant glance. The message was clear enough: *She blames you.* Of course Harmony blamed me. Why wouldn't she? I was the root of all evil.

"So what?" asked Big Bank. "What can she do? Deny it?"

Doug shook his head. "She can try, but the voice analysts will nail her. She's essentially screwed. The problem is that there's nothing stopping her from telling the press all about us."

The Judge aimed his fury at me. "That's because she *knows* all about us! I told you from the start it was a bad idea! Now she's going to bury us!"

"She's not going to bury you," I said impatiently. "She's going to bury me."

"Bullshit."

"No, he's right," said Maxina. "She's going to bury Scott."

Try as they might, the others couldn't make the leap. I let Maxina explain it.

"All the tape proves is that there's a plot to frame Jeremy, not a plot to save him. If Harmony tries to reveal the rest, the press won't buy it. It's too crazy. It's too self-serving. And she won't have any credibility left anyway. The story would flutter around the mainstream for a day or two, but that's it. If it doesn't die on its own, we can always kill it ourselves."

On Fox News, a split-box graphic floated over the news anchor's shoulder. One side had an unflattering shot of Harmony. The other side had a generic male silhouette with a question mark in it. The sight of it made my stomach drop.

"Unlike us, Scott is linked to the story through hard evidence. If Harmony wants to take him down with her, she can. And make no mistake: Harmony wants to take him down with her."

"But he'll go down as part of the white conspiracy," she added.

I would *be* the white conspiracy. Alonso and Harmony would simply be my race-traitor lackeys. The tables were about to turn real hard, real fast. Some people would call it poetic justice. I suddenly wondered if Maxina was one of them.

Hunta gawked at me. "Wait a second. You saying I'm saved and you're screwed?"

"Yeah," I said, while keeping my sights on Maxina. "Enjoy the twist."

He had every right to gloat at my downfall, but he was too stunned to fit me into the equation. The Bitch had really worked him over these past two weeks, to the point where he couldn't tell up from down, left from right, black from white. He was the world's hostage. Whether he was rescued or merely exchanged for another prisoner, who the hell cared? It was an open door. Despite his earlier claims that it no longer mattered, it mattered.

"Don't fuck me with now," he said. "Don't tell me this shit is over if it ain't really over."

"It ain't really over," Maxina dryly responded while meeting my stare. "We've established that Harmony is Scott's problem. What we don't know is whether or not Scott's going to be our problem."

Naturally, everyone turned to me. I crossed my legs and rested my head against my fist, playing coy, even though my gut wrenched.

"So that's the sticky wicket, is it?"

"Don't fuck with us," the Judge snapped. "What are you going to do?"

"What *can* he do?" asked Big Bank.

"Scott's a thoroughly cautious man," said Maxina. "I have no doubt that he recorded at least some of our key meetings. He probably has each and every one of us on tape. What I can't tell from his impassive young face is whether or not he plans to use it."

She was right, as usual. Thanks to my Palm Pilot recorder and a lifetime of vigilant thinking, I had everything I needed to blow up the world. I even had some incentive.

"Well, I'll be honest." I sighed. "I'm not happy about that tape being leaked. Somebody screwed me over. Worse, somebody screwed Harmony over. The more I think about that, the angrier I get. I mean she had a chance. If she had just confessed, the press and the public would have given her a chance to redeem herself. And she would have. With or without me, she would have built from this and become . . . who knows? She would have become something. But now? Forget it. Now she's just another criminal caught on Fox. She's fucked for life. I'm fucked for life. And why? Because somebody in this room got nervous. That doesn't just make me angry. That makes me cynical."

Maxina sat forward. "Just from your glares, I can tell who your chief suspect is."

"Yeah. You're sharp that way."

"It wasn't me," she attested. "If it was me, I'd tell you. And I'd tell you why."

"I already know why. You were afraid that Harmony and I were still in cahoots together. That we faked this whole blowout between us. That we were secretly scheming to pull some last-minute trick that would screw you all and set us up for life. So you beat us to the punch line. You took a calculated risk. And you know what? It paid off."

She raised her palms, speaking to me as if I were a hysterical child. "That's not what happened at all. Look, you're very upset right now—"

"You're goddamn right I'm upset! You ruined her life! You ruined her life and she thinks I did it!"

I'd famously yelled at the Judge before, but none of them had ever seen me like this. I was sliding down toward something ugly, and it was clear for everyone to see. I clenched my teeth. I dug my fingers into the cushion. I would not break down. Not here. Not in front of them. Like Madison, I would appear mature and professional to my last spiteful breath.

In this case, it was a last spiteful sneeze.

"Bless you," said Maxina.

"Thank you."

I took a tissue out of my pocket and wiped my nose. "Don't worry. I'm not going to be a problem. I'm not going to strike back. I know how the game's played. If I leaked my own recordings, the press would just take it out on Jeremy, and I have absolutely no interest in seeing that happen. I've already pissed enough in his bed."

It wasn't often in life that I got to seize the moral high ground. The view from here was nice. Their mildly astonished expressions were invigorating to me. They vindicated me, but only mildly. There were no loved ones of mine in the room. The thoughts and impressions of these five people—clients, associates, accomplices, whatever—ultimately meant nothing to me. So they had gotten me all wrong. So they finally started to realize that. So what? I'd never let them in.

"So what are you going to do?" the Judge asked again.

The network continued to stretch out the last few minutes before the grand premiere of the audiotape. They were merely pumping up their numbers, hogging our precious eyeballs for as long they could. They showed us Harmony's momentous first walk down the media gauntlet. For the thousandth time, Alonso escorted her from her front door to his shiny black Audi. Even in replay, her frightened face had a paralyzing effect. Her wide eyes screamed her distress at me. They screamed my name.

"Scott?"

What could I do? I was plummeting into the depths right alongside Harmony. Her I had let in. She was a loved one of mine. The fact that she hated me, the fact that she was blind to me, the fact that she was falling, these were all things I couldn't quite handle. I couldn't just tell her I meant well. She wouldn't believe me. And even if she believed me, she wouldn't forgive me. And even if she forgave me, it still wouldn't save her. By this point in the game, she needed more than words. She needed hard proof. She needed rescue.

By this point, I was in a unique position to offer both.

"I'm going to go home," I replied, still watching Harmony. "I'm going to take a long, hot shower, until the steam clears me up and I sound like myself again. Then I'm going to break out my handy voice recorder, and I'm going to make a confession."

Typically, the Judge and Doug reacted in loud knee-jerk fashion. Maxina held up a hand to them.

"It'll be pure fiction," I assured them. "I'll confess that I was hired by unnamed parties to frame Hunta. Our sole objective was to keep rap in the headlines until the U.S. Senate called for a brand-new round of obscenity hearings. So I enlisted Harmony Prince. I met her at the Flower Club and promised her fame, fortune, the whole nine yards. Initially, she refused, but I also promised that the case would never go to trial and that Jeremy would never go to jail. Once I had her on board . . . Shit, we're going to have to find a way to explain that restraining-order request. And we'll have to exonerate Alonso. If not, he might—"

"We'll work out the details," said Maxina, failing to hide her amazement. "Just go on."

Unlike the others, she could see where I was going. I rose to my feet and paced the room. I had to keep moving or I'd lose my nerve.

"Shortly after her debut, Harmony started to have serious misgivings about the whole operation. She couldn't deal with the fact that she was ruining the life of an innocent man. She didn't want to do it anymore but obviously I couldn't let her quit now. Using the bodyguards, I kept her a virtual prisoner of the hotel. She screamed at me every day, begging me to let her go, threatening to go public with the truth."

I stopped moving. I closed my eyes.

"So, to my own deep regret, I had no choice but to threaten her back. I let her know just how powerful my clients were, and just how short and difficult they could make her life. And the lives of her roommates."

"Whoa, man," said Hunta.

"That's crazy," said Big Bank.

"That's why she broke down on *Larry King*," I continued. "That's why she didn't confess when Simba implored her to. She wanted to desperately, but she knew there'd be horrible consequences."

"Scott, do you know what you're doing?"

I turned to the Judge. "Yes. I'm sending the tape to Miranda Cameron-Donnell. She's a reporter at AP who's been sniffing after me. This won't answer all her questions, but she'll have no choice. She'll have to run with what I give her."

"But if you admit all this, you're going to jail!"

I sat on the wing of the love seat, glancing out the sunny east window. "I'm not going to jail, Doug. I'm going to disappear. I'm going to go liquid. Anything with my name on it, I'll leave behind. My apartment. My car." My gin. My medicine. "If I change my hair a little, if I live off cash, they'll never find me. They won't even spend that much time looking. I mean, crime-wise, I'm small potatoes. I'm just a hoaxster with a guilty conscience. I'll be fine."

I let out a brief and wild chuckle. "I'll be Scott Free."

The room was silent until Doug's watch beeped in the new hour. It was nine o'clock. My voice was seconds away from hitting the nation. At best, I had six hours before my name and face followed. Six hours to tie up all the loose ends in my life and become a permanent specter. Jesus Christ. I was really doing this.

"There are other ways to help her," Maxina said. "Ways that are less extreme."

"And less effective," I replied. "You know how it works."

"Still," the Judge said, "you're sacrificing your whole future for this woman. And not even to save her life, just to save her public standing. Why?"

With a wet sniff, I shrugged. "I'm the one who found her. I'm the one who got her into this. What kind of man would I be if I didn't get her out?"

For a wonderful moment, I felt as brave and noble as I sounded. Then, as usual, I ruined it all by thinking. I ran myself through my own debunking devices. Thanks to whoever leaked the tape, my future was already sacrificed. All I was doing was dodging the scariest consequences. The long arm of the law. The long nails of the Bitch. The betrayal of Madison. The inevitable flameout with Jean. I lacked the strength to face any one of those enormities. I certainly couldn't face them all. Better to run. Better to fly east, into the sunrise, and reincarnate myself on the opposite shore.

Considered that way, I didn't seem very brave at all. I didn't even seem that noble. I wasn't saving Harmony so much as I was killing her misconception of me. That was the one thing I couldn't outrun. She had to know. She had to know that I'd meant well, or I wouldn't be able to exist in any shape or form.

Shit. I knew it was too good to be true. I knew I'd never fall for my own act. Still, for such a cowardly and selfish deed, it must have looked great on the outside. For once I would play well in the theaters.

Maxina emitted a heavy sigh. "What can we do to help?"

The Judge's watch beeped. So did Big Bank's.

"Just make sure Harmony knows what I'm doing. She's not dumb. She'll know her best option now is to go along with the lie. But she'll need someone to coach her on the details. She'll need a dedicated publicist to help her with the backlash. Maybe Kathy Oh. Or Jeff Hawn. He's good. Oh, and make sure she gets the other half of my fee, please."

"What can we do to help *you*?"

It was Maxina's question again, but I found myself looking to Hunta. It occurred to me that if I gave him Madison's phone number, he could tell her the whole story himself. She could hear straight from the horse's mouth that he was never really betrayed by me. It was just a trick, a stunt, a media play that blew up toward the end. But ultimately, Slick took the heat of the blast. He did the right thing. He did right by everyone.

"Uh . . ."

While everyone watched me, I watched the television. At long last, it was showtime. The sound was off, but a transcript of the dialogue began to wipe onto the screen, word by word, right between a still shot of Harmony and that sinister graphic of Question-Mark Man.

```
Harmony: This the craziest s*** I ever heard in my life.
Man: Hey, I don't blame you for being skeptical, Harmony. Tell me
which part worries you the most, and I'll see if I can clarify.
```

I was running short on time. I had to get out of here and get started on my task list. But I couldn't leave without asking Hunta for this one favor. Worse, I couldn't ask him without breaking down. Madison was a load-bearing wall. If I brought her up now, if I even mentioned her name, I'd crumble to the ground in a cloud of dust.

But something on the TV . . .

```
Harmony: Which part? How about all of it? You want me to yell
"rape" against a man who never even touched me...
Man: We don't really want to call it rape.
```

Something wasn't right.

```
Harmony: But I won't have any evidence!
Man: You won't need evidence.
```

"This isn't right," I said.
Everyone followed my gaze.
"What isn't right?" asked Doug.

```
Harmony: But what if people don't believe me?
Man: What, that Hunta sexually abused you?
Harmony: Yeah.
Man: [laughs] That's not an issue. Trust me.
```

"That's not what we said," I told them.
"What the hell you talking about?" asked Hunta.
"The dialogue. It's all wrong. It's not what was on the tape."

```
Harmony: How you gonna prove he had the opportunity?
Man: Well, first there's your paycheck, which shows you were at the
```

> Christmas party. Then there's a hotel slip, which proves he got
> a room that night.

"He's right," said Maxina.

Without taking her wide eyes off the screen, she reached for the remote and turned up the volume. The voices were crackly, tinny, and almost submerged in the background hum of an auto engine. The conversation was obviously recorded in a moving car. But it wasn't my car. It wasn't my voice.

> Harmony: Damn. You really thought this whole thing out.

And that wasn't Harmony.

"Can someone please tell me what the fuck is going on?"

Nobody was prepared to answer Hunta. Once Maxina switched off the television, the six of us sat in pure silence, staring absently at various points in the room. I zoned in on Hunta's bare feet. Christ, even they were perfect-looking. Even at wit's end, he was a daunting sexual presence. If Jean were here, sitting right next to me, she'd pass me a grin and her handheld.

> I'M CRAZY ABOUT YOU, MY DEAR, BUT IF THAT MAN THREW ME OVER HIS
> SHOULDER AND CARRIED ME TO THE BEDROOM, I WOULDN'T PUT UP A FIGHT.

No. I couldn't imagine many women would. I suppose it wasn't fair of Mother Nature to favor a man so, but Fate had more than compensated for the bias. Fate was a real bitch to Jeremy Sharpe. If anything proved that, it was this latest twist. Although he didn't know it yet, the tables had just turned back. Suddenly I was saved and he was screwed.

"It's a fake," I said, still gazing at his feet. "The tape is a complete fake."

Doug was stumped. "It's weird. I mean the man sounded nothing like you, but are you sure that woman wasn't Harmony?"

"It wasn't. Someone just did a very good impression of her."

"But that don't make sense," said Hunta. "Who would do that?"

Apparently I was the only one who figured it out. Even Maxina was left flailing in the dark, but she was just a minute away from piecing it together. I didn't want to be here when that happened.

The Judge chimed in. "It could be any jokester. There are always people messing with the news."

"Or it could be the news itself," Big Bank added. "Maybe they did it for the ratings."

"Yeah, but why this? Who would play a trick on 'sweet little Harmony'?"

"It wasn't a trick on her," I explained to Hunta. "It was a trick on you."

Yet again, all heads turned my way. My mind was still reeling from the implications. If I didn't stay focused on the negatives, if I didn't stay focused on Hunta, I'd probably start laughing. If I started, I probably wouldn't stop.

"Over the next few hours, a whole bunch of audio experts are going to compare the voice on that recording to Harmony's voice on *Larry King Live*. They're all going to come to the same conclusion: it's not her."

Doug went agape. "Holy shit. That's right."

"And if that's not Harmony," I continued, "then the press will conclude that somebody set her up. Somebody made a cheap attempt to destroy her credibility."

The Judge lowered his head into his hands. "Oh Jesus . . ."

"They're going to blame us," said Doug. "We're the only ones with a motive. They're going to think we did it!"

"Oh Jesus Christ . . ."

"Wait. This shit ain't over? You saying this shit ain't over?"

"No," said Doug. "They'll think you're guiltier than ever now. They'll think we're all guilty now."

"We got framed," said Big Bank, astounded. "We got framed for framing her."

For framing Hunta. Scheme-wise, it was a marvelous structure, a hoax within a hoax within a hoax. It was so artful in its simplicity and so devastating in its thorough effectiveness.

"But can't we stop this?" the Judge asked me. "Can't we just release the real tape and end this once and for all?"

I shook my head. "No. That was the point. She didn't do this to frame us. She did it to jam us."

"What are you talking about?"

"*Who* are you talking about?"

Finally, I looked to Maxina. Her face was a stone mask, as always, but behind it I could hear the pieces snapping together. Snap. Snap. Snap.

"It was Harmony," I told them with splendorous awe. "She got us."

The expressions on the men's faces varied from skeptical to distrustful to downright incredulous.

"You can't be serious," said Big Bank.

"How can you be sure?" asked Doug.

"The voices may not have been ours, but the dialogue was. That whole script was a medley of things that Harmony and I actually said to each other, in private, unrecorded anywhere except her brain and mine. She wrote that scene herself, and she did it from memory."

The Judge was locked in denial. "Wait. No. You're telling me this girl—this squeaky little mouse—just orchestrated a huge and elaborate media stunt on her very own, in less than twenty-four hours?"

"It's not that elaborate. It probably took her one hour to write it, two hours to produce it, and three hours for a trusted pal to leak it to Fox News. In fact, I bet the female voice on that tape is her best friend Tracy. As to who played me . . . I don't know. I guess whichever one of her roommates does the best white-man impression."

"But why would she do a thing like that?" asked Big Bank. "That's a crazy risk."

"It's not that crazy. She knew all about our audiotape. I told her. She knew that if she didn't cooperate with us, the tape would be released and the voice experts would nail her. I told her that, too. So what does she do? She beats us to the press with her very own decoy, knowing damn well it'll be exposed as a fake, knowing damn well it'll block us from releasing our own tape."

"That's bullshit." With wide, desperate eyes, the Judge turned to Maxina. "That's bullshit. Ours is the real thing. We've got her! If we play it for the media . . ."

Maxina had no intention of responding. She simply kept her cold gaze on me. Snap. Snap. Snap.

"It won't matter," I told the Judge. "Once Harmony's cleared, there's no force on earth that'll get the media to consider a second recording. It's like double jeopardy. They won't try someone twice for the exact same crime, especially when the first trial blew up in their faces like a gag cigar."

Doug's wonder wasn't as glowing as mine. "God. That's why she insisted on having a whole night to write her confession speech. She was stalling us."

"But how did she get this plan?" asked Big Bank. "Where'd she come up with it?"

"We gave it to her!" I answered. "The idea was right there all along! She framed herself and then exonerated herself. Doesn't that sound awfully familiar? Don't you get it? She jammed us the exact same way we jammed Lisa Glassman! She used our very own trick against us!"

"*Our* trick?" the Judge inquired accusingly.

"My trick," I corrected. "Yes. I taught her everything she knew. I just didn't expect her to be such a good listener. Or such a quick learner. I guess I underestimated her again."

"You unbelievable bastard," said Maxina at long last.

Once again, the room fell into silence. In my frazzled state of mind, my peaked state of being, my practical engine finally stopped running. It was clogged on irony to the point of malfunction. With my mind shut down, there was nothing left for me to do but coast on involuntary reactions.

I lowered my head and laughed.

"Oh yes," I said. "Yes, of course it would be me. Of course it only makes sense if I'm the mastermind behind this."

"Scott, are you familiar with Occam's Razor?"

I kept chortling. "Why, yes, Maxina. Yes I am."

"Good," she said without a trace of levity. "So what do you see as the simplest explanation? That we were all outsmarted by a nineteen-year-old hostess dancer with partial brain damage? Or that she once again took her cue from an extremely devious and talented publicist who just happens to be infatuated with her?"

"Or maybe it was someone else's idea!" I said, still painfully amused. "Maybe it was Alonso!"

Even as I said it, I didn't buy it. Alonso's version of a clever idea was cybersex with Jesus. Face it, Slick. This was Harmony's brainchild. She just adopted it from you.

But that wasn't even the simplest explanation. Immediately, the men in the room glommed on to Maxina's theory. Big Bank gaped at me, appalled.

"You motherfucker . . ."

"You planned this from the beginning," said the Judge. "You were scheming with Harmony all along."

"That's why you made us give her half your money," Doug added. "You tried to make us give her *all* your money. You knew we'd never pay you if this thing happened, so you tricked us into paying her."

I couldn't stop chuckling. It was too much. Too ironic. Too surreal.

"You put on this whole show," said Maxina, motioning around. "Right here. Just now. You accused us. You lectured us. You played this whole 'noble sacrifice' bit when you knew all along what was happening . . ."

Big Bank shot to his feet. "You motherfucker!"

Winded, I threw my hands up. "Wait! Wait! Everybody . . . just stop. Stop."

Amazingly, they did. It took several deep breaths, but I managed to regain myself. Somewhere in my mind was a perfectly cogent argument for my defense, and yet I couldn't seem to find it. I couldn't even find a reason to acquit myself. I did this. I gave Harmony all the ingredients, all the tools, all the incentive she ever needed to get the last laugh, and still I didn't see it coming. All this effort, all this stress, and it turned out I only saved her by accident.

The strangest part was that she'd accidentally saved me, too. I didn't have to worry about media exposure anymore. I didn't even have to worry about Miranda. As long as Harmony didn't say my name, Miranda didn't have a smoking gun. And Harmony had every reason now to keep me a secret. We were locked in a covenant of silence. Together, we were airtight, unsinkable. No matter what happened, no matter how the Judge or Maxina retaliated, we were protected. It would take nothing less than a full double confession to bring us down, and that would never happen.

Sober again, I wiped my eyes, ran a quick finger under my nose, then looked around the room.

"Uh . . ."

The only one who didn't meet my gaze was Jeremy, the ultimate victim of all this. He stared down at his feet, shaking his head, rocking back and forth. He knew now that he'd never get the deliverance I promised him. I gambled his future, I lost, and now I was about to walk away from the table. What could I possibly tell him in this instance? What could I possibly say?

"Jeremy . . ."

"Get him out of here," he said. "Get him the fuck out of here."

"All right. I'm going."

I stood up so fast, I became dizzy. I held my hands out, standing perfectly still until the room stopped spinning.

"I'm going."

"I'll walk you out," said Big Bank with ominous inflection.

"No," Maxina replied. "I'll do it. Someone help me up."

Big Bank pulled her to her feet. Honestly, I would have preferred his send-off to Maxina's. I would have preferred a good punch to the gut. But I wasn't in a position to voice my preferences.

The Judge, Doug, and Big Bank glared as Maxina met me at the archway. She walked me through the foyer.

"I noticed the little love mark on your neck," she said.

"Yeah. I'm sure that was evidence, too."

"Scott, I'm working at about thirty percent capacity right now. And about five percent of that thirty percent is considering the possibility that you didn't orchestrate this. But whether this happened on purpose or by accident, whether you're malicious, incompetent, or just plain jinxed, it doesn't matter now. All that matters is that this did not end well."

"No," I said, glancing back into the house. "No, I guess it didn't."

"There's going to be plenty of blame to go around behind the scenes, and I'll certainly get my deserved share. But the biggest slice is going to you. Fair or not, that's just the way the game is played. Fair or not, I feel compelled to tell my colleagues what a horrible mistake it was for me to hire you."

"Then do it."

She opened the door for me, gazing out at the sunny street. "I have a lot of colleagues, Scott. And they have a lot of colleagues."

"I know how it works."

She looked up at me again. We were both having a terrible morning, and we were both a shade of our usual selves, but even our shades were bright enough to speak in soft language. She was asking for a reason not to ruin my career. I couldn't offer one. All I could give her was my blessing. The decision stabilized me. I couldn't leave Doug's house unscathed. I couldn't get away Scott Free.

With a long and weary sigh, Maxina squeezed my shoulder. "I'll keep the Judge off your back."

"Keep him off Harmony's back."

"He won't touch her," she replied. "I can't even touch her now."

I grinned. I couldn't help it. For Jeremy's sake, and for the sake of my own conscience, I didn't want to take pleasure in Harmony's ultimate triumph. But I was only human, and she was a loved one of mine.

It took five minutes to get back to my car. Once again I focused on my ailing body. It screamed at me, clamoring for food, warmth, rest, and maybe a little human contact. It wanted to be caressed again, the way it was caressed last night.

I didn't meet any of its demands. I simply sat in the car with my left hand on the wheel and my right hand on the key in the ignition. My attention was captured by that damn red phone on the floor. Ever since yesterday, I'd been afraid to pick it up, as if it were burning hot. But now that everything had reversed itself, now that up was down, left was right, black was white, I figured it would be cool to the touch again. I figured Harmony would love to hear from me.

One last time, I called her up. She answered after the very first ring.

"Hey baby!"

"Harmony."

She hesitated. "Oh. Gosh. I'm sorry. I was expecting someone else. Who is this?"

"You know who this is."

Another pause. "I'm afraid you have the wrong number, sir."

"Harmony, it's Scott."

"You definitely have the wrong number, then. This ain't Harmony. And I don't know any Scott."

At first I was annoyed. I thought this was an act of childish petulance. Then I realized she was just being cautious.

"It's okay," I assured her. "I'm not recording this."

"I didn't say you were. I just said you got the wrong number."

"So who am I talking to, then?"

She mulled it over. "Danesha."

"Well, hi, Danesha. My name is Scott. Scott Singer."

"Is it now?"

"Yeah. Turns out it really is."

"I don't know," she mused. "It's kind of hard to believe you when it sounds like you're disguising your voice."

I laughed. No wonder she got antsy. "I'm not disguising my voice. I just have a cold. I got it from standing in the ocean yesterday. Remember?"

"No. Why should I? I don't even know you."

I was no longer amused. "All right. You know what? This was a bad idea. I'm sorry I bothered you. Take care of yourself."

"No. Wait. Don't go yet."

I paused. "Yes?"

"Did you say you were calling for Harmony?"

"I did."

"As in Harmony Prince?"

"The one and only," I patiently replied. "Is she around?"

"No, but she's all I see on the news nowadays. What do you think about her?"

I smiled. "There's no simple answer to that question."

"Well, what do you think about her future? I mean, this shit with the tape . . ."

"Nah. The tape's a fake. If there's one thing I know, it's Harmony's voice. And that's not it. I figure by lunchtime, she'll be completely exonerated."

"And after that?"

"After that, she's home free."

She squealed with delight. She must have been on pins and needles, wondering if her bold gambit would work. There was no point in keeping her guessing. She deserved to hear it, especially from me.

"Yeah." I sighed. "That woman is unstoppable."

"Really, now? I thought maybe you'd tell me there's some people coming after her."

"What, you mean like hired thugs? No. No. That's not what she needs to worry about."

"What does she need to worry about?"

I let out a long, hot breath. "Well, there's that little blond girl in Wisconsin who's going to go missing in a week or two. Or maybe it'll be another cute little Cuban boy caught up in an international custody battle. Or maybe the next Annabelle Shane is loading up her daddy's pistol as we speak. I don't know. I'm not a psychic. I just know that these are the people coming after Harmony. If I were her publicist, I'd tell her to work hard, work fast, and use every bit of the limelight while she's got it. With luck, she might really go places."

Her silence was lukewarm. "You really sound sick."

"I know. That's what I get for standing in the ocean."

"Yeah? You regret it?"

Absently, I stared out the windshield at the endless row of neat little houses.

"I regret it," I told her. "More than anything I've ever done in my life."

"And I bet you'd do anything to take it back," she replied cynically.

"No."

"No?"

"No. There are some things I wouldn't do."

"Like what?"

I was going to tell her that I'd never sacrifice an innocent man. Not on purpose, anyway. But there was no point in splitting hairs. We were both the architects of Jeremy's fate. Unlike me, Harmony was smart enough to see that somebody had to lose this dirty game I'd started. There was no point in faulting her when in truth I was just so damn impressed. I was so damn impressed that she managed to win, and that she did it by my very own rules.

"It doesn't matter," I said. "I can't take it back. But if I could wish for anything in the world right now, I'd wish for ten more seconds of credibility with Harmony Prince. I'd even settle for five."

"Five seconds."

"Five seconds," I echoed. "Five seconds where my words go past her defenses, around her doubts, beyond her suspicions, and straight on through to her core beliefs."

"That's asking a lot."

"I'm not asking. I'm wishing."

"What makes you think you even deserve five seconds?"

"It doesn't matter what I think. It's what Harmony thinks."

She thought about it for a few moments.

"Why don't you try me instead? I'll be Harmony. And you'll be whoever you claim to be. I'll give you five seconds. How does that sound?"

"Discouraging."

"Well, you're just gonna have to take your chances, mister. You ready?"

"Sure."

"Okay . . . go."

"I wish you well."

I ran out the clock in silence. Harmony laughed. "That's it?"

"That's it."

"That was hardly even one second!"

I shrugged. "I guess I didn't need the whole five."

"You are so strange."

"It doesn't matter what you think. It's what Harmony thinks."

Her laughter died down. Now she opened her balcony doors and stepped out into the high ocean breeze. I listened to a good eight seconds of wind static.

"I met this guy once," she told me. "He was a strange man, just like you, but he was all charming and funny to me. And he had a nice face. Even though he was older than me, and white, I got a little bit of a crush on him. He seemed kind of sweet on me, too, but he had a job to do and he was fixed on doing it. See, he had this crazy idea. He had this crazy thing he wanted me to do for a client of his. Nothing dirty. Just crazy. And somehow, God knows how, he talked me into doing it."

"You regret it?"

"Well, that's the thing. Right before I agreed, I asked him to promise me something. I asked him to promise me that when this was all over, when everything was said and done, that I wouldn't hate him."

I gripped the steering wheel. "Do you?"

"It don't matter. He didn't promise that. He just guaranteed that when this was all over, when everything was said and done, I'd be glad I met him."

"Are you?"

"That don't matter either," she replied thoughtfully. "Turns out it ain't over."

We were both silent again. I stared at the empty passenger seat. It was hard to believe that our relationship had begun only ten and a half days ago, when she dropped my ticket into the punch clock at the Flower Club. The meter had been running ever since. At 40 hours, we shared a kiss, and then forever disappeared inside each other's red phones. At 80 hours, she became famous, and then suddenly turned me on. At 230 hours, I called her a bitch, and then slowly began to crumble. And just fifteen minutes ago, at the 250-hour mark, I made plans to immolate myself. For her well-being. For her forgiveness. For my own peace of mind. I'd been ready to break her fall with my very own body. That was a pretty dramatic affair for a man like me. It was a pretty remarkable run for a courtship that—at Flower Club rates—would cost a mere six thousand dollars, before tip.

"I don't love you, Scott," she said, finally abandoning the facade. "But I don't hate you, either. I could have easily hated you for what you did and said to me yesterday. But we been through too much together. And given everything that's happened, given everything that's changed and everything I learned, I have to say I'm glad I met you."

I leaned my head back, smiling, squeezing out tears.

"But you're a stranger to me now. That's the way it has to be. You understand?"

Wiping my eyes, I nodded.

"You there?"

"I'm here," I said. "I hear you."

And she could hear me. It wasn't the most theatrical of breakdowns, especially when parsed through a cellular link, but she could hear my choked-up voice. She knew I was crying. It was the closest I'd ever come to standing naked in front of her: exposed, vulnerable, all out of tricks, all out of angles. I was glad it was Harmony. I was glad she was the ear-witness to such a rare emotional event.

But if she was affected, she hid it deep within her. Her voice was strong and hard.

"You know, I've been waiting for this one guy to call," she said facetiously, "but I don't think it's gonna happen. So you know what? I think I'm gonna get rid of this phone. I think I'm gonna drop it right off the balcony."

"Just be careful. You could hurt someone."

"Yeah, well, if I do, I'll just have to live with it."

"Just live well, all right?"

"You take care of yourself now, stranger."

"You too."

"I'm dropping the phone now."

"Do it."

She did it. I could hear the wind whistle through the receiver as Harmony let me go. When the phone hit the pavement, the resulting noise was so loud, I had to turn my head away. Ka-CHINK! It was like an aluminum bat hitting a stack of quarters right behind a megaphone. I couldn't even imagine the number of high-tech fragments spread out on the sidewalk. I wished I could have dropped my phone with her. They could have died thematically together, bleeding circuitry so far and so wide that people wouldn't be able to tell where one device began and the other one ended.

It wasn't meant to be, I suppose. But I couldn't complain. This was a fine way to end our arrangement. A fine way to clock out. As for my own red phone, it would have to die elsewhere. Symbolically, there was no better place than the ocean itself. It was in for a cold, dark swim soon. Not now, but soon. I wasn't in a hurry. I wasn't going anywhere.

By a quarter after three, my mind and body were both mush. I'd spent the last five hours wrapped up in a blanket, laid out on my sofa, napping, waking, napping again. All the while, my television infused me with a running drip of zeitgeist, courtesy of Turner Classic Movies. The current distraction was *Babes in Arms,* a 1939 Busby Berkeley number with Mickey Rooney and Judy Garland. I knew I was in trouble when I started laughing at the jokes.

Madison came back from the kitchen with a hot cup of lemon tea. She placed it on the coffee table. Funny that she came to work in a turtleneck sweater. So did I. My brain wasn't entirely dead. I still had secrets to hide.

"Thank you. You know, you really don't have to take care of me."

"Oh, shut up," she said, sitting down on the floor. "What else am I going to do here?"

"Yeah. I'm sorry about that."

"I still can't believe they fired you."

I sniffed. "Yeah, well, that's the way it works sometimes."

Harmony's plan had reached fruition sometime around noon. Much ado was made about the fake recording, the evil attempt to frame her. I didn't watch the news. I heard about it from Madison. I assured her the tape wasn't made by anyone from the Hunta camp. In fact, they fired me simply because they thought I was the one behind it. That was sort of true.

"Is this going to be bad for your freelance business?"

I sighed. "Yeah. Things are going to be real quiet around here for a while."

"That's just not fair."

With considerable effort, I wriggled my way down to the floor, between the couch and the coffee table. I took the mug in my hands.

"It's all right," I told her, sipping. "We'll manage."

"But what are you going to do now?"

"I'm going to finish this nice cup of tea you made me. I'm going to lie back down on the sofa. And then I figure I'll either get better or die. I haven't decided which."

She smirked. "Don't die."

"Why not?"

"Because I'd miss you."

After a few long moments, I put the tea back down and muted the television. Despite my minor release in the car, there was still a tempest brewing inside of me. I was filled with emotions that were constructive and otherwise, positive and otherwise. I would not expose my cherished assistant, Jean's daughter, to such untested energies. Otherwise . . .

"I'd miss you, too," I said.

"God. I can't stand seeing you like this."

"I'm all right," I assured her, unconvincingly. "I'll be all right."

I tried to meet her gaze, but she stared me down in three seconds.

"Scott, can I please give you a hug?"

"That's sweet of you. Really. But I don't want to get you sick."

"It's all right. My mom's already coming down with something. If I don't get it from you, I'm going to get it from her."

I let out a weak laugh. Doesn't it figure?

"Still, I don't know if she'd want us crossing certain professional boundaries . . ."

"Scott."

Madison crawled her way over to me, curling up against my side. She threw her arms around me, then rested her head on my shoulder.

"It's a hug," she said. "There's no crime. There's no scandal. It's just a hug. You need it."

After a few awkward beats, I put my hand on her back. Damned if she wasn't right. Damned if this wasn't all the medicine I needed right now.

"I told you I was a business jinx," she said, with limited jest. "I told you at the very beginning. You should have listened to me."

"Madison, hiring you is one of the few things I don't regret."

"You make it sound like this whole thing's your fault."

"Well, I wouldn't say it's all my—"

"You didn't form the Bitch Fiends," she declared. "You didn't put a gun in Annabelle Shane's hands. You didn't tell the media that lynching Hunta was a perfect way to spend sweeps. And you definitely didn't tell Harmony Prince to lie."

She was three for four, but this wasn't the day to correct her. Thank God this wasn't the day. Thank God, thank Fate, thank Harmony.

"I don't know," I said. "It's still a rough trade. You sure you want to go into it?"

After a brief contemplation, she sighed across my chest. "I might as well now. I mean, you were right. Once you get that X-ray vision, you can't turn it off. I see the business angle behind everything now. All I see are dirty tricks, ulterior motives, and colored words. I see lots of colored words."

On TV, Mickey Rooney and his flock of happy halflings continued to dance, jump, and kick to music we couldn't hear.

"I guess it never used to be that way," she mused.

"There were still plenty of illusions back then. They were mostly just happy illusions."

"Do you think people are getting worse, Scott? Or are we just getting more cynical?"

I mulled it over. "I don't really know. I mean I've worked for some of the world's most disreputable businesses. The gun industry, the liquor industry, big oil, big tobacco, polluters, pill pushers, pornographers. And now rap. The strangest thing is that I've met some of the nicest people at these places, and I've met some real assholes at nonprofits and charities. You just can't tell at a glance."

The movie ended with a grand splash, and the credits began to roll.

"But there are good people out there," I said, rubbing her back. "There always will be."

"There'll always be liars, too."

"Yeah, but that's nothing new. There have always been liars and there have always been lies. It's human nature. That'll never change."

I kept my pensive gaze on the credits. "But sometimes . . . I don't know. Sometimes I wonder when we all got so good at it, you know? When did we all get so goddamn slick?"

It was quite a stumper indeed, but with Madison bunched up next to me, what did it matter? I held her close, resting my head on hers. The poor girl. She was going through such a hard time at home. At school. Everywhere. She was carrying such a load on her narrow shoulders. She wasn't ready to share it with me. I certainly wouldn't force the issue. There was no need to chip away at her brave face. In this apartment, she could wear whatever face she wanted. Around me, she could be whoever the hell she wanted to be.

That was pretty damn decent for a man who was quietly, gradually, and cautiously falling for his cherished assistant's mother. There'd be hell to pay when Madison caught that twist. Another issue. Another challenge. Another crisis to manage. It would keep until I got better.

Madison curled in my grasp, yawning, closing her eyes. "So what do you think's going to happen with them?"

"With who?"

"With Harmony. With Jeremy. Everyone."

I didn't have the slightest clue. The story was long out of my hands, and the future loomed ahead of me in branches. Maybe Harmony will get everything she wants out of life, every success she deserves and every success she doesn't. Or maybe she won't. Maybe Jeremy will slip his way out of the Bitch's fingers, into the background, into the forgiving arms of his estranged wife and daughter. Or maybe he won't. Maybe Maxina won't try very hard to ruin my career. Or maybe I'll try to find a new one. Maybe I'll track down Ira and turn his Move My Cheese thing into a profitable business venture for both of us. Or maybe I won't.

One thing I know for sure is that somebody, at some point, will try to tell the story behind the story of Harmony Prince. Long after the stage has changed and the great American play has moved on to new victims and new villains, new things to shout and scream about, somebody will revisit the tumultuous events of February 2001 and try to set the record straight. Maybe it'll be an investigative report by Miranda. Or a strategic mea culpa from Alonso. Who knows? Maybe Harmony herself will be the one to come clean. I'd surely trust her version above all others, even if she embellishes the details. Even if she makes me out to be the villain of the piece.

Will it be fair? Will it be accurate? Who can say? I just know it'll make an interesting story. It might even make a great movie. Heck, I'd go. I'd relish the chance to sit in the theater, listening to the audience's reactions as they watched the big-screen version of me: the cold and conniving bastard who schemed and toyed with other people's lives like they were pieces on a chessboard. I'd look up with the rest of the crowd, but unlike them, I'd simply shake my head and smile. I'd smile because I'd know it wasn't really me up there. They got me all wrong. The actor they cast won't act a thing like me or sound a thing like me. He probably won't even look like me. He'll probably be short.

ACKNOWLEDGMENTS

I acknowledge that this was not a thin book. So let me first thank you, the reader, for sticking with *Slick* to the very end.

I also acknowledge that prior to writing this novel, I knew close to squat about PR and media manipulation. I would still be clueless if not for the many authors and experts who illuminated me through their brilliant works. The bibliography to *Slick* would be a small book in itself, but I'd like to single out (or in this case, double out) Sheldon Rampton and John Stauber. Their website—www.prwatch.org—and their books on corporate disinformation—*Toxic Sludge Is Good for You!* and *Trust Us, We're Experts!*—are critical reading for anyone who wants to take a Madison-style journey through the looking glass.*

Next I'd like to thank everyone who supported me in my thirty-month endeavor to create *Slick*. Although I suffered the occasional lapse of funds and stamina (not to mention sanity), I was fortunate to have an endless supply of encouragement and feedback from some very fine people. You know who you are, but here are your names anyway: Mary Ann Bastian, Pamela Brown, Fritz Cambier-Unruh, Jill Flomenhoft, Mike Gavin, Karine Hovsepian, Drew and Jennifer Hoyt, Chris Jordan, Camilla Lawlor, Erika Lawrence, Adam LeBow, Josh Lipking, Jimena Lopez, Kris McGrew, Charlotte Miller, Kelly Milner, Jen Preston, Liz Nagle, Mick Soth, and my highly supportive cat, Jake.

---

*For more information on the topics and research featured in *Slick,* please visit my Author's Guide at www.slicknovel.com/guide. In it, I go chapter by chapter and separate the stuff that really happened from the stuff I made up. I also answer questions from readers.

Special thanks to my stepmother, Joan Bar-Zeev, for her enthusiasm in both reading and promoting my book. There'll be a big fat sales spike in Wilmington, North Carolina, and I'll know why.

Extra-special thanks to these folks, for reasons they damn well know: Jennifer Gennaco, Tara McDonough, Craig Mertens, Huan Nghiem, Krista Stein, and Dév Tandon.

Crucial thanks to my tireless advocates at the Lazear Agency: Julie Mayo, Christi Cardenas, and of course Jonathon Lazear. And on the subject of agents, I thank my lucky stars every day for Stuart M. Miller, the man who discovered me and quite possibly invented me.

Eternal gratitude to all at Random House, who took a big fat chance on *Slick* in an age and a business where big fat chances are rarely taken. Special thanks to Claire Tisne for the world domination, Evelyn O'Hara for the organization, Daniel Menaker for the reconsideration, and Will Murphy for just about everything. Make a note, authors: Will Murphy is the editor from heaven.

And finally, there are the people who have the thankless job of being related to me. My nuclear family went fission some years ago—as families do—but despite our being scattered across the landscape, I feel fortunate all the way down to my genes. I come from a clan of folks who are so damn unique, so damn brilliant, so damn benevolent in so many different ways that even as a writer, I'm at a loss to describe them. I can't adequately express my gratitude to them, although I plan to try more often. So, to Ruth Jensky (the grandmother), Avi Bar-Zeev (the brother), Yona Bar-Zeev (the father), and Ricki Bar-Zeev (the mother, who shaped both me and *Slick* in more ways than can be listed), I owe you everything. All that I am, and all that I have. Just thought you should know.

ABOUT THE AUTHOR

DANIEL PRICE is a writer living in Los Angeles. He runs AbusedbytheNews.com, a website of media criticism and satire. *Slick* is his first novel.

ABOUT THE TYPE

This book was set in Bembo, a typeface based on an old-style Roman face that was used for Cardinal Bembo's tract *De Aetna* in 1495. Bembo was cut by Francisco Griffo in the early sixteenth century. The Lanston Monotype Company of Philadelphia brought the well-proportioned letterforms of Bembo to the United States in the 1930s.